KILL THE MESSENGER

**Also by Tami Hoag
available from Random House Large Print**

Dark Horse
Dust to Dust

TAMI HOAG

KILL THE MESSENGER

RANDOM HOUSE
LARGE PRINT

Copyright © 2004 by Indelible Ink, Inc.

All rights reserved under International and Pan-American Copyright Conventions. Published in the United States of America by Random House Large Print in association with Bantam Books, New York, and simultaneously in Canada by Random House of Canada Limited, Toronto. Distributed by Random House, Inc., New York.

The Library of Congress has established a Cataloging-in-Publication record for this title.

0-375-43299-x

www.randomlargeprint.com

This Large Print edition published in accord with the standards of the N.A.V.H.

To Jester
My little pal who came to me
when I needed him most,
and left far too soon.
Always missed. Always loved.
R.I.P.

Acknowledgments

As always, I have a number of people to thank for helping me with either technical, psychological, or moral support during the writing of this book. So here goes.

My sincere thanks to Detective 2 Jeffrey Sandefur, LAPD, and Detective 2 Humberto Fajardo, LAPD, to whom I was directed by way of John Petovich, LAPD, retired; Jim Stith, Esq., simple country lawyer and international man of mystery; Eileen Dreyer, who always knows the answers to the questions about the gross, the sick, and the weirdly perverted.

To Dr. Toni Bernay and Dr. Robert Gerner. Gray O'Brien and the staff at Robert Forster Physical Therapy. You all know what your contributions were. My mind and body thank you.

To Nita, Irwyn, Danielle, Andrea, et al., for your extreme patience. You may have been pissed as hell, but not in my face, and I appreciate that more than you know. The muse waits for no one, but everyone must wait for the muse.

And finally, to Lynn Cardoso, Betsy Steiner, and the Divas-Eileen, Karyn, Kim-for the hand-holding, the listening, the sympathy, the empathy, the counseling, and for being the inner circle. Friends in need, friends indeed. Seasons and men come and go, but girlfriends are forever.

KILL THE MESSENGER

1

L A traffic.
Rush hour.

Rush hour at four hours and counting. Every Angelino busting it to get home before the heavens opened up like a bursting bladder and the rains came in a gush. The city had been pressed down beneath the weight of an anvil sky all day. Endless, ominous twilight in the concrete canyons between the downtown skyscrapers. The air heavy with expectation.

Legs pumping. Fingers tight on the handlebars. Fingertips numb. Eyes on the gap between a Jag and a FedEx truck. Quads burning. Calves like rocks. The taste of exhaust. Eyes dry and stinging behind a pair of swim goggles. A bag full of blueprints in cardboard cylinders riding his back.

The two-way strapped to his thigh like a six-gun barked out bursts of static and the rock-crusted voice of Eta Fitzgerald, the base dispatcher. He didn't know her real name. They called her Eta because that was what they heard out of her all day, every day: **ETA? ETA sixteen? Base to Jace. ETA? What's your twenty, honey?**

He had three minutes to make it to the developer's office on the seventeenth floor of a building still blocks away. The guard at the front desk was a jerk. He locked the doors at six on the dot and had no sympathy for anyone standing on the street trying to get in. The guy would have turned his back on his own mother, if he had one, which Jace doubted. He looked like something that had sprouted up out of the ground. A human toadstool.

Shift his weight to the right. Cut around the Jag.

He caught the blast of its horn as he ran on his pedals to put a few inches between his back wheel and the car's front bumper. Just ahead of him the traffic light had turned yellow, but the FedEx truck was running the intersection. Coming up on the right side of the truck, Jace reached out and caught hold above the wheel, letting the truck carry him through the intersection and down the block.

He was a master at riding the blind spot. If the person behind the wheel saw him and didn't want him there, a messenger could become a bug on a windshield in a hurry. The FedEx drivers were usually cool. Simpatico. Messenger to messenger. They were both connections between people who didn't give a rat's ass who they were unless they were late with a delivery.

The building was in sight. Jace checked over his shoulder, let go of the truck, and dipped right again, cutting across another lane, drawing another blaring horn. He angled to jump the curb in front of a fire hydrant and behind a Cadillac idling in a red zone. The car's passenger door swung open as the bike went airborne.

Shit.

Jace turned the wheel hard right and twisted his hips left as the bike came down. The old lady getting out of the car screamed and fell back into the Cadillac. The bike's front tire hit the sidewalk clear.

Jace held his position as tight as a tick on the back of a dog. He touched the brakes with little more than his imagination. Just enough to break the chaos.

Don't panic. Panic kills. Ice water, J.C. Steel. Focus. Calm.

He kept his eyes on his target. He could see the security jerk walking toward the front doors, keys in hand.

Shit!

Panic. Not at threat of injury, but at threat of being locked out. The customer wouldn't care that he had sent the delivery impossibly late or that the messenger had nearly been killed by the door of a Cadillac. If the package didn't make it, there would be hell to pay.

He dropped the bike ten feet from the door, sick at the thought that it might be gone by the time he got out of the building, but there was no time to lock it. He bolted for the door, tripped himself, fell like a boulder, and tumbled and skidded, arms and legs bouncing like pickup sticks. Cardboard blueprint tubes shot out of his bag and rolled down the sidewalk.

No time to assess damage or recognize and catalog pains.

He forced himself to his feet, tripping, stumbling, trying to scoop up the tubes even as his momentum carried him forward. The security jerk stared at him through the glass. A lumpy gray face, twisted with sour disapproval. He turned the key in the lock and walked away.

"Hey!" Jace shouted, slamming into the glass. "Hey, come on!"

The guard pretended not to hear him. Son of a bitch. One minute to six and this guy had nothing more on his mind than getting on the freeway and creeping out to Pomona or to the Valley or to whatever nondescript shithole suburb he squatted in every night. He wasn't staying three extra minutes to log in a delivery.

Having the power to walk away was probably the only power he had in his miserable life.

"Asshole!" Jace shouted. He would have kicked the door, but with his luck the damn thing would shatter and he'd be hauled off to jail. Not that he couldn't have used the rest and three squares a day. In Jace Damon's life, rest was not an option.

Juggling the cardboard tubes in one arm, he yanked his bike up off the sidewalk and climbed back on. The entrance to the underground parking garage for the building was on the side street. The chain gate would be down, but as soon as a car rolled out, he could slip in. If there was a God in heaven—which he doubted, except in times of dire need—someone would still be in the developer's office on the seventeenth floor. Hopefully it would be Lori, the receptionist, who was blond and bouncy and would give him a Snickers bar from the stash in her bottom drawer. He hadn't eaten since breakfast—a day-old bagel and a shoplifted PowerBar.

He parked himself to the right of the garage entrance, back just far enough so as not to be noticed by anyone coming up the ramp. He had learned a long time ago to fly below the radar, to be invisible and furtive and resourceful. Survival skills of the street kid.

His radio made a sound like Velcro tearing free. "Sixteen? You out there? Base to Jace. Base to Jace. Hey, Lone Ranger, where you at? I got Money chewing my ass."

Money was Eta's word for a customer. The developer was on the phone screaming at her.

"I'm in the elevator," Jace answered. He keyed the radio on and off, on and off. "You're breaking up, Base."

A nasty-looking snot-green Chrysler nosed its way up out of the garage. The security jerk was behind the wheel. Jace gave him the finger as he turned into the drive and shot the bike down the ramp.

The Korean guy in the ticket booth barely looked at him as Jace darted around the lowered arm that prevented cars from simply rolling in. He rode the bike straight to the elevator and jumped off as the doors opened and an assortment of well-dressed professional people stepped out, freed from their cubicles for the day. A woman with a helmet of blond hair and a leopard-print raincoat gave him a look like he was dog shit and clutched her designer bag to her as she stepped around him.

Jace forced a grin. "How's it going?"

She sniffed and hurried away. People in suits and offices tended to look at bike messengers with wary suspicion. They were rebels, road warriors, fringe citizens in strange costumes invading the orderly, respectable world of business. Most of the messengers Jace knew had tattoos all over their bodies and more piercings than a colander. They were walking billboards for life on the edge, their individuality screaming from their very pores.

Jace made no such statements. He wore what he could get for little or nothing at Goodwill— baggy shorts and sweatshirts with the sleeves cut off, worn over bike shorts and a long-sleeved T-shirt. His hair stuck up in spikes through the openings in his helmet. The swim goggles made him look like an alien.

He pulled the goggles down and rubbed at the grit in his eyes as he rolled the bike into the elevator and punched 17. He could smell himself—stale sweat and exhaust fumes. He had run twenty-three packages that day and could feel the filth of the city clinging to him like a film. He had skinned his knee on the sidewalk out front. Blood was running in a slow, thick trickle down his dirty bare shin to soak into the top of his baggy gray sock.

When he finally got home and could take a shower, the day would come off him like a mud slide and he would become a blond white kid again. He would spend a couple of hours with his little brother, Tyler, then hit the books until he fell asleep on them. Too soon it would be five-thirty and another day would begin with him shoveling ice into the coolers at the fish market they lived over in Chinatown.

My life sucks.

He allowed himself to acknowledge that fact only once in a while. What was the point in dwelling on it? He didn't plan on staying where he was in the grand scheme of things. That was the thought to focus on: change, improvement, the future.

He had a future. Tyler had a future—Jace had made sure of that, and would continue to make sure of it. And their futures would be a thousand times better than anything life had given them so far. It was only a matter of time and focus and will.

The elevator dinged and the doors pulled open. The developer's office was down the hall on the left. Suite 1701. Major Development. Lori the cute receptionist was gone, along with the chance for a free Snickers. Mr. Major Development was standing at her desk, shouting into the phone. He stopped abruptly and slammed the receiver down as Jace walked in with the blueprint tubes.

"Well, it's about fucking time!" Major shouted. "My eighty-year-old mother could have gotten here faster with her walker!"

"Sorry," Jace said, handing over the manifest. He offered no excuse or explanation. He knew from experience it wouldn't matter. What mattered to Mr. Major Development was that he now had his blueprints and could get on with his life.

Major snatched the manifest away from him, scribbled a signature, and shoved it back at him. No thanks, no tip, no nothing. Lori the receptionist might have noticed the scrape on his knee and given him a Band-Aid and sympathy along with the Snickers bar. All he got was the fantasy. At least in his imaginary social life he could afford to take a girl out someplace decent.

Back out on the street, he radioed Base to confirm the delivery. He would make it back to the base office in fifteen and spend half an hour matching his delivery receipts with Eta's floaters—the notes she made assigning jobs to messengers. By seven-fifteen he could be standing in the shower.

"Sixteen to Base. Jace to Base. Got POD on Major Pain In The Ass."

"Ten-four, angel. You'll go to heaven yet."

"I don't believe in heaven."

"Darlin', you got to believe in a better world than this."

"Sure. It's called Malibu. I'm gonna get a house there when I'm rich and famous."

"And I'll come be your kept woman. Give you a big ol' dose a brown sugar, baby boy."

Eta weighed more than two hundred pounds, had three-inch purple fingernails and a Medusa's head of braids.

"You'll have to get in line behind Claire Danes and Liv Tyler."

"Honey, I'll eat them skinny white girls for lunch and pick my teeth with their bones."

"Eta, you're scaring me."

"That's good. How else can I boss you around and tell you you got one more run?"

The groan came from the deepest part of his soul. "No way. Not tonight. Call someone else."

"Ain't no one else left. You're it, Lone Ranger, and baby, you're the best."

She gave him the address for both the pickup and delivery and told him he could use the tip he would get to buy her a diamond ring.

Jace sat on his bike under the security light beside the garage entrance and stared at the note he'd written with the names and addresses, and he thought of the only tip anyone had ever given him that was of any real value: It's better to be lucky than good.

As he folded the note, it began to rain.

2

The television was playing in the overflowing bookcase across the room as Lenny Lowell prepared the packet for pickup. His office was an oasis of amber light in an otherwise dark strip of low-end storefronts—a yoga place, a psychic, a nail salon frequented by hookers. Across the street and down the block, the bail-bonds/check-cashing place was open, and farther down a 76 station lit up the night with more lights than a prison yard.

The gas-station attendant would already be locked in his booth like a veal calf behind a couple of inches of bulletproof Plexiglas. But there wouldn't be much crime tonight for either the station attendant or the bail bondsman to worry about. It was raining. In LA even the criminals don't do rain.

On the TV, a hot brunette was reporting on the latest crime of the century. Jury selection continued for the upcoming trial of actor Rob

Cole, accused in the brutal murder of his wife, Tricia.

Lenny watched with one eye, listened with one ear. Only his jealousy was fully committed. Cole had retained the services of Martin Gorman, whose client list read like a Who's Who of Hollywood's most famous screwups. Lenny's client list read like a Who's Who of LAPD's best-known dirtbags.

Not that he hadn't done well for himself. The world was full of recidivists too flush for a public defender and too stupid to keep from getting caught. Lenny had a thriving practice. And his extracurricular activities of late had netted him a new Cadillac and a ticket to Tahiti. Still, he had always coveted the spotlight claimed by lawyers like Martin Gorman and Johnnie Cochran and Robert Shapiro. He had just never found a way to get there that didn't involve talent and social connections.

A photograph of Tricia Crowne-Cole filled the television screen. She wasn't especially attractive, kind of pudgy and mousy with brown hair too long for a woman her age. (She had to be fifty-something—significantly older than Cole, provided he was the forty-something he claimed to be.) She wore glasses that made her look like a spinster librarian.

You would've thought the daughter of a bazillionaire would have used some of that money to jazz herself up a little. Especially in this town, where women kept the numbers of their plastic surgeons and their favorite designers on speed dial. A bazillion dollars could make plain look pretty damn gorgeous.

It was hard for the average person to imagine why anyone would have wanted her dead. She had devoted her life to overseeing her father's philanthropic trust. There wasn't a disease Norman Crowne wasn't trying to cure, a liberal social cause he didn't champion, a highfalutin art he didn't support—via Tricia. She was her father's social conscience.

It was impossible for the average person to imagine how anyone could have killed her so brutally, strangling her, then smashing her face in with a piece of sculpture the size of a bowling ball. Lenny was not the average person. He had heard it all a thousand times and knew full well what people were capable of, what jealousy and hate could drive them to.

Word around town was that Tricia, fed up with Cole's infidelities and endless dramas, had been about to dump Rob Cole off the gravy train at long last. Cole had tanked his career with sulkiness, stupidity, and a shallow store of talent. He had run through all of his money and plenty of hers. A lot of it had gone up his nose.

A lot had gone to rehab clinics—charitable donations, as it turned out. Rob Cole didn't have the character to pull himself out of the train wreck, or sense enough to keep his weaknesses private.

The tailor-made Leonard Lowell client, Lenny lamented. He could have made a big name for himself getting Rob Cole off the hook—a name that would be recognized even by people who didn't have rap sheets. But Rob Cole was Martin Gorman's headache. Lenny had other fish to fry.

The front buzzer sounded, announcing the arrival of the messenger. As he rounded the desk, Lenny glanced at the brochures he had gotten from the redhead at the travel agency on the second floor and wondered if he could sweet-talk her into going with him. The Cayman Islands and a hot broad. Paradise.

Jace leaned on the buzzer a second time, even though he could see Lenny Lowell coming out of the office and into the dark cubicle occupied in daylight hours by Lowell's secretary—a woman with cotton-candy blond hair and cat-eye glasses, known only as "Doll." Lenny was like a character out of an old movie where all the men wore hats and baggy suits, and everybody smoked cigarettes and talked fast.

Jace had been to Lowell's office many times. A lot of a messenger's runs were to or from lawyers of one kind or another—much to the displeasure of the messengers. Lawyers were notoriously cheap and impossible to please. At the annual Thanksgiving bash—Cranksgiving—the messengers always had a piñata in the image of their least favorite attorney of the year. They made the thing extra tough so everyone could get their chance to beat on it repeatedly.

Jace played along with the game and kept to himself the fact that he intended to join the ranks of the loathed someday. Growing up the way he had, he had seen the law work against a lot of people, especially kids. He meant to turn it in his favor—turn his life around, and hopefully some others' too. But he was taking only two college courses a semester, so most of his messenger cohorts would be dead or gone by the time he passed the bar. If Jace was ever to be immortalized as a piñata, it would be strangers beating the stuffing out of him.

In the meantime, he always made an effort to chat up any lawyers he could, trying to make a good impression, trying to pick up whatever he could about the profession and the people in it.

Networking. Working toward the day when he might be looking for a job, a recommendation, career advice.

Lowell pulled the door open, an unnaturally white smile splitting his long, horsey face.

"Neither rain, nor smog, nor gloom of night," he boomed. He'd been drinking. Jace could smell the bourbon hanging over the bad cologne.

"Hey, Lenny," he said, pushing his way inside. "It's raining, man."

"That's why they pay you the big bucks, kid."

"Yeah, right. I'm rolling in it," Jace said, resisting the urge to shake himself like a wet dog. "I just do this gig for the rush."

"You got a simple life," the lawyer said, weaving his way back to his office. "There's a lot to be said for that."

"Yeah, like it sucks. Believe me, Lenny, I'd rather be driving your new Cadillac than my bike. Especially tonight. Man, I hate the rain."

Lowell waved a big bony hand at him. "Nah. It never rains in Southern California. Unless you're some poor stiff like Rob Cole. Then you get a shitstorm on your head."

Jace glanced around the office piled with books and papers and file folders. Next to a bowling trophy dated 1974, two framed photographs sat on the desk—one of a racehorse in the winner's circle with a bunch of flowers around its neck, and one of a pretty young woman with long dark hair and a confident smile—Lenny's daughter, Abby. A law student, Lenny had told him.

"Gorman will get him off," Jace said, picking up the bowling trophy to read the inscription: 2ND PLACE TEAM, HOLLYWOOD BOWL, 1974. It wasn't difficult to picture Lenny in one of those bowling shirts from the fifties, his hair greased back. "Gorman is good. Better than good."

"It's better to be lucky than good, kid," Lowell returned. "Martin's betting against the house in a rigged game. Money talks. Remember that."

"I would if I had any." Jace put the trophy back and scratched his arm under the sleeve of his cheap plastic rain jacket. He had bought half a dozen at the 99 Cent Store because they came folded to the size of a wallet and didn't take up any space in his messenger bag. One seldom lasted more than a single storm, but the odds were good that six would last him the winter.

"Here," Lowell said, thrusting a twenty at him. "For your trouble, kid. Don't let it shoot its mouth off all in one place."

Jace wanted to hold it up to the light.

Lowell snorted. "It's real. Jesus. The last pa-
perhanger I defended went to San Quentin in
1987. Counterfeiting is all Russian mob now. I
don't want any part of that. Those bastards
make Hannibal Lecter look like a moody guy
with an eating disorder." He raised his glass in a
toast to himself. "To long life. Mine. You want
a toot, kid?"

"No, thanks, I don't drink."

"Designated driver?"

"Something like that."

Designated adult, as long as he could remember, but he didn't tell Leonard Lowell that. He
never told anyone anything about his life.
Below the radar. The less people knew, the less
curious they would be, the less apt to want to
"help." An extra twenty bucks was the only kind
of help Jace wanted.

"Thanks, Lenny. I appreciate it."

"I know you do, kid. Tell your mother she
raised a good one."

"I will."

He wouldn't. His mother had been dead
six years. He had mostly raised himself, and
Tyler too.

Lowell handed him a five-by-seven-inch
padded manila envelope. He hung a cigarette
on his lip and it bobbed up and down as he
spoke while he fished in his baggy pants pocket

for a lighter. "I appreciate you dropping this off for me, kid. You've got the address?"

Jace repeated it from memory.

"Keep it dry," Lowell said, blowing smoke at the dingy ceiling.

"Like my life depends on it."

3

Famous **last words,** Jace would think later when he looked back on this night. But he didn't think anything as he went out into the rain and pulled the U-lock off his bike.

Instead of putting the package in his bag, he slipped it up under his T-shirt and tucked the shirt and the package inside the waistband of his bike shorts. Warm and dry.

He climbed on the bike under the blue neon of the PSYCHIC READINGS sign and started to pedal, legs heavy, back aching, fingers cold and slipping on the wet handlebars. His weight shifted from pedal to pedal, the bike tilting side to side, the lateral motion gradually becoming forward motion as he picked up speed, the aches gradually melding into a familiar numbness.

One last run.

He would leave his paperwork 'til morning. Drop this package, go home, and crawl into that hot shower. He tried to imagine it: hot water pounding on his shoulders, massaging out the knots in the muscles, warm steam cleansing the stink of the city from his nostrils and soothing lungs that had spent the day sucking in car exhaust. He imagined Madame Chen's hot and sour soup, and clean sheets on the futon, and did his best to ignore the cold rain pelting his face and deglazing the oil on the surface of the street.

His mind distracted, he rode on autopilot. Past the 76 station, take a right. Down two blocks, take a left. The side streets were empty, dark. Nobody hung around in this part of town at this time of night for any good reason. The businesses—a glass shop, an air-conditioning place, a furniture-stripping place, an auto-body shop—in the dirty, low, flat-roofed buildings closed up at six.

He might have thought it was a strange destination for a package from a lawyer, except that the lawyer was Lenny, and Lenny's clients were low-end career criminals.

He checked address numbers as lighting allowed. The drop would be the first place on the right on the next block. Except that the first place on the right on the next block was a vacant lot.

Jace cruised past, checked the number on the next available building, which was dark, save for the security light hanging over the front door.

Apprehension scratched like a fingernail on the back of his neck. He swung around in the street and rode slowly past the vacant lot again.

Headlights flashed on, blinding him for a second.

What the hell kind of drop was this? Drugs? A payoff? Whatever it was, Jace wasn't making it. Only a fool would ride into this and ask for a signature on a manifest.

Now he was pissed. Pissed and scared. Sent to a vacant lot in the dead of fucking night. Fuck that. Fuck Lenny Lowell. He could take his package and shove it up his ass.

Jace stood on his pedals and started to go.

The car lurched forward, engine roaring like a charging beast as it made straight for him.

For a split second it seemed Jace didn't—couldn't—move. Then he was going, legs pumping like pistons, the bike's tires slipping on the wet street. If he ran straight, the car would be on him like a cat on a mouse. He turned hard left instead. The bike's back end skated sideways on the slick pavement. He stuck a foot down to keep from falling, pulled the bike back under himself. Then he was charging the car.

Heart in his throat, he juked right, nearly too late, jumped the curb back into the vacant lot, shooting past the car—big, dark, domestic. He heard the grind of metal on pavement as the car went off the curb and bottomed out. Tires squealed on the wet street as it swung a wide, awkward, skidding turn.

Jace made for the alley as hard as he could go, praying it wouldn't dead-end. In the heart of downtown he was like a street rat that knew every sewer pipe, every Dumpster, every crack in a wall that could offer a shortcut, escape, shelter, a hiding place. Here he was vulnerable, a rabbit caught in the open. Prey.

The car was coming after him. The predator. The headlights bucked up and down in the gloom as the car banged back up over the curb.

Jace had had cars come after him in traffic—kids screwing around, men with rage disorders pissed off that he had cut in front of them or skitched a ride up a hill or knocked a side mirror. Assholes trying to make a point, trying to give him a scare. He had never been set up. He had never been hunted.

If he could get to the end of the alley before the car turned down it and spotlit him, he had a fifty-fifty shot at ditching it. The end of the alley looked nine miles away.

And it was already too late.

The high beams slapped at his back like a paw reaching out to tag him. The car came, as loud as a train, sending trash cans scattering like bowling pins.

Shit, shit, shit.

His luck was running out faster than the alley was. He couldn't outrun the car. He couldn't turn and ditch the car. To his left: buildings shoulder to shoulder, backed with Dumpsters and boxes and discarded junk—an obstacle course. To his right: a chain-link fence crowned with razor wire. On his ass: the angel of death.

Jace reached back with one hand and jerked his U-lock out of his messenger bag. The bumper kissed his back tire. He nearly fell onto the hood of the car. Moving as close as he could against the fence, Jace touched his brakes, dropped just behind Predator's bumper.

Jace swung the heavy U-lock left-handed into the windshield. A spiderweb of cracks exploded across the span of glass. The car swerved into him, drove him sideways into the fence. Jace turned and grabbed hold of the chain-link fence with both hands, hanging on hard as the bike was yanked out from under him. The toe of his right shoe hung up in the pedal clip and his body jerked wildly sideways as the car pushed the bike forward.

The fence bit into his fingers as the bike tried to drag him. It felt like his arms were tearing out of their sockets, that his foot was being wrenched off at the ankle, then suddenly he was free and falling.

He landed on his back on the cracked asphalt, rolled, and scrambled up onto his knees, his eyes on the car as his bike went under the back tire and died a terrible death.

His only transportation. His livelihood. Gone.

He was on his own. On foot. And one foot was missing a shoe. Pain burned through his wrenched ankle as Jace pushed himself to his feet and ran for the buildings before the car could come to a complete stop.

The voice of his survival instinct screamed through his brain. **Go, go, go!!!**

He was young, he was fast, he was highly motivated. He set his sights on a half wall blocking the space between two buildings. He would hit it running, vault over the side, and be gone. Bum ankle or no, he could damn well outrun the asshole driving that car.

But he couldn't outrun a bullet.

The shot hit the Dumpster a foot to Jace's left almost simultaneously as he heard the report.

Fuck!

He had to get over that wall. He had to get over it. Get over it and run like hell.

Footfalls were coming hard behind him.

The second shot went wide right and hit another Dumpster.

A man shouted, "Fuck!"

Too close. Too close.

Footfalls coming hard behind him.

Jace launched himself at the wall and was summarily yanked backward as his pursuer grabbed hold of the messenger bag he wore strapped across his back.

He fell into the man, and momentum carried them both backward, their feet tangling. Predator's body cushioned the fall as they went down. Jace scrambled to get his feet under him, to wriggle away. Predator hung tight to the messenger bag.

"Fucking little shit!"

Jace swung an elbow back, connected hard with some part of the guy's face. A bone cracked nearly as loudly as the gunshot had, and for a split second the bastard's hold let loose and he cursed a blue streak. Jace ducked down and twisted out of the bag's strap and lunged toward the wall again.

Predator grabbed hold of the back of Jace's rain slicker with one hand and swung at him with the other. The cheap poncho tore away like wet tissue. The butt of the gun glanced off the back of Jace's helmet. Stars burst bright before his eyes, but he kept moving.

Over the wall! Over the wall!

He hit it running, scrambled up and over,

and tumbled ass-over-teakettle as he landed, rolling through mud and muck and garbage and water.

The canyon between the buildings was pitch-black, the only light at the end of the tunnel the dim silver glow of a distant sodium vapor light. He ran toward it, never expecting to reach it, expecting to feel the thump and burn of a bullet passing through his back, tearing through his body, ripping apart organs and blood vessels. He would probably be dead before he hit the ground.

But still he ran.

The bullet didn't come.

He broke out of the alley, turned left, and raced past the fronts of dark buildings, jumping shrubbery and low walls of tired landscaping. As he landed on the other side of a row of bushes, his bad ankle buckled beneath him and he fell, gravel tearing at his hands as he tried to break the impact. He expected to hear footfalls behind him, another shot aimed at his back, but no one was coming yet.

Panting, dizzy, Jace rose and stumbled down the narrow corridor between two buildings. He stopped and fell against the rough concrete wall, wanting to puke, afraid the sound would draw his predator and get him killed.

Doubled over, he cupped his hands over his

mouth and tried to slow his breathing. His heart felt like it would burst through his chest wall and flop out onto the ground, bouncing and twitching like a beached fish. His head was spinning. His brain felt like it was swirling around in a toilet bowl, ready to be sucked down the drain.

Oh, God. Oh, my God.

The God he didn't believe in.

Someone's trying to kill me.

Jesus H.

He was shaking violently, suddenly cold, suddenly aware of the winter rain pouring down on him, soaking his clothes. Pain throbbed and burned in his ankle. A sharper pain pierced his foot. He felt along the bottom of his wet sock and pulled out a sliver of broken glass. He sank down into a squat, hugged his arms around his legs as he leaned against the wall.

The two-way was still strapped to his thigh. He could try to call Base, but Eta was long gone home to her kids by now. If he had a cell phone, he could call the cops. But he couldn't afford a cell phone, and he had no faith in the police. He had no real faith in anyone but himself. He never had.

The dizziness was swept away by a wave of weakness, the wake of the initial adrenaline rush. He strained to hear past his own breathing, past the sound of his pulse pounding in his ears. He tried to listen for the sounds of pursuit. He tried to think what to do next.

Best to stay where he was. He was out of sight and had an escape route if his assailant did flush him out. Unless there were two of them—**assailants,** plural. One on either end of this tunnel and he was cooked.

He thought of Tyler, who would by now be wondering where he was. Not that the kid was sitting alone somewhere, waiting. Tyler was never alone. A brainiac little white kid living in Chinatown and speaking fluent Mandarin sort of stood out. Tyler was a novelty. People liked him and were bemused by him at the same time. The Chens treated him like some kind of golden child sent to them for good fortune.

Still, the only true family the Damon brothers had was each other. And that bond of family with Tyler was the strongest thing Jace had ever known. It was the thing he lived for, the motivation behind everything he did, every goal he had.

Gotta get out of here.

Footfalls slapped on pavement. Jace couldn't tell from where. The alley? The street? He made himself as small as he could, a tight human ball tucked against the side of the building, and counted his heartbeats as he waited.

A dark figure stopped at the end of the building, street side, and stood there, arms slightly out to his sides, his movements hesitant as he turned one way and then the other. There wasn't enough light to make out more than the vague shape of him. He had no face. He had no color.

Jace pressed his hand against his belly, against the envelope he had tucked inside his shirt for safekeeping. What the hell had Lenny gotten him into?

The dark figure at the end of the tunnel turned and went back the way he had come.

Jace waited, counting silently until he decided Predator wasn't coming back. Then he crept along the wall through scraps of trash and puddles and broken glass, and cautiously peered out. A Dumpster blocked his view. He could see only one section of taillight, glowing like an evil red eye in the dark some distance down the alley.

His bike lay crumpled on the ground somewhere behind the car. Jace hoped against hope that the frame wasn't shot, that maybe only a wheel had been mangled. He could fix that. He could fix a lot of damage. If the frame was bent, that was something else.

He could hear Mojo now, telling him the bike was cursed. Mojo, the tall, skinny Jamaican who had dreads down to his ass and wore the kind of black wraparound shades meant for blind people. Mojo was maybe thirty, an ancient among the messengers. A shaman to some. He would have plenty to say about that bike.

Jace had inherited the thing, in a manner of speaking. That was to say no one else would touch it when it had suddenly become available two years before. Its previous owner, a guy who called himself King and worked nights as an Elvis-impersonating stripper, had lost control dodging street traffic and ended up under the wheels of a garbage truck. The bike had survived. King had not.

Messengers were a superstitious bunch. King died in the line. Nobody wanted a dead guy's bike if he died in the line. It sat in the back hall at Base for a week, waiting to be claimed by King's next of kin, only it turned out he didn't have any, at least none that gave a shit about him.

Jace didn't believe in superstition. He believed you made your own luck. King went under the wheels because he was cranked up on speed most of the time and had poor judgment. Jace believed in focus and hustle. He had looked at the bike and seen a strong Cannondale frame, two good wheels, and a gel-cushioned seat. He saw himself cutting his delivery times, making more runs, making more money. He waved off all warnings, left the piece of shit he'd been riding leaning against an **LA Times** box for anyone who wanted to steal it, and rode home on the Cannondale. He named it The Beast.

The car's engine revved and the taillight disappeared from view. Predator was going home, calling it after a hard day of trying to kill people, Jace thought. Chills shook his body, from the rain and from relief. This time when he thought he was going to puke, he did.

Headlights flashed past on the street. Predator passed by, the big car growling like a panther as sirens whined in the distance.

Jace went back to the scene where his fallen mount lay, the rear wheel mangled beyond saving. If it were a horse, someone would shoot it, put it out of its misery. But it was a bike, and the frame was still intact. A miracle from God, Preacher John would have said. In his downtime between runs, Preacher John stood on the corner of Fourth and Flower in front of the upscale Bonaventure Hotel and recited the Bible for all those unfortunate enough to have to pass by him.

Jace didn't believe in miracles. He'd caught a break. Two, considering he was still alive.

He looked around for his bag, but it was gone. Taken as a trophy by Predator, a consolation prize. Or maybe he thought he'd accomplished his true mission. Someone wanted whatever the hell was in Lenny Lowell's packet, held tight against Jace's belly by his bike shorts.

Whatever it was, Jace was going to find out. Lenny had a lot to answer for.

He picked up the bike, tilted it up onto the front wheel only, and started walking.

4

"Don't step on his brain," Kev Parker warned. Kev Parker, forty-three, Detective 2, kicked down to one of the lesser divisions to finish out his career in disgrace and oblivion.

Renee Ruiz, his latest trainee, looked down at her stylish beige suede and leopard-print shoe. The spike heel was already stuck in a squishy gob of gray matter that had splattered some distance away from the body.

"Jesus Christ, Parker!" she squealed. "Why didn't you tell me?"

"I just did."

"I could have ruined my fucking shoe!"

"Yeah? Well, your fucking shoe is the least of your problems. And since you were standing behind a door when they handed out common sense, I'll tell you again: Don't wear stiletto heels on the job. You're supposed to be a detective, not a hooker."

Ruiz narrowed her eyes at him and spat a few choice words in Spanish.

Parker was unfazed. "You learn that from your mother?" he asked, his attention going to the body on the floor of the office.

Detective trainee Ruiz stepped wide of the mess to try to get in Parker's face. "You gotta treat me with respect, Parker."

"I will," he said, not even glancing at her. The dead body had his undivided attention. Massive trauma to the head. Whoever killed this guy enjoyed his work. "When you deserve it," he added.

Again with the Spanish.

Parker had been breaking in new detectives for going on four years, and this one was at the top of his shit list. He didn't have a problem with women. He didn't have a problem with Hispanics. He had a problem with attitude, and Renee Ruiz had attitude coming out of her pretty Jennifer Lopez–esque ass. Or she would have, if her skirt hadn't been so damn tight. Parker had been working with her for less than a week and already he wanted to strangle her and throw her body into the La Brea tar pits.

"Are you paying attention here?" he said impatiently. "In case you hadn't noticed, we're at a homicide. There's a dead guy on the floor and his head is bashed apart like a rotten cauliflower. What are you supposed to be doing instead of giving me shit about your shoes?"

Ruiz pouted. She was a knockout. A body that would turn any unsuspecting straight man with a pulse into a drooling idiot. Her lips were full and sexy. She outlined them in a color three shades darker than the shiny wet gloss she used to fill them in. The "Mall Mexican" look was the way Detective Kray described it.

Kray, another of their Homicide team, had problems with women **and** Hispanics, and blacks, and Jews, and every other definable ethnic group that wasn't a stupid, racist, redneck cracker from Bumfuck, Louisiana—which was how Parker described Kray.

"Where's your notebook?" he demanded. "You have to write everything down. And I mean **every thing.** You should have started writing the second you got this call. What time the call came, who told you what, what time you wedged your ass into that skirt and put on those ridiculous shoes. What time you arrived at the crime scene, who you spoke to first, what you saw when you came in the front door, what you saw when you came into this room. Position of the body, location of the murder weapon, which way his brain splattered and how far the pieces flew, whether or not his fly is open. Every damn thing in sight.

"You leave something out and I can guarantee you some dirtbag defense attorney will get you on the stand and ask you about that one seemingly insignificant item, and he'll unravel the DA's case like a cheap sweater. The worst two words in the English language, babe: **reasonable doubt.**"

Parker refused to call her "Detective" Ruiz one second before she had her shield in hand. She was not his peer, and he would remind her in subtle and not-so-subtle ways every day of her training period. He didn't have control over a hell of a lot in his job, but for the time he was partnered with Ruiz, he had at least the illusion of control over her.

"And measure the distances," he said. "If you find a booger on the carpet, I want to know exactly where it is in relation to the body. Put the exact measurements in your personal notes, approximate measurements in the notes you'll take to court. If you put your exact measurements in your official notes and your measurements don't match the criminalists' to the millimeter, you'll have a defense attorney all over you like a bad rash."

Ruiz came back with the attitude. "You're

lead. It's your case. Why don't you do the scut work, Parker?"

"I will," Parker said. "I sure as hell am not trusting you to do it right. But you'll do it too, so when the next vic comes along and you get the lead, you at least look like you know what you're doing."

He looked around the room cluttered with crap and crime-scene geeks. One of the uniforms who had answered the initial call stood by the front door, logging in every person who entered the scene. The other one—older, heavyset, and balding—was on the other side of the room, pointing out to one of the geeks something he thought might be significant evidence. Jimmy Chewalski. Jimmy was good people. He talked too much, but he was a good cop. Everyone called him Jimmy Chew.

Ruiz looked right through the crime-scene techs and the uniforms. Having passed the written detective exam, she now considered herself above them. Never mind that she had been in a uniform herself not that long ago, she was now a princess among the lowly hired help. To Ruiz, Jimmy Chew (Choo) was a pair of fuck-me shoes.

Parker made his way over to the officer, leaving Ruiz to figure out how to bend down and look at evidence without flashing her ass to everyone at the scene.

"Jimmy, where's the coroner's investigator?" Parker asked, stepping gingerly around the body, careful to miss a sheaf of papers that were strewn on the floor. The coroner's investigator had the first dance. No one could so much as check the dead body's pockets until the CI had finished his or her business.

"Could be a while," Chewalski said. "She's helping out at a murder-suicide."

"Nicholson?"

"Yeah. Some guy blew away his wife and two kids 'cause the wife brought home a bucket of regular KFC instead of extra-crispy. Then he goes in his bathroom and blows his head off. I heard the scene was so bad, the detectives had to take umbrellas in the bathroom with them. Most of the guy's face ended up on the ceiling. And, as we all know, what goes up must come down. I heard an eyeball dropped and hit Kray in the head."

Parker chuckled. "Too bad he couldn't have scooped up some of the gray matter. Then at least he'd have half a brain."

Chew grinned. "That guy's head is so far up his ass, it's popped back out of his shoulders again. He's a fucking French knot."

Parker turned his attention to the dead body again. "So what's the story here?"

Chew rolled his eyes. "Well, Kev, we have here dead on the floor an unlamented scum-sucking member of the bar."

"Now, Jimmy, just because a man was a soulless, amoral asshole doesn't mean he deserved to be murdered."

"Excuse me? Who's in charge here?"

Parker swiveled his head around to see a pretty twenty-something brunette in a smart Burberry trench coat standing three feet away, near the hall to the back door.

"That would be me. Detective Parker. And you are?"

Unsmiling, she looked directly at him with steady dark eyes, then at Officer Chewalski. "Abby Lowell. The scum-sucking member of the bar, the soulless, amoral asshole lying dead on the floor, is my father. Leonard Lowell."

5

Jimmy Chew made a sound like he had been impaled with something. Parker took it on the chin with just a hint of a flinch around his eyes. He pulled his hat off and offered his hand to Abby Lowell. She looked at it like she figured he never washed after going to the john.

"My condolences for your loss, Ms. Lowell," Parker said. "I'm sorry you heard that."

She arched a perfect brow. "But not sorry you said it?"

"It wasn't personal. I'm sure it's no surprise to you how cops feel about defense attorneys."

"No, it's not," she said. Her voice was a strong, slightly hoarse alto that would serve her well in a courtroom. The withering gaze never wavered. She had yet to look at her father's body. She kept her chin up, Parker thought, to avoid seeing him. "I'm in law school myself. Just so you can get a head start coming up with new and different derogatory ways to describe me."

"I can assure you, we treat every homicide the

same, Ms. Lowell. Regardless of who or what the victim was."

"That doesn't instill much confidence, Detective."

"I have an eighty-six-percent clearance rate."

"And what happened to the other fourteen percent?"

"I'm still working them. I'll work them 'til they're cleared. I don't care how long it takes. I don't care if by the time I close those cases the perps are hunchbacked old men and I have to chase them down with a walker," Parker said. "There's not a homicide cop in this town better than me."

"Then why aren't you working with us, Parker?"

Bradley Kyle, Detective 2 with Robbery-Homicide—LAPD's glamour squad, bastion of hotshots and arrogant assholes. Parker knew this firsthand because he had once been one of them, and a more arrogant, hotshot jerk had never walked the halls of Parker Center. In those days he had been fond of saying the building had been named for him. Stardom was his destiny. The memory bubbled up inside him now like a case of acid reflux, burning and bitter.

Parker scowled at Kyle moving toward him. "What is this? A party? And how did your name get on the guest list, Bradley? Or are you just out slumming?"

Kyle ignored him and started looking around the crime scene. His partner, a big guy with no neck, a blond flattop, and horn-rimmed glasses, spoke to no one as he made notes. Parker watched them for a moment, a bad feeling coiling in his gut. Robbery-Homicide didn't just show up at a murder out of curiosity. They worked the high-profile cases, like O.J., like Robert Blake, like Rob Cole—LA's celebrity killer du jour.

"Don't piss on my crime scene, **Bradley.**" Parker emphasized the name, dragged it out, knowing Kyle hated it. He wanted to be called Kyle—or at the worst, Brad. Bradley was a name for an interior decorator or a hairstylist, not a kick-ass detective.

Kyle glanced at him. "Who says it's yours?"

"My beat, my call, my murder," Parker said, moving toward the younger detective.

Kyle ignored him and squatted down to look at the apparent murder weapon—an old bowling trophy, now encrusted in blood and decorated with Lenny Lowell's hair and a piece of his scalp.

Kyle had been on his way up in Robbery-Homicide while Parker was being driven out. He was at the top of his game now and eating up the spotlight every time he got the chance, which was too often.

He was a good-looking guy, good face for television, a tan so perfect it had to have been airbrushed on him. He had an athletic build, but he was on the slight side, and touchy about it. Made a point of telling people he was five eleven and a half, like he'd knock anyone on their ass for making something of it. Parker, who was himself a hair under six feet, figured Kyle for five nine and not a fraction more.

Parker squatted down beside him. "What are you doing here?" he asked quietly. "What's Robbery-Homicide doing cruising the murder of a low-rent mouthpiece like Lenny Lowell?"

"We go where they send us. Isn't that right, Moosie?" Kyle tossed a look at his partner. Moose grunted and kept on making notes.

"What are you saying?" Parker asked. "Are you saying you're taking this? Why? It won't even make the paper. This guy's clients were scumbags and dirtballs."

Kyle pretended not to have heard him, and stood up. Ruiz stood a scant few inches away from him. In her ridiculous heels she was almost at eye level with him.

"Detective Kyle," she purred in a hot phone-sex voice as she offered her hand. "Detective Renee Ruiz. I want your job."

This in the same tone she might have used to say "I want you inside me," not that Parker had any desire to find out. He stood up and gave the dead eyes to his partner. "**Trainee** Ruiz, have you finished diagramming the crime scene?"

She huffed a petulant sigh at Parker, then tossed a sexy look at Kyle and walked away like a woman who knew a guy was watching her ass.

"Forget it, Kyle," Parker said. "She'd grind you up like lunch meat. Besides, she's too tall for you."

"Excuse me, gentlemen." Abby Lowell joined them. "If I might intrude on your little game of who has the biggest dick—" She offered her hand to Kyle, all business. "Abby Lowell. The victim is—was—my father."

"I'm sorry for your loss, Ms. Lowell."

"You're with Robbery-Homicide," she said. "I recognize you from the news."

"Yes." Kyle looked as pleased as a second-rate dinner-theater actor thinking he was about to be asked for his autograph.

Parker expected Abby Lowell to say "Thank God you're here." Instead, she looked Kyle square in the eyes and said: "Why are you here?"

Kyle gave her the poker face. "Excuse me?"

"Come on, Detective. I've been around my father's business all my life. His clients and their accused crimes should be way below your radar. What do you think happened here? Do you know something I don't?"

"A man was murdered. We're homicide cops. Do you know something **I** don't? What do **you** think happened here?"

Abby Lowell took in the mess as if seeing it for the first time since she had entered the room: the files and paperwork everywhere, the overturned chair, maybe from a struggle, maybe from a ransacking after the murder.

Parker watched her carefully, thinking there was a whole lot stirring beneath the thin facade of calm. He could see it in her eyes, in the slight tremor of her lips. Fear, shock, the struggle to control her emotions. She kept her arms crossed tight, holding herself, keeping her hands from shaking. She was very careful not to look at the floor in front of her.

"I don't know," she said softly. "Maybe a disgruntled client, maybe a family member of a victim in a case Lenny won. Maybe someone wanted something here Lenny didn't want to give up."

Her gaze landed on a credenza at the far side of her father's desk. A cube-shaped black safe that was maybe two feet square squatted in the cabinet, the door open. "He kept cash in that safe."

"Did you check the safe, Parker?" Kyle asked, the Man In Charge.

Parker turned to Jimmy Chew. "Jimmy, did you look in that safe when you got here?"

"Why, yes, Detective Parker, I did," Chew said with false formality. He didn't so much as glance at Kyle. "When my partner and I arrived at nineteen hundred hours and fourteen minutes, we first secured the scene and called in Homicide. While looking around the office, my partner observed the safe was open and that it appeared to contain only documents, which we did not examine."

"No cash?" Parker asked.

"No, sir. No money. Not in plain sight anyway."

"I know there was money," Abby Lowell said with an edge in her voice. "A lot of Lenny's clients preferred to pay him in cash."

"There's a surprise," Jimmy Chew muttered, retreating.

"He never had less than five thousand dollars in that safe—usually more. He kept it in a bank bag."

"Was your father having problems with any of his clients?" Kyle asked.

"He didn't talk to me about his clients, Detective Kyle. Even scum-sucking dirtbag attorneys have their ethics."

"I didn't mean to imply otherwise, Ms. Lowell. I apologize on behalf of the department if anyone here may have given you that impression. I'm sure your father had ethics."

And he probably kept them in a jar at the back of a cupboard, next to the pickled onions and some ten-year-old canned salmon, never to be opened, Parker thought. He'd seen Lenny Lowell at work in the courtroom. Short on scruples **and** ethics, Lowell would have impugned the testimony of his own mother if it meant getting an acquittal.

"We'll need to see his client records," Kyle said.

"Sure. As soon as someone rewrites the Constitution," Abby Lowell returned. "That information is privileged."

"A list of his clients, then."

"I'm a student, not stupid. Unless a judge tells me I have to, you get nothing confidential out of this office."

Color began to creep upward from Kyle's starched white collar. "Do you want us to solve your father's murder, Ms. Lowell? Or is there some reason you'd rather we didn't?"

"Of course I want it solved," she snapped. "But I also know that I now have to look out for my father's clients and for the best interest of his

practice. If I just hand over privileged information, that could open my father's estate to lawsuits, compromise ongoing cases, and could
very well keep me from my chosen profession. I
don't want to be disbarred before I even take the
bar exam, Detective Kyle. This has to be done
by the book."

"You don't need to compromise yourself, Ms.
Lowell. Names and addresses aren't privileged,"
Parker said calmly, pulling her attention away
from Kyle. "And it's not necessary for us to access your father's files. The criminal records of
his clients are readily available. When was the
last time you spoke with your father?"

He saw more value in trying to get Abby
Lowell on his side than in bullying her into an
adversarial position. She wasn't some weak, hysterical woman, terrified of the police, which was
what Kyle wanted her to be. She had already
dug in her heels, put a chip on her shoulder, and
dared him to knock it off.

She rubbed a slightly trembling manicured
hand across her forehead and let a slightly shaky
sigh escape, showing a tiny crack in the armor.
"I spoke with Lenny around six-thirty. We
were supposed to meet for dinner at Cicada. I
got there early, had a drink, called him on my
cell phone. He said he might be a little late,"

she said, her voice tightening, her dark eyes filling. She blinked the tears back. "He said he was waiting for a bike messenger to pick something up."

"Did he say what?"

"No."

"Late in the day to call a messenger."

She shrugged. "Probably something he needed to get to a client."

"Do you know what service he used?"

"Whichever could pick up and deliver the fastest and the cheapest."

"If we can find out which service, their dispatch office will have the address the package was going to, maybe a vague description of what was in it, and the name of the messenger they sent," Parker said. "Do you know if the messenger ever arrived?"

"No. I told you, when I last spoke with Lenny, he was waiting."

Parker glanced over at the safe, frowning.

"That would be stupid," she said, reading his mind. "Like you said, his dispatch office will have the messenger's name."

Which could very well not be real, Parker thought. Bike messengers weren't known for being stable, family types. They tended to be loners, oddballs, living a hand-to-mouth existence.

The way they raced the downtown streets—balls-out, no fear for life or limb, no regard for themselves or anyone else—it wasn't a stretch to imagine more than one of them was hopped up on something.

So some down-on-his-luck junkie messenger shows up for a package, gets a look in Lowell's open safe, decides to elevate his social standing, kills Lowell, takes the money, and vanishes into the night, never to be seen again. The guy could be on a bus to Vegas while they stood around talking about it.

"It's not my job to draw conclusions, Ms. Lowell. I have to consider all possibilities.

"Who called 911?" he asked, turning again to Jimmy Chew.

"The ever-popular anonymous citizen."

"Anything around here open or inhabited?"

"Not on a night like this. There's a 76 station and a bail-bonds place down the street, on the other side. And the 24/7 Laundromat."

"Go see if anyone at the Laundromat has anything to say."

"They're closed."

"I thought you said it was called 24/7."

"It's raining," Chew said, incredulous. "Me and Stevie cruised past around six-fifteen. The place was locked up tight. Besides, they quit being open twenty-four after their night clerk was robbed and raped six, eight months ago."

Kyle smirked. "Great neighborhood you work, Parker."

"Killers are killers, no matter what neighborhood you're in, Bradley," Parker said. "The only difference is, you can't make the news off the murders here."

He turned back to Abby Lowell. "How were you notified of your father's death, Ms. Lowell?"

She looked at him like she thought he might be pulling something on her. "One of the officers called."

Parker looked at Chew, who held up his hands in denial, then looked at Chew's partner, who shook his head.

"Someone called you. On your cell phone," Parker said.

Abby Lowell's eyes bounced from one man to another, uncertain. "Yes. Why?"

"What did the caller say to you?"

"That my father had been killed, and could I please come to his office. Why?"

"May I see your cell phone?"

"I don't understand," she said, hesitantly pulling her phone out of a pocket in her trench coat.

"LAPD wouldn't tell you something like that over the phone, Ms. Lowell," Parker said. "An officer or detective would have come to your residence to give you the news."

Her eyes widened as the implication sank in. "Are you telling me I was on the phone with my father's killer?"

"What time did you get the call?"

"Maybe twenty minutes ago. I was at the restaurant."

"Do you have a call list on that thing?" Parker asked, nodding toward the phone she clutched in her hand.

"Yes." She scrolled through a list of commands and brought up the screen that listed calls received. Her hand was trembling. "I don't recognize the number."

"You didn't recognize the voice?"

"No. Of course not."

Parker held his hand out. "May I?"

Abby Lowell handed him the phone. She couldn't jerk her hand back from it quickly enough, as if it had just been revealed to her that the thing was in fact a live reptile. Parker checked the number, hit the button to call it back, then listened as it rang unanswered on the other end.

"Oh, my God," Lenny Lowell's daughter breathed. She pressed a hand to her lips and blinked away the gathering tears.

Parker turned back to Chew. "Track down

the owner of the Laundromat. Find out who was working and what time they closed. I want that person located. I want to know if there was a single living being in proximity of this office between six-thirty and seven-fifteen. If a rat crawled by the back door and someone saw it, I want to know."

"Roger that, boss." Chew flipped Kyle's smirk back at him as he went to speak to his partner.

Parker went to the vic's desk. The old Rolodex was closed. He flipped the cover up with the tip of a pen, then turned to the Latent Prints tech. "Cynthia, I want every print you can lift off this thing, inside and out. Every frigging card, but priority on this one."

Abby Lowell's. Beneath her name was her home number, her cell number, her address.

"Go ahead and cover the bases for us, Parker," Kyle said tightly as he stepped in beside Parker behind the desk. "But don't get too cozy. If the word comes down from the mountain, you're out."

Parker stared at him for a second, then a new voice called from the front office. "Parker, please tell me your DB had a heart attack. I need a nice simple 'natural causes' so I can go home. It's raining."

Diane Nicholson, coroner's investigator for

the County of Los Angeles, forty-two, and a long cool drink of gin to look at. She took no shit and no prisoners—an attitude that had earned her the fear and respect of cops all over the city. No one messed with a Nicholson crime scene.

She stopped just inside the door to Lowell's private office and looked down at Lenny Lowell. "Oh, shit." This with more disappointment than horror. There wasn't much that shocked her.

She looked at Parker with flat eyes, giving away nothing, then looked at Kyle and seemed offended at the sight of him.

"Parker is the detective of record," she announced. "Until I hear differently from someone more important than you, Bradley, I talk to Parker."

She didn't wait for a response from Kyle. What he might have to say was of no interest or consequence to her. She worked for the coroner's office. The coroner might jump to the bark of big dogs in Parker Center; Diane Nicholson did not.

She pulled on a pair of latex gloves and knelt down to begin her examination of the body.

Lenny Lowell's pants pockets yielded forty-three cents, a Chiclet, and a laminated, faded, dog-eared pari-mutuel ticket from a horse race at Santa Anita.

"He carried it for luck."

The voice that had been so strong and forceful earlier was now barely audible. Parker looked at Abby Lowell, watched her eyes fill again as she stared at the small piece of red cardstock in Nicholson's hand. She didn't try to blink the tears back this time. They spilled over her lashes and down her cheeks, one fat drop at a time. Her face was white; the skin appeared nearly translucent, like fine porcelain. Parker thought she might faint, and brushed past Kyle to go to her.

"The ticket," she said. She tried to force a sardonic smile at some private joke, but her mouth was trembling. "He carried it for luck."

Parker touched her arm gently. "Is there a friend you can stay with, Ms. Lowell? I'll have an officer drive you. I'll call you tomorrow and we'll set up a time for you to come into the station and talk more about your father."

Abby Lowell jerked her arm away without looking at him, her gaze nailed to the floor, to her father's wingtips. "Don't pretend concern for me, Detective," she said bitterly. "I don't want your phony sympathy. I'll drive myself home."

No one said anything as she walked away and hurried down the hall and out the back door.

Nicholson broke the silence, slipping Lenny Lowell's good-luck charm into an envelope in case it might turn out to be relevant later on. "I guess he should have cashed it in while he had the chance."

6

Jace worked his way back to Lenny Lowell's neighborhood through alleys and between buildings, avoiding streetlights and open spaces, his heart racing every time a car crossed his field of vision. He had no way of knowing where Predator had gone. He had no way of knowing whether or not the son of a bitch was half a block away, parked at the curb, rifling through the messenger bag for the packet that had to have been his objective in the attack—and discovering that it wasn't there, that he hadn't finished his job.

It seemed to take for-fucking-ever to walk The Beast back to familiar territory. He tried to balance the mangled bike up on its good front wheel and at the same time balance his own weight against the bike like a crutch. His wrenched ankle was throbbing. He had at least recovered his boot, but the swelling in his ankle prevented him from tying the laces tight. If he were a gazelle, like on those nature shows Tyler soaked up from the Discovery Channel, the next lion to come hunting would take him down.

He came to the 76 station from the alley, propped The Beast up against the back wall of the building, then leaned around the corner and peered out of the darkness toward the island of fluorescent light surrounding the gas pumps. No one was buying gas. There were few cars on the street. Those that drove past went with purpose, going somewhere and determined to get there on what was in their tank.

It was still raining. Jace was shaking with cold and fear, adrenaline and exhaustion. He felt weak and faint and on edge, all at once. Home was still a long walk away. As soon as he could find a pay phone that worked, he would call the Chens and ask to speak to Tyler. There was no phone in the Damons' three rooms above the fish market. Jace couldn't afford one, and had no one to call on a regular basis anyway.

He wished that wasn't true tonight. It would have been a damn good night to call a friend for a ride. But he had no friends, only acquaintances, and it seemed best not to drag anyone into the mess in which he found himself. Instinctively, he thought in terms of isolation, keeping his life as uncomplicated by other people as was possible. He sure as hell could have done without knowing Lenny Lowell tonight.

His stomach rumbled and started to cramp. He needed to put something in it, needed fuel for what the rest of the night might bring. Lenny Lowell's twenty-dollar tip was in his pocket. He could buy himself a soda and a candy bar. Unlike a lot of the messengers, Jace never stored money or anything of personal value in his messenger bag. He knew too well that anything could be taken from him at any time.

An overhang along the front of the booth offered shelter from the rain. A thin, dark guy in an orange turban sat in the booth behind the bulletproof glass. He startled at Jace's sudden appearance, grabbed his microphone, and said with a crisp British accent: "The police are just down the block."

As if he had already called them in anticipation of being robbed.

"A Snickers and a Mountain Dew." Jace dug two damp, crumpled bills out of his pocket and stuck them in the pay tray.

"I have no more than fifty dollars in the till," the man went on, his voice sounding tinny and distant through the cheap speaker. He pointed to the sign stuck to the window among the many warning stickers. Exposure to gas fumes could cause birth defects. Cigarettes caused cancer but if a person didn't care and wanted them anyway, 76 stations would ask for an ID, in accordance with the law. The night clerk had no more than fifty bucks in the cash register.

"And I have a gun."

He pulled a big-ass handgun out from under the cluttered counter and pointed it at Jace's face, even as he snagged the two dollars from the tray with his other hand.

"Isn't that glass bulletproof?" Jace asked.

The clerk scowled. "Yes, you cannot shoot me."

"I don't have a gun," Jace said. "And if you try to shoot me, the glass will stop your bullet, maybe even bounce it back into your face. Did you ever think of that?"

Jace spread his hands where the clerk could see them. "I'm not robbing you anyway. I just want a Snickers and a Mountain Dew. Come on, man. It's raining."

From the corner of his eye Jace caught the watery red intermittent flash of a police strobe down the street, and his pulse kicked up a beat. The car wasn't moving. Nor were any of its companions parked around the same small chunk of real estate.

"What's going on down there?"

Maybe Lenny had called the cops when he figured out the package hadn't been delivered. Maybe the envelope was stuffed with cash and everyone assumed the bike messenger had taken off with it. Maybe there was even now, as Jace stood trying to buy a candy bar from a guy in an orange turban who pointed a gun at him, an APB out on him, and LAPD cruisers were trolling the streets in search of him.

The clerk put his gun down on the counter, as casually as if he were putting a cigarette on the lip of an ashtray. "A murder," he said. "I listen to the scanner."

Jace felt the blood rush out of his head.

"Who?" he asked, still staring at the congregation of vehicles the next block down, on the other side of the street.

"Maybe you," the clerk said.

Jace looked at him, a weird current of déjà vu going through him. Maybe he had been murdered? Maybe he was dead. Maybe he hadn't gotten away. Maybe Predator's bullet had gone through him, and this surreality he found himself in was the afterlife. Maybe this guy was the guardian at the gate.

"Maybe you are the killer," the clerk said, then laughed as if he hadn't three minutes ago assumed Jace was there to rob him.

"Who was killed?" Jace asked again. The

shaking he had in part attributed to hunger was growing stronger, but he'd already forgotten his empty belly.

"They call no names, only codes," the clerk said. "Codes and the address."

He repeated the address aloud. Jace's mouth moved along like a ventriloquist's dummy's, the words and numbers forming but no sound coming from him.

Lenny Lowell's address. There was no one in Lenny's office to kill except Lenny.

Jace wondered if the attorney had been murdered before or after Predator had tried to turn him into roadkill. Could have gone either way, he thought, if what the killer was after was the package tucked inside the waistband of Jace's pants. Or maybe Lenny had blown away Predator. That could have happened. Except that the attorney had been too drunk to walk a straight line, let alone shoot a gun and actually hit somebody.

An LAPD black-and-white crawled up the street and turned in at the gas station. Jace quelled the urge to run. His hands were shaking as he removed his junk-food dinner from the pay tray. He stuffed the candy bar in his pocket, opened the soda, and gulped down half of it.

The cops pulled up maybe ten feet in front of the building. The cop riding shotgun opened the door and got out. A doughy-faced guy on the heavy side, all of him draped in a rain slicker.

"Hey, Habib," the cop called in a voice too jovial for the weather. "Hell of a night, huh?"

"Jimmy Chew!" Habib exclaimed, a wide grin splitting his face. One of his upper front teeth was discolored gray and rimmed with gold. "It's raining! I swear I should never have bothered to leave London!"

The cop laughed. "It's fucking raining! Can you believe it?

"I need my usual, Habib," he said. He produced a wallet from somewhere under his rain gear. Head bent, water running in a stream off his hood, the cop dug out a couple of bills. He flicked a glance at Jace. "Hell of a night," he said again.

"Yeah," Jace answered. "Fucking rain."

"Your car break down, kid?"

"Something like that." Jace raised the soda can to his lips again, trying to be nonchalant, but his hand was shaking and he knew the cop saw it.

"What happened to your face?"

"What about it?"

Chew pointed to his chin and jawline. "That's some case of razor burn."

Jace lifted a hand to his face and winced as he

touched the part of his chin he had skinned falling on the gravel as he was running for his life. His knuckles were scrubbed and torn too.

"I fell," he said.

"Doing what?"

"Nothing. Minding my own business."

"You got a place to stay, kid? Father Mike at the Midnight Mission can give you a hot meal and a dry bed."

The cop had taken him for homeless, a street kid with nowhere to go. He probably figured Jace was either turning tricks or selling dope to stay alive, and that some lowlife pimp or dealer had smacked him around. Jace supposed that was what he appeared to be as he stood there wet and ragged and pathetic.

"I'm okay," he said.

"You got a name?"

"John Jameson." The lie tripped off his tongue without hesitation.

"You got ID?"

"Not on me. You gonna card me for buying a Mountain Dew?"

"How old are you?"

"Twenty-one."

He knew the cop didn't believe him, that he figured Jace was trying to pass for a legal adult. Compact and wiry, he had always looked young for his age. Wet and beat-up, standing there like a stray dog, he probably looked even younger.

"What are you doing out on a night like this?" the cop asked. "No hat, no coat."

"I was hungry. I didn't think it was raining that hard."

"You live around here?"

"Yeah." He gave an address two blocks away and waited for the cop to call his bluff.

"Are you come for the murder, Jimmy Chew?" Habib asked in the same kind of pleasant tone he might use to ask if his friend had come for a party. "I heard on the scanner."

Chew answered the question with another question. "You see anything going on around here earlier tonight, Habib? Around six-thirty, seven?"

Habib pursed his lips and shook his head. He put a king-size Baby Ruth candy bar and two cans of Diet Coke in the drawer and shoved it out to the cop. "Cars go by. No fast getaways. Some poor bastard went past on a bicycle earlier. Can you imagine?"

"What time was that?"

"About when you said. I didn't look at the clock. I'm working on my screenplay," he said, gesturing to a mess of printed pages on the counter. He had slipped his gun out of sight.

"What direction did he come from?" Chew asked.

"The way you came. He went past and turned to the right at the corner."

Jace felt like his heart had lodged at the base of his throat, the beating of it interrupting his ability to swallow.

"What'd he look like?"

Habib shrugged. "Like a miserable bastard riding a bicycle in the rain. I wasn't really paying attention. For heaven's sake, who would ride a bicycle to go commit a murder?"

"We're just looking for anyone who might have been around, maybe saw something go down. You know how it is," the cop said casually, including the gas station clerk in the cop process, as if Habib was some kind of auxiliary officer. He flicked another glance at Jace. "How about you? You hanging around this street six-thirty, seven o'clock?"

"I don't own a watch," Jace lied. "And I didn't see anything."

"You didn't see a guy on a bike?"

"Who's stupid enough to ride a bike in the rain?"

"A bike messenger, for one. You know any of those guys?"

"Why would I?"

"They hang out under the bridge at Fourth and Flower," Chew said. "I just thought maybe you might have run into them."

"I mind my own business," Jace said, fronting attitude over the fear. "Can I go now? Am I under arrest?"

"Any reason you should be?"

"Yeah. I robbed the Mint," he lipped off. "I'm just hanging around here for old times' sake. Can I go? It's fucking raining."

The cop considered for a moment that seemed like half an hour. Jace kept his perturbed, defiant gaze steady and right on Jimmy Chew's eyes.

"In a minute," the cop said.

Jace watched Chew go back to the car, and wondered if running wasn't his best option. The cops would probably just think he was a homeless kid who didn't want a hassle. Or maybe Chew had taken Jace's trembling hand as a sign he was on something, maybe had some rock cocaine in his pocket to smoke or to peddle.

If the cop decided to shake him down, looking for drugs, he would find a package with the return address of a murder victim.

The muscles in Jace's calves and thighs tightened. He centered his weight over the balls of his feet, hoped the bum ankle would be able to support him in a sprint.

The cop stuck his head inside the car, said a few words to his partner, and came back out with something in his hand.

Jace lowered his center of gravity a couple of inches, so he could dodge either way, wheel, and run.

"Here, kid."

Chew tossed what he held in his hand. Jace caught it on reflex. When he looked at what it was, he almost wanted to laugh. A blue disposable rain poncho from the 99 Cent Store.

"Better late than never," the cop said. "You can get dry clothes at the mission, if you need them."

"Sure. Thanks," Jace mumbled.

"Sure you don't want a ride? We can drop you—"

"No. That's okay. Thanks anyway."

"Suit yourself," the cop said, shrugging him off. Jace knew Chew hadn't bought any of his crap but had just deemed him not important enough to bother with. "Habib, you'll call if you hear something?"

"You'll be the first to know, Officer," the clerk's delighted voice crackled over the speaker.

Maybe he thought he would hear something that could break the case. Maybe the killer would confess as he prepaid for his gas. Then Habib could write a screenplay about that and maybe star in the movie, or at least see his name roll in the credits. LA. Everybody wanted to be in show business.

The patrol car rolled back out onto the street and took a right at the corner. Jace watched them go as he chugged his Mountain Dew. Then he tossed the can in the trash, threw a casual "See you" to Habib, and walked away as if he didn't have a care in the world.

Five blocks later, his knees were still shaking.

7

W hat a creep."

Parker walked into the bedroom naked with a glass of wine in each hand. A nice, full-bodied Cab from Peru. He had hardly touched the hard stuff since about two months after he had gotten sent down from Robbery-Homicide. In those two months he had downed enough booze to float a boat. Then he woke up one day, said enough was enough, and took up tai chi instead.

"Was it something I said?"

The woman in bed didn't take her eyes off the television. Her face was sour with disgust. "Rob Cole, that piece of dirt. I hope he gets the needle. And after he's dead, I hope we can dig him up and kill him all over again."

"That's what I like about you, Diane. Overflowing with the milk of human kindness."

He handed her a glass, set his on the night table, and slipped between the covers.

He and Diane Nicholson had what they both considered to be the perfect relationship. They liked and respected each other, were a pair of animals in bed, and neither of them had any interest in being anything other than friends.

Parker because he didn't see the point in marriage. He'd never seen one that worked. His parents had been engaged in a cold war for forty-five years. Most of the cops he knew had been divorced at least once. He himself had never had a romantic relationship that hadn't crashed and burned, primarily because of his job.

Diane had her own reasons, none of which she had ever confided in him. He knew she had been married to a Crowne Enterprises executive who had died of a heart attack a few years past. But when she spoke of him, which was hardly ever, she talked about him without emotion, as if he were a mere acquaintance, or a shoe. Not the great love of her life.

Whoever had put her off the idea of everlasting love had come after the marriage. Curious by nature and by vocation, Parker had nosed around for an answer to that question when they had first gotten involved, almost a year before. He hadn't found out a thing. Absolutely no one knew who Diane had been seeing after her husband's death, only they believed she had been seeing someone and that things had ended badly.

Parker figured the guy was married or a muckety-muck in the coroner's office or both. But he dropped the unsolved mystery, figuring that if Diane had been so careful, so discreet that not even her friends knew, then it was none of his business. She was entitled to her secrets.

He liked having his secrets too. He had always figured the less anyone knew about him, the better. Knowledge was power, and could be used against him. He had learned that lesson the hard way. Now he kept his personal life personal. No one at LAPD needed to know who he saw or what he did with his time off the job.

She scoffed at his milk-of-human-kindness line. "This guy deserves an acid bath."

They were watching **CNN Headline News.** Diane had televisions all over the house and sometimes had them all on at once so she could go from room to room without missing anything.

It was late, but it always took a while to wind down after a murder. Uniforms had knocked on doors within viewing distance of Lowell's office, but the shops were empty for the night and there wasn't a soul to speak to. If there had been, Parker would've worked through the night. Instead, he had locked down the scene, gone to the station to start his paperwork, making Ruiz go with him instead of chasing after Bradley Kyle like a cat in heat. From there he had gone to Diane's Craftsman bungalow on the Westside.

"Fifty-five-gallon drum, and forty gallons of acid," he said matter-of-factly. "Keep the drum in your basement, leave it for the next home-owner, who leaves it for the next one after that."

Most women would probably have been ap-palled that he had that kind of stuff in his head. Diane just nodded absently.

The story running was about jury selection for Cole's upcoming trial, and a recap of the whole sickening mess—from the discovery of Tricia Crowne-Cole's body; the funeral with Norman Crowne sobbing on his daughter's closed casket, his son leaning over his shoulder, trying to comfort him; all the way back to her wedding to Rob Cole. An incongruous photo-graph: Cole posing like an Armani tuxedo model, Tricia looking like maybe she was his older, dowdy sister who had been left at the al-tar. She would have been better off.

"Look at this clown," Diane said as they ran file footage of Cole starring in his short-lived TV drama, the aptly named **B.S.: Bomb Squad.** "Looking like he thinks he's somebody."

"He used to be."

"In his own mind. That guy is all about one thing: himself."

There was never any gray area with Diane. Rob Cole was an instant ON button for her opinions. She had worked the murder scene more than a year ago now. She and Parker had had numerous variations of this conversation since. Every time some new phase of jurisprudence kicked Cole's name into the headlines again, she resurrected her ire and outrage.

"I met him at a party once, you know," she said.

"The memory is as vivid as if I had been there myself," Parker remarked dryly. She must have told him a hundred and ten times since the murder. Somehow the mere mention of Cole's name shut down her short-term memory.

"He hit on you."

"He told me he was trying to put together a new series and maybe I could help him out with the research. The main character was going to be a coroner's-investigator-slash-private-eye. What crap."

"He just wanted to get in your pants," Parker said.

"With his wife standing not ten feet away," she said with disgust. "He's only got eyes for me. He's the bad boy. He's all charm. He's the big white grin."

"He's the guy all the guys want to be and all the women want to go home with," Parker said.

"He's a jerk."

"I guess you still haven't signed on to the 'Free Rob Cole' Web site," Parker said, bringing his hand up to massage the back of her neck. The muscles were as taut as guy wires.

She scowled. "People are idiots."

Parker slid his arm around her. She sighed softly as she let her head fall against his shoulder.

"No argument there," he murmured. "No matter how rotten, how guilty a criminal may be, there are always people who don't want to hear it."

"Like I said. And these are the same people who can't get out of jury duty. Cole will end up being the new millennium's Ted Bundy and have some dumb-as-dirt woman marry him from the witness box in the middle of his murder trial."

Parker didn't give a shit about Rob Cole. LA was a "what have you done for me lately" kind of town, and aside from being accused of murder, Cole hadn't done anything noteworthy in a decade. One production deal after another had gone down the drain. Starring roles had tapered off to guest roles of diminishing importance on episodic television, and a slew of forgettable movies of the week for those powerhouse networks: Lifetime and USA.

Parker's attention was on the file footage of Cole being brought into Parker Center by a posse of Robbery-Homicide hotshots, Bradley Kyle and his pal Moose among the pack. Cole, red-faced and bug-eyed with anger, a drastic contrast in mood to his corny trademark fifties vintage bowling shirt; the Robbery-Homicide boys stone-faced in sharp suits and ties, mirrored shades hiding their eyes. Everyone costumed and playing their parts to the hilt.

"Why were Kyle and the Hulk there tonight?" Diane asked.

Parker shrugged as if it didn't matter to him. "I don't know. I didn't invite them."

"You think the dead guy was connected to something big and juicy?"

"The Lenny Lowells of the world are the Lenny Lowells of the world because they can't hook on to something big and juicy even if they trip and fall in it."

"He tripped and fell in something. And it killed him. Something smelly enough for the Parker Center boys to come sniffing."

"It's my case until my captain tells me it's not," Parker said. "Then I'll walk away."

Diane laughed, a throaty, sexy sound that moved her shoulders on its way out. "You liar.

You wanted to run Bradley out of there like a tiger protecting its kill."

"Well, I **do** hate the guy."

"You're entitled. He's a prick. I hate the guy too. Everybody hates the guy. I'll bet his mother hated him in utero," she said. "But that's all beside the point. I just don't get what RHD would want with the murder of a bottom-feeder like that lawyer."

"I don't know," Parker said as the **Headline News** anchor jumped from the Cole story to a story about the sudden surge in sales of vintage bowling shirts in Los Angeles. "But I'll find out. Crack of dawn, I'm finding that bike messenger."

8

The Chinatown of LA is not the Chinatown of San Francisco. There are no pretty cable cars. Shops selling cheap souvenirs and knock-off designer handbags are fewer, and far from being the largest part of the economy.

The Chinatown of LA was the first modern American Chinatown owned and planned by the Chinese themselves, home now to more than fifteen thousand people of Asian heritage. In recent years it has begun to attract artists and young professionals of all races, and has become a hip place to live.

The Chinatown of LA is about the thriving avant-garde mix of people who make it their home, who live and work there. The streets are lined with meat markets with duck carcasses hanging in the front window, fish markets where the fishmongers wield razor-sharp knives, and places to buy herbs and medicinal cures that the Chinese have been using for thousands of years. Signs in windows are written in

Chinese. The primary language spoken is Chinese in a multitude of dialects. But alongside the traditional Chinese shops are contemporary art galleries, and boutiques, and yoga schools.

Jace had moved himself and Tyler to Chinatown after their mother died. They had dumped their meager possessions in a couple of laundry bags pilfered from the back of a delivery truck parked behind a restaurant, and jumped on a bus. Every evening when he returned to Chinatown, Jace recalled the day he had led his brother by the hand beneath the Gate of Filial Piety and to a place no one would ever come looking for them.

Alicia Damon had died as a Jane Doe in Good Samaritan Hospital. Jace knew this because he had taken her to the emergency room himself, "borrowing" the car of a junkie neighbor who was too wasted to notice the scrawny kid next door taking his keys.

His mother had not given the admissions clerk her name or address. She had not allowed Jace to appear to be with her, or to attract attention to himself in any way, or to give anyone his name or tell anyone where they lived.

Alicia had trusted no one in any position of authority, her greatest fear being the Children and Family Services people, who had the power to take her sons away from her. What little mail they got came to a rented box, never to whatever crappy apartment they were living in at the time. They had no phone. Jace had been registered in public school under the name John Charles Jameson. They lived on what money Alicia could make at menial jobs that paid cash, and on a Social Security check that came monthly, made out to Allison Jennings.

They had no family friends. Jace had never brought any school friends home with him. He had never met his father, or even seen a photograph of him. When he was younger, he had asked why, but he had stopped asking by the time he was six, because it upset his mother so much that she would go into another room and cry.

He had an idea who Tyler's dad might be—a bartender from a dive his mother had worked at briefly. He had seen the guy a couple of times because he had secretly followed his mother to work, afraid to stay alone in the room they were renting at the time. Twice he had seen them through a window, kissing after everyone else had gone from the bar. Then suddenly the Damons picked up and moved to another part of the city. Some months later, Tyler was born. Jace had never seen the bartender again.

Whenever Jace had asked for an explanation

about the way they lived, Alicia would only re-
ply: "You can't be too careful."

Jace had taken her at her word. After her
death, he had made no claim on his mother's
body, because people would ask questions, and
questions were never a good thing. He had been
just thirteen at the time, and knew without having to be told that Children and Family Services
would swoop in like hawks and he and Tyler
would be put into foster care, probably not even
together.

There was no money for a funeral anyway.
And besides, the mother he and Tyler had
known was gone. The dead body had nothing
really to do with who she had been and would
never be again. And so the body had been
shipped off to the LA County Coroner's building to be stored in the morgue with the other
three hundred or so Jane and John Does that
came in every year, waiting in vain for someone
to remember them and care enough to come
looking for them.

With stubby candles in cobalt blue votives
from the Catholic church three blocks from
their apartment, and wilted, unsalable flowers
from the Korean market down the street, Jace
and Tyler had made their own memorial to their
mother. They had set up a little altar of sorts

in the living room. Their centerpiece: a photograph of Alicia, taken long ago, in better times.

Tyler had dug the picture out of a cloth-covered box their mother had had as long as Jace could remember. He had looked through it many times when his mother had been out, but not with her there. She hadn't offered to share it. A box of memories with no stories, no explanations. Photographs of people Jace had never known, taken in places he had never been. Secrets that would forever remain secrets.

Jace had given a short eulogy, then he and Tyler had each named the qualities about their mother they had loved most, and would miss most. They had said their good-byes and put out the candles. Then Jace had held his little brother tight, and both of them had cried, Jace as silently as he could because he was all they had now, and he had to be strong.

Alicia had told Jace never to worry if something ever happened to her, that in the event of tragedy, he should call a phone number she made him memorize, and ask for Alli. Only, when Jace called the number from a pay phone, he was told it was no longer in service. And so there was no Alli, and there was plenty to worry about.

The next day Jace had gone looking for

another place for them to live. He had set his
sights on Chinatown for a number of reasons.
One, because he wanted Tyler to grow up in a
place where he didn't have to worry some junkie
would beat his head in for a nickel or take him
and sell him to a pedophile to get money for his
next fix. Two, because the community was so
eclectic, no one would think them out of place
there. And three, because he figured if he could
actually get them in among the Chinese, he
wouldn't have to worry someone would rat
them out to Children and Family Services. The
Chinese ran their community their own way,
discouraging intrusion from the outside world.
Family was more than just a word defined by
the County of Los Angeles. The difficulty
would be in getting accepted.

Jace had gone up and down the streets, looking for a menial job, being turned down again
and again. Nobody wanted him, nobody trusted
him, and most of them conveyed the sentiment
without speaking a word of English.

At the end of the third fruitless day, when
Jace had been almost ready to give up, Tyler had
dragged him into a fish market to look at the
live catfish in the tank in the front window.

Typical Tyler, he had gone right up to the
person who looked most likely to have answers,
and proceeded to ask half a million questions

about the catfish—where had they come from, how old were they, what kind were they, were they boys or girls, what did they eat, how often did the tank have to be cleaned.

The person he had chosen to ask was a tiny Chinese woman with the bearing of a queen, nicely dressed, dark hair done up in a bun. She was probably fifty-something, and looked as if she could have balanced a glass of champagne on top of her head and walked to the end of the block without spilling a drop.

She listened to Tyler's stream-of-consciousness questions with one brow lifted, then took him by the hand, went to the fish tank, and patiently answered each of them. Tyler soaked up the information like a sponge, like he had never learned anything more fascinating. He looked up at the woman with wide-eyed eager wonder, and the woman's heart melted.

Tyler had that sort of effect on people. There was something about him that seemed both wise and innocent at once. An old soul, Madame Chen called him. She had fed them dinner in the small restaurant next door, where everyone jumped to please her as she snapped at them in Chinese.

She had quizzed Jace about their background. He had been as vague as possible about most of it, but had told her about their mother's death and that they had no relatives. He had admitted that they were afraid of being put into foster care, separated, possibly never to see each other again. Tyler was likely to be adopted, because he was young. Placing a teenage boy was a whole other thing.

Madame Chen had weighed all these matters as she sipped her tea. She was silent for so long, Jace was certain she was going to tell them to get lost. But when she finally spoke, she looked from Jace's eyes to Tyler's and back, and said: "Family is everything."

The line reverberated in Jace's head as he limped down the back alleys of Chinatown in the dead of night. In the best of times he felt detached from most of the world, the outsider, the loner. He relied on no one, confided in no one, expected nothing from anyone. He had been raised not to trust, had seen many reasons not to trust, so he didn't trust.

But he liked the Chens, and was deeply grateful to them. He enjoyed the company of the other messengers, though he didn't think he could call them friends. These were his connections, the circle of people around himself and Tyler, tied to him by thin threads that could be easily broken if necessary.

Someone had tried to kill him. The police wanted him for questioning at the very least, to charge him with the murder of Lenny Lowell at the worst. He couldn't go to anyone he knew to share those burdens. Relying on someone else meant risking too much by dependence. And why would any of the people he knew risk part of their lives for him?

Jace could see that loose circle around him coming apart, sending the people of his life away from him like so many particles of a meteor as it hurtled through Earth's atmosphere. He was surprised to realize how much those casual connections meant to him. He hadn't felt so bleakly, completely alone since the days after his mother died.

Family is everything.

His only real family was a ten-year-old boy, and Jace would go to any lengths to keep this danger from touching him.

He had managed to get back to Chinatown without arousing the suspicions of anyone except for a few street people camping out in boxes in the alleys Jace had taken. But tomorrow the cops would be making the rounds of the messenger agencies, trying to track down the messenger who had picked up a package at Lowell's office. He would become the center of everyone's suspicions then. For all Jace knew, his would-be killer would be making those same rounds, trying to get a name and address, trying to get to the package that was still pressed against his belly beneath his clothes.

Whoever was looking would have a hard time finding him. The address he had put on his job application at Speed wasn't where he and Tyler lived. He gave that address to no one. He was paid in cash under the table—not an uncommon practice among the shadier agencies in the messenger game. Getting paid in cash meant none of his money went to the government; therefore, the government didn't know he existed, and the agency didn't have to provide him with health insurance and workers' comp.

It was a risky proposition at first glance. If he was injured on the job, he had no medical coverage. And injury was inevitable. Statistics showed that the average cyclist could expect to have one serious accident every two thousand miles on the bike. Jace figured he clocked two thousand miles every couple of months, give or take. But he made more money this way—a straight fifty percent on the price of every run—and if the agency had to cover him, he might have his hospital bills paid once, but he probably wouldn't have a job waiting for him when he got out. The company would consider him a risk and dump him.

No one could track him through utility bills,

because he paid the Chens in cash for water and power, and for the cable feed to the television in the apartment. Rent was traded for work shoveling ice for the cases in the fish market. He never brought visitors home, wasn't close enough to anyone to have reason to. He rarely dated, had no time for a relationship. The few girls he had gone out with knew little about him or where he lived. As he had been trained from a very young age, he left no paper trail that could lead anyone to him and Tyler.

Even knowing how difficult it would be for anyone to find him, Jace felt skittish about going home. Despite the fact that he hadn't run into the cops or seen Predator's car again, he couldn't escape the feeling that someone was watching him, following him. Some omniscient evil floating over the city just beneath the storm clouds. Or maybe it was just the onset of hypothermia making him shake as he let himself in the back door of the fish market and climbed the stairs to the tiny apartment.

He heard voices as he neared the door. Male voices. Angry voices. Jace held his breath, pressed his ear to the door, and tried to make out the conversation over the roaring of his pulse in his ears. The voices went silent. His heart pounded harder. Then a louder voice shouted to shop for a car at Cerritos Auto Square.

"We save more, so you save more! Cerritos Auto Square."

Jace exhaled and let himself into the apartment.

The only light came from the television in the corner of the room, splashing colors across the small space and over the two bodies on the futon: Tyler, sprawled, head and one arm hanging over the edge of the cushion, legs splayed; and the old man Tyler called Grandfather Chen, the ancient father of Madame Chen's deceased husband. Grandfather Chen sat upright on the futon, his head back, his mouth open, his arms out from his sides with palms up, like a painting of some tormented saint pleading with God to spare him.

Jace went to his brother, moved the boy's dead weight up onto the cushion, and covered him with a blanket that had fallen to the floor. Tyler didn't stir, didn't open his eyes. Grandfather Chen made a crying sound and jerked awake, raising his arms in front of his face defensively.

"It's okay. It's only me," Jace whispered.

The old man put his arms down and scowled at Jace, scolding him in rapid-fire Chinese, a language Jace had not managed to master in his six years of living in Chinatown. He could say **good morning,** and **thank you,** and that was about it. But he didn't have to understand Grandfather Chen to understand that it was very late and Tyler had been worried about him. The old man went on like an automatic weapon, pointing to his watch, pointing to Tyler, shaking his finger at Jace.

Jace held his hands up in surrender. "I'm sorry. Something happened and I'm late, I know. I'm sorry."

Grandfather Chen didn't even take a breath. Outraged, he held his thumb and pinkie up against the side of his head and pantomimed talking on the phone.

"I tried to call," Jace said, as if it would do him any good to explain. In fifty years of living in the United States, the old man had made no attempt to learn the language, turning his nose up at the very idea, as if it were beneath him to speak English for people too ignorant to learn Chinese.

"The line was busy." Jace mimicked talking on the phone and made the busy signal.

Grandfather Chen huffed a sound of disgust and threw his hands at Jace as if to shoo him from the room.

Tyler woke then, rubbing his eyes, looking at Jace. "You're really late."

"I know, buddy. I'm sorry. I tried to call Madame Chen. The line was busy."

"Grandfather Chen was on his computer, looking at Chinese girly sites."

Jace cut a look of disapproval at the old man, who now wore the cold, inscrutable expression of a stone Buddha.

"I don't want you looking at porn sites," Jace said to his brother.

Tyler rolled his eyes. "They weren't naked or anything. He's shopping for a mail-order bride."

"He's a hundred and twelve, what's he going to do with a mail-order bride?"

"He's ninety-seven," Tyler corrected him. "In the Chinese way of counting birthdays, where the day of your birth is considered your first birthday. So he's only ninety-six by our way of celebrating, by the **anniversary** of our date of birth."

Jace listened patiently to the lesson. He tried never to be short with his brother. Tyler was as bright as a spotlight but very sensitive about Jace's approval or disapproval.

"Anyway," Jace said. "He's an antique. What's he want with some young bride?"

"Technically, he's not an antique, because he

isn't a hundred years old. As for the bride—"
Tyler gave an exaggerated shrug. "He says: If she
dies, she dies."

He looked up at the old man beside him and
rattled off something in Chinese. Grandfather
Chen replied, and they both laughed.

The old man ruffled Tyler's hair fondly, then
slapped his hands on his thighs and rocked himself off the futon. He was Jace's height, his posture straight as a rail, his body thin, almost to
skeletal proportions. His face was sunken in like
a shrunken head, the skin as transparent as wet
crepe paper, a road map of blue veins running
just beneath the surface. He squinted at Jace's
face, frowning, brows knit. He pointed to
the bruises and abrasions, and said something
in a serious voice, too softly for Tyler to hear.
Concern, Jace thought. Worry. Disapproval.
Grandfather Chen figured—rightly—that whatever had caused Jace to be so late wasn't anything good.

The old man said good night to Tyler
and left.

Tyler turned on the table lamp and soberly
studied his big brother. "What happened to
your face?"

"I had an accident."

He lowered himself onto a hardwood

Chinese stool and took his boots off, careful not to pull too hard on his right foot. The ankle was throbbing.

"What kind of accident? I want to know **exactly** what happened."

They had been over this ground before. Tyler wanted to be able to visualize every aspect of Jace's job, down to the smallest detail. But he was particularly obsessed with any kind of accident his big brother—or any of the messengers—might have.

Jace wouldn't tell him. He had made that mistake once, then came to find out that his brother was fretting about him to the point of making himself sick, playing out every horrible possibility over and over in his mind, fearing the day Jace would go out and never come back.

"I fell. That's all," he said, dodging Tyler's too-serious stare. "Got doored by an old lady in a Cadillac, twisted my ankle, and got some scrapes. Bent a wheel on The Beast and had to walk it home."

The short version of the story. Tyler knew it, too. His big eyes welled up with tears. "I thought you weren't coming back. Ever."

Ignoring the fact that he was sopping wet, Jace moved to the futon and sank down beside the boy, sitting sideways to look into his brother's face.

"I'll always come back, pal. Just for you."

One tear slipped over the rim of Tyler's lower eyelid, over the eyelashes, and down his cheek. "That's what Mom used to say too," he reminded Jace. "And it wasn't true. Stuff happens that a person can't do anything about. It just happens. It's karma."

He squeezed his eyes shut and recited from memory what he had read in the dictionary he studied every evening: "Karma is the force generated by a person's actions to per-pet-uate transmigration, and in its ethical consequences to determine his destiny in his next existence."

Jace wanted to say it was all bullshit, that there was no meaning in anything, and there was no "next existence." But he knew it was important to Tyler to believe in something, to search for logic in an illogical world, so he made the same lame joke he always did. "And while you're distracted worrying about it, you'll step out into the street and get hit by a bus.

"Here's what I can control, buddy: that I love you and I'll be there for you, even if I have to crawl on my hands and knees over broken glass to get there."

He pulled the boy close and gave him a fierce hug. Tyler had reached the age where he was starting to think a real man didn't need hugs, and the fact that he still needed them was embarrassing. But he gave in to that need and pressed his ear against Jace's chest to listen to his heartbeat.

Jace held his brother close for a moment, wondering what karma would dish out to him for withholding the whole truth from Tyler. Tonight, more than any other night, he was too aware of his own mortality. Death had come calling and sucked him into a dark vortex where he had no control over anything but his own will to come out of it alive. Even as Tyler leaned into him, he could feel Lenny Lowell's package pressing against his belly beneath his shirt.

In the morning he would have to explain some things, but he wouldn't do it now. Now all he wanted was a hot shower and some sleep. The world would not look brighter come morning, but he would have more strength to deal with it.

After Tyler had gone to bed and fallen asleep, Jace went into their small bathroom and squinted at himself in the small mirror over the small sink and beneath the small light fixture that stuck out from the wall like a glowing wart.

He looked pretty damn bad. His face was pale and drawn, his only color the black circles beneath his eyes, a smear of mud on his cheek, and the angry red abrasions on his chin. His lower lip was split, the line drawn in clotted blood. No wonder the cop, Jimmy Chew, had taken him for a homeless kid.

He washed his hands, wincing at the sting of soap in the torn skin of his fingertips and palms. He lathered his face, with the same resulting pain, and splashed it clean with ice-cold water that took his breath for a second. Then he stood straight and carefully worked his way out of his wet sweatshirt and tight T-shirt. His shoulders hurt, his back hurt, his chest hurt. There was hardly a body part that wasn't aching, throbbing, swollen, bleeding, or bruised.

Lenny Lowell's package was still tucked inside the waistband of his tight bike pants. The padded envelope felt damp but otherwise undamaged. Jace pulled it free, stared at it as he turned it over and over in his hands. He was shaking. In normal circumstances he would never open a client's package, no matter what it was. Rocco, the guy who ran Speed Couriers, would fire him in a heartbeat. Now he almost wanted to laugh. He had bigger problems than Rocco.

He sat down on the lid of the toilet and picked at the edge of the envelope flap until he could get his finger inside and tear it open.

There was no note of any kind. There was no thick wad of money. Sandwiched between two pieces of cardboard was a waxy envelope of photographic negatives. Jace took them out of the envelope and held a strip of them up to the light. Two people exchanging something or shaking hands. He couldn't really tell.

Someone was willing to kill for this.

Blackmail.

And I'm in the middle of it.

With nowhere to turn. He couldn't go to the cops, didn't trust the cops. Even if he turned the negatives over to them, he would still be a target for Predator, who couldn't afford to wonder what Jace knew or didn't know. Predator wouldn't know whether or not Jace had looked at the negatives, or that he hadn't had them developed or given them to the cops. He was a loose thread a killer couldn't leave dangling.

If this was karma, then karma sucked.

He wouldn't wait to find out. Jace had never felt he was a victim of anything in his life. His mother had never allowed it, not for Jace, not for herself. Shit happened and he dealt with it and moved on, moved forward. He had to look at this situation in the same way. That was always the way out, to move forward.

Shit happened. And he was up to his neck in it. There was nothing to do but start swimming.

9

Jace hobbled slowly down the stairs from the apartment in his socks, boots tied together and slung over his shoulder. He had slept maybe a total of an hour and a half. He had just drifted off again around four when Tyler had crawled onto the futon with him and whispered that he was scared. Jace told him it was okay, and to go to sleep.

Tyler was still young enough to believe him about things he wanted to believe. Jace couldn't remember ever having been that young. He'd never had the luxury of a buffer. Alicia may have wanted to protect him but hadn't believed she should. Instead, she had given him the best gift she thought she had to give: survival skills.

She had always told him not to waste valuable time panicking. There was no point in it, no benefit to be gained. Still, it was partly panic—and pain—that had kept his brain running like a hamster in a wheel those few precious hours he should have been sleeping. At four-thirty he slipped out of bed, onto the floor on his hands and knees, taking stock of what hurt most.

The ankle felt thick and difficult to move. He had packed it in ice bags overnight, trying to bring down the swelling, hoping he could get by with taping it, that he hadn't done more damage to the ligaments than he thought. Slowly, slowly, he braced a hand on the Chinese stool, took a deep breath, and struggled to stand.

Even a normal, hectic day on the job could come back the next morning like a bad hangover. Back hurting, hamstrings tight, Achilles tendons hard as rocks. Bruises, cuts, scrapes. Lungs aching from breathing exhaust. Eyes stinging, fingers frozen in a curl from gripping the handlebars.

Today seemed no worse than any bad day after a wreck, except for the idea that someone wanted to kill him.

He went into the bathroom, took a quick cold shower to clear his pounding head, then taped the ankle as tight as he dared. It was half again the size it should have been, but he could put weight on it, and that was all that counted.

At the bottom of the stairs he sat down and

worked his boot on, clenching his jaw at the discomfort. Small beads of sweat popped on his forehead. He could hear the ice delivery truck idling outside the big door of the loading dock. The first call of morning in Chinatown, and most other ethnic neighborhoods Jace knew: deliveries to the small family grocers, the meat markets, the restaurants. Once a week the butcher across the street received crates of live chickens and ducks, adding to the wake-up call. Jace found the noise and routine comforting, the way he imagined he would feel if he had been born into a big family.

The rattle of a chain. The grinding of the motor that lifted the overhead door. The voice of Madame Chen's nephew, Chi, barking orders to third cousin Boo Zhu. The scrape of metal against the concrete as Boo Zhu hopped off the dock and dragged his shovel with him.

Jace pulled in a deep breath of damp, fish-scented air, and went to work. He said nothing to Chi about being injured. Chi didn't ask. Chi, who ran the day-to-day business of the fish market, disliked Jace and disapproved of his aunt's decision to take the Damon brothers in. In six years he had not changed his mind.

Jace didn't care about Chi. He did his job and gave Chi no reason to complain about anything other than the fact that Jace wasn't Chinese and didn't speak Chinese. Something Chi found impossible to tolerate despite the fact that he had been born in Pasadena and spoke English as well as anyone.

Madame Chen had very bluntly pointed out to Chi that bilingual skills were not a requirement for shoveling shaved ice from one place to the next. Boo Zhu, who was twenty-seven and mentally handicapped, barely spoke any language at all, and managed to get through his work without a problem.

The rain had become a thick, cold drizzle. Still, Jace was sweating like a workhorse, feeling nauseous and weak as pain burned through his ankle with every shovelful of ice. Fifteen minutes into the job, Madame Chen appeared on the loading dock, a tiny figure swallowed up in a trench coat, a huge Burberry plaid umbrella in hand. She called to Jace to come into her office, earning him a withering glare from Chi.

"My father-in-law tells me you are hurt," she said, shutting the umbrella as she led the way into the cramped, cluttered space.

"I'm fine, Madame Chen."

Frowning, she stared up at his face—wet, pale, scraped, bruised. "Fine? You are not fine."

"It was just an accident. Being a messenger is sometimes a dangerous job. You know that."

"I know you are never coming home so late at night from your job. Are you in some kind of trouble?"

"Trouble? Why would you ask that? I've been hurt before. It's nothing new."

"I don't like answers that are not answers, JayCee."

Hands on his hips, Jace looked away, fixing his gaze on a wall calendar from a local bank, which wished everyone a happy Chinese New Year. Madame Chen turned on the small space heater beneath her desk, and the thing made a humming sound and released a hot electrical smell that was unnerving. He thought for a moment about what to tell her. She probably deserved the truth, out of respect alone, but he didn't want to involve the Chens in this mess. He didn't understand it all himself yet. No one could trace him to this address, so there seemed no reason to alarm her.

"A truth does not take so long to tell," she said firmly. "Only a fiction requires so much thought."

Jace sighed. "I was making a delivery late yesterday, and someone almost ran me over. I took a bad fall."

"And you called the police to report this, which is why you were so late in returning home," she said, clearly not believing that to have been the case.

"No. It was dark. It happened fast. I couldn't get the license plate number."

"Instead, you went to the emergency room to be examined by a doctor."

Jace looked away again, more out of aggravation than evasiveness. Madame Chen was the only person besides his own mother he could not lie to successfully. He could fool and trick anyone else into believing anything he wanted them to believe. Because no one else cared enough about what he was telling them. He was just a messenger, and they heard what they wanted to hear, what was easiest to accept.

"I walked home," he said. "It took a long time because it was a long way and my bike is broken."

Madame Chen said something in Chinese that was probably not very ladylike.

"You don't call a cab?"

"Cabs cost money."

"You don't call me?" she said, offended.

"I tried to call. The line was busy."

"You have no respect," she said, jamming her hands on her hips. "Six years I worry about you. You have no respect for me."

"That's not true," Jace protested. "I respect

you very much, Madame Chen. I don't want to worry you."

She hissed like a snake and shook a finger at him. "You are like Boo Zhu now? With stones in your head? You think **I** am like Boo Zhu?"

"No, ma'am."

"You are like my family, JayCee," she said quietly.

Jace felt a burning at the backs of his eyes. He never allowed himself to want that, not in any way less abstract than the loose sense of community he had thought about earlier. Tyler was his family.

"I'm sorry," he said.

"That you offended me, or that I consider you family?"

A crooked smile twisted his mouth. "Both, I guess. I don't like to burden you."

She shook her head sadly. "You were old in the womb. Not in the way of your brother, but in the way of a man who has seen too much."

It wasn't the first time she had made this particular comment. Jace never replied. There was no point in stating the obvious.

"I have to go, Madame Chen. I have business to take care of. I have to get the bike fixed."

"And how will you get where you are going? On a magic carpet?"

He didn't answer. She pulled a set of keys off

a nail on the wall. "Take my car. And don't tell me you can't. You will."

"Yes, ma'am. Thank you."

Madame Chen owned a two-year-old Mini Cooper, black with a cream-colored top and a moon roof. Jace carefully wedged The Beast into the car and crept out into the early traffic. The car gave him a disguise of sorts. Predator wouldn't be looking for a Mini Cooper.

The trick of the day would be getting in and out of the Speed offices without being seen by anyone watching the building. He needed to get to Eta before the cops did.

10

"Here's your shit work," Ruiz said, throwing a single sheet of paper down on Parker's desk. The paper floated and settled gently on a stack of files, ruining her big show of affront.

Parker glanced at it. A list of messenger companies within a five-mile radius of Lenny Lowell's office. It had to have taken her all of three minutes to get it off Yahoo!

"You do realize 'plays well with others' is a part of your evaluation, don't you?" he said, as he got up to go to the coffee machine.

It was 6:43 A.M. He'd had roughly two hours' sleep. There were two other detectives in the room. Yamoto and Kray had caught the family annihilation Nicholson had been at before she showed up at Lowell's office. Multiple murders and a suicide. An all-nighter just dealing with the paperwork.

Yamoto, another trainee, was writing reports on a snazzy laptop computer he'd brought in himself. He was neat, courteous, professional, and wore better than average suits. Kray didn't deserve a trainee like Yamoto.

Kray was facedown on his desk, sound asleep, drooling a puddle onto a bright green memo reminding everyone that it wasn't too late to sign up for the stress-management seminar: Life and Death Don't Have to Kill You.

Parker went back to his chair and sat down. "You've got to learn to lock down that temper, doll," he said seriously. "What happens when you get some dirtbag killer in the box and he starts in with you?" he asked. "He'll call you names filthier than any even you know. He'll suggest you let him perform eighty-three different kinds of unnatural acts on your naked body. You need to get a confession out of the guy, and you go off calling him a fucking whatever? That's not acceptable."

"I wouldn't do that," she pouted.

"You just did it with me."

"You're not a suspect."

"No, I'm your immediate boss. You have to respect that whether you like it or not. You're always going to have a boss in this business, and a lot of them will make me look like a prize. Chances are better than even, you'll be answering to one or another asshole from now until you need your first face-lift."

He rose and dumped the coffee in the trash. Two slugs of it was enough to jump-start a truck engine. "Fire in the belly is a good thing. Use it while you've got it. But if you don't learn to control it, you won't last on this job. Anger alone won't keep you going. It clouds your judgment. You'll alienate people you need, and piss off people you shouldn't."

"You're the voice of experience on that," she said.

"Yeah," Parker said quietly. "I am. You're learning from a master."

He felt a hundred years old, most of them spent running up mountains, cocky and sure of himself, then skidding down the other side face-first.

Parker shrugged into his charcoal raincoat, an Armani take on the classic trench. A recent splurge courtesy of his other life. He flipped the collar up and reached for the old fedora he'd had since he made detective. A detective had worn it before him, and another before him, going like that all the way back to the thirties. The good old days when LA was still a frontier town and the Miranda warning wasn't even a twinkle in the court's eye. Back when cops used to meet gangsters as they got off the plane from New York or Chicago, beat the hell out of them, and send them back to where they came from.

"Come on," he said to Ruiz. "We're starting on these messenger companies. We'll start
with the ones closest to Lowell's office and
work our way outward until we find who got
the call."

"Can't we just do it on the phone?" she
whined. "It's raining."

"You don't learn how to read people over the
damn phone," Parker snapped. "You want to
solve mysteries over the phone, get a job with
the Psychic Friends Hotline."

She gave him the finger.

Such a lady.

The first agency they tried had gone out of business. Six days ago, according to the bag lady
camped in the shelter of the empty office's doorway. Parker thanked her, gave her his card and
twenty bucks.

"Why'd you do that?" Ruiz asked as they got
back into the car. "Crazy, psycho bag lady. Man,
did you get a whiff of her?"

"They don't offer steam showers and aro-
matherapy at the Midnight Mission. Besides,
she's not a psycho. She was lucid, at least she
was today. Who knows what she might see living out here. If a couple of bucks makes her
think more kindly about talking to cops . . ."

Parker shot Ruiz a look out of the corner of his eye. "How long have you been on the job?"

"Five years."

"And in five years you haven't learned anything? Do you have pictures of the chief with a farm animal?"

"Maybe I'm just cheap," she returned, holding back the temper.

"I'm not even touching that. It's too easy."

"I **mean,** I can't afford to run around handing out money to street people."

"Right. That would put a dent in your shoe budget."

"And you can afford to pass out money to whoever?"

Parker frowned at her. "Twenty dollars? I'm not exactly going to have to give up eating red meat. Investing in a person like Mary there is like putting a few on a long shot at the track. Maybe you lose, but maybe you win and get a nice payout. You didn't have snitches on that gang task force?"

"Not my job. I worked undercover—and no wiseass remarks," she cautioned.

Parker raised his brows. "I didn't say a word."

"And don't talk to me about shoes. Those Tod's wingtips on your feet are like six hundred fifty dollars. I don't know any other cops wearing six-hundred-fifty-dollar shoes."

"Except yourself."

"That's different."

"How so? I'll bet your closet is stacked with Manolos and Jimmy Choos. You haven't worn the same pair twice in a week. Me, I've got maybe five pairs of shoes."

"So maybe I have a friend who likes to buy me nice things. Clothes, shoes—"

"You have a friend?"

She didn't take the bait. "So maybe you have a friend like that," she said slyly. "Maybe you have hidden talents. What about it, Parker? Are you some rich lady's boy toy? Is that where you got that Jag you drive on the weekends? If you're that good, you might be worth a second look after all."

"What do you know about my car?"

She shrugged and played coy. "I've heard rumors."

Parker glanced at her then away as a traffic light ahead turned green. "I don't think it's wise for a cop to accept expensive gifts. You never know. That special someone might be in a real jam with the law one day. Maybe he or she asks for a big favor. Even if you don't grease some wheels for that person, someone's going to find out you're wearing a gold Rolex courtesy of the defendant, and then it's your anatomy in the wringer. Impropriety, bribery. Next thing you know, you've got some Internal Affairs parasite crawling up your ass."

"If you haven't done anything wrong, you don't have anything to hide," Ruiz commented.

"Everybody's got something to hide, sweetheart."

"Yeah? What have you got to hide, Parker?"

"If I told you, I wouldn't be hiding it. Never reveal a fear or a weakness, doll. Someone will spin around and knock you flat with it when you least expect it."

They rode in silence for a moment, creeping down the street in the morning traffic. Lawyers and more lawyers, accountants and more accountants, bankers and more bankers going to their offices in the tall buildings of downtown. Mercedeses, BWMs, Porsches. The car the detectives got was a nondescript domestic sedan of questionable vintage. Robbery-Homicide got better rides. They had to look good on TV. The main requirement of cars in Parker's division was that they not be tempting to car thieves.

At the second messenger agency—Reliable Couriers—a good-looking young guy in J.Crew and hip glasses, Rayne Carson, spelled his name out so he would get proper credit in any future report. He told them Leonard Lowell was on their list of deadbeat customers who had racked up a bill then refused to pay. They no longer did business with him.

"Can you believe most of that list are attorneys?" he confided to Parker, pointing to the list taped to the wall behind the desk.

"The only debts lawyers want paid are for billable hours," Parker commiserated.

The phone rang and Rayne Carson held up a finger and flashed an apologetic look as he punched a button on the phone console and listened to the caller via his wireless headset, pen in hand poised over a notepad.

He looked like he should have been a concierge at some happening hotel or a waiter in a trendy restaurant in West Hollywood, Parker thought. But times were tough. The well-tipped professions were staffed with out-of-work writers and actors, victims of the reality TV craze.

Ruiz looked at Parker, rolled her eyes, and gave the Big, Bored Sigh. "I think he wants to ask you out," she mumbled.

Carson made the "talk, talk, talk" motion with his hand, then pointed at Parker and mouthed: "Great hat."

"Everybody wants me, doll," Parker muttered to Ruiz in a Bogart accent. "That's the curse of being me."

"I don't want you."

Rayne Carson ended his call with a very pointed, "I have to go, Joel, the police need to speak with me about a very important matter. . . . No, it's not about you. But I could change that."

He rang off and apologized to Parker. "My agent—such as he is. I'm perfect for a new gay reality show Fox is putting together, and this clown can't get me arrested."

"We could," Ruiz said sweetly.

"Can you get me on **America's Most Wanted**? A couple of days reenacting some horrible crime. It takes up space on the résumé."

"Some other time," Parker said. "Do you have any idea what messenger company someone like Lowell would go to, with his bad track record?"

"One of the small companies. Desperate and disreputable. Cheap and dirty."

"Such as?"

"Right Fast, Fly First, Speed Couriers."

11

Eta Fitzgerald was a creature of habit. Every morning at quarter of six she dumped the last of her wake-up coffee in the sink, kissed her elderly mother on the cheek, and hit the road.

She lived with her mother and four children in a nondescript little tract house in a nice working-class neighborhood beneath one of the more commonly used flight paths for jets in and out of LAX. The Fitzgerald family had migrated to Los Angeles from New Orleans eight years earlier, during a booming economy, before bankruptcy and terrorist scares cut a swath through the airline industry. Her husband, Roy, a jet mechanic, had taken a job with Delta, and never missed a day's work in six years, until a platform collapsed while he was working on a 747 and he fell to his death.

At quarter of six it took Eta no time to get downtown. By quarter of seven the trip would be twice as long. By quarter of eight the roads would be bumper-to-bumper and so slow that she would be able to read the **LA Times** front to back before she got where she was going.

Her first stop downtown was always the Carl's Jr. at Fifth and Flower, where she would sit down for a second cup of coffee and a greasy, calorie-busting, artery-clogging egg and sausage sandwich. More often than not she saw some of her messengers there as they fueled up for the day. Sometimes she would chat with them and catch up with their lives off their bikes. Sometimes she only observed.

She could have found a better-paying job. She had worked dispatch for the New Orleans Police Department, and for a couple of years with a private ambulance company in Encino. But she'd had her fill of life-and-death situations, and she didn't need to make a million. Roy's insurance and pension took good care of the family. Eta liked working at Speed. The messengers were strange and interesting characters, a ragtag bunch of kids and grown men who had never been able to take any road but the one less traveled. They were a family, of sorts. Eta was their mother hen.

Mojo raised a hand to acknowledge her. He stood at the far corner booth with one foot up on the seat, leaning forward as he told two messengers from another agency one of the fantastic stories that made up his past. He was a wild-looking guy, that Mojo. The dreads, the black black skin stretched taut over a tall, bony frame. He dressed in layers of rags, like a homeless person, and when his eyes went wide, he looked crazy.

Mojo had been known to put voodoo curses on cabdrivers who had cut him off—had nearly got himself thrown in jail once for chasing a driver into a noodle shop, grabbing him by the collar, and screaming curses at him as he shook his necklace of chicken bones and claws and God knew what all in the man's face.

That was Mojo's gig, his thing that kept folks from looking too closely at him. Eta happened to know his real name was Maurice, and he read poetry and played a badass saxophone open-mike nights at a jazz club in West LA.

She sipped her coffee and looked around for any of her other "children." Gemma, a red-headed girl in bike pants and a tight colorful jersey, was sucking on the straw of a super-size Coke, looking through the **LA Weekly.** She was taking a year off from college to make some money and to experience urban life.

Through the window Eta could see Preacher John pacing up and down the sidewalk, already beginning his rant of the day. Mojo liked to play crazy, Preacher John was the real deal, but somehow he managed to get his deliveries made.

Divine intervention, Eta supposed. He did his job as long as he stayed on his meds. When he went off them, he would disappear for weeks at a time. The boss, Rocco, kept John on because he was a nephew or something, so the family could keep tabs on him.

Eta dumped her tray in the trash and went back out into the early-morning gloom. Preacher John came toward her, shaking his worn-out old Bible at her, calling, "Sister! Sister!"

"Don't you be coming at me with that wife of Heber shit!" Eta warned, holding up a hand. "I am a God-fearing, churchgoing Christian, John Remko."

He pulled up and tilted his head sideways, lucid enough to be sheepish. "Eta! Eta, my queen of Africa!"

"I'm the queen of your ass," she barked. "You better take your happy pills, honey, and get yourself down to Base."

She shook her head as she went to her van, muttering, "How that boy hasn't been killed in traffic, I don't know."

She hefted herself into the driver's seat of her minivan and reached to put the key in the ignition. The hand was over her mouth before she could even realize where it had come from.

"Don't scream."

The hell I won't, she thought, trying to throw herself forward to break his hold. Her eyes went to the rearview mirror. She wanted to see him so she could tell the cops what he looked like before she beat his sorry face in.

"It's me."

The hand fell away, and the tension rushed out of her in a gust of air.

"Boy, you done scared three lives out of me!" she snapped, still looking at him via the rearview.

"I'm sorry," Jace said. "I knew you would react. If you screamed, you might have attracted somebody. Like a cop."

Eta swiveled around, scowling at the boy crouching on the floor of her backseat. Boy. He claimed he was twenty-one, but she didn't believe him and couldn't look at his sweet face and call him anything other than a boy.

"And just why don't you want cops looking at you?" she asked, taking in the scrapes and bruises on his face. "What you been into, Lone Ranger?"

"Someone tried to make roadkill out of me on that last run last night."

"People in this town get crazy when it rains."

"Did you see anything on the news about the lawyer Lenny Lowell?"

"I don't stay up for the news. Ain't never anything on it that ain't bad. Who's Lenny What?"

"Money," Jace said. "My last run. The lawyer."

"Oh, yeah. What about him?"

He tossed a folded section of the **Times** on the passenger seat. "It's in there. Someone killed him last night. After I made the pickup."

Eta stared at him. This boy would no more kill someone than her mother would get up and dance the hoochie-coochie. But he was afraid of the cops, and someone was dead.

"The cops are looking for me," he said. "I might have been the last person to see the guy alive—except for who killed him."

"So you tell them what you know," Eta said.

"No way. No way I go to the cops. I was in that office last night. I touched things. My fingerprints are there. They get me in the box, match my prints . . . It's a slam dunk for them. No."

"But, honey, someone tried to kill you," Eta said reasonably.

Jace looked incredulous. "And you think they'd believe me? I don't have any proof of that. I don't have any witnesses."

"Honey, have you looked in a mirror today?"

"All the more reason to consider me a suspect. There was a struggle. Eta, you've got to help me out here. The cops are going to show up at Speed sooner or later. They're going to ask a lot of questions."

"You want me to lie to the police?" she asked, frowning. "That's not good, son. If you've got nothing to hide, then don't hide nothing. I've known a lot of cops in my day, a lot of homicide detectives. They get the scent of something, they're gonna track it down. And the harder you make it for them, the harder they'll make it on you."

"Eta, please. You don't have to lie to them. Just—just stall them."

The boy had the clearest, bluest eyes she'd ever seen. And all they were filled with now was fear.

He reached out and put his hand on her forearm. "Just tell them you don't know anything about me."

I don't **know anything about you,** she thought. In the couple of years she'd known him she hadn't learned a thing about him. She didn't know if he had family, didn't know where he lived, didn't know what he did away from the job. He was still a mystery. He wasn't antisocial, he was quiet. He wasn't an introvert, he was a watcher. If he had a steady girlfriend, no one at Speed knew about it. He laughed at a joke, had a smile that could have sold movie tickets, but most of the time the look in his eyes was . . . careful. Not quite suspicious, but not inviting anyone in either.

Eta sighed. "What you gonna do, J.C.? You gonna run?"

"I don't know," he said.

"That's no good answer, you. You run, I guarantee they'll hang this thing on you. Then what? You run for the rest of your life?"

He closed his eyes, took a deep breath that made him wince, then sighed. "I'll figure it out. I have to. I just need some time."

Eta shook her head sadly. "You won't let anyone help you."

"I'm asking you to help me. Please."

"What do you need? You need a place to stay?"

"No, thanks, Eta." He glanced away, embarrassed. "If you could advance me some cash . . . You know I'm good for it."

"I don't know anything about you," she said, starting the van. "I got money in the safe at the office."

"I can't go there."

"You can keep your skinny ass right where you at. I'll park at the back door and bring the money out to you."

"What if the cops are watching the place?"

"What do you take me for? Honey, I done forgot more about cops than you'll ever know."

Or so she wanted to think. Suddenly she wanted to ask him everything she didn't know about him, but she knew he wouldn't give her the answers. "Baby, that dead lawyer, he ain't no crime kingpin. He ain't running the mob out of some nasty office in some nasty strip mall. He ain't worth the money it'd cost the taxpayers to set up surveillance on every courier service in LA. First they gots to figure out who done the pickup. Unless that man was the neat-and-tidy kind, keeping notes of who done what, when, why. He strike you like that?"

Jace shook his head.

"Then lay down on the floor and stay there 'til I tell you something else."

"You're the best, Eta."

"You're damn straight I am," she grumbled, pulling away from the curb. "Y'all don't appreciate Miss Eta. Hanging my big black bootie out there for y'all. I don't know what you'd do without me."

12

Speed Couriers. Stylish logo. A forties deco look. All caps, letters slanted steeply to the right, a series of horizontal lines extending to the left to suggest fast movement. The sign had probably cost more than a month's rent on the dump it hung over.

The space had once been an Indian restaurant, and still smelled like it, Parker noticed as they went inside. The stale, sour ghost of old curry had permeated the royal blue walls and gold- painted ceiling. Ruiz wrinkled her nose and looked at Parker like it was his fault.

"Welcome to our house." The guy who opened the door and stood back to let them in was tall and thin with the dark, shiny eyes of a zealot.

A punked-out kid with three nose rings and a blue Mohawk sat smoking a cigarette at a small table near the front window. After a furtive gaze at Parker and Ruiz, he put on a pair of curved

silver shades, slipped out of his chair and out
the door as they moved into the room.

"All guests are welcome, all sinners redeemed," their doorman told them. He arched
a brow in disapproval as he looked down on
Ruiz and the red lace bra playing peekaboo out
of her black suit jacket. "Are you familiar with
the story of the wife of Heber?"

Parker looked around. The wall going down a
long, narrow hall was covered with cheap, sta-
ple-riddled fake wood paneling and served as a
giant bulletin board. Playbills and political
propaganda. RAGE AGAINST THE MA-
CHINE—WAGE WAR AGAINST THE CAR
CULTURE. A flyer advertised a messengers'
race that had happened two months previously.
A poster recruited blood donors for cash.
Snapshots showed a motley assortment of messengers at parties, on their bikes, clowning
around. Hand-scrawled notes on torn scraps of
paper advertised stuff for sale. Someone was
looking for a nonsmoking roommate. Someone
was moving to Holland, "Where the weed is
legal and the sex is free. Bye-bye you cock-
suckers!"

Parker showed his badge to their spirit guide.
"We need to speak with your dispatcher."

Their doorman smiled and gestured toward a
scratched-up Plexiglas and drywall cubicle,

where a large woman with a head of braids held back by a bright-colored scarf and a phone sandwiched between her shoulder and her ear was taking notes with one hand and reaching for a microphone with the other. "Eta, Queen of Africa."

The woman's voice boomed over a tinny speaker. "John Remko! Get your crazy ass on a bike! You got a pickup. Take this manifest and get the hell out of here!"

Frowning, the man went to the window cut into the hall side of the cubicle. "Miss Eta, such language—"

The woman's eyes were bulging. "Don't you give me no lip, Preacher John! You ain't my cousin's uncle's son. You get out of here or you ain't gonna be nobody's relative no more, 'cause I will have done killed you!"

Preacher John took the manifest and disappeared down the dark hall, a retreating specter.

Parker stepped up to the window. The woman didn't look at him. She slapped her note up on a magnet board. The magnets each had a word printed on them—MOJO, JC, GEMMA, SLIDE. She secured the note to the board with PJOHN.

"You want a job, honey, fill out the yellow form. You got a job for us, fill out the top of the manifest," she said, reaching for the ringing phone. "You want something else, you ain't gonna get it here.

"Speed Couriers," she barked into the phone. "What you want, honey?"

Parker reached inside the window and slipped his shield into her line of sight. "Detective Parker, Detective Ruiz. We need a few minutes, ma'am. We have some questions."

The dispatcher looked at the badge, not at Parker, as she listened to the person on the other end of the call.

"Well, whatever you got, Todd, babydoll, you better die of it. I'm already short a messenger. . . . Walking pneumonia? I don't need you walking, honey. I need you on a bike." She listened for a moment, huffed in offense, and said: "You don't love me. That's all there is to it."

She slammed the receiver down, swiveled her tall wheeled stool around, and faced Parker with an imperious glare. "I got no time for you, Blue Eyes. You ain't nothing but trouble. I can see that comin' now. A sharp-dressed man with a hat ain't never nothin' but trouble. You gonna cost me nothin' but time and money."

Parker swept his fedora off, grinned, and held his raincoat open. "You like the suit? It's Canali."

"I'll like it better from a distance. Aks what

you gonna aks, honey. This ain't the offices of **GQ** magazine. I got me a real business to run."

"Did you send a messenger to the office of Leonard Lowell, Esquire, for a pickup last night around six-thirty?"

She stuck her chin out and didn't blink. "We close at six P.M."

"Good for you," Parker said with a hint of a half smile. A dimple cut into his right cheek. "But that's not what I asked."

"I send out a whole lotta messengers on a whole lotta runs."

"Do you want us to interview each of them?" Parker asked politely. "I can clear my calendar for the rest of the day. Of course, they'll have to come down to the station. How many are there? I'll have my partner call for a van."

His nemesis narrowed her eyes.

"What do you call those notes you put up on that board?" Parker asked.

"Floaters."

"Every order gets put on a floater. The floater goes on the board under the name of the messenger going on the run. Is that how it works?"

"You want my job?" she asked. "You need another line of work? You want me to train you? You can have this job. I'll go file my nails and watch Oprah and Dr. Phil every day."

Her fingernails were as long as bear claws, with metallic purple polish and hand-painted pink rose details.

"I want you to answer a simple question, ma'am. That's all. You can answer me, or I can take all the floaters you wrote yesterday back to the station and go through them one by one. And what about the manifests? I'm guessing you match the two things up at the end of the day. We could take them too. Let you get on with your business."

"You can get a damn warrant," Eta barked. She grabbed her radio mike by the throat as incoming static and garbled words crackled over the speaker. "Ten-nine? Ten-nine, P.J.? What the hell do you mean you're lost? You ain't gone but two minutes. How could you be lost? You're lost in your brain, that's where you're lost. What's your twenty? Look at a damn street sign."

The messenger answered, and Eta rolled her eyes. "You're hardly across the damn street! I swear, John Remko, if you ain't taking your meds, I'm gonna feed 'em to you my own self! Get yourself turned around and get gone before I got Money chewing on my tail."

Ruiz stuck her nose into the mix. "We can get a warrant," she said aggressively. "We can make your life hard. Do you know the meaning of **obstruction?**"

Eta looked at her as if Ruiz were an annoying child. "Sure I do," she drawled. "You ought to take some Metamucil for that, honey. There's a Sav-on Drugstore the next block up."

Ruiz flushed red. The dispatcher sniffed her disdain. "Honey, I worked dispatch for the New Orleans Police Department for eight years. You don't scare me."

The phone rang again, and she snatched it up. "Speed Couriers. What you want, honey?"

Parker cocked a look at Ruiz, one corner of his mouth tugging upward. "She's something."

Ruiz was pouting, angry, offended at being made the butt of a joke.

"Don't push too hard," Parker murmured. "We want her on our side. Finesse beats force every time with a woman."

"Like you would know," Ruiz grumbled. "You threatened her first."

"But I did it politely and with a charming smile."

The dispatcher moved from phone to microphone, one hand scribbling out the order. "Base to Eight, Base to Eight. Gemma, you there, baby?"

The messenger answered, and was dispatched to pick up a package from a downtown law office and deliver it to an attorney at the federal building on Los Angeles Street. The floater went up on the board under the GEMMA magnet.

"I'm curious," Parker said, leaning on the counter with both elbows, settling in. "You haven't asked once why we want to know if you dispatched a courier to this office. Why is that?"

"It don't concern me."

"A man was murdered there last night. His daughter told us he was waiting for a bike messenger. We're thinking the messenger might be able to tell us something that could be valuable to the case."

Eta heaved a sigh. "May the Lord have mercy on his soul."

"The victim? Or the messenger?" Ruiz asked.

"You're making me suspicious, you know," Parker said casually, giving her the up-from-under look—intimate, as if they had known each other for years and he had gotten his way with this look before. "Being difficult like this. Makes me think you've got something to hide."

The woman looked away, thinking. Maybe weighing pros and cons, maybe realizing she'd made a mistake taking the hard line.

"We'll find out one way or the other," Parker pointed out. "Better for everyone if we do it the friendly way. You don't want us to get warrants, haul away half your office and all of your messengers. Do you own this business, Ms. . . . ."

"Fitzgerald. No, I do not."

"So you would have to answer to your boss, explain to him why he's losing a day's income, why his files are being confiscated, why the police want to look at his employee files and payroll records." He shook his head sadly. "That won't be good for you."

She stared at him, hard, maybe wondering if she dared call his bluff.

"I know these kids," she said. "They march to their own drummer, but they ain't bad kids."

"We just need to ask him some questions. If he didn't do anything wrong, he's got nothing to worry about."

Eta Fitzgerald looked away and sighed again, her presence deflating as she admitted defeat to herself. The phone rang, she picked it up and politely asked the caller to hold.

"It was a late call," she said to Parker, staring down at the counter.

"Where's the manifest?"

"The messenger's still got it. He didn't make it back to match up his paperwork. It was raining. I closed up and went home to my kids."

"And is he working today?"

"He ain't been in yet."

"Why is that?"

She made a sour face. "I don't know! I'm not his mother. Some of these kids drift in and out.

Some of them got other jobs besides this one. I don't keep track of them."

Parker pulled his notebook out of his inside coat pocket. "What's his name?"

"J.C."

"What's J.C. stand for?"

"It stands for J.C.," she said, perturbed. "That's what we call him: J.C. Number Sixteen."

"Where does he live?"

"I have no idea."

"Must say something in his employee file."

"He's 1099. We got no file."

"He's an independent contractor," Parker said. "No paperwork, no health insurance, no workers' comp."

"That's right."

"I'll hazard a guess and say he might even get paid in cash."

"That ain't my department," Eta snapped.

"Do you want me to call for the warrant?" Ruiz asked Parker, taking her cell phone out of her purse.

Parker held up a hand to hold her off. His attention was steady on the dispatcher. "You have his phone number."

"He don't have no phone."

Ruiz sniffed and started punching numbers.

"He don't! I got no number for him."

Parker looked dubious. "He's never called you? Called in sick, asked for something, let you know he's running late?"

"He calls on the two-way. I got no phone number for the boy."

Ruiz spoke into her phone. "Detective Renee Ruiz, LAPD. I need to speak with ADA Langfield regarding a warrant."

"Maybe I got an address," the dispatcher said grudgingly.

The phone was lighting up like a pinball machine, one call on hold, another coming in. She grabbed up the receiver, hit the second line button, and said, "You gotta call back, honey. I'm in the middle of a police harassment."

She went to a file cabinet in the corner of the cubicle and dug through a drawer, pulling out what looked like an empty file folder.

"It's just one of those mailbox places," she said, handing it over. "That's all I know. I wouldn't say any different if you tortured me."

Parker raised his eyebrows. "I hope we won't have to find out. Can you tell me what he looks like?"

"He looks like a blond-haired, blue-eyed white boy."

"Any pictures of him up on that wall?" he asked, nodding toward the paneled wall.

"No, sir."

"Thank you for your cooperation, Ms. Fitzgerald. You're a good citizen."

Eta Fitzgerald scowled at him and grabbed her ringing phone, dismissing him. Parker opened the folder, scanned the single sheet of paper—a job application—for pertinent info.

NAME: J. C. Damon

Parker closed the folder and handed it to Ruiz. Instead of turning for the front door, he started down the hall toward the back of the restaurant-cum–courier service. The dispatcher jerked the telephone receiver away from her head and shouted at him.

"Where do you think you're going?"

Parker waved her off. "We'll let ourselves out, Ms. Fitzgerald. Don't worry about us. We're parked closer to the back."

He glanced into what used to be a small private dining room, now converted to office space for Speed's executives, neither of whom had yet made it in to work. By the state of the place, it was safe to assume there was no high ladder of success to climb and nowhere lower to go. There were two beat-up desks littered with paperwork, and a dirty, bottle-green ashtray sitting on a coffee table in front of a sofa that looked like it might have been found along the freeway.

Farther down the hall, what had been a coatroom now was a dark red closet crammed with file cabinets.

Parker hit the swinging door into the kitchen, where conversation and cigarette smoke hung in the air, along with the slight, sweet, faded scent of pot. The kid with the blue Mohawk was sitting on a stainless-steel prep table. He froze like a small animal that knew it had been spotted by a predator that would kill it if it moved. A wild-looking Rasta man stood leaning back against a sink, smoking a cigarette. He seemed neither surprised nor alarmed to see a pair of cops walk in.

"May we help you good folks?" he asked. Jamaican.

"Either of you gentlemen know J. C. Damon?"

Mohawk said nothing. Rasta Man took a drag on his cigarette. "J.C.? Yes."

"Seen him around today?"

"No. Not today."

Parker did a slow scan of the space that had clearly been claimed by the messengers as their own. A couple of street-ravaged bikes leaned up against a wall. Random bike parts, beer bottles, and soda cans littered the counter. The room had been gutted of its commercial appliances. A filthy, old, once-white GE refrigerator stood in a fraction of the space occupied by what had been there before it. A nasty green sofa squatted where the range had been. A table and mismatched chairs sat near the back door, magazines and messy paperwork scattered over the table. The centerpiece was a hubcap being used as a giant ashtray.

"You know where he lives?"

Rasta Man shook his head. "What you need him for, mon?"

Parker shrugged. "He might have seen something go down last night."

No reaction.

Ruiz stepped toward Mohawk. "What about you? What have you got to say for yourself?"

"I don't know nothing about nobody." Attitude now. He couldn't run, he couldn't hide, he went with attitude. "Nice bra."

Ruiz tugged her coat into place. "The guy works here. How can you not know him, smart-ass?"

"I didn't say I didn't know him. I said I didn't know anything about him."

"Would you know him if I threw you up against that wall and found dope in your pockets?"

Mohawk frowned. Parker shook his head and rolled his eyes. "I apologize for my partner. She's got a short fuse. One brutality charge after another."

Ruiz cut him with a look. "He's wasting our time. What do you want to do? Stand around and smoke a joint with them?"

"That would be against regulations," Parker said easily.

She called him a turd in Spanish.

Rasta Man exhaled smoke through his nostrils. "J.C. We call him the Lone Ranger."

"Why is that?" Parker asked. "Does he wear a mask? Carry a silver bullet? Shack up with an Indian?"

"Because he likes to be alone."

"No man is an island."

The courier pushed away from the sink. Standing beneath his spectacular head of gray-brown dreadlocks was a body as strong as a tree. His thigh muscles, clad in black spandex, looked as if they had been carved by a master sculptor. He walked over to the hubcap ashtray, the clips on the toes of his bike shoes clacking on the concrete floor.

"That one is," he said.

Parker took out his wallet, flashing a stack of green bills as he dug out a business card and flicked it onto the worktable, in the direction of Mohawk. "If you hear from him, he should give me a call."

He put his wallet away and went out the back
door. Ruiz nearly knocked him down, shoving
her way around him, trying to get in his face.

"What the fuck was that about?" She kept her
voice low, but caustic nonetheless.

"What?"

"You could have gone with me. Backed me
up on the drug thing. We could have twisted
the little punk."

Parker looked at a couple of bikes chained to
a gas meter. "I could have. But that's not the
way I wanted to play it. My case, follow my
lead. Your case, I'll let you alienate as many
people as you want."

The alley was like any alley downtown,
a narrow, dirty valley between brick buildings.
The strip of sky above was the color of soot.
The limited parking spots behind the businesses were crowded with delivery vans hud-
dling together like horses in the soft rain.

"And your lead is to bribe everybody?" Ruiz
said.

"I don't know what you're talking about, Ms.
Ruiz. No money changed hands."

A dark blue minivan sat wedged into a parking space between a wall and a green Dumpster.
PROUD PARENT OF AN HONOR STUDENT was
neatly affixed to the back window. Eta
Fitzgerald's car.

"The **idea** of available money is out there," Parker said, walking around the van. "Doesn't mean anything to me. I didn't make any offers. But you never know. Mohawk might think an offer was implied. The notion might influence him to tell us something he otherwise wouldn't have."

Ruiz didn't want to calm down. Parker thought she enjoyed being angry. Anger was the fuel for her energy. And it probably made her feel bigger than she was, stronger than she could ever physically be.

"And then what?" she demanded. "He comes forward, tells you something, and you stiff him?"

"He comes forward, tells me something, I save him from you. I should be so lucky to have someone do that much for me."

He took a peek inside the van through the windows. The usual load of family crap. A football helmet, action figures, and a black Barbie. Loose bottles of Arrowhead water that had to roll around like bowling pins when the car was in motion.

"What are you doing running around with that much money anyhow?" Ruiz demanded crossly.

"You don't know how much money I have. I could have twenty dollars in ones, for all you know. It's none of your damn business anyway."

She decided to pout, crossing her arms over her chest, shoving her cleavage upward, red lace tempting the eye. "What are we looking for?"

Parker shrugged. "I just like to have the lay of the land."

"Let's go find this guy. I'm freezing."

"Sixty percent of your body heat escapes out the top of your head."

"Shut up."

He started to move away from the van, then glanced back, something catching his eye. He frowned, and went back into the building, Ruiz at his heels like a terrier.

Eta Fitzgerald, once again juggling phone and radio mike, froze and stared at them as they approached her window. "What now?" she demanded. "You're just a bad penny, you. Why don't you go spend yourself somewhere else?"

Parker grinned at her and put a hand against his chest. "You're not happy to see me? I'm crushed."

"I'd like to crush something. Get on with it. You're worse than a child."

"It's your car," he said. "Can you come out back with us for a minute?"

She turned ashen, cut the mike, and hung up the phone. "My car? What about my car?"

Parker motioned for her to follow, and went back down the hall.

Outside, the mist was thickening again, raindrops falling spontaneously around them. Parker adjusted his hat and went to the back of the van.

The dispatcher followed reluctantly, her breathing short and labored, as if she'd run a race.

"It's your taillight," Parker said, pointing. "Busted out. Not a lot of damage, but still . . . You'll get pulled over for it on a day like this."

Eta Fitzgerald stared at the back of the van. Her expression was one of sudden nausea.

"Not by me," Parker went on. "They don't let me write tickets anymore. Something about road rage . . . I just wanted to give you a heads-up."

"Thank you, Detective," she said softly. "I appreciate that."

Parker tipped his hat. "We're here to serve."

13

Jace watched from across the alley, from inside a soggy cardboard box that had been left behind an Italian furniture store. Crumbs of Styrofoam packing peanuts clung to him like fleas.

Staying in Eta's backseat was too risky. He'd been a captive there, trapped, vulnerable. No good. He needed space, a vantage point, escape routes. As soon as she'd gone inside, he had slipped out of the van and gone across the alley. The box squatted, half-hidden, in front of the furniture store's delivery truck. The store didn't open for another couple of hours. He was safe to squat there for a while.

Eta had promised to come back out with the money right away, but half a minute after she had gone inside, Preacher John had shown up, chained his bike to the Dumpster, and gone in. Then came Mojo, then the guy they called Hardware because of his body piercings. They had probably cut out on their paperwork from the day before, wanting to get home and out of the rain, and had come in early to do it before they started their runs.

No Eta. No Eta.

All she had to do was put the cash in an envelope and step out to put it in her van. There was no sign of Rocco, the boss, or of his sidekick, Vlad, who seemed to do nothing all day but smoke, talk to other Russians on his cell phone, and putt golf balls around the office. Rocco usually showed up by nine. Vlad usually turned up around noon, and was almost always hungover.

Come on, Eta. Come on.

Jace huddled back into his oversize army jacket and looked at the newspaper page he had tried to show her in the van. He reread the piece for the hundredth time. Lenny Lowell's violent passing from the world had been reduced to two column inches buried in the depths of the **LA Times.** It said the lawyer had been found by his daughter, Abigail (a twenty-three-year-old student at Southwestern Law), that he had been bludgeoned to death in his office. An autopsy was pending. Detectives from the LAPD were following all leads.

Abby Lowell. The pretty brunette in the photograph on Lenny's desk. A law student. Jace wondered if she had seen anything. Maybe she'd seen Predator fleeing the scene. Maybe she knew who would want her father dead, and why. Maybe she knew who the people in the negatives were.

Speed's back door opened, and two people came out. A man first: average height, average build, expensive-looking raincoat, and a hat like a 1940s movie detective. Sam Spade. Philip Marlowe. With a petite woman in a black suit, a flash of red in the V of the neckline. Pissed off. Hispanic. Sam Spade ignored her.

Cops. At least the guy was—even though he was really too well-dressed. Jace had a sixth sense for cops. They held themselves a certain way, walked a certain way, moved a certain way. Their eyes never stopped scanning the territory when they came into a new situation. They were taking in everything about their surroundings in case they needed to remember details later on.

This one walked around Eta's van, slowly, looking in the windows. A chill swept over Jace, pebbling his skin with goose bumps. The woman seemed more interested in chewing out the guy than she was in the van. Neither of them tried to open a door, and then they went back inside the building.

Jace shivered. Why would the cops be interested in Eta's van, unless someone had told them to be? She'd told him to go to the police. Maybe she had made the decision for him.

He told himself he couldn't be disappointed, because he never really expected anything from anyone. Except that he **was** disappointed. People never meant what they said. Or they meant to keep a promise in the moment it was made, but not under pressure. That was always the fine print in a deal—**Does not extend past the introduction of extenuating circumstances.**

Eta treated the messengers like she was their cranky, surrogate mother. She had a good heart. But why would she put her neck on the line with the cops for him? She had her own life, her own real kids. He wasn't part of her family. Or maybe she was the kind of mother who did things for her children "for their own good," which almost always turned out to be bad.

Jace told himself he'd been stupid going to her for help, asking her to lie for him. Involving other people meant losing absolute control of the situation. But he'd seen a quick way to get his hands on a couple hundred bucks. Money he could use to lay low for a while, if he had to. He didn't want to take money out of his bank, which was not a bank at all but a fireproof lockbox he kept hidden inside an air duct in the bathroom at the apartment. That money was for Tyler to live on, in case something happened.

Something **had** happened.

Time to go.

Using the delivery truck for cover, Jace crawled out of the box. He flipped up the collar of his coat, hunched his shoulders, held the newspaper like a tent over his head, and started down the alley. He tried not to limp, tried to look like he wasn't in a hurry, like he had nowhere to go, like he didn't want to run. He kept his eyes on the ground.

What now, J.C.?

The negatives were in their envelope under his shirt, strapped around him with athletic tape. He had to find a place to hide it, someplace away from Tyler, and away from the Chens. Obviously, it was valuable to someone. He could use it for leverage, use it as an insurance policy if things went further south than they already had. He needed to find safe, neutral ground. A public place. And he needed to get to Abby Lowell.

A car turned in at the mouth of the alley, crawling toward him. Maybe the two cops.

A dark sedan.

A cracked windshield.

Fear hit Jace in the belly and shot through his

veins like mercury. Quick, toxic. He wanted to look, to put a face on his hunter. Humanize the monster. See that in the light of day the guy was just a small, inadequate man who posed no real threat. But of course none of that was true. He wanted something Jace had, and even if Jace simply gave it to him, the guy would probably kill him anyway because Jace knew too much— even though he really knew nothing at all.

The car slowed as it neared him. Jace's chest tightened. He was on the driver's side. Could the guy put a face on him? Flashes of the night before burst behind his eyes. He was on the bike, swinging his U-lock into the windshield. He couldn't remember the driver's face; could the driver remember his? He'd had his helmet on. And his goggles.

He glanced over out the corner of his eye as the car came even with him.

A head like a square block of stone, small, mean eyes, dark hair buzzed short. The guy's skin was pale with blue undertones beneath his beard. He had a piece of white tape across the bridge of his nose, and a black mole on the back of his neck. The kind of mole that was more like a growth, sticking out, the size of a pencil eraser.

The sedan cruised past like a panther in the jungle, quiet, sleek, ominous.

Jace kept walking, refusing the urge to look back. His legs felt like jelly.

The guy was cruising the Speed office. Of course he knew where Jace worked. He had Jace's messenger bag. Another flash of memory: being grabbed and yanked backward by the strap of his bag. There was nothing much in the bag—a tire pump, a spare tube, a couple of blank manifests . . . with the Speed logo and address in red at the top of the page.

Next the guy would try to find out where Jace lived, just as the cops would. But none of them would be able to, he assured himself. The only address Speed had for him was the old P.O. box. And the only address the P.O. box people had on file was an old apartment he had lived in briefly with his mother before Tyler was even born. No one would be able to find him.

But the sharks were in the water, moving, hunting.

Two cops and a killer.

I never wanted to be the popular guy, he thought as he crossed the street. The position came with too much trouble.

He chanced a look back over his shoulder. The sedan's taillights glowed at the far end of the alley.

Jace broke into a jog, pain throbbing in

his ankle with every footfall. He couldn't afford to feel it. He didn't have the luxury of time to heal. All his energy had to go to survival now.

He needed to find Abby Lowell.

14

Whats your opinion?" Parker asked as they eased back into traffic.

"That I'm glad I don't have a shit job like that," Ruiz said, checking her hair in the mirror on the back of the sun visor. It was frizzing from the humidity.

"So now we know where the suspect works," she said. "But he's not going back there anytime soon. We know where he gets his mail, but we don't know where he lives. There's nothing to make much of."

Parker made the rude sound of a game-show buzzer. "Wrong. First of all, we could have his prints on the job ap. We know his name, or an aka at least. We can kick up his sheet if he has one. Scrutinize his prior bad acts. And there's a good chance he has priors. He keeps to himself, gets paid in cash, mail goes to a box; no address, no phone. He operates like a crook."

"Maybe he's homeless," Ruiz pointed out. "And what if he doesn't have a sheet?"

"If Latent can pull a clear print off the job ap, and if they can match it to a print on the murder weapon, we'll have that. And the dispatcher knows more than she's saying."

"Yeah, but she's not saying it."

"She's got a conscience, she doesn't like breaking rules. But she's protective of her messengers. They're like a family, and she's the mom. We'll give her a little time to think about it, then go back to her. I think she wants to do the right thing."

"I think she's a bitch," Ruiz grumbled.

"You can't take it personally. You make it personal, you lose your perspective. It worked well in this situation to play her off you. You make a good bad cop, Ruiz," he said. "You've got good tools. You have to learn not to throw the whole box at the head of every witness or perp you run into."

From the corner of his eye he could see her watching him. She didn't know what to make of him. She bristled at his suggestions, and didn't trust his compliments. Good. She needed to be kept off balance. She had to learn how to read people and how to adapt. She should have learned it day one in a uniform.

"Jesus," he mumbled. "I sound like a teacher."

"You are a teacher. Allegedly."

Parker didn't say anything. His mood had turned south. Most of the time he tried to keep a narrow focus on his goal in the department. He didn't think of himself as a teacher. He was waiting for the chance to make a comeback.

He could have quit. He didn't need the money or the hassle. The job he had on the side had paid off his debts, bought him his Jag and his wardrobe. But he was too stubborn to quit. And every time a case took hold of him, and he felt the old adrenaline rush, he was reminded that he loved what he did. He was old-fashioned enough to be proud that he carried a badge and did a public service.

And every time a case took hold, and he felt that adrenaline rush, he was reminded that somewhere deep inside him he still believed **this** could be the case that turned it all around. This could be the case where he proved himself, redeemed himself, regained the respect of his peers and his enemies.

But if this was the kind of case with the potential to turn his career around, Robbery-Homicide was sure to muscle in and take it away from him.

He turned the car into the tiny parking lot of a little strip mall with a collection of food shops: Noah's Bagels, Jamba Juice, Starbucks. The driver picked the radio station, the passenger picked the restaurant. Parker usually chose a cop hangout for breakfast, not because he liked too many cops, but because he liked to eavesdrop, pick up the mood of things on the street, catch a scrap of gossip that might be useful. Ruiz picked Starbucks. Her order was always long and complicated, and if it didn't turn out exactly to her liking, she made the barista do it over, sometimes by making a scene, sometimes by batting eyelashes. Bipolar, that girl.

Parker went into Jamba Juice and got a fruit smoothie loaded with protein and wheatgrass, then went into Starbucks and commandeered a table in the back with a clear view of the door, took the corner chair, and picked up a section of the **Times** a previous customer had abandoned.

He kept thinking about the fact that Robbery-Homicide had come sniffing around his crime scene. There had to be something to that. They were front-page guys working front-page cases. Lenny Lowell had not made the front page. The **Times** probably wouldn't waste any ink on him at all.

"Watching your girlish figure?" Ruiz asked as she joined him.

Parker kept his attention on the newpaper. "My body is a temple, baby. Come worship."

He hadn't seen or spoken with anyone at the scene resembling a reporter, and he was the detective of record . . .

. . . but there it was, a couple of sentences stuck in a lower corner on a left-hand page beside an ad for a sale on tires. ATTORNEY FOUND DEAD.

Leonard Lowell, the victim of an apparent homicide, found by his daughter, Abigail Lowell (twenty-three, a student at Southwestern Law), bludgeoned to death in his office, blah, blah, blah.

Parker stopped breathing for a moment as he called up his memory of the night before. Abby Lowell arriving on the scene, carefully controlled. Jimmy Chew had said the call had been phoned in by an anonymous citizen. Abby Lowell said she'd received a call from an LAPD officer notifying her of her father's death while she was waiting for him at Cicada.

It was too early to call the restaurant to check her alibi.

The byline on the story was "Staff Reporter."

Ruiz was paying no attention, too busy sipping her extra-hot double venti half-caf no-whip vanilla mocha with one pink and one blue sweetener, and making eyes at the hunky barista.

"Ruiz." Parker leaned across the table and snapped his fingers at her. "Did you get a name for that phone number I gave you to check out? The number from Abby Lowell's cell phone call list?"

"Not yet."

"Do it. Now."

She started to object. Parker slid the paper across the table and tapped a finger on the piece. He got up from his chair, dug his phone out of his pocket, and scrolled through the address book as he went out the side door into the damp cold.

"Kelly." Andi Kelly, investigative reporter for the **LA Times.** A fireball in a small red-haired package. Tenacious, wry, and a lover of single malt scotch.

"Andi. Kev Parker."

There was a heavy silence. He pictured confusion then recognition dawning on her face.

"Wow," she said at last. "I used to know a Kev Parker."

"Back when I was good for a headline," Parker remarked dryly. "Now you never call, you never write. I feel so used."

"You changed your phone number, and I don't know where you live. I thought maybe you'd gone to live in a commune in Idaho with

Mark Fuhrman. What happened? They didn't approve of your smoking, drinking, womanizing, arrogant ways?"

"I repented, gave all that up, joined the priesthood."

"No way. Cool Kev Parker? Next you'll be telling me you've taken up yoga."

"Tai chi."

"Fuck me. Where have all the icons gone?"

"This one crumbled a while ago."

"Yeah," Kelly said soberly. "I read that in the papers."

Nothing like a public flameout to win friends and influence people. The cocky, arrogant Robbery-Homicide hotshot Parker had been made the whipping boy by an equally cocky, arrogant defense attorney in a high-profile murder trial.

The DA's case had been good, not watertight, but good, solid. A mountain of circumstantial evidence had been gathered against a wealthy, preppie UCLA med student accused of the brutal murder of a young female undergrad.

Parker was second on the team of detectives sent to the crime scene, second lead in the investigation. He had a reputation for shooting his mouth off, for riding the edge of the rules, loving the spotlight, but he was a damn good detective. That was the truth he had held on to during the trial while the big-bucks defense team shredded his character with half-truths, irrelevant facts, and outright lies. They had impugned his integrity, accused him of tampering with evidence. They couldn't prove any of it, but they didn't need to. People were always eager to believe the worst.

Anthony Giradello, the ADA set to make his career on the case, had seen Parker dragging down his ship, and had done the cruel and certain thing any ADA would have done: He took up his own whip and joined in the beating.

Giradello had done everything he could to distance his case from Parker, to downplay Parker's role in the investigation. Sure, Parker was an asshole, but he was an **unimportant** asshole who hadn't really had anything much to do with the investigation or the gathering or handling of evidence. The liberal LA press had joined in the feeding frenzy, always happy to eviscerate a cop doing his job.

Andi Kelly had been a single voice against the mob, pointing out the defense was employing the shopworn but tried-and-true "When All Else Fails, Blame a Cop" strategy. A shell game devised to draw attention away from overwhelming forensic evidence, to plant a seed of doubt in the minds of the jury. All they needed was to convince one juror that Parker was some kind of rogue, that he wouldn't think twice about planting evidence, that he had some kind of racial or socioeconomic bias against the defendant. One juror, and they would hang the jury.

They managed to convince all twelve. A murderer walked free.

The political fallout had been ugly. The DA's office had pressed for Parker to be fired, to continue to deflect the spotlight away from the fact that they had lost and a killer had walked free. The chief of police, who loathed the DA and feared the police union, had refused to get rid of Parker, despite the fact that every brass badge in the department wanted him gone. He had been painted as a problem, a loose cannon, insubordinate. The public spotlight was on him. He was a black eye on a department that couldn't take another scandal.

The only interview Parker had granted during all of it was to Andi Kelly.

"So how you doing, Kev?" Kelly asked.

"Older, wiser, like everybody," Parker said, slowly pacing the sidewalk.

"Know anything going on in the Cole case?"

"You'd know more than I would. You're the one at the courthouse every day. I'm just a peon now, you know. Training the next crop of wolf cubs," Parker said. "For what it's worth, I have it on good authority Cole is an asshole."

"That's news? He beat his wife's head in with a sculpture worth three-quarters of a million dollars."

"He came on to a friend of mine with the missus standing right there."

"Everybody knows he cheated on her. Robbie's not smart enough to pull off total discretion, despite his best efforts. Everything Tricia Crowne put up with with that clown, it's hard to believe she didn't pull a Bobbitt on him years ago," Kelly said. She released a big sigh. "Well, if you don't have a scoop for me, Parker, to hell with you."

"That's harsh. Now that I'm down on my luck, living in the gutter, eating out of garbage cans, can't you do an old friend a favor?"

"If you're such a good old friend, why didn't you stop me from marrying Goran?"

"You married a guy named Goran?"

"I believe you just made my point," she said. "But never mind. I managed to divorce him without you too. What do you want, Man-I-Haven't-Heard-From-In-Years?"

"It's nothing much," Parker said. "I'm working a homicide. Happened last night. There's a couple of lines in the **Times** this morning. I'm curious who wrote it. Can you find out?"

"Why?" Like every good reporter, Kelly was always keen for the scent of a story. If she'd been a hunting dog, she would have been on point.

"It just struck me as odd," Parker said casually. "No one spoke to me. I was on the scene half the night, and I didn't see any reporter."

"Probably some staff flunky picked it up off the scanner. Who's the vic?"

"Low-end defense attorney. I'm surprised the **Times** wasted the space."

"And?"

"And what?"

"And why do you care it was in the paper if the guy's a nobody?" Kelly asked.

"They got a couple of details wrong."

"So?"

Parker sighed and rubbed a hand over his face. "Christ, I don't remember you being such a pain in the ass."

"Well, I always have been."

"It's a wonder your mother didn't put you in a sack and drown you when you were two years old."

"I think she tried," Kelly said. "I have issues."

"Honey, I can trump your issues any day of the week."

"Now you're making me feel inferior."

"Why did I call you?" Parker asked, exasperated.

"Because you want something, and you think I'm a whore for a good story."

"You're a reporter, aren't you?"

"Which brings us back to my last question. What do you care about two sentences buried in the **Times**?"

Parker glanced back into Starbucks. Ruiz was still on her phone, but was making a note. He considered and discarded the idea of telling Kelly about Robbery-Homicide's unofficial appearance at the scene. He believed in playing his cards one at a time.

"Listen, Andi, it's nothing I can put my finger on yet. I'm just getting a weird vibe here. Maybe I'm just hinky because they don't let me out of my cage enough."

"Still in the minors, huh?"

"Yeah. Ironic, isn't it? They wanted to get rid of me because they thought I was a rotten cop, so they sentenced me to train new detectives."

"Management at its finest," Kelly said. "There's a method to that madness, though. Anybody else they would have sent down to South Central to work drug murders and body-dump jobs, but they knew you'd thrive there. They had a better chance making you quit by boring you to death."

"Yeah, well, I showed them," Parker said.

"So what do you say? Can you make a couple of calls?"

"And if this turns into something . . . ?"

"Your number is in my phone, and I'll buy you a bottle of Glenmorangie."

"I'll get back to you."

"Thanks."

Parker stuck his phone in his pocket and went back into the coffeehouse.

"The number is a prepaid cell phone," Ruiz said. "Untraceable."

"Every criminal's favorite toy," Parker said. Every drug dealer, gang banger, and thug in the city carried one. The number was sold with the phone. No paperwork, no paper trail. He grabbed the newspaper and started for the door. "Let's go."

"Who were you talking to?" Ruiz asked as they got back into the car.

"I called an old friend for a favor. I want to know who wrote that bit."

"Because they got it wrong?"

"Because what if they didn't? If the daughter found the body—"

"Then she's a suspect."

"She has to be considered anyway. Most murder victims are killed by people they know. You always have to look at the family."

"But she has an alibi."

"I want you to check it out later today. You'll need to speak with the maitre d' and the waiter at Cicada. Was she there, when did she get there, when did she leave, what was she wearing, did she speak to anyone, did she use the house phone, was she absent from the table for any length of time."

"But if she found the body, how did this reporter find out and not us?"

"That's my question," Parker said, starting the car. "Chances are, it's just a screwup. Some low face on the totem pole at the **Times** picked up the call on the scanner, got a detail third-hand from one of the crime-scene geeks while they were sitting in a bar. Who knows? Half of what gets printed in the paper is bullshit. You can stand there and tell a reporter a story word for fucking word, and they'll still get it wrong."

"I guess you'd know about that," Ruiz said.

Parker shot her a glance. "Baby, I could write a book. But right now we've got better things to do."

15

According to the Pakistani woman who had been managing the mailbox place for the last three months, Box 501 belonged to a woman named Allison Jennings, whom she did not know. The box had been rented to Ms. Jennings in 1994. The rent was paid by a money order left in the box once a year. These facts had been noted in the file, each year's note in different handwriting. It seemed a lot of people had used Box-4-U as a stepping-stone to bigger things.

Box-4-U occupied a deep, narrow space between a Lebanese take-out place and a psychic who was running a special on tarot card readings. The mailboxes made a corridor from the front door back to an area with a counter, shelves stacked with shipping cartons, padded envelopes, rolls of tape, bubble wrap, and giant bags of foam packing peanuts.

From the back it took an effort to see past all the stuff to the mailboxes if one cared to pay attention to who was going in and out. Probably the great majority of box renters entered and left in anonymity. As long as they paid their rent on time, no one cared who they were.

The manager who had rented Box 501 to Allison Jennings had made a copy of her driver's license and stapled it to the rental form as required. The license was from Massachusetts. The photo on the copy was nothing but black ink. Parker had the manager make copies of both sheets, and he and Ruiz went back out onto the street, where they had parked in a loading zone.

As they got into the car, Parker paused to look at the psychic's storefront. A lavender neon sign read: "Madame Natalia, Psychic to the Stars." She gladly accepted Visa and MasterCard.

"You want to go inside?" Ruiz asked. "Maybe she can see your future."

"Why would anyone go to see a psychic in a shithole place like that? If Madame Natalia can see the future, why hasn't she won the lottery by now?"

"Maybe that's not her destiny."

Parker put the car in gear and pulled away from the curb. He had been about to say people make their own destiny, but that didn't reflect kindly on himself, so he said nothing at all. He knew he had set himself up for his fall from

Robbery-Homicide by being too cocky, too mouthy, too visible. And he had made his own choice to stay where he was now, a sidetrack to nowhere. He had also decided he would prove himself again, go out a winner. But according to Ruiz's logic, maybe that wasn't his destiny.

Ruiz called in the DL for Allison Jennings. Who knew? Maybe the woman would turn out to be a fugitive.

The physical address the woman had listed on her renter's form for Box-4-U was a redbrick building in a dicey downtown neighborhood where everything, including the population, had been neglected for decades. Street people decorated the landscape, digging in garbage cans, sleeping in doorways. Across the street from Allison Jennings's building, a crazy guy in a parka that had once been white marched up and down the sidewalk, screaming epithets at the construction crew working on the building.

The place had been gutted and was being redone for downtown's newest invasion of urban hipsters. The sign advertising the development company promised one-, two-, and three-bedroom luxury apartments in LA's hippest, most happening new district. The artist's rendering of the finished project did not show the screaming homeless guy.

"Are they crazy?" Ruiz asked. "No one in their right mind would move down here. There's nothing here but crack houses and schizo street people."

"Wait 'til they put a Starbucks on the corner," Parker said. "There goes the neighborhood. Bring in the young urbanites, next thing you know, the price of illicit substances is through the roof. The average pipehead won't be able to afford to live here. It's a social tragedy."

"You think this woman is still around here?"

Parker shrugged. "Who knows? She filled out that form ten years ago. She could be dead by now, for all we know. This Damon kid maybe bought the box off her, or took it over. He's got to be around here someplace if he's using it."

"Someplace" covered a lot of territory. Central Bureau policed four and a half square miles of downtown LA, including Chinatown, Little Tokyo, the financial district, the jewelry and fashion districts, and the convention center. A lot of ground, a lot of people.

Parker pulled the car into the lot at the station and turned to his partner. "First thing, take Damon's job ap to Latent. See if they can get a match with anything off the murder weapon. Then call Massachusetts. Then look for any local Allison Jenningses. Then get on the computer and see if you can find any crimes similar to the Lowell homicide in LA over the past two years. And call the phone company for the local usage details on Speed Couriers."

Ruiz looked perturbed. "Anything else, Master?"

"Start going through the calls. Maybe this Damon kid doesn't have a phone, but maybe he does. And get the phone records for Lowell's office and for his home."

"And what will you be doing while I'm doing all of this shit?"

"I'm going to talk to Abby Lowell. Find out how she got her name in the paper. She'll like talking to me more than she'd like talking to you."

"What makes you so sure of that?"

He flashed her the famous Kev Parker grin. "Because I'm me, doll."

With Ruiz out of his hair, Parker drove directly to Lenny Lowell's office. He wanted to walk through the crime scene and around the street in daylight, without the distractions of the uniforms and the criminalists, a trainee, and the Robbery-Homicide goons. He found it centering, calming in a macabre sort of way, to spend time in the place where a victim had died.

He wasn't sure he believed in ghosts, but he

believed in souls. He believed in the essence of what made a being, the energy that defined a person as being alive. Sometimes when he walked a scene alone, he believed he could feel that energy around him, lingering. Other times there was nothing, emptiness, a void.

He had never paid attention to such ideas in his former life as an RHD hotshot. He had been too full of himself to sense much about anyone else around him, alive or dead. One good thing he had gained in his loss: awareness, the ability to step back from himself and see a clearer picture of what was around him.

The neighborhood was no more attractive in daylight than it had been at night, in the rain. Less so, actually. In the stark light of a gray morning, the age and dinge and tiredness of the place couldn't hide.

The little two-story strip mall where Lowell's office was located looked to have been built in the late fifties. Hard angles, flat roof, metal panels of faded color—pale aqua, washed-out pink, puke yellow. Aluminum frames around the windows. Across the street, the 24/7 Laundromat squatted, a low brick building with no discernible style.

The better scum defense attorneys had offices in Beverly Hills and Century City, where the world was beautiful. This was the kind of place where the lower end of the food chain hung their shingles. Though it seemed to Parker that old Lenny had been doing pretty well for himself.

Lowell's Cadillac had been towed away from the back door of the office, taken away to be checked for evidence. The car was new but had been vandalized. His home address was a condo in one of the new downtown hotspots near the Staples Center. Pricey stuff for a guy whose clients used the revolving door at the bail bondsman's office.

Parker wondered why the killer would have risked smashing the Cadillac's windows if all he had wanted was to steal the money in the safe.

Was it an act of punitive rage? A former client, or a family member of a client who hadn't beaten the rap, and blamed Lowell? Had the motive for the murder been revenge and the money a bonus? Or had the killer been after something he hadn't found in the office? If that was the case, this murder was a much more complicated affair. Besides the money in his safe, what could a guy like Lenny Lowell have that would be worth killing for?

Parker unsealed the crime-scene tape and let himself in the back door of the office. The smell of stale cigarette smoke clung to the fake wood paneling, and had been absorbed into the acoustic-tile ceiling, dyeing it an oily yellow. The carpet was flat and utilitarian, and a color chosen to camouflage dirt.

There was a bathroom on the left. The criminalists had gone over it, dusting for prints, plucking hairs out of the sink drain, but they had found no trace of blood. If the killer had gotten Lenny Lowell's blood on him, he'd been smart enough not to try to clean himself up here.

Lowell's office was next. A decent-size space now awash in paper, and fingerprint dust residue, and bits of tape marking evidence locations on the rug. The lawyer's blood had soaked into the carpet in a barely discernible stain (another selling point for the manufacturers: hides large bloodstains!). Drawers had been pulled out of file cabinets, out of the desk.

"You're disturbing a crime scene," Parker said.

Abby Lowell, sitting behind her father's desk, startled and gasped, and banged her knee trying to stand up and back away.

"Oh, my God! Oh, my God, you scared me!" she scolded, her splayed hand pressed to her chest as if to keep her heart from leaping out.

"I have to ask what you're doing here, Ms.

Lowell," Parker said, taking a seat across the desk from her. The arm of the chair was speckled with blood. "We seal crime scenes for a reason."

"And do you make funeral arrangements?" she asked, gathering her composure around her again like the cashmere sweater she wore. "Do you know where my father kept his life insurance policy? Will you call the company for me? And what about his will? I'm sure he has one, but I have no idea where it is. I don't know if he wanted to be buried or cremated. Can you help with that, Detective Parker?"

Parker shook his head. "No, I can't. But if you had called me, I would have met you here and helped you look. I would have known what you touched and what you moved. I would have known if you had taken something other than your father's will or his life insurance policy."

"Are you accusing me of something?" she asked, sitting a little taller, arching one dark, elegant brow.

"No. I'm just saying. That's how a crime scene works, Ms. Lowell. I can't care that the victim was your father. It can't matter to me if you think you have a right to come into this office. My job is very clear to me. The second your father ceased to breathe, he became my responsibility. I became his protector."

"Too bad for my father you weren't here to protect him from being killed. And by 'you' I don't mean you personally, I mean the LAPD."

"We can't predict when and where a crime is about to happen," Parker said. "If that were the case, I'd be out of a job. And frankly, you would be ahead of us in expectation of being able to protect your father. You knew his habits, you knew his friends, you probably knew his enemies. Maybe you knew he was into something that could have gotten him killed."

She looked incredulous. "Are you now saying it's my fault some thug broke into my father's office and killed him? You're incredible. How insensitive can you be?"

"You wouldn't want to find out," Parker said. He took his hat off and crossed his legs, settling in. "You didn't seem all that sensitive yourself last night, if you don't mind me saying, which you probably do. You walk into a room, your father is posing for the big chalk outline. You seemed more upset that your dinner plans had been disturbed."

"Why? Because I didn't fall down weeping? Because I didn't become hysterical?" she asked. "I'm not the hysterical type, Detective. And I do my crying in private. You don't know anything about my relationship with my father."

"Fill me in, why don't you? Were you and your father close?"

"In our own way."

"What way was that?"

She sighed, looked away, looked back. The relationship, like most relationships, was more complicated than she wanted to attempt to articulate—or more complicated than she expected him to understand.

"We were friends. Lenny wasn't much of a father. He wasn't around. He cheated on my mother. He drank too much. His idea of quality time with me when I was a child was to drag me along with him to the racetrack or to a bookie bar, where he would promptly forget I existed. My parents divorced when I was nine years old."

"Why didn't you hate him?"

"Because he was the only father I had. And because, for all his faults, Lenny wasn't a bad guy. He just couldn't live up to expectations."

Restless under scrutiny, she got out of her father's chair and started a slow pace back and forth in front of his bookcases, arms crossed, eyes scanning the few things that hadn't been knocked from the shelves in the ransacking. She was model gorgeous in the sapphire sweater and matching skirt, a pair of very nice black boots on her feet. "I was angry with him for a long time after he left. Mostly because I was stuck with my mother."

"But you forgave him?"

"We sort of found each other when I started college. Suddenly I was an adult. We could have a conversation. I wanted to become an attorney. He took an interest in me."

"You became friends," Parker said. "Which is why you call him Lenny instead of Dad."

She looked away again, not wanting him to see her have an emotional reaction to her memories of her father. But it was there—a thin sheen of tears in the dark eyes, a tightening along the jawline. That was some kind of steely control, Parker thought.

He supposed maybe that was what a little girl learned to do while her father was busy handicapping the sixth race at Santa Anita. And what a little girl did when she was caught between warring parents, what she did when her father left, what she did when he reappeared in her life. She maintained control. She suppressed reactions. She could survive any challenge if she didn't let anything penetrate her armor.

"Did you know your father's friends?" Parker asked quietly. "His enemies? Whether or not he was into something dangerous?"

She seemed to laugh a little to herself. Some private joke she had no interest in sharing with him.

"Lenny was always looking for an angle. Maybe he finally found one. I don't know. If he was involved in something . . . I don't know. He didn't tell me. We talked about my classes. We talked about him wanting me to work with him after I pass the bar. We went to the racetrack."

Her voice strained on the last sentence. Her relationship with her father had gone full circle, only this time around they were pals and he gave her the attention she had craved as a child. Craved so badly she had gone into her father's profession to please him—consciously or not.

Parker said nothing for a moment, letting his gaze move without focus over the stuff on the desk. Abby Lowell continued her slow pace. She wanted out, he supposed. Not even innocent people wanted to be around cops. He had no way of knowing how innocent she was or wasn't.

"You're in charge of making the funeral arrangements?" he asked. "Does he have any other family?"

"He has a brother in upstate New York. He has a daughter from his first marriage, Ann. I haven't seen her in years. I think she moved to

Boston. And three ex-wives. None of them would cross the street to spit on his corpse."

"You're the only forgiving one in the bunch."

She didn't comment, didn't acknowledge that he had spoken. She picked up a black Coach leather tote from the floor, and put it on the desk. It matched her boots.

"Do you mind if I smoke, Detective?" she asked, already digging a cigarette out of a pack of Newports.

He let her get it to her mouth, lighter poised, before he said, "Yes, I do."

She cut him a look from under her brows and lit up anyway. As she blew a stream of smoke at the nicotine-stained ceiling, she said, "I only asked for form's sake."

She leaned against the side of the desk. Her profile belonged in an Erté drawing, the long, graceful, subtly curving lines of the early Art Deco movement. Her skin was like porcelain. Her hair spilled down behind her like a dark waterfall. There appeared to be nothing of Lenny in her looks. Parker wondered if the other daughter had been so lucky. He wondered if this one was trying to distract him.

"Did you speak to anyone last night after you left here, Ms. Lowell?"

"No. I went home."

"You didn't call your mother? Tell her her ex checked out?"

"My mother died five years ago. Cancer."

"I'm sorry," Parker said automatically. "You didn't call a friend? A boyfriend?"

She sighed, impatient, stubbed out the cigarette, started to move again. "What are you trying to get at, Detective? If you have a question, ask it. We don't have to play twenty questions about my personal life. I have arrangements to make, and I have a class at eleven. Can we get on with it?"

Parker cocked a brow. "A class? No day off to mourn, to try to grasp the idea that your father was murdered less than twenty-four hours ago?"

"My father is dead. I can't change that." Her pace picked up a step. "He was murdered. I can't grasp that idea. I don't know how anyone possibly could. What good would it do me to stay home in my pajamas, contemplating the meaninglessness of life?" she asked. "I may seem cold to you, Detective Parker, but I'm dealing with this the only way that makes any sense to me—moving forward, doing what has to be done because no one else is going to do it for me."

"Cope now, fall apart later," Parker said, rising from the bloodstained chair. He positioned himself where she had been, leaning against the end of the desk. "I've been a cop nearly twenty years, Ms. Lowell. I know survivors deal with grief in their own way.

"I had a case once," he said. "A woman murdered in a carjacking. Her coat caught in the door when the perp shoved her out. She was dragged nearly a block. It was horrible. Her husband was a reasonably successful artist, a painter. His way of coping, of exorcising grief and guilt, and all the rest of it, was to lock himself in his studio and paint. He painted for thirty-six hours straight, no sleep, no food. For thirty-six hours he raged in that studio, hurling paint, brushes, cans, anything he could put his hands on. The whole time he was screaming and shouting and sobbing. His assistant called me because she was afraid he'd had a psychotic break, and worried he might try to kill himself.

"Finally everything went silent. The guy came out of the studio, spoke to no one, took a shower, and went to bed. The assistant and I went into the studio to see what he'd been doing all that time. He'd done a dozen or so big canvases. Incredible work, brilliant, miles beyond anything he'd done before. Pollock would have wept to see it. Every emotion tearing this man apart was up there, raw, angry, crushing grief.

"When the guy woke up, he went back into the studio and destroyed every one of them. He said they were private, not meant for anyone else to see. He buried his wife, and went on with his life."

Abby Lowell was staring at him, trying to figure out how she was supposed to react, what she was supposed to think, what kind of trick this might be.

Parker spread his hands. "Everyone handles it the only way they can."

"Then why were you judging me?"

"I wasn't. I need to know the why of everything, Ms. Lowell. That's my job. For instance, I need to know why it said in the **Times** this morning that you, a twenty-three-year-old student at Southwestern Law, discovered your father's body."

Something flashed in her eyes, across her face, there and gone. Not anger. Surprise, maybe. Then the poker face. "I don't know. It isn't true. You know it isn't true," she said defensively. "I was at the restaurant when I got the call. And I don't know any reporters. I wouldn't talk to them if I did."

"And you didn't speak to anyone after you left this office last night?"

Exasperation. "I told you. No." She checked her watch, shifted her weight, put her hand on her purse.

"How about before? Did you call anyone from the restaurant or from your car on your way over here? A friend, a relative?"

"No. And I'm sure you can get my cell phone records if you don't believe me." She put the strap of her bag over her shoulder and looked toward the door to the front of the office. "I have to go," she said bluntly. "I have a meeting with a funeral director at eleven."

"I thought you had a class."

The dark eyes snapped with annoyance. "The class is at one. I misspoke. I have a lot on my agenda, Detective. You know how to contact me if you need anything more."

"I can find you."

She started past him to leave. Parker reached out and gently caught her by the arm. "Wouldn't you like to know when your father's body is going to be released from the morgue? I'm sure the funeral director will need that information."

Abby Lowell looked him in the eye. "His body won't be released until after the autopsy. I'm told that could be several days, or as much as a week. I want everything arranged so I can get this over with as soon as possible."

Parker let her go. She had the composure of a knife-thrower's assistant, he had to give her that. He wondered if there was anything more behind it than a lonely little girl protecting herself.

His gaze drifted across the desk as he tossed these thoughts and observations around in his head. She'd left empty-handed, no sign of the things she had come here to look for. Lenny's life insurance policy, his will.

He went out to the car, got the Polaroid camera out of the trunk, and went back in. He shot photographs of the desktop, the open filing cabinets, the floor around the desk. Then he carefully lifted a long black plastic envelope out of a half-opened desk drawer. In gold stamped letters across the front: CITY NATIONAL BANK. It was empty. The impression of a small key had been left in one frosted plastic pocket. Safe-deposit box.

Parker eased himself into Lenny Lowell's big leather executive's chair and looked around the room, trying to imagine what Lenny would have seen as he surveyed his domain. What he would have focused on. Abby's photograph had been knocked over on his desk. He looked down beside the chair. A couple of travel brochures lay at cockeyed angles half under the desk. Parker inched them out with the toe of his shoe.

LOSE YOURSELF IN PARADISE. THE CAYMAN IS-LANDS.

"Well, Lenny," he said to the empty room. "I'd hope you're in another paradise now, but I imagine you've gone where all scum defense attorneys go. I hope you took your sunscreen."

16

Jace took The Beast to a bike shop in Korea Town, where he knew no one and no one knew him.

"I need some work done."

The guy behind the counter was busy watching Court TV on a television hanging up near the ceiling. He barely flicked Jace a glance. "Three day."

"No. I need it today. It's an emergency."

The counter guy scowled up at the TV screen. "Three day."

"You don't understand, sir," Jace said, trying to lean into the guy's field of vision. "I need the bike. I'm a messenger. I need the bike to work."

"Three day."

The guy still hadn't looked at him. He suddenly pointed a finger at the television and went off in Korean. Martin Gorman, attorney to the stars, was standing at a podium bristling with microphones, giving a press conference. At the bottom of the screen, it read: "Tricia Crowne-

Cole: Death of a Debutante." By the photograph of the woman in the lower left-hand
corner, she looked like maybe she'd been a
debutante during the Kennedy administration.

Jace sighed, cleared his throat, thought about
walking out, but he couldn't spend the day
looking for another bike-repair shop.

"I'll pay extra," he said. "I'll pay cash. An extra twenty bucks."

The clerk turned to him and said, "Twenty
now. Come back in two hour."

It pained Jace to give up the money, but he
had no choice. So much for his tip from Lenny.
He only had two hundred forty in his pocket.
He thought of Eta and the advance, and felt
a pang of something. Disappointment, fear,
uncertainty. He didn't want to believe she
had talked to the cops. Family was everything to
Eta, and she considered her messengers family.

"I'll wait for it," Jace said.

The clerk made a sour face. Jace held up the
twenty, just out of the man's reach.

"For twenty I want it done now."

The man said something nasty under his
breath, but he nodded. Jace lowered his arm
and the clerk snatched the bill away from him
so quickly, he was tempted to check his hand to
see if he had fingers missing.

The guy working on the bikes in the back

room had a goatee and a red rag on his head. He looked like a pirate. His hands were black with grease and oil. The clerk told him tersely that he had to stop what he was doing to fix Jace's bike.

"Very important customer," the clerk said, then went back to his own important matters.

The mechanic looked at Jace. "How much did you give him, man?"

"Why? Are you gonna shake me down too?" Jace asked. "I'm a bike messenger, for Christ's sake. Do I look like I'm rolling in dough?"

"Nah, I'm not gonna shake you down," he said. "I'm gonna shake him down."

There were twelve Lowells listed in the phone book. Three of them had first names beginning with the letter **A:** Alyce, Adam, and A. L. Lowell. Abby Lowell was a student at Southwestern University School of Law, located on Wilshire Boulevard, about two miles west of downtown. Assuming that Lenny's daughter lived near school, assuming that she had a listed phone number, A. L. Lowell was a good bet.

Jace put the rejuvenated Beast in the back of the Mini, and headed west. His two-way radio lay on the passenger's seat, the crackle and chatter familiar and comforting in a way, like he wasn't all alone, like he was surrounded by friends. Only he didn't really have friends, he had acquaintances. And he sure as hell was alone.

His head was pounding, his ankle was throbbing. He pulled into a 7-Eleven and bought a desiccated hot dog, a cheese burrito, a bottle of Gatorade, and some Tylenol. Fuel for the engine. He took a five-finger discount on a couple of PowerBars. He didn't like stealing, but his first obligation was to survive. That law overruled a petty misdemeanor.

He ate in the car, careful not to spill anything—Madame Chen was very particular about her Mini—and tried to figure out what he would do if he found Abby Lowell at home. Knock on the door and say, "Hi. I'm the guy the cops think killed your father"? No. Who would he say he was? A client of Lenny's? A reporter looking for a story?

He liked that angle. Lenny's clients were criminals. Why would she open the door to one? But a young reporter searching for the truth . . . If she didn't slam the door in his face, he might get to ask some questions, and get some answers. She'd probably take a look at him through the peephole and call 911. He looked dangerous or crazy or both with his face beat up and a day's growth of beard. Who in their right mind would open a door to him?

"Base to Sixteen. Base to Sixteen. Where you at, Lone Ranger?"

An electric jolt of surprise hit him and he jumped a little. Eta.

"Base to Sixteen. I got a pickup for you. Sixteen, do you copy?"

He looked at the radio, but let it alone, his mind racing. Were the cops standing there beside her, making her try to lure him in?

"Base to Sixteen. I got money, honey. Never let money wait."

Did she mean Money, as in a customer? Or did she mean money, as in cash? Cash made good bait. Jace thought about the two cops in the alley. The guy in the hat and the curvy **chica.** He still wasn't sure she was a cop, but the hat was. Homicide, he supposed.

Jace reminded himself that just because they knew where he worked didn't mean they could find him. If worse came to worse, and things heated up, he could always grab Tyler and go. But that would have to be a last resort. The idea of uprooting Tyler, wrenching him out of the only real home he'd ever known, taking him away from the surrogate family that made him feel safe and loved, tore at Jace's heart. But what else could he do?

The answer lay in his stomach like a rock, heavier than the burrito he'd eaten. He wouldn't acknowledge it. His mother hadn't raised him to quit, to cut and run. Tyler was his only family. Jace wouldn't leave him.

A. L. Lowell lived in a two-story rectangular stucco building with a few understated Spanish details on the facade. Built in the twenties or thirties, when people had style. The neighborhood was a funky mix of West Hollywood edgy hip, Hancock Park yuppie chic, and mid-Wilshire working-class run-down. Depending on the street, the area was dangerous, quiet, rough, family-oriented, or a place where you could pick up a transsexual hooker.

Jace cruised past the building, looking for signs of life.

By the size of the place and the configuration of the windows, front and side, he figured there were four units, two up, two down. There was no concierge, no uniformed doorman.

He parked the Mini just around the corner and across the street, where he still had a vantage point of the front entrance but couldn't be suspected of casing the place. And he sat and waited.

It was the middle of a cold, damp, gloomy day. No one wanted to be out. With all the trees lining the streets and standing sentinel in the yards, the quality of light was as dim as the interior of a forest. Huge old maple trees made a canopy over the street in front of A. L. Lowell's building.

This was the kind of neighborhood Jace had always imagined he would have grown up in if his life had been normal. People here probably knew one another, stopped and chatted on the sidewalk as they were walking their dogs or pushing strollers. No one here lived in one location under one name, got their mail somewhere else under another name, picked up and moved out in the middle of the night.

A stooped elderly woman with a tall white poodle emerged from the Lowell building. Both she and the dog were wearing clear plastic rain hats tied under their chins. They came down the sidewalk at a snail's pace, the dog dropping turds behind it as it walked, like a horse would. The woman didn't seem to notice, not that she could have bent over to pick up the mess if she had. The pair crossed the street, in Jace's direction.

It took them about a year to get past the Mini Cooper. Jace watched in the rearview mirror until woman and dog, still dumping shit as it went, were far enough down the block. Maybe the trail of turds was necessary for them to be able to find their way home. Like a trail of bread crumbs.

It was time to do something, plan or no. He got out of the car and casually walked across the street to the building. He was going to visit someone. No reason to act nervous or secretive.

The tenants' names were each listed next to a call button on the wall beside the front door, but it didn't matter, because the old lady hadn't opened the door with enough force to make it latch when it closed behind her. Jace checked the apartment numbers and went in.

A central staircase led to the second floor, where there was one apartment on either side of the hall. Jace went to the neighbor's door first, to listen for anyone home. The only sound was some kind of bird squawking and clucking to itself.

Jace knocked softly on the door to the Lowell apartment a couple of times. No one answered. He checked behind him, then tried the knob, expecting it to be locked, but it turned easily. He checked over his shoulder again, then went inside, wiped the knob off with the sleeve of his sweater, and closed the door behind him.

The apartment looked like the neighborhood had suffered an earthquake of huge magnitude. Everything that had been on shelves or in cabinets was on the floor, chairs were overturned. Someone had slashed the upholstery on the couch and an armchair, and pulled the stuffing out. Cereal boxes had been opened and dumped on the floor.

Jace took it all in, trying so hard to process everything that he forgot to breathe. Someone had been looking for something. He wondered if that something was taped to his belly.

Even trying to step carefully, he crunched something under his boot as he made his way past the kitchen and down the hall. The small bathroom was in the same shape, but someone had taken red lipstick and written on the mirrored medicine cabinet: NEXT YOU DIE.

"Holy crap," he murmured. "This is a fucking movie. I'm living in a fucking movie."

Only, in this movie the bullets were real, the bad guys were real, and people actually died.

Now he was breathing shallow, quick breaths. He had begun to sweat. He closed his eyes for a few seconds, trying to gather himself, trying to think what to do.

He had to get out. The fleeting thought crossed his mind that he should find Lenny's daughter and warn her. But how was he supposed to find her? Go sit in the hall of the Bullocks Wilshire Building at Southwestern Law and wait for her to happen past? Go wait

in the car until she showed up here, then run up
to her to tell her someone was threatening to
kill her? She would probably think that someone was him.

He put his hands over his closed eyes and
rubbed at the tension in his forehead.

The blow to his back was so unexpected,
it took a second to register what was happening. Without his permission, Jace's body
hurtled forward. The sink hit him in the groin.
His head bounced off the mirror. Stars of
swirling color bursting before his eyes, he tried
to shove backward. The assailant grabbed him
by the hair and slammed his head against the
medicine cabinet again and again. He heard
the glass crack, felt a shard slice his cheek.

Maybe this was the part of the movie where
he died in a surprise twist. This idiotic thought
swam through his head as his assailant let him
fall. His chin hit the porcelain sink with the
force of a hammer. Then he was on the floor,
waiting to be kicked at the least, shot at the
worst, torn between wanting to fight back and
wanting to lapse into unconsciousness, though
he didn't really have a choice.

Jace wasn't sure how long he lay there, drift-
ing in and out. Gradually, his vision came into
sharper focus. The floor was a sea of old one-
inch octagonal white tile with dingy grout. He

could see the lines of the old white bathtub, and, nearer, the base of the pedestal sink, the rusty water lines that came out of the wall and snaked up under the sink to the faucets.

You have to get up, J.C. You have to get out of here.

He couldn't seem to pass the message from his brain to his body.

Slowly, he became aware of something wet beneath his cheek. He brought himself to his hands and knees and saw the pool of blood smeared on the floor where his face had been. Head swimming, arms and legs trembling and rubbery, he grabbed the edge of the sink and slowly pulled himself to his feet.

His mouth and chin hurt like someone had hit him in the face with a bat. Blood dripped, bright red, into the bowl of the sink. The reflection looking back at him in the broken mirror was from a horror show. His right cheekbone and eyebrow were swollen from being slammed into the medicine cabinet. His cheek was cut and bleeding, his nose was bleeding. Some of the lipstick from the message on the mirror was smeared on his cheek like war paint.

Gingerly, he felt his nose to see if it was broken. The left side of his chin had a knot on it, already turning black and blue from bouncing off the sink. Wincing, he felt along the jawbone for a break. He'd split his lip and chipped a tooth.

The apartment was quiet. Jace hoped that meant his attacker had gone, rather than that he was waiting until Jace came around so he could beat on him again.

Still feeling weak, still trembling, he turned on the faucets, washed his face, washed his hands, found a towel, dried himself, and wiped the sink out. Bending over to mop up his blood from the floor, he went down on one knee as everything tilted around him. Somehow he ended up sitting on the floor with his back against the bathtub.

He had to get out of there. He wanted to go slowly, casually, so as not to draw attention to himself, but his face was going to attract plenty of attention if someone came near him, passed him on his way out, passed him on the street, saw him from a window as he got into the Mini and drove away.

The apartment door opened and closed. Jace sat up straighter, straining to listen. Someone going out or someone coming in?

He waited for some exclamation of surprise, but he heard nothing for a moment. If Abby Lowell had walked in to see the mess, to see that her home had been violated, she would have gasped or made some sound of being shocked. Maybe she would have gone back out to find a neighbor and get help. Call the cops.

He could hear someone moving through the front rooms slowly, as if trying to take it all in, or trying to find something. Objects being moved.

Maybe the guy had panicked when Jace came in, and bolted without whatever it was he had come here to find. Maybe he'd come back to get it. Maybe he'd come back with a weapon.

A weapon. He needed a weapon.

A long triangular shard of glass stuck out from the broken mirror. Jace wrapped the bloody towel around his hand and plucked it free. He stepped behind the bathroom door and waited.

Maybe a neighbor had already called the cops, and there were two uniforms picking their way toward the back of the apartment with guns drawn.

The shattered mirror gave a distorted, surreal reflection of the person stepping cautiously into the room—an eye here, a nose there, a live Picasso painting.

Jace dropped his weapon, kicked the door shut, and grabbed Abby Lowell, clamping his hand over her mouth to muffle her scream. She tried to jab him with her elbow, kicked backward, connecting a boot heel to his shin. Jace tightened his arm around the middle of her, kept his palm flat over her mouth as she tried to bite him. She was strong and athletic and determined to get away from him. Jace shoved her forward, as his assailant had done to him, trapping her up against the sink.

"Don't scream," he ordered quietly, his mouth brushing the shell of her ear. "I'm not here to hurt you. I want to help. I knew your father. He was a good guy."

She was watching him in the mirror, her brown eyes round with fear and distrust.

"I came here to see you, to talk to you," Jace explained. "Someone had ransacked the place. He beat the shit out of me and left."

His chin was on her shoulder. He could see himself in the broken mirror. With the swelling and bruising and bleeding, he looked like a freak from a horror movie. Abby Lowell's attention had gone from him to the message on the glass. The red lipstick had smeared on the word **you,** but the message was clear enough.

Next You Die.

"I didn't put that there," Jace said. "I didn't get a look at the guy who did, but I swear it wasn't me."

She had gone still in his arms. He loosened his hold on her slightly.

"You won't scream?" he asked. "I'll take my hand away if you promise you won't scream."

She nodded her head. Slowly, Jace took his hand away from her mouth. She didn't scream, didn't move. He loosened his hold across her stomach, stepped back a couple of inches so that she was no longer pressed against the sink, but he could pin her there again if she tried to bolt.

"Who are you?" she asked, still watching him in the broken mirror.

"I knew your father."

"How? Were you a client?"

"I did some work for him once in a while."

"What kind of work?"

"That's not important."

"It is to me," she said. "How do I know you didn't kill him? How do I know you didn't do this to my home?"

"And then beat myself into a stupor?" Jace said. "How did I manage that?"

"Maybe Lenny did that to you before you killed him."

"And I'm still bleeding? Maybe if I'm a hemophiliac."

"How do I know you didn't kill him?" she said again. "And now you're here to kill me."

"Why would I want you dead? Why would anyone want you dead?"

"I don't know. One minute my life was normal, and the next my father is dead, and I'm being questioned by detectives, and having to make funeral arrangements, and now this," she said, her eyes filling with tears. She pressed a hand to her mouth and tried to steel herself against the emotions threatening to overwhelm her.

"I know," Jace said softly. "I know."

She twisted around to face him. They stood as close as lovers sharing a secret. He could smell her perfume, something soft and musky. "Do you know what happened to him?"

"I know he was killed," Jace said. "I read in the paper you found his body."

"That's not true. I don't know how that got in there."

"They seemed to know a lot about you."

She looked away, upset by the idea. "I wasn't there. Not until . . . after."

"So you didn't see anyone leaving the scene?"

"No. The police were there by the time I got there. Why would you want to know that? Do you have some idea who killed him?"

Jace shook his head, though in his memory the dark sedan slid past him, and he saw the stone-faced guy behind the wheel. "No. Do you?"

"I was told it was a robbery."

"What about this place?" he asked. "The perpetrator of a random crime kills your father, then seeks you out to rob you and leave a death threat on your mirror? That's pretty far-fetched. I'd say somebody was looking for something here. Do you know what?"

"I can't imagine," she said, watching him like a poker player. "Do you know?"

"Was anything missing from Lenny's office?"

"Money. I don't know how much. There was money in the safe. He was waiting for a bike messenger last night. The police think the messenger did it. Killed Lenny, took the money, and skipped town."

"Doesn't look to me like the killer skipped town," Jace said.

"Maybe it wasn't the killer who did this. Maybe this was just a thief."

"And why would a common thief write that on your mirror?" he asked. " 'Next you die.' It would be a pretty amazing coincidence if the night after your dad was murdered, an unrelated serial killer just happened to single you out to be his next victim."

Abby Lowell put her hands over her face, rubbing at the tension, trailing her manicured fingers down her throat as she tipped her head back and sighed. "I need to sit down."

Jace didn't stop her as she slipped past him to sit on the edge of the bathtub. He lowered himself onto the closed toilet. He wanted to lie down. His head felt like someone was hitting him over and over with a lead pipe. He raised a hand to his face to check for bleeding.

"Who are you?" she asked again. "Why would you come here? I don't know you. You're not the usual sort Lenny did business with. Even if you were, why would you come to me? Why is this any of your business?"

Jace studied her for a moment. She sat with her back straight and her legs crossed, elegant and ladylike. How the hell had Lenny ever managed to produce a daughter like this? Maybe she was adopted.

"You haven't answered my questions," she said.

She tilted her head, dark hair spilling from behind her ear like a curtain. She pushed it back and looked at him, sort of up-from-under. Sexy.

"If you know something about Lenny's death," she said, "you should go to the cops. Ask for Detective Parker. If you know something about why this unknown assailant broke into my apartment, you should go to the cops. You can use my phone," she offered. "Or I can make the call."

Jace glanced away. She was cornering him. He stayed cool. "I'm not interested in talking to cops."

"I didn't think so."

"Do you know what your father was involved in?"

"I didn't know he was involved in anything."

"Someone thinks you do," Jace said, looking at the mirror. "Someone thinks if they didn't get what they wanted from your father, then you must have it."

"Why don't you want to talk to the police?" she asked. "If you aren't involved in something yourself. If you don't know anything about it, why are you asking all these questions?"

"I have my reasons."

"Because you know something," she said, standing. She was getting angry, agitated. She paced a couple of steps one way, then the other. "And the only way you could know something is if you're involved."

"Someone tried to kill me last night," Jace said, coming to his feet as his own anger bubbled up. "That's what I know. I was doing something for your father, and someone tried to kill me. And on my way back to ask Lenny what the fuck he'd gotten me into, I found out he was dead. I think that gives me a right to be interested, don't you?"

"You're him, aren't you?" she said. "You're the bike messenger."

In a heartbeat she was out the door, yanking it shut behind her. Jace bolted, flinging the door back and running after her.

She grabbed a portable phone on her way toward the door, then stumbled over books that had been flung to the floor in the ransacking.

Jace lunged at her, knocking her down, landing on top of her. She cried out for help, and twisted beneath him enough so that she could swing at him with the phone. She landed a glancing blow off his right eyebrow. Stars burst before his eyes. He blocked a second blow, and tried to knock the phone out of her hand.

"Goddammit, stop fighting!" he growled. "I don't want to hurt you!"

"What the hell's going on up there?" a male voice called from somewhere outside the apartment.

Abby started to shout again for help. Jace clamped a hand over her mouth. Footsteps sounded on the stairs in the hall.

"Miss Lowell? Are you all right?"

She twisted her head to the side to slip his hold, and bit down hard on a finger. Jace yanked his hand back and she shouted "No!" before he could cover her mouth again.

Out in the hall the man shouted to someone else, "Call 911!"

"Shit!"

Jace pushed himself up off her and bolted for the door.

Goddammit, goddammit, goddammit!

An older man, with thinning gray hair and wild eyebrows, jumped back, startled. He had a big wrench in his hand.

Jace shoved past him and ran down the stairs so fast, he couldn't believe he didn't fall on his face. The poodle woman was sticking her head out a door at the bottom of the staircase, eyes wide, mouth hanging open.

Jace skidded around the base of the staircase and ran for the back door, feet slipping on the old polished pavers. He kept his eyes on the double doors and the courtyard beyond.

He hit the doors running. Burst outside. The little courtyard had flowers and shrubs, and a seven-foot stucco wall surrounding it.

Don't think. Act. Don't think. Act.

He grabbed a wooden bench, dragged it to the wall.

Stepped back, took a deep breath.

The guy with the wrench came through the doors, shouting.

Jace hit the bench seat running. Launched himself.

Grabbed the top of the wall. Hurled himself over.

He couldn't help crying out as he hit the ground on his feet and pain exploded in his ankle and shot up his leg like glass shattering.

Don't stop. Don't stop. Don't stop.

Jaw clenched, he struggled to his feet and moved forward, limping heavily. He had to get gone. He couldn't hide. The cops would bring a dog. And a chopper wouldn't be far behind.

Across the street, down the alley. Cut between houses. Across another street, down another alley. Doubling back toward the Mini. If he'd been riding The Beast instead of driving a car, he could have jumped on and been gone, flying down side streets and alleys in a blur. No one could have touched him.

His head was pounding. He couldn't hear. He couldn't hear a siren. He couldn't hear anything but the jarring thud of his feet beating the ground, the rasping of air sucking in and out of his lungs.

He could see the car. He stuck his hand in his coat pocket and yanked out the keys, nearly fumbling them.

Unable to stop his momentum, he ran into the side of the Mini, pushed himself back, yanked the door open, spilled into the driver's

seat. He was dizzy. He felt sick. He couldn't get
the key in the ignition.

Now a siren sounded in the distance.

The engine turned over and he threw the car
into gear and started to spin a U-turn in the
middle of the street. A horn blasting, tires
screeching. The nose of a minivan just clipped
the Mini, knocking the tail of the car sideways
as its tires spun on the street, squealing.

And then he was moving. Right turn, left
turn, right turn, left turn, headed east.

He slowed his pace as quickly as he dared. He
didn't want a trail of complaining citizens for
the cops to follow.

A radio car would arrive on the scene at Abby
Lowell's building. There would be confusion,
excitement. It would take time to sort it all out.
Maybe there wasn't a chopper cruising the skies
nearby. If a chopper got on him, he was
screwed.

He kept moving east at a normal pace, like a
normal human being in a normal situation.
Behind the wheel he was shaking, sweating, his
heart still racing. His throat squeezed closed
every time he thought he saw a black-and-
white.

He couldn't have fucked up any bigger than
he had. What had he thought, that Abby Lowell
would offer him a drink and they would sit

down and discuss the situation calmly? Her father was dead. And as innocent as she pretended to be, she had to know something. Why else would some thug leave a death threat on her mirror? **Next You Die.**

Next, as if Lenny had been a warning, or just the first on a list of things to do.

Jace put a hand against his stomach and felt the package. He wondered how she would have reacted if he had told her he had it.

Shaking himself free of his thoughts for a second, Jace glanced to either side of the car. He had worked his way north and east, north and east, all the way to Silverlake, about five miles northwest of downtown.

Silverlake had been a happening place in the twenties and thirties, when silent film stars and movie moguls built homes and studios in the area. The hills above the reservoir were full of homes from that era that had been refurbished for modern, hip, artsy types with bucks.

Jace found a place to pull over and park near the reservoir. He got out of the car to move and stretch and gather his thoughts. He walked to the back of the car and swore under his breath. Madame Chen's pride and joy was no longer pristine. Half the taillight cover was gone, left shattered on the street where the minivan had clipped him. Scratches and paint marks from the pale-colored van highlighted the area below the taillight.

What now?

Now he was wanted for a murder **and** an assault, home invasion, and vandalism. And for stealing who knew how much out of Lenny Lowell's safe.

He played back the few minutes he had been in Lowell's office last night. He remembered thinking the place was a mess. He had glanced around, looked at the television, touched Lenny's bowling trophy and left a great set of fingerprints. He didn't remember any safe being open.

Sitting back against the hood of the car, he drank some of the Gatorade he'd bought at the 7-Eleven, and washed down three Tylenol. He needed to keep his energy level up and try to minimize the pain enough to think through it. His brain was what kept him alive on the streets every day. The ability to see a couple of jumps ahead, yet to focus on the moment.

He took his life into his own hands every day on the streets as a messenger. Risking his own life and having someone else put him at risk were very different scenarios. He chose to put himself on the street. He knew the risks, he knew his abilities. If he went under a bus, a bus killed him, not the people on the bus. If he made a mistake, it was on him.

None of this mess seemed within his control. He'd been thrown into the middle of the mix like he'd been sucked into a tornado. The only thing he could control was his own mind, and in the end, that would be the only thing that could save him.

He wished he knew what he was up against— **who** he was up against. He could easily call to mind the blockheaded guy in the dark car. But when he called up the memory of the attack in Abby Lowell's apartment, he came up blank. In his mind's eye he tried to see things he hadn't seen. He tried to look in the mirror, to see the guy behind him, but it hadn't happened that way.

What the hell is going on, and why do I have to be in it?

Luck of the draw. If he hadn't been late with the blueprints, he would have gone home that night like any night, and Eta would have told Lenny Lowell they couldn't take his package. Lenny Lowell would have been a story buried in the paper. Jace probably wouldn't have paid any attention to it, just as the majority of Angelinos wouldn't have paid any attention to it. Nobody blinked at an ordinary, run-of-the-mill murder. Murders happened every day. There had to be a hook. Something kinky, something twisted, and/or a celebrity.

Jace wondered if the people in the negatives taped to his belly might be famous. Some celebrity being blackmailed over deviant sexual behavior. The kind of seedy story that made up the gritty side of LA. City of angels, city of sleaze. It depended on who was looking, and where.

The reservoir was the gray of gunmetal, reflecting the heavy clouds that hung above it, but shining metallic where the low western sun skipped rays across it. The sky in the west was the color of molten lava, purple twilight seeping down toward it. It would all disappear into the ocean soon, and darkness would fall like a cloak over the city. He would go home and maybe he would be able to sneak upstairs through the shadows, and escape Madame Chen's scrutiny.

He wanted to go home, to be home, to stay home, or to throw his books into his bag and jump the Gold Line train to Pasadena for his social sciences class at City College. He wanted to do something normal. He wanted to help Tyler with some project for school, watch television, make popcorn. Maybe he would do that, he thought, mail Lenny's package to Abby, get a new job, start over again, pretend none of this had ever happened.

As he slid behind the wheel of the car and reached to turn the key, the two-way on the passenger seat gave a blast of static, then Eta's voice. "Base to Sixteen. Base to Sixteen. Where you at, baby?"

Jace reached over and touched the radio, fingered the call button, but he didn't push it. He didn't dare.

"Base to Sixteen. Where you at, Lone Ranger? You gotta come on home to Mama, sugar. ASAP. You got that? I'm still holding money for you. You copy?"

"I'm in the twilight zone, Eta," he murmured. "I'm going home."

17

"Abby Lowell's story about Cicada checks out," Ruiz announced as Parker approached the building from the parking lot. She stood outside the doors, smoking a cigarette under cover from the rain that had started to spit down in slow, fat drops.

"What else did you find out at the restaurant?"

"They have a wonderful poached pear salad," she said.

"Did you sample the wine cellar too?"

"No, but I got a date with a really cute waiter," she said, preening. "He's going to be the next Brad Pitt."

"Aren't they all? You spoke with the maitre d' who was there last night?"

"Yes. He said she seemed impatient, kept checking her watch."

"Was she upset? Crying? Did she look shaken?"

"Impatient was all he said. They were busy."

"What about her waiter?"

She shook her head. "They never seated her. The maitre d' showed her to the bar. The bartender said she had a vodka tonic. A couple of guys tried to hit on her. She wasn't interested. He saw her on her phone a couple of times. She left a nice tip, but he didn't see her leave."

Parker frowned, looking out at the gathering gloom as evening crept near. "I want her phone records, home and cell."

"You think she had something to do with it?" Ruiz asked, puzzled.

"I caught her at her father's office this morning. She said she was looking for his life insurance policy and his will."

"That's cold, not criminal."

"She violated a sealed crime scene," Parker said. "And she didn't leave with an insurance policy. She left with documents and a key to a safe-deposit box at City National Bank. She went there directly after leaving the office and tried to get access to her father's box."

"They didn't let her in?"

"She gave the manager her sob story, but she wasn't authorized by Lowell to sign for the box. The manager told her she needs to file a probate petition along with an affidavit, and get a court order. Ms. Lowell was not a happy girl."

"Did you get in the box?" Ruiz asked.

"We'll have a court order first thing tomorrow," Parker said. He yawned as he moved toward the doors. "I need a cup of something."

"I called Massachusetts," Ruiz said as they went toward the squad room. "They ran the DL number we have for Allison Jennings. It came back to a woman living in Boston."

"Did you get a phone number?"

"I did better than that," Ruiz said smugly. "I called her. She said she has no idea how her license turned up here. Said she had her handbag stolen and lost her driver's license with it once a long time ago. Maybe that's it."

They went into the squad. Parker hung up his raincoat and his hat and went directly to the coffee machine. He poured a cup and leaned back against the cupboard. The coffee tasted three times worse than it had in the morning.

"You were just a regular whirling dervish while I was out," he said. "I'm impressed."

She looked at him like she was waiting for the nasty punch line.

"I do say nice things every once in a while," Parker said. "When earned."

Ruiz seemed not to believe him, but she didn't call him on it. She leaned back against her desk and crossed her arms, pushing the red lace bra and its contents up into sight. "Latent has Damon's job ap. They haven't called back. And

I got the local usage details for Speed, and for the victim—office and home."

Parker squinted at her. "Who are you? And what have you done with Ms. Ruiz?"

She gave him the finger and went on. "The number off Abby Lowell's cell phone call list? Leonard Lowell called that number yesterday from his office at five twenty-two in the afternoon. The call lasted one minute, twelve seconds."

Parker frowned and thought about that. At 5:22 P.M. Lenny Lowell had called an untraceable cell phone number. A little more than an hour later someone using that same cell phone had called Abby Lowell and told her that her father was dead.

How did that tie in with the bike messenger? It didn't. The lawyer had called the Speed office to arrange the pickup.

Even if the phone belonged to Damon, it didn't make sense. Why would Lowell have called him directly, then set up the pickup through Speed? There wouldn't have been any reason to.

And then what? Damon shows up, kills Lowell, takes the package and the money from the safe, turns the office inside out looking for something, bashes in Lowell's car window on the way out, then calls a woman he doesn't know to tell her her father is dead?

"This isn't working for me," Parker muttered, going around the desks to lower himself into his chair. He yawned and rubbed his hands over his face. He needed a second wind. His shift might be over, but his day wasn't.

The first couple of days of a homicide investigation were crucial. Trails cooled fast, witnesses started losing the details of their memories, perps slithered away into holes. To say nothing of the fact that oftentimes three days was as much priority time as they could devote to a case before another dead body turned up and they had to move on that one because the first couple of days were crucial . . . And round and round they went.

There was no luxury of time. The LAPD employs roughly 9,000 cops for a city of 3.4 million people. The NYPD has a force of 38,000 for just over twice the population.

"What?" Ruiz asked, perturbed. "Looks pretty neat to me."

"That's why I have the number **two** in my rank and you don't. Most murders are easy. A guy kills another guy because the second guy has something the first guy wants. Money, drugs, a woman, a leather jacket, a ham sandwich. A guy kills his wife or girlfriend because she's been screwing some other guy, or because she burned the pot roast, or because he's just a plain vanilla mentally unbalanced asshole.

"Same thing for women. It's usually straightforward. They kill someone they know because they're jealous. It's always jealousy with women. Sometimes jealousy mixed with greed, but mostly just jealousy."

Parker shook his head. "There's something wrong with this picture. A bike messenger is dispatched by chance. He gets in Lowell's office, sees money hanging out of the safe, kills Lowell, steals the money, beats it out of Dodge. Lowell didn't call him up beforehand and say, 'Hey, come steal my money and beat my head in.'

"And if it was a crime of opportunity," he went on, "the messenger doesn't take the time to look up Abby Lowell's cell phone number and call her to pretend he's a cop and tell her to go to her father's office. Why would he? What's it to him?" The phone on Parker's desk rang. He snatched up the receiver. "Parker."

"Kev, it's Joan Spooner over at Latent."

Parker flashed the grin, even though she couldn't see it. "Tell me something I want to hear, Joanie. What have you got for me besides your heart?"

"A husband," she said dryly.

"A podiatrist," Parker said with distaste. "A

guy who comes home every night smelling like other people's feet. When you could have me. A lot of women would kill to have me."

"Right. They do. They're called perps," she said. "What a sad commentary that you have to put women in handcuffs to have them go anywhere with you."

"Some like it that way," he purred into the phone. "Don't knock it 'til you try it, Joanie."

Across the desk, Ruiz rolled her eyes.

"Enough out of you, mister. Put both hands on the table and pay attention. I've got a possible match for you on those prints from the Lowell homicide. You can't hang your hat on it in a courtroom, but it's something you can play off of. I've got a thumb and a partial middle finger on the murder weapon, and a partial thumb on the job application."

"And they match?"

"In court I'd have to say a possible match on the thumb, and a defense attorney would have me for lunch. Between you, me, and the lamppost, I think it's probably the same person."

"I love you, Joanie," Parker crooned.

"So you say, Kevin. One of these days it's going to be put up or shut up."

"Careful what you wish for, doll."

He thanked her and hung up.

Ruiz tried to lean into his line of sight. "Hey, Romeo, what did she say?"

Parker chewed on his thumbnail for a moment, staring into the middle distance, thinking. "A probable match of a thumbprint on the murder weapon and on the job ap."

"He's our guy."

Parker shook his head. "Play devil's advocate. If you were Damon's defense attorney, how would you punch holes in Latent's evidence?"

Ruiz sighed. "I would say that we concede Damon was in Lowell's office. He went there to pick up a package. So he touched a bowling trophy. So what?"

"Exactly. And where on the murder weapon are these prints located? To beat Lowell's head in, he held the trophy upside down. The marble base did all the damage. Do we have photos back?"

"No."

"Call SID now before they all go home like regular folks. You need to talk with the guy who lifted the prints off the murder weapon. And I need photos of the back of the desk, and the area around the desk."

"What am I? Your secretary?" Ruiz complained. "My shift is over, and I'm hungry."

Parker tossed a roll of Mentos across the

desks. "When you're with me, there are no shifts working a homicide, babe. Eat a breath mint. You'll be fine. Your clothes will fit better."

His phone rang again and he grabbed it up. "Parker."

"Detective Parker?" The smoky voice was trembling a little. "It's Abby Lowell. My apartment has been broken into. By that bike messenger. I thought you should know."

"I'll be right there."

He hung up the phone and pushed himself to his feet. "Get those photos ASAP," he ordered Ruiz as he went to the coatrack and shrugged into his raincoat. "And get going on the phone records from Speed. We need to get a line on Damon. Abby Lowell says he broke into her apartment today."

"And where are you going now?" Ruiz whined.

Parker bobbed his eyebrows and put on his hat. "To the damsel in distress."

18

Abby Lowell lived outside the lines of Central Bureau. Parker flashed his badge to the uniforms standing in the foyer of the building. One nodded him past. The other was engaged in conversation with a potbellied older guy who was expounding on his theory regarding the downfall of our once-great nation.

A pair of detectives from West Bureau, Hollywood Division, stood in Abby Lowell's living room, looking around like they were sizing up the place to redecorate. Everything was everywhere. The living room had been tossed like a salad. A Latent Prints guy Parker knew was dusting.

"Some party," Parker said. "Mind if I join the fun?"

The older of the two Hollywood cops, a square-headed guy with a Marine buzz cut, curled his lip like a dog about to growl.

"What are you doing here, Parker? I thought they had you writing parking tickets."

"Your vic called me in. Apparently you failed to impress her with your commanding presence."

"Crawl back in your hole, Parker. This is ours. We'll send you a copy of the reports."

Parker curled his own lip and took a step forward. "You think I want your fucking lousy B&E? File all the paper you want, then go chase some 7-Eleven bandits, go scare up some wannabe starlets moonlighting on their backs. Do whatever it is you people do over here." He twirled a finger around, indicating the room. "This is part of my homicide, ace. You can't piss the fence higher than I can."

"The always-charming Detective Parker."

Abby Lowell stood in the archway leading to the private rooms of the apartment, leaning one shoulder against the wall. She was still dressed in the same sapphire knit outfit she'd had on that morning, but had pulled on an old oversized gray cardigan. She was hugging the sweater around her. Her hair was mussed. Her mascara was smudged beneath her eyes as if she had been crying.

Parker went to her. "You're all right?"

The smile was wry, fragile, quivering at the corners of her mouth. She looked down just to the right of his feet, and combed a strand of hair back behind her ear with a trembling hand.

"He didn't kill me, so I'm better off than the last Lowell he ran into."

"Where do you keep your booze?" Parker asked.

"In the freezer. Grey Goose. Help yourself."

"Not my poison," he said, picking his way over the aftermath of the ransacking as he went into the kitchen. He found a glass, poured some of the vodka over ice, and handed it to her. "How long ago did this happen?"

She sipped the drink, leaning her hip against the counter. "A couple hours, I guess. I didn't realize this was out of your area until they showed up. They didn't want me to call you."

"Don't worry about them. You did the right thing. Besides, I'm like a wolf. I've got a big territory. What happened?"

"I came home, walked in, the place looked like this. I went down the hall, went into the bathroom, and he grabbed me."

"Did he have a weapon?"

She shook her head.

"What'd he look like? Tall, short, black, white. . . ?"

"Not as tall as you. Blond. Young. White. He looked like he had been in a fight or something."

"I'll need you to get with our sketch artist

first thing tomorrow," Parker said. "How did you know he was the bike messenger?"

"He wouldn't tell me who he was. But he said he knew my father, that he'd done some work for him, and I just knew it was him."

"What did he want? Why would he come to you?"

"I don't know. I didn't want to find out. I was sure he was going to kill me. I ran, and he chased me, and I was almost to the door, and then he was on me. . . ."

The dark eyes glistened with tears. She leaned back against the counter and put a hand over her face. Parker watched her for a moment, then walked away from her and went down the hall. The bathroom was on the left. A small space with a tub/shower combo, a toilet, a pedestal sink. The mirror of the medicine cabinet above the sink was broken, with shards missing.

He squatted down and checked out a pale rust-colored smudge on the old octagonal tile. Blood, he figured. Some had seeped into the grout between the tiles, staining it dark.

He stood and looked closely at the broken mirror and the inscription someone had written on it in red lipstick. NEXT YOU DIE.

Why would the bike messenger want Abby Lowell dead if killing Lenny and stealing the

money from the safe had been a crime of opportunity? He wouldn't. Whoever was behind
the murder, behind this, had a more complicated motive. And as far as Parker was concerned, that ruled out Damon.

Abby appeared in the shattered glass, a multitude of tiny, fragmented images, as if she was
inside a giant kaleidoscope.

"What's this guy looking for?" Parker asked,
turning to face her.

"I don't know."

"Your place gets turned upside down, someone threatens to kill you, and you don't
know why?"

"No, I don't," she said, stiffening. "If Lenny
was up to something, he didn't include me
in it."

Parker cocked a brow. "Really? Isn't it strange,
then, that shortly before he was murdered,
Lenny made a phone call to his own killer? And
that after your father was dead, the killer called
you to tell you about it? I find that strange.
Why would Lenny feel free to give his killer
your cell phone number and address?"

She wasn't ready to cry now. She was getting
pissed off. The brown eyes were nearly black.
She didn't like it that he wasn't as sympathetic as
she wanted him to be.

"Maybe he got it out of Lenny's Rolodex."

"But why? Why terrorize you if you can't give him what he wants?"

"I shouldn't have to remind you, Detective, I'm the victim here."

"Why didn't you tell me about your father's safe-deposit box?" he asked bluntly.

Her breath caught in her throat. She opened her mouth to answer, but nothing came out.

"What this killer is looking for—what he was looking for in your father's office, what he was looking for here—am I going to find it in that box when I open it tomorrow?"

"I don't know what you're talking about. I'm still looking for Lenny's will and life insurance. I thought they might be in the bank."

"I'll let you know," Parker said. "I'm not hindered by probate. As soon as I have the court order in hand, I get to find the prize in the Cracker Jack box."

She had nothing to say about that, but neither did she look nervous. If Lenny's will was in the box, it probably didn't contain a paragraph beginning with **In the event of my violent death, my daughter was in on it.**

"I find it odd that you didn't include a trip to the bank in your list of reasons to get away from me this morning," Parker said.

"I wasn't trying to get away from you. I have a lot to take care of."

"I'm sure you do, Ms. Lowell. And how was your class, by the way?"

"I didn't go."

"What was the subject again?"

"I didn't say."

"Now's your chance."

She had that I-want-to-hurt-you look in her eyes. "What's the difference? I didn't go."

"And which funeral home are you using?"

"I haven't decided."

"But you were at one today? After the bank, before you came back here?"

She took a deep breath and let it out. "If you don't mind, Detective, I need to go lie down. I'm really not up to being interrogated tonight."

"You should probably stay with a friend," Parker suggested.

"I'm going to a hotel," she said tightly.

Parker stood too close to her as he leaned toward the door. "Sleep well, Ms. Lowell," he purred, holding her gaze with his, nearly close enough to kiss her. "Call me if you need me."

"That's not likely." She didn't blink, didn't flinch. Hell of a poker player . . .

Parker edged past her through the door, and

went back down the hall. Buzz Cut was on his cell phone, standing by the front door. Parker approached the younger detective, who was still making notes.

"Anybody see this guy get away?"

The guy tried to look around Parker to see his partner.

"You can answer me now, junior, or I can have my captain crawl up your captain's ass, and we can all have a bad time. I don't want to do that," Parker said apologetically. "I got no beef against you, kid, but I'm working a homicide. I don't have a lot of time to screw around."

The big sigh. The look to the side. "One of the neighbors got a partial plate," the kid said quietly. "A dark green or black Mini Cooper."

"A Mini Cooper?" Parker said, taken aback. "What the hell kind of a crook drives a Mini Cooper?"

The shrug. The head cock. The kid flipped back a few pages in his notebook and showed his notes. "He got clipped by a minivan when he pulled a U-turn in the middle of the street. Knocked out some of the plastic from the Mini's driver's-side taillight and scratched the paint."

"Did the driver get a good look at him?"

"Not really. All she could say was young, white male. It happened too fast."

"You got a card?"

The young detective pulled a business card out of his pocket and handed it over. Joel Coen.

"Thanks, Joel," Parker said, jotting the tag number down on the back of the card. "If I get something, I won't forget you."

He stuck the card in his pocket and went to the Latent Prints guy to tell him they were looking for a possible match to prints found at the Lowell homicide. He told him to talk to Joanie.

Buzz Cut was closing his phone as Parker made his exit.

Parker tipped his hat and said sarcastically, "Thanks for the hospitality, Buzz. I'll call as soon as I've solved it for you."

19

Eta heaved a sigh as she locked the front door from the inside. The iron grates were already down. The place was a damn fortress. Otherwise, the windows would have been busted out, and there would have been bums and winos and crazy people all over the damn place. Tonight, though, she thought it felt more like a prison inside.

She had been trapped all day, daring to try only periodically to make contact with her Lone Ranger. Not that it would have mattered if she had tried every twenty minutes to reach him. Either he didn't have the radio with him, or he wouldn't answer because he was afraid of some kind of trap.

She'd damn near had a heart attack when Parker had asked her to go out back. Something about her van. But Jace hadn't been in it. And where he'd gone, she didn't know. She fretted that he might have thought she had brought the detectives in, if he'd seen them. She had gone back out after Parker and his hoochie-mama partner had gone, but she couldn't see any sign of the boy.

And then that dirt-for-brains Rocco had gone off on her. She'd better not think about trying to harbor a fugitive. He couldn't have a criminal associated with his business.

Eta had pointed out to him that half his damn family were criminals, and that a place like this one couldn't be waiting around for altar boys and Eagle Scouts to come through the door. Like Rocco was particular who was around him, she'd said, rolling her eyes at his friend, Vlad, who was putting golf balls, ash falling from the end of his cigarette onto the rug.

Rocco would have sold his sister for a dime if he thought that would keep his ass out of trouble. He didn't want no truck with LAPD, and the word **loyalty** was foreign to him.

"Worthless, spineless weasel," Eta mumbled as she set the place to rights, dumping ashtrays, throwing out soda cans and beer bottles. "Someone shoulda put him in a sack at birth and dropped him in a hole."

When the second round of cops had come calling—some bug-up-his-ass Robbery-Homicide pretty boy and his mute partner—Rocco had been so far up their digestive tracks, they must have tasted that god-awful cologne he dipped himself in every day. He didn't have a clue about Jace Damon or anyone else who worked for him, but he was quick to bad-mouth just the same. The detectives wanted Jace, therefore he must have done whatever they said he'd done, and Rocco had always had a bad feeling about that kid.

Eta had her doubts Rocco could pick Jace out of a lineup.

He had ordered Eta to tell the detectives everything she knew. She looked at him like he was stupid—which he was—and walked away from the lot of them. Until she knew more about the situation, what little information she had was staying right in her brain.

"Man needs a whuppin'," she grumbled, working her way toward the back. As she went to turn the lights out in her office, the phone rang.

All she knew about Jace was that once she had been shopping in Chinatown, and she had seen him across the street with a boy about eight or nine. They had probably been there for fun. She had watched them go into a fish market. When she had mentioned it to him the following Monday, he had denied being there. Must have been someone else, he'd said, but she knew it hadn't been.

She wouldn't have answered the phone, but she thought it might be him.

"Speed Couriers," she said. "What you want, honey? We closed for the day."

"This is Detective Davis, ma'am. I need to ask you a few questions."

Eta scowled at the phone, as if he could see her. "Don't you people talk to each other? What am I paying taxes for? For y'all to all go running around asking the same questions over and over like a bunch of damn morons?"

"No, ma'am. I'm sorry, ma'am. I just have a couple of questions about one of your messengers, J. Damon."

"I know that," she said with annoyance. "You got to get up to speed. What are you? The third string? I got better things to do with my night than talk to you, honey. I got babies at home need me. I'm hanging up."

She slammed the receiver down, her gaze going to the radio. One last try.

She keyed the mike. "Base to Sixteen. Where you at, Lone Ranger? You gotta come home to Mama, sugar. ASAP. You got that? I'm still holding money for you. You copy?"

Silence. No static. No nothing. She had no idea if he even had his two-way with him. She wondered where he was, what he was doing.

She tried to picture him safe someplace. She could only picture him alone.

Eta shut off the lights. As she made her way toward the kitchen, she pulled on her raincoat. It was late already. If Jace was going to call, he would have done it by now. She had her own two-way with her, just in case.

The alley was black as pitch. It had started to rain again. The light above the door had gone out like it did every time it rained. She'd told Rocco to call an electrician the last time it happened, but of course he hadn't. He'd wait until the entire electrical system shorted out and burned the damn building to the ground.

Eta shook her head at the hopelessness of thinking Rocco might one day have some sense in his head. She dug her car keys out of her tote bag.

And then a light was in her face, blinding her.

"Detective Davis, ma'am," he said.

This isn't right, Eta thought. If he'd been back here all along, why wouldn't he have just come inside to see what she was up to? Why call on the telephone?

"I really need to get an address from you, ma'am."

Eta inched her way to the side, a strange feeling crawling over her. This wasn't right. She wanted to go. "What address?" she asked, inching toward the van.

"Your messenger, Damon."

"I don't know how many times I got to say this," Eta complained, taking another step. "I don't have no address for the boy. I don't have no phone number. I don't know where he lives. I don't know nothin' about him."

The light moved closer. Davis moved closer. "Come on. He's worked here awhile, hasn't he? How can you not know anything about him? You can't keep that up."

"I can and I will. I can't tell you nothin' I don't know."

Her escape ended at the side of her van. She clutched the keys in her hand.

The light moved closer. She had nowhere to go.

"You want to do this the hard way?" he asked.

"I don't want to do this at all," Eta said, sidling toward the back of the van. If she could get in the van, lock the doors . . . She turned her key ring in her hand.

"I don't care what you want, bitch," he said, and lunged.

Eta brought her hand up, pressing the trigger on the mini-can of pepper spray she kept on her key chain. She guessed where his eyes might be and fired, a primal shout tearing up out of her throat.

Davis yelped and swore. The flashlight beam went straight up, then came down, the heavy flashlight missing her head, hitting her shoulder.

Eta cried out, kicked blindly, connected with some part of his anatomy.

"Fucking cunt!"

Davis spat the words at her, grabbed a handful of braids as Eta tried to bolt. He probably thought he could stop her in her tracks, or pull her back. But Eta was a large lady, and for once that was in her favor.

She kept her momentum moving forward. Davis swore and flung himself on her back, trying to knock her down. The flashlight went flying, beam flashing up, down, skimming the ground as it rolled.

One knee buckled beneath her and she fell, throwing him off. She tried to scramble up off the ground, but she was awkward and unbalanced, and she fell against the van, and had to get her feet back under her and try again.

Davis threw himself at her, slamming her back against the vehicle. She clawed at him, her long nails scratching down his face, and he cried out again. He hit her hard across the face. And then his body was pressed up against hers, and something sharp was at her throat.

"Tell me," he demanded, his voice low, breath rasping in and out of his lungs, bitter with the scent of stale cigarettes and sour beer.

"I don't know," Eta said. Her own voice was unrecognizable to her, soft, shaking, frightened. She was crying. She thought of her kids. Her mother would have them at the dinner table by now. Jamal would be begging to stay up late. Kylie would be talking nonstop about what had gone on in fifth grade today.

"You want to live, bitch?"

"Yes," she whispered.

"Where is he? Answer me and you go home to your family."

She was trembling. She was going to die for keeping a secret she had no answer for.

The knife caressed her throat. "Give me an answer. You go home to your kids. If it's the truth, I won't come back for you—or them."

Eta didn't know the truth. She gave him the only answer she could.

"I seen him in Chinatown."

"Chinatown."

She drew breath to answer him, but when she tried to speak no words came out of her mouth, just strange wet sounds. Davis stepped back from her, picked up the flashlight, shined it on her. She lifted a hand to touch her throat and felt her life running out of her. Her hand was red with it.

Horrified, she wanted to scream, but she couldn't. She wanted to shout for help, but she seemed not to have control of her tongue. She needed to cough, but she couldn't breathe. She was drowning in her own blood.

She staggered forward. Her legs buckled beneath her. She fell like an anvil to the wet, oily pavement.

She thought of her husband . . . and then she went to him.

20

Diane Nicholson sipped at a glass of mediocre champagne and rolled an eye around the elegantly appointed room, bored. The Peninsula Beverly Hills Hotel was the epitome of class and wealth, two things required to attend a political fund-raiser for the district attorney of Los Angeles. But very little in the political world impressed Diane. The glow had worn off long ago.

Her husband had spent a dozen years involved in city politics. Joseph's second great love. His job was his first, the love that made him a wealthy man. Diane had been ranked somewhere further down the list—after golfing and his boat. The last couple of years of the marriage, the most they saw of each other had been at events like this one. And even then, all she had been was an accessory on his arm, like a pair of diamond cuff links.

At his funeral all his friends had given her their sympathy and had gone on about how much she would miss him. But they had seen more of him than she ever had. Joseph's absence from her life was an absence of the anxiety of wondering what was wrong with her that the man who was supposed to love her would rather have been golfing than with her.

He had married her for her potential as a social asset. She had a good look, was well-dressed, well-informed, well-spoken. But her career was an embarrassment to him, and Diane had refused to give it up. And the more strained their relationship became because of it, the harder she had hung on to it, afraid to let go of the one thing that was a sure thing, because her husband's love was not.

Better to have loved and lost, the saying went. What bullshit. She had learned that lesson the hard way, twice.

She allowed herself to be dragged to these events now because she enjoyed eavesdropping, and because appearing with someone warded off matchmakers. Also, she had agreed to come on the condition her date buy her dinner afterward.

Her date was Jeff Gauthier, forty-six, handsome, an attorney for the city of Los Angeles, chronic bachelor. He had been a friend for years and years. After Joseph's death, Jeff had talked her into becoming each other's event date. Jeff considered it bad policy to drag a real date to these rubber-chicken affairs. Not so much to spare his date-of-the-month the brain-numbing experience, but because he felt showing up with dates-of-the-month was bad for his image.

"I'm having the most expensive thing on the menu," she said, leaning toward him and snagging a stuffed mushroom off the tray of a passing waiter. "And dessert."

"That's what you always do."

"I might even order an extra dessert to take home with me."

"We only have to stay long enough for me to be seen with three prominent people."

"Do I count?"

"You're notorious, not prominent."

"I like that better, anyway." This crowd had never known what to make of her. Married to someone as successful as Joseph, yet working for the county touching dead bodies every day.

She scanned the crowd. The usual suspects. District Attorney Steinman and his wife, the mayor and his wife, ADA Giradello and his ego, the assorted LA movers and shakers who thrived on this kind of thing, newspaper photographers and reporters, crews from the local television stations here for a sound bite for the late news. The media could have saved themselves the trouble and simply run photos and footage from the last event this crowd had gathered for. They all looked alike.

"I'm going to slip a twenty to one of the waiters if he'll start spinning plates on a stick," she said.

"Why don't you just get up on a table and sing us a song?" Jeff suggested, herding her toward a big-deal downtown developer.

They did the meet and greet. A couple of flashes went off. Diane smiled and complimented the developer's wife on the vintage brooch she was wearing.

"Did I hear you sold the Palisades house?" the woman asked.

"I didn't want that much house," Diane replied. "I'm trying to downsize and simplify my life."

The woman would have looked puzzled if not for the Botox in her forehead. "Barbra Sirha said she thought you bought something in Brentwood."

"West LA." A much less impressive zip code than star-studded Brentwood or Pacific Palisades. Diane could sense the woman's need to ask her if she'd lost her mind.

Gazes passed like ships in the night as everyone looked for the next important person to move on to.

And then that person walked into the room.

Norman Crowne was a man of average height and slight build, gray hair, and a beard precisely trimmed. Unassuming at first glance for a man who wielded the kind of power he did. People expected him to be an imposing figure, tall, broad-shouldered, with a booming voice. None of those traits applied to him, yet he still possessed an aura of power that preceded him through the crowd.

He was followed by his son, Phillip, and a pair of bodyguards who looked like they had come straight from the Secret Service. All four of them were impeccably turned out in dark suits and stylish ties. The crowd parted before them as if they were royalty, and the senior Crowne went directly to the district attorney and offered his hand.

The son, a product of Crowne's ill-fated second marriage, turned to Anthony Giradello and was greeted warmly. They were of an age, and both graduates of Stanford Law, but Phillip had been born a Crowne, with all the opportunities and privileges that came with it. He had gone to work for his father and held a cushy position in Crowne Enterprises. Giradello had been spawned in a small town near Modesto, the son of fruit ranchers, and had hustled for every chance he could grab, clawing his way up the ladder in the DA's office.

"One big happy family," Diane murmured into Jeff's lapel as they moved through the crowd in search of his second significant person of the evening. "That's blatant. The trial of his daughter's murderer is about to start, and Norman Crowne is all but laying money on the table for the DA in front of every media source in Los Angeles."

Jeff shrugged. "So? There's no conflict of interest. Giradello hardly needs to be bribed to go for the throat on this one. He wants to convict Rob Cole so badly, he can hardly stand it. Cole is his O.J. He's not going to mess that up. To say nothing of using this trial to blot out the memory of that preppie murder your friend Parker screwed up for him."

"Parker was a scapegoat. Giradello didn't do his homework. That trial was his first big lesson in 'money buys justice.' This is his second," Diane said. "You don't think every average person in America isn't going to look at this picture on the morning shows tomorrow and say Norman Crowne is buying himself a conviction? That more expensive lab tests of forensic evidence will be done, more expert witnesses will be called; that a bigger effort will be made to nail Rob Cole to a cross than to convict a gangbanger in South Central who's killed five or six people."

"Well . . . I don't care, frankly," Jeff said. "And I don't see why you would, either. You'd have them stick Rob Cole's head on a pike and feed his remains to dogs at the city pound. What's your problem with Norman Crowne's influence?"

"Nothing. He can have the pike custom-made. I just don't want to see grounds for appeal."

"Lady Justice," Jeff chuckled, pointing her toward one of the DA's biggest backers, a radio talk-show host with on-air politics so far to the right he should have fallen off the planet. "There's the Diane we know and love."

"I'm not making nice with this blowhard," she said between her teeth.

"You know, for a faux date, you're a lot of work."

"Quality doesn't come cheap."

Jeff introduced himself to the blowhard. Diane gave him the cursory acknowledgment nod with the Novocain smile, and turned to get a bead on the Crowne clan, now joined by Tricia's daughter from her first marriage.

Caroline Crowne was just twenty-one, short and somewhat stubby, like her mother had been, though Caroline had done a lot more with herself than Tricia ever had. Packaged in conservative designer labels and balancing on a pair of Manolos, her curly mop of auburn hair was stylishly cut in a chin-length bob. She gave the appearance of a well-heeled young executive type, and was supposedly slowly inserting herself into her mother's role of seeing to the Crowne charitable trust.

Shortly after Tricia's murder, the tabloids had hinted at the possibility of something sordid going on between Caroline Crowne and her stepfather, but the rumors had been squelched like a slug on the sidewalk, and Norman Crowne's granddaughter had abruptly ceased to be of any interest to the press.

What a list of headlines an affair between Caroline Crowne and Rob Cole would have generated. Poor old Tricia whacked to make way for a May-December romance between her daughter and her sleazy rotten rat-bastard husband. Caroline had been nineteen when her mother died. Barely legal.

It wasn't all that hard for Diane to imagine.

"One more and we're out of here," Jeff said through his teeth as he smiled and raised his glass to someone off to his right.

"I can already taste the sea bass," Diane said, letting him steer her toward the district attorney.

From the corner of her eye she caught a door swinging open, maybe six, eight feet to her

right. Bradley Kyle and his partner came in
looking like kids who were being sent to the
principal's office. They were headed in the same
direction that Jeff was taking her—toward the
DA and the ADA, and Norman and Phillip
Crowne.

Giradello turned and looked at the detectives,
frowning.

Diane drifted a step in their direction
as Giradello excused himself from Phillip
Crowne and moved two steps toward the cops.
Eavesdropping was the real reason she came to
these things.

Jeff interrupted her briefly to introduce her to
the district attorney, whom she'd met fifty times
before. She smiled, shook the man's hand, and
tuned him out, her gaze sliding just to the right
of him.

The conversation was terse, Giradello's face
darkened, Bradley Kyle turned his hands palms-
up, like, What do you want me to do about it?
Only the odd word escaped for the casual ear to
catch. **Do, what, can't, know.** Somebody was
supposed to have done something, but hadn't
been able to.

Kyle and his partner had worked Tricia
Crowne's murder. Not as leads, as second team.
As the trial began they would be called on to
double-check, to dig up and polish off notes

and memories, to pick at any tiny fibers that could become loose ends.

Rob Cole's attorney, Martin Gorman, would know everything about them—who they were on the job, who they were off the job, whether one or the other had ever made a derogatory re-mark about Rob Cole or about actors in general or about too-handsome jerks who went around in vintage bowling shirts no matter what the oc-casion. Odds were good Gorman had spies in this very room, watching Giradello's every move, looking for anything that could give him an edge, an opening, or at the very least keep him from getting surprised.

A trial as big as this one was a chess game with layers and layers of strategy. The pieces were being jockeyed into position. Giradello was bringing his army into line. Somebody was supposed to have done something but hadn't been able to. She wondered what that some-thing was.

Steinman said something. Jeff laughed po-litely. Diane smiled and nodded.

A word, a curse, a growl, a name she didn't recognize . . . and one that she did.

21

Ruiz was long gone by the time Parker returned to the station. He wanted to be pissed off, but he couldn't manage it. It was important to have a life away from the job if you wanted to stay sane **on** the job. He'd learned that lesson the hard way, so consumed by his rise to stardom in Robbery-Homicide that when that train came off the tracks he hadn't known what to do or who he was. He'd invested everything in his career.

It would have been nice to go home himself, take a steam, put on some jazz, have a glass of wine, order in some wonton soup and Mongolian beef from the restaurant down the street. He had a script to read, and notes to make. And sleep sounded like a good idea too.

He had a great bed and a view of Chinatown's neon lights for when he didn't want to or couldn't sleep. He could stare out those windows and lose all track of time. A three-dimensional abstract of the streets four stories below. He found the colors soothing, or maybe it was the juxtaposition of vibrant light and sound on the streets with the quiet dark around him in his haven, his cocoon.

He wouldn't be going home soon. There were too many things he needed to know, and he needed to know them quickly. His instincts had already been on point with this case, and that sense was only getting keener. The oddities of the break-in at Abby Lowell's apartment— and with Abby Lowell herself—were rubbing against the grain.

She was a study in contradictions. Courting sympathy, giving the cold shoulder, vulnerable, tough as nails, victim, suspect. All applied. The hell she didn't know what her burglar was after. She was after it herself.

Lenny Lowell's death was no random act of opportunity. And what the hell would a bike messenger, assigned by the luck of the draw, have known about this mysterious something Lowell apparently possessed that was worth killing for? The money gone from the safe— provided there had ever been any, and they had only Abby Lowell's say-so on that point—had been nothing but a bonus for the killer.

A simple robbery didn't send a perp on to his victim's daughter to toss her apartment and threaten to kill her. Parker's instincts told him the words scrawled on Abby Lowell's bathroom mirror had an implied "unless" to them. **Next you die . . . unless I get what I'm after.** Which implied the assailant believed Abby Lowell knew what he was after.

And why had the mirror been broken? How had the mirror been broken? The damage had been done after the message had been written on it. Abby Lowell hadn't had a mark on her, nor had she said anything about a struggle in the bathroom, the mirror getting broken, someone bleeding.

She said the guy told her he'd done some work for her father. What was that about? The Emily Post etiquette rules for murderers? **Hello, here's who I am, my references, my connection to you. So sorry, I'm going to kill you now.** What crap.

And the guy drives away in a Mini Cooper.

Parker reminded himself the Volkswagen Bug had been the car of choice for serial killers in the seventies. Cute cars were nonthreatening. How could anyone driving a Bug be a bad person? Ted Bundy had driven a Bug.

Parker ran the partial plate from the Abby Lowell break-in through the DMV, and waited, impatient. He made himself a cup of tea, paced while it steeped. Kray's trainee, Yamoto, was at his desk, studiously working on a report. Ruiz was probably out salsa dancing with the sugar daddy who kept her supplied in Manolo Blahniks.

Girl most likely to marry money. Parker wondered why she hadn't done so already. She probably figured she had a better shot at a big fish if she went up the career ladder to a better class of crime. Make Robbery-Homicide, become high-profile, start hanging out with political and Hollywood types, and boom: rich husband.

On impulse, he picked up the phone and dialed the number of an old friend who worked Homicide in South Central.

"Metheny," a gravel-choked voice barked on the other end of the line.

"Hey, Methuselah, you got it under control down there?"

"Kev Parker. I thought you died."

"I kind of wished I had there for a while," Parker admitted.

Metheny growled like a bulldog. "Don't let the motherfuckers get you down."

"I had that one tattooed on my dick. How'd you know?"

"Your sister told me."

Parker laughed. "You old son of a bitch." He had partnered with Metheny a thousand years ago when Parker had been cutting a swath through the food chain to get to Robbery-

Homicide. Metheny liked him anyway. "You got any contacts working Latin gangs in your neck of the woods?"

"Yeah. Why?"

"I've got a trainee did some task force work down your way. I'd like to find out how she was."

"Trying to get in her head or her pants?"

"Her head is scary enough for me. Her name is Ruiz. Renee Ruiz."

"I'll see what I can find out."

They traded a few more insults and hung up. Parker turned his attention to the results of his DMV search.

Of Mini Coopers registered in the state of California, in the Los Angeles area, seventeen matched the possible combinations of numbers and letters Parker had offered for the search. Of those, seven were listed as being green, five black. None of them were registered to Jace or J. C. Damon. None of them had been reported stolen.

The detectives at Abby Lowell's break-in would be looking for the car too, though Parker doubted they would get to it until the next day. Their case was basically a B&E. No serious violence. They wouldn't be excited enough to stay late—unless it was just to spite him.

Parker couldn't let them go hunting first.

Maybe they were good at what they did, and they would pull it off without a problem. But he thought it more likely they would go charging through the clutch of Mini Cooper owners like stampeding cattle, bolting the lot of them, tipping off Damon. He couldn't risk losing his suspect because of stupidity and territorial bullshit.

He dug a map of the city out of his desk drawer and spread it across Ruiz's desk, then took his Thomas Guide and began locating the addresses of the Mini Cooper owners. He marked the places on the map. None were in the immediate vicinity of the mailbox rented to Allison Jennings and passed on to J. C. Damon.

Working his way outward from that location, Parker found one of the owners lived in the Miracle Mile area, not far from Abby Lowell's apartment. That car was registered to Punjhar, Rajhid, DDS. One was in Westwood, near UCLA. One was registered to a Chen, Lu, who lived in Chinatown—on his way home.

He plotted all twelve, and stared at the map with his splotches of red ink like bloodstains scattered over the city. Which car did Damon have access to? Where the hell did he live? Why was he so secretive about it? He didn't have a record. And if he had one under another name,

who in his day-to-day life would know? If he
was living under an alias, the only way he was
going to be found out was to be arrested or have
his fingerprints turn up at a crime scene. They
had the partial prints from the murder weapon,
but not enough to get a hit running them
through the system.

Maybe the kid was a career criminal. Or
maybe he was hiding from someone. Whatever
the reason for all his secrecy, Damon was driving around in somebody's Mini Cooper. And if
he hadn't killed Lenny Lowell, why would he
search out Lenny's daughter? How would he
know anything about this missing something
everyone wanted so badly?

And why had Robbery-Homicide shown up
at that scene?

Parker put his head in his hands and rubbed
his face, his scalp, the corded muscles in the
back of his neck. He needed fresh air, and he
needed answers. He put his coat on and went
outside in search of both.

The clock had struck rush hour two hours
ago. The streets were nose-to-tail cars, everyone
in such a hurry to get somewhere that no one
was getting anywhere. A few people came out of
Central Bureau and headed for cars—stragglers.
The shift had changed a couple of hours ago,

and the business day was over. Things would soon be settling down for the night.

Parker walked to his car and slipped behind the wheel. This one was the workhorse, a five-year-old Chrysler Sebring convertible. He drove it to work, drove it to crime scenes when he was on call. Time off the job was for the bottle-green vintage Jag, his beautiful, sexy, secret lover. He smiled a little at that. Then the smile faded as he remembered Ruiz asking him about the car. She'd heard rumors, she'd said.

He dug his cell phone out of his coat pocket, dialed Andi Kelly, and opened with: "What have you done for me lately, gorgeous?"

"Jesus, you're a pushy son of a bitch. I have priorities other than you, you know. Cocktail hour is at hand, my friend. I have a date with a seventeen-year-old."

"Still pounding down the scotch, huh?"

"How do you know it isn't a young man?"

"Because you're too smart to tell me if it was. Seventeen isn't legal, not that you didn't already know that."

"Besides which, it would be gross," Kelly declared. "I'd be old enough to be the kid's mother. That's way too Demi Moore for me. I've never been interested in boys, anyway, only men," she purred.

Parker cleared his throat. "So? Do you have anything for me?"

"My memory isn't so good before dinner," she said. "Meet me at Morton's in West Hollywood. You're buying."

22

Jace parked Madame Chen's car in the narrow space reserved for her behind the office. He wiped down the interior with wet paper napkins, trying to erase any sign he'd been behind the wheel, or touched a door, or left a handprint on a seat. Then he stood beside the car for he didn't know how long, trying to decide what to do next.

A thick fog had rolled in off the ocean and settled into the nooks and crannies of the city, a milky filter softening the lines of buildings, diffusing the yellow light glowing in windows. He felt like he was a character in a dream, like he could be gone in the blink of an eye and no one would quite remember him.

Maybe that was what he was supposed to do—go underground completely. That was what Alicia would have done. She would have packed them up without a word, moved out in the middle of the night. They would have popped up like toadstools in another part of town, with new names and no explanation why.

Jace had wondered why, many times. When he was Tyler's age, he had dreamed up all kinds of stories about his mother, always painting her as the heroine. She was protecting her children from one kind of danger or another. As he had grown older and wiser, more savvy about life and the streets, he had wondered all the time if Alicia had been evading the police.

Why, he couldn't imagine. His mother had been a quiet, kind person who had made him cry after she caught him shoplifting just by telling him how disappointed in him she was.

Maybe she was like me, he thought now, **in the wrong place at the wrong time.**

"Why don't you want to come into the light, JayCee?"

Madame Chen came into focus as she spoke, as if she had just magically appeared beneath the dim light over the office door.

"I have a lot on my mind," Jace said.

"Your thoughts are heavy like stones."

"I'm sorry I'm so late with your car, Madame Chen."

"Where did you go to fix the bicycle? The moon?"

Jace opened his mouth to answer, but his

voice stuck in his throat like a ball of dough. He thought again of the day his mother had caught him stealing.

"I have to talk to you about something important," he said at last. "In private."

She nodded and went back inside. Jace followed, head down. She motioned him to a hard wooden straight-backed chair beside her desk, and kept her back to him as she made two cups of tea from the ever-present hot pot perched precariously on the window ledge above the cluttered desk.

"They have no phones on the moon, I suppose," she said matter-of-factly. "Moon men have no families worrying about them."

"I'm in a bad situation, Madame Chen," Jace said.

"You are in trouble," she corrected him, turning to face him. She couldn't hide her reaction. The color left her face, her small mouth formed an O of shock.

He had tried to clean up with some paper napkins and a bottle of water he got out of a vending machine outside a Mexican market in Los Feliz. Water didn't wash away cuts or bruises or swollen knobs of flesh. He knew he looked like he'd been on the wrong side of a prizefight.

Madame Chen said something in Chinese,

her voice soft and frightened. Her hand was shaking as she set a cup on three square inches of desktop not covered in paperwork. She lowered herself to her chair. Jace could see her gathering her composure, trying to come up with a strategy for a situation completely beyond her experience.

"Tell me," she said. "Tell me everything."

Jace tried to take a deep breath and let it out. His body reminded him not to do that. He had gone round and round in his mind trying to decide what to tell her, what not to tell her, what would be safer for her, for Tyler.

"You might hear some things about me," he said. "Bad things. I want you to know they aren't true."

She arched a brow. "You think so little of my loyalty that you would say this to me? You are like a son to me."

If her son was living a secret life under half a dozen aliases. If her son was wanted for murder and assault. If her son had someone trying to kill him.

Madame Chen had no children. Maybe she stuck with him because of that, Jace thought. She had no frame of reference.

"The attorney I was delivering a package for last night was found murdered after I'd been in his office. The police are looking for me."

"Bah! They are crazy! You would never kill a man!" she said emphatically, offended at the idea. "You did not kill him. They cannot put you in jail for something you didn't do. I will call my attorney. Everything will be fine."

"It's not that simple, Madame Chen. They probably have my fingerprints from the office." **And I was caught in the victim's daughter's ransacked apartment,** he added mentally. **I had a conversation with her. She can identify me. She'll say I attacked her. . . .**

"Why would the police think you would kill this man?" she asked, calmer. "What motive would you have to do such a terrible thing?"

"I don't know. Maybe he was robbed or something."

"An innocent man has nothing to hide. You have to go to the police, tell them what you know."

Jace was shaking his head halfway through the last sentence. "No. If they have evidence, if they can make an easy case against me, they will."

"But you aren't guilty—"

"But I **look** guilty."

She sighed and reached for the phone. "Let me call the attorney—"

"No!" Jace came up out of his seat, reached across the desk, and pushed the receiver back down in the cradle with more force than he wished he had. For a second, Madame Chen looked at him as if she had never seen him before.

"I can't go to the police," he said quietly, sinking back down. "Please understand. I can't take that chance."

He started to rub a hand over his face and winced as he brushed the cut where the broken glass of Abby Lowell's mirror had sliced his cheek open. He probably needed stitches, but he wouldn't be getting them.

"If I go to the police," he said, "then it's all over."

"Your life is not over—"

"I'll go to jail. Even if I eventually get off, I'll go to jail first. It takes months for cases to go to trial. What happens to Tyler? If Children and Family Services find out about Tyler, they take him. He goes to foster care—"

"I would never allow that to happen!" Madame Chen said, angry he would consider the possibility. "Tyler belongs with us. His home is here."

"CFS won't see it that way. They'll take him, and they sure as hell won't ever give him back to me."

"There is no need for foster care."

"That doesn't matter to them," Jace said bitterly, his mother's warnings branded in his head, along with the cautionary stories he'd heard on the street, read in the paper. "They're all about rules and regulations, and laws made by people who never have to deal with them. They'll look at you and see someone who isn't in their system, who hasn't filled out their paperwork. They'll look at you and say, what's this Chinese woman doing with a motherless little white kid who isn't in any of their files."

"You exaggerate—"

"No," Jace said angrily. "I don't. They'll give him to people who take kids in just to get the check, and they won't tell anyone where he is. They could lose track of him—that happens, you know. Jesus, for all I know, you might even be in trouble for having him here in the first place. You could be fined, or charged with something. Then what?"

"Let me talk to the attorney."

Jace shook his head vehemently, more afraid of the prospect of losing Tyler to the system than he had been of getting killed in Abby Lowell's bathroom.

"I can't take that chance," he said again. "I won't. I want him to be safe. I'd rather leave him here with you. He'd be safer with you, but I'll take him if I have to. I'll take him and we'll just go. Now. Tonight."

"You talk crazy!" Madame Chen argued. "You can't take him! You can't go!"

"I can't stay!" Jace argued back. His voice was shaking. He tried to pull himself together, lowered his voice, tried to sound rational. "I can't stay here. I can't come back until it's over. I don't want you in danger, Madame Chen, or your father-in-law. I don't want Tyler in danger, but I can't leave him if I have to worry he won't be here when I come back."

Neither of them said anything for a moment. Jace couldn't bring himself to look at this woman who had been kind enough to take the Damon brothers in, give them a home, treat Tyler like family. Treat **him** as family. He wished he hadn't told her. He should have followed his instincts, just plucked his brother out of bed in the dead of night and vanished.

God, what a mess. Damned if he did, damned if he didn't.

If he went to the police and they took him into custody, that news would make the papers. Reporters would want to know more. If they found Tyler and the Chens, Predator could find Tyler and the Chens.

If he got rid of the evidence or gave it back somehow, or gave it to Abby Lowell, he had still seen the negatives. They hadn't meant anything to him, but he had seen them, and Predator wasn't going to leave a loose end that might come back and hang him. He wouldn't leave witnesses.

"I'm so sorry I'm dragging you into this," he said softly, aching in a way that had nothing to do with the beatings he had taken. "I wish I didn't have to tell you, but I don't see a way around it. If someone comes here looking for me . . . if the police come . . . You deserve to know why. I owe you that. I owe you more—"

One sharp knock warned them a split second before Chi opened the office door and stuck his head inside. He gave Jace a hard look.

"What happened to you?" he asked bluntly.

Jace's eyelids went to half-mast. He wondered how long Chi had been standing outside that door. "I fell," he said.

"You didn't total my aunt's car? It was gone so long, I thought it was stolen. I was ready to call the police."

Jace didn't answer. He didn't like or trust Chi. His show of caring for his aunt, of looking out for her interests, was just a veneer. Chi would always do whatever would most benefit Chi. He had himself first in line to take over the business.

Chi glanced at Madame Chen and said something in Chinese.

Her face was like iron, her back straight. "If you have something to say, Chi, speak English. Have more respect than to be rude in my presence."

Chi's dark eyes were like cold stones as he looked at Jace. He didn't apologize. "I was wondering if all my help will be here in the morning, or if I get left in the lurch again because some people are unreliable."

Jace stood up. "If you want to have a conversation with me, Chi, why don't we step outside?"

"You don't look up to it," Chi said, one corner of his mouth turning.

"Only Chi is going outside," Madame Chen said firmly, staring at her nephew. "If you have waited to go home for such an insignificant reason, Chi, you have little value for your time."

Chi was still watching Jace. "No, Aunt. I've used my time very well."

Jace said nothing as Chi left the room. He wouldn't say anything against the man to Madame Chen. But Chi's parting remark left him with a sick feeling curdling in his stomach.

"It shouldn't be easy for anyone to trace me here," he said quietly. Unless Chi dropped a dime on him, or someone had gotten the license plate number on the Mini Cooper as he sped away from Abby Lowell's apartment. "I don't give out this address to anyone. But I want you to be prepared in case the police show up."

"What will you do?" Madame Chen asked. "If they think you killed this attorney, and you act like a guilty man, how will they know to look for someone else? They will look only for you. The true killer will go free."

Jace put his head in his hands and stared down between his boots. His head was pounding. His ankle was pounding. He could feel the swelling flesh pressing over the top of the boot. A nasty combination of nausea and hunger washed around in his belly.

"Is that what you want?" she asked. "For this evil person to go free to do more harm?"

He wanted to say he didn't care so long as he was out of it, so long as nothing threatened Tyler, but he knew that wasn't what Madame Chen wanted to hear. And he knew it couldn't be that way, no matter what he wanted.

"No, that's not what I want. I just need to figure it out before I . . . I'll work it out . . . I'll figure it out. I just need time."

"If the police come," Madame Chen said softly, sadly, "I will tell them nothing."

Jace looked up at her.

"I don't agree with what you are doing, JayCee, but my loyalty is to you, as I know yours would be to me. And I know you did not commit this crime."

One of the few truly good people Jace had ever known in his life, and he was putting her in the untenable position of having to lie for him. Possibly putting her in harm's way. All because he had answered one last call for one last run on the shittiest night of the year. A favor to Eta. Another few bucks to support himself and his brother.

He could almost hear Lenny Lowell saying it: **No good deed goes unpunished, kid.**

23

Tyler knew every inch of the building, from the secret hole in the ceiling of the apartment's bathroom, where Jace hid stuff, to the loading dock below, the storerooms, the closets, the space under the cupboard at the back of the employee break room, where Tyler sometimes hid to eavesdrop on Chi and the others.

He was small for his age, which helped in his efforts to go unnoticed. It would have helped even more if his hair was black and he didn't stand out like a yellow duck among the Chinese. He had dyed it once when he was eight, buying a box of Clairol that had been on clearance at the drugstore for $3.49.

The process had been a lot messier than he had counted on. By the time he finished, his head was black, his ears were black, his neck was black, his hands were black—on account of the latex gloves included in the package had been way too large for him and had kept coming off. He had the stuff on his forehead, smeared across one cheek, and dotted on the tip of his nose.

Jace had said that for a smart kid he did some pretty stupid things, and Tyler had spent the next few hours scrubbing the bathroom with Comet. And then he'd gotten a good scrubbing himself.

It had taken weeks for the stuff to come out. The kids at the school he went to were mostly Chinese. They had made fun of him until his hair had grown out enough to buzz the dyed stuff off. In another couple of weeks he had started to look like that yellow duck again.

Now when he wanted to be anonymous, he wore a faded black sweatshirt with a hood. The shirt was Jace's from who knew when, and who knew who had had it before him. It was soft with age, and the color Tyler imagined a ghost would be, like fog over darkness. The sleeves were long enough to cover his hands to the tips of his fingers, the hood so deep it swallowed his face.

Going unnoticed was a skill Tyler had honed from an early age. Jace always wanted to protect him from everything, shelter him like he was a baby or something. But Tyler wanted to know everything about everything. Knowledge was power. Knowledge diminished the chance of unpleasant surprises. Forewarned was forearmed.

Tyler believed all of these things. He was just
a little kid, and too small to control his world by
physical means, but he had an IQ of 168. He
had taken all kinds of tests on the Internet. Real
tests, not the stupid, made-up kind. His brain
was his strength, and the more he could learn—
through books, through observation, by experi-
mentation—the stronger he became. He might
never be able to push around someone like Chi,
but he would always be able to outsmart him.

He stayed back inside the hood now as he
cracked open the door of the broom closet just
down the hall from Madame Chen's office, and
spied Chi with his ear to the office door, trying
to listen in. Tyler had never liked Chi. He was
always tense and sour. Grandfather Chen said
Chi had swallowed the seeds of jealousy as a
child, and that the roots were now intertwined
with every part of him, and nothing would ever
dig them out.

Jace had been late coming home. Again. Tyler
had watched for him out the small window in
the bathroom, had seen him drive in, had
watched him standing like a statue beside the
car, as if he was trying to decide what to do
next. As soon as he had headed for Madame
Chen's office, Tyler had grabbed his secret cloak
of invisibility and beat it downstairs in his

stocking feet, scurrying like a little mouse to get to the broom closet.

He knew something was wrong, and he knew it was worse than Jace just taking a fall from The Beast. He had known it the instant Jace had spoken to him the night before. There had been a tension in him. He hadn't quite looked Tyler in the eyes when he'd said he'd had an accident and that was all.

Tyler was sensitive that way. Because he'd spent a lot of time observing people, listening to people, studying people without them knowing he was studying them, he had developed an uncanny sense of whether or not a person was telling the truth. He knew Jace hadn't been, but Tyler had been too scared to call him on it.

Grandfather Chen said lies could be more dangerous than vipers. Tyler believed him.

But now, as he crouched in the broom closet that shared part of an uninsulated wall with Madame Chen's office, he wondered if the truth wasn't just as bad.

The police thought Jace had killed a guy! Tyler's eyes filled as his mind raced, picturing all the things Jace was saying about going to jail and child services dragging him—Tyler—off to foster care.

Tyler didn't want to have to give up his home,

or the school Madame Chen had gotten him into, a small private school where no one seemed to think it strange at all that a Chinese woman showed up for his parent-teacher conferences. His stomach started to hurt at the idea of being forced to leave Madame Chen and Grandfather Chen, being forced to go live with strangers.

Strangers wouldn't know what he was like, what he liked to eat, what he liked to do. Strangers wouldn't know that even though he had an IQ of 168, he was still a kid, and sometimes he was afraid of stupid stuff like the dark or a bad dream. How would strangers understand that?

Maybe they would be good people, and mean well, and try hard—Madame Chen and Grandfather Chen had been strangers once, he reminded himself—but maybe they wouldn't be. And no matter what they were, good or bad, they wouldn't be family.

Tyler barely remembered his mother. When he thought of her, he thought of the sound of her voice, the touch of her hand, the scent of her skin. What specific memories he did have, he wasn't sure his brain hadn't manufactured. He knew that could happen, that the brain could fill in the blanks, and bridge the gaps between real events and what might have happened, or what a person wished had happened.

Tyler wished a lot of things. He wished his mother hadn't died. He wished they could all live in a house together—a house like families on television lived in, like in those old shows like **Leave It to Beaver**—him and Jace and their mom. And he wished they had a dad, but they didn't.

And he wished now with all his heart that Jace wasn't in trouble, that there wasn't a chance of him going away and never coming back.

Tyler tucked himself into a little ball with his arms wrapped around his legs, and his cheek pressed against his knees, and he held himself tight like that, squeezing his eyes shut against the burning tears.

It wouldn't do him any good to cry, no matter how much he wanted to. He had to think. He had to try to gather as much information as he could, and lay it all out, and reason through it, and come up with some ideas of what to do and how to help. That was what he was supposed to do with his 168 IQ.

But even knowing that, he was still a little kid, and he'd never been so scared in his life.

24

For a woman the size of a pixie, Andi Kelly's capacity for food seemed to defy the laws of nature. She ate like a wolf, like she would actually snap at the hand of an unsuspecting busboy trying to take her plate away before every molecule had been devoured.

Parker watched her with amazement. LA was a town where eating real food was frowned on for women. Half the women he knew would come to Morton's, order endive salad and a piece of shrimp, and go throw it all up afterward.

But then, Andi Kelly didn't fit any particular mold. In Parker's limited experience with her, it seemed Andi was who she was 24/7. No apologies, no subterfuge, no games. She said what she wanted to say, did what she wanted to do, wore what she wanted to wear. She was a breath of fresh, cinnamon-scented air—he'd noticed her perfume during the kiss hello. She greeted him like he was an old dear friend she'd seen just two days ago, sat down, and started chatting.

Parker was getting too keyed up to eat much himself. The nervous tension that wound inside him during an investigation like this one—a case that had snagged his interest, intrigued and challenged him—revved him up to a point where he didn't want to stop moving, not to eat, not to sleep. He wasn't quite to that point yet, but he knew all the signs. He could feel them now like the subtle foreshocks of an earthquake.

"So this kid, Caldrovics, says he got a tip on your murder," Kelly informed him between bites of prime Angus beef.

Parker nursed a glass of Cabernet. "From who?"

She rolled her eyes. "You're kidding, right? These little devil spawn come out of the womb ready to claw your throat out so they can feed on your blood then step over your rotting corpse to move up the mountain to stardom. He won't tell me."

"Beat it out of him," Parker suggested, deadpan.

"What do you think I am? A cop?"

"So you're saying you're old and you're marked for death?"

Kelly snarled and sliced another juicy chunk

off her steak. "I'm too mean to die. I know I look sweet, and everyone remarks on how pleasant and agreeable I am, but I have a dark side," she informed him, pointing her steak knife at him. "I'll turn this little shit inside out and pick my teeth with his bones if there's something in it for me." She gave Parker the hairy eyeball. "There had better be something in it for me."

"You're not the only one who's after something in this," Parker confessed quietly, his gaze casually scanning the territory around them.

Tucked back in lush landscaping on Melrose in trendy West Hollywood, Morton's was a throwback to the days of old Hollywood glamour and still a hangout for deal-makers and power players. Particularly for the old-time heavy hitters, the generation that had never stopped eating red meat. They all had their designated tables forward of the second palm tree, where they could see and be seen.

Looking around, Parker wondered if an eavesdropper might tune in to his conversation with Kelly and mistake it for a movie pitch.

"Lowell's daughter is holding back on me," he said. "Someone tossed her place today, threatened to kill her. Assaulted her, she said."

"She said?" Kelly arched a brow.

"Knocked her down. She didn't look any the worse for wear to me."

"Don't you know it's politically incorrect to doubt the victim?"

"My victim is Lenny Lowell, who's dead on a slab in the morgue. For all I know, the daughter had him whacked. She's looking for something besides her father's will, and she lied to me about it. Whoever tossed her place was looking for something, and she claimed not to know what. If she was at that murder scene before I got there, I need to know about it. That's why I want an explanation from your little friend down there at the Daily Planet."

Sitting back, Kelly gazed with satisfaction at the puddle of blood and grease on her otherwise empty plate. She patted her mouth with her napkin, took a breath, and let it out. "Here it is, Kev: The kid says he picked up the call on the scanner—"

"Bullshit. He was never on the scene. If he caught it on the scanner, why didn't he come to the scene? He never talked to me. Nobody said anything to me about a reporter."

"Well, he claims he talked to someone who knew what was what, and that he confirmed with someone else at the coroner's office."

"Who at LAPD? Who at the coroner's office?" Parker demanded, as if Kelly had given the kid written directions herself.

"Hey, don't kill the messenger," she said, reaching for the last of her scotch. "You asked me to find out what I could. I'm telling you what I found out. I got this from the boss."

Parker sighed, scowled, turned the news over in his mind. "And it's okay with him the kid won't reveal his sources on this nothing little story?"

"A newspaperman? We're all wrapped in the cloak of the First Amendment, or did you forget you've had your fill of 'unnamed sources'? Nobody had to tell you where they got the dirt to smear you with."

"It's obstruction," Parker complained. "This is a murder investigation. If this little jerk has something, if he talked to someone—"

"Maybe you can put the fear of God into him yourself," Kelly said. "You've got more leverage than I do. He'll think I'm trying to screw with him, get him in trouble, steal his story. You can, oh, I don't know, pistol-whip him or something. Threaten to arrest him for a traffic violation then stick him in jail and lose his paperwork while he gets to know his cell mates on an intimate level."

"So I'm buying you a steak at Morton's so you

can tell me all you have to give me is his name," Parker said.

"Actually, that's all you asked me to do. Think of it as goodwill that will pay off later," Kelly suggested with a sweet smile. Her eyes were an amazing shade of French blue. Her hair was the color of an Irish setter, and looked like maybe she'd cut it herself with pinking shears. It stood up in a messy little spiky cap on her head. It suited her.

Parker shook his head, smiling. "You're a trip, Andi."

"To paradise," she murmured dramatically, then bobbed her eyebrows.

"How'd this story make the paper at all?" Parker asked.

"Slow news day. They got down to press time and needed filler on the page. Caldrovics had two inches of ink for them."

Parker's pager vibrated at his waist. He unclipped it from his belt and squinted at the screen. Diane's cell phone number.

"Excuse me," he said, standing up. "I have to make a call to someone much more important than you."

Kelly rolled her eyes. "You're just trying to stick me with the tab."

Parker ignored her and went out of the restaurant to return the call.

The marine layer had crept into the city, a cold, silver mist tinged with salt. Parker could feel it envelop him and seep into his bones, making him wish he'd grabbed his trench coat.

Diane answered before the first ring had finished. "Did I tear you away from a hot date?" she asked.

"Not exactly."

"Where are you?"

"Morton's. Where are you?"

"The Peninsula. A fund-raiser for the DA. I just overheard your name in a conversation."

"Yeah? And then did they all turn their heads and spit on the ground?"

"It was Giradello," she said. "And Bradley Kyle."

Parker said nothing. Everything seemed to freeze in and around him for a few seconds as he tried to process the significance of the information.

"Kev? Are you there?"

"Yeah. Yeah, I'm here. What was the context?"

"I only caught a few words. I got the impression Kyle was supposed to have done something about something, but hadn't."

"And my name was in there somewhere?"

"First there was a name I didn't recognize. Yours came later in the conversation."

"The first name—do you remember what it was?"

"I don't know. It didn't mean anything to me."

"Try." Parker held his breath and waited.

Diane hummed a little as she searched her memory. "I think it started with a **D.** Desmond? Devon, maybe?"

A rush of internal heat went through Parker like a flash fire. "Damon."

25

Parker went back into Morton's, hailing the waiter en route to the table and making the universal hand signal for "Check, please."

"Let's go," he said to Kelly. He pulled out his credit card and handed it to the waiter, then grabbed his coat off the back of his chair and started shrugging into it.

Kelly looked up at him. "No dessert? Some date you are."

"Sorry," Parker said. "You know, I'm not the kind of guy your mother would like anyway."

Kelly rolled her eyes as she stood up. "She'd like you fine—for herself. What's the big rush?"

Parker's eyes did a quick scan of the tables. The waiter hustled back with his credit card, and Parker hurriedly added a generous tip and scrawled his signature at the bottom of the slip. He didn't speak again until they were out the door.

"I've got a dead low-end defense attorney nobody should care about but his nearest and dearest," Parker said as they walked just past the valet parking stand. "Why do you think Robbery-Homicide and Tony Giradello would have an interest in that?"

Kelly drew a breath as if she had an answer, but nothing came out. Parker could all but hear the wheels in her head whirring like Swiss watch parts. "They wouldn't," she said. "But you're telling me they do?"

"A couple of Robbery-Homicide humps showed up at the crime scene last night. Kyle and his partner. Tried to throw their weight around."

"But they didn't take over the case?"

Parker shook his head. "No. I called their bluff and they backed down, and I don't get that at all. What the hell were they doing there if they weren't there to steal the case? And I mean **there,** Johnny-on-the-spot, not their usual MO."

The Division cops always locked down the scene on a homicide, and Division detectives usually began the initial investigation. Then if the case was big enough or bad enough or glamorous enough, and Robbery-Homicide decided to take over, they would waltz onto the stage and take over with attitude and press conferences.

"No fanfare," Parker said. "No trumpets,

no warning, no press, except this clown Caldrovics—"

"Who won't name his sources on a nothing story about a nobody lawyer."

"And now I'm told those same Robbery-Homicide hotshots reported to Giradello in the middle of a fund-raiser tonight."

Kelly shrugged it off. "That could have been about anything. They're preparing for the Cole trial. Just because you're paranoid—"

"Why would my name get mentioned in that conversation?"

Kelly looked at him like she thought she must have missed out on something earlier in the conversation. "You didn't have anything to do with Tricia Cole's homicide investigation."

"No, nothing. No regular grunts like me were involved. The body was discovered by the daughter, who called Norman Crowne. The Crowne brain trust called the chief directly. The chief sent Robbery-Homicide."

"I know," Kelly said. "I was there. That was my story, **is** my story. So why would Giradello be talking to Robbery-Homicide cops about you?"

"The only common denominator between me and Bradley Kyle is Lenny Lowell," Parker said, carefully omitting the fact that the name of his chief suspect had also come up in the same conversation.

It was one thing to dangle a carrot in front of Kelly; giving her the store was something else. Parker wouldn't compromise his case by selling himself out. As a cop, he had had a healthy hatred of reporters drilled into him long ago. But he liked Kelly, and he owed her, and he certainly wasn't above siccing her on Bradley Kyle or Tony Giradello. As Parker saw it, it was a mutually advantageous arrangement.

"But why would Giradello have any interest in your stiff?"

"That's the sixty-four-thousand-dollar question, Andi," Parker said, digging his ticket out of his coat pocket and turning toward the valet. "Why don't you ask someone who might know."

Kelly handed her ticket over. "And get back to you."

"Symbiosis, my friend," Parker said. "In the meantime, we're going to go ask your little pal Jimmy Olsen if Bradley Kyle is a secret friend of his."

Kelly's face dropped. "We?"

"Well, I don't know the guy. You do."

"He's not my child, for Christ's sake. How would I know where he is?"

"You're an investigative reporter. Where would you investigate if you were looking for young, asshole reporters?"

The big sigh. Parker's Chrysler rolled up. "Maybe I can get a pager number."

"Maybe you can do better than that," Parker said, as Kelly's car pulled to the curb behind his. "Where do the young monkeys hang out to drink and beat their chests these days?"

They each went to their respective driver's door.

"If you kill him," Kelly said. "I get the exclusive."

The only single group of people Parker knew who drank as much as cops were writers, all kinds of writers. Screenwriters, novelists, reporters. The nearest watering hole was where the animals gathered to commune and commiserate. As solitary as writers were by nature, they had the particular stresses and paranoias of their work in common. And no matter what the profession, misery consistently loves company.

The bar Kelly led him to was a downtown die-hard joint that probably didn't look much different than it had in the thirties. Except that in the old days, the air would have been white with smoke, and the clientele would have been predominantly male. In the new millennium it was illegal to smoke damn near anywhere in LA, and women went wherever they pleased.

Kelly snagged a pair of stools at the front corner of the bar that tucked them back from the crowd but allowed a view of the room and the front door.

"Back when your hat was in fashion," she said, "this place would have been full of cigar-chomping newspapermen. Now that it's fashionable to listen to Frank Sinatra and drink cocktails again, it's overrun with young professionals looking for sex partners."

"The world's gone to hell on a sled," Parker observed.

He ordered a tonic and lime for himself. Kelly asked for the best scotch in the place, then raised an eyebrow at Parker. "You're still paying, right? I'm counting this as part of the date."

"We're not on a date."

"You want something from me, and you bought me dinner in hopes of getting it," she said. "How is that different from a date?"

"There's not going to be sex involved."

"Well, Jesus, reject me to my face, why don't you?" she said, pretending outrage. "You're brutal. At least most of the guys I date are too cowardly to be blunt. There's something to be said for that."

Parker chuckled. "You've still got it, Andi. You know, I'd kind of forgotten that. During that whole mess with the preppie murder, you were the only person who made me laugh."

"I'm not quite sure how to take that."

"As a compliment." He turned toward her on his stool, going serious. "You were decent to me on that. I don't know that I ever said thank you."

She blushed a little, looked away, took a sip of her scotch, caught an errant drop from her upper lip with the tip of her tongue.

"Telling the truth is my job," she said. "I shouldn't have to be patted on the back for doing what's right."

"Well, still . . . You stood up when it wasn't the popular thing to do. I appreciated that."

Kelly tried to shrug it off, even though Parker knew she had taken flak for it at the time.

"I don't see Caldrovics," she said. "But that little pack in the fourth booth down is the one he might run with. The obnoxiously young and hungry," she said with disgust. "I have jeans as old as they are."

"You're not old," Parker scoffed. "If you're old, I'm old. I don't accept that."

"Easy for you to say. A sexy guy is a sexy guy until he becomes incontinent and has to use an ear trumpet to hear. Look at Sean Connery. The guy has more hair coming out his ears than on his head, and women still fantasize about him. A girl hits forty-something in this town, and she's culled from the herd."

"Are you fishing for compliments, Kelly?"

She scowled. "No. I'm casting a fucking net. What are you? Stupid? Has training recruits had the same effect on you as a frontal lobotomy?"

"You look great," Parker said. "You haven't aged a day. Your skin is luminous, and your ass looks fantastic in those pants. How's that?"

She pretended to pout. "You hit the key points, but you could score better on sincerity."

"I'm out of practice."

"That's hard to believe."

"I'm telling you, I'm a quiet homebody now," he said. "So tell me about Goran."

"There's nothing much to tell."

"You married the guy."

"Seemed like a good idea at the time," she said, looking down into her drink, waiting for Parker to drop it, but he was waiting her out, and she blinked first.

"I thought he was the love of my life. Turned out I wasn't the only one who thought that." She shrugged and made a funny face that didn't quite reach her eyes. **"C'est la vie.** Who needs it, right? I don't see a ring on your finger."

"Nope. I'm still working on the joy of being me."

"There he is," Kelly said, nodding across the
room. "Caldrovics. He's coming from the back.
Must have been in the men's room. Greasy hair,
scruffy goatee, looks like a homeless person."

"Got him," Parker said, sliding off the bar
stool.

"And for God's sake," Kelly said, "whatever
you do, don't mention my name."

He put some bills on the bar to cover the tab,
then made his way across the room, through the
yuppies in heat, past a couple of old bulldogs
arguing about the president's Middle East poli-
cies. None of Caldrovics' pals noticed him ap-
proaching their booth. They were too caught up
in themselves and in some tale Caldrovics was
telling as he stood at the end of the booth with
his back to Parker.

Parker put a hand on the kid's shoulder. "Mr.
Caldrovics?"

The expression was unpleasant surprise with
a base of suspicion. He was maybe twenty-four,
twenty-five. He still had acne. He was probably
still having flashbacks of being sent to the principal's office.

"I'd like to have a word with you, please,"
Parker said. He cupped his shield in his hand
and flashed it discreetly to Caldrovics.

Before the rest of the table could become interested, Parker moved away from it, his hand still resting firmly at the base of the kid's neck.

"What's this about?" Caldrovics asked, dragging his feet.

"Doing your civic duty," Parker said. "You want to do your civic duty, don't you?"

"Well—"

"I'm sorry, I don't know your first name."

"Danny—"

"Can I call you Danny?" Parker asked, walking him toward the back hall. "I'm Detective Parker, Kev Parker. LAPD Central Division, Homicide."

"Homicide?"

"Yeah. When one person kills another person, that's called homicide."

"I know what it means."

They went out the back exit to an alley where a couple of bar staffers were having cigarettes and looking bored.

"Let's take a walk, Danny," Parker suggested.

"This isn't a very safe area."

"Oh, don't worry. I'm carrying a loaded weapon," Parker said, tightening the tenor of his voice a little more with each word. "Two, actually. Do you have a gun, Danny?"

"Shit, no!"

"Well, that's all right. I'm sure you'll never need one."

Caldrovics tried to put the brakes on. "Where are we going?"

"Just over here," Parker said, giving him a little shove as they passed a Dumpster, where they couldn't be seen by the employees behind the bar. "I thought a little privacy would be a good thing. I don't like people eavesdropping on conversations. You know, like reporters. They never get the facts right, do they, Danny?"

He pulled his service weapon from his belt holster and kicked the side of the trash container. The sound reverberated like a gong. "Everybody out!"

Caldrovics jumped back, wide-eyed. "Shit, man! What are you doing?"

"Damn pipeheads," Parker complained. "They're always back in these alleys like rats in the garbage. They'll slit your throat for a dime."

The security light behind the building had the astonishing white brightness of a full moon. Parker could see the kid's every expression but the kid couldn't see his. The brim of his hat cast a shadow over his face.

"I need to ask you a couple of questions, Danny," he began. "About that little bit you had in the paper this morning regarding the murder of Leonard Lowell, Esquire."

Caldrovics took a step back toward the Dumpster.

"I'm the primary investigator on that case," Parker said. "That means everything comes through me. Everyone who has anything to do with or to say about that case has to come to me."

"I don't have—"

"It's protocol, Danny. I'm a stickler for protocol."

"That's not what I've heard," Caldrovics muttered.

"Excuse me?" Parker said, taking an aggressive step forward. "What did you just say?"

"Nothing."

"Are you trying to piss me off?"

"No."

"Then you're just stupid. Is that it?"

Caldrovics backed up another step, but Parker closed the space between them by another foot. "You're so stupid you'd stand here and disrespect me to my face?"

"I don't have to take shit from you, Parker," Caldrovics said. "I did my job—"

"You're not impressing me here, Danny. You've really gotten off on the wrong foot."

"You can't harass me like this," Caldrovics said.

"What are you going to do? Tell on me?" Parker laughed. "You think I give a shit what anybody thinks of me? You think anyone gives a shit about what you have to say with no corroborating witness?"

They were close enough to kiss. Caldrovics was nervous, but doing a good job of trying not to show it.

"What have you got in your pockets, Danny?" he asked quietly. "You got a tape running?"

"No."

Parker stuck a hand in the left pocket of the kid's army surplus jacket, then in the right. He came out with a microcassette recorder.

"It's not smart to lie to me, Danny," Parker said, clicking the thing off. "The fuse on my temper right now is the size of an eyelash. I've got a murder that smells like week-old oysters, and you've got information I need. And now you're lying to me."

"I don't know who killed the guy!"

"No? You seem to know things the rest of us don't. How is that? Maybe you killed him."

"You're fucking crazy! Why would I kill him? I never met the guy in my life!"

"For money, for a story, for him having pictures of you doing bad things with little boys—"

"This is shit," Caldrovics declared. He tried to sidestep Parker. Parker shoved him back against the Dumpster.

"Hey!" Caldrovics snapped. "That's assault!"

"That's resisting arrest." Parker put both hands on him, turned him around, and slammed him face-first against the steel container. "Danny Caldrovics, you're under arrest."

"For what?" Caldrovics demanded as Parker pulled one arm and then the other behind him and slapped on cuffs.

"I'll think of something in the car."

"I'm not getting in a car with you, Parker."

Parker jerked him away from the Dumpster. "What's the matter, Danny? I'm a police officer. Didn't your mother tell you that the policeman is your friend?"

"What the hell is going on back here?" Andi Kelly rushed around the side of the Dumpster and skidded to a halt at the sight of Caldrovics in cuffs and Parker pushing him toward the alley.

"Kelly?" Caldrovics looked at her, astonished.

"I saw you go out the back way with him," she said. "It didn't look right."

"Butt out, Kelly," Parker snapped. "What the hell are you doing out here? Looking for a head-line?"

"What are **you** doing, Parker? What's this about?"

"Your little pal here is under arrest. He's withholding information on a felony murder. That makes him an accessory after the fact, if not before."

Caldrovics twisted around toward him. "I told you: I didn't have anything to do with any murder!"

"And I'm supposed to believe you? You're a proven liar, Caldrovics, and I know for a fact you're withholding information."

"You never heard of the Constitution, Parker?" Kelly said sarcastically. "The First Amendment?"

"You people make me sick," Parker said. "You put the First Amendment on like a fashion ac-cessory. You don't give a shit what happens to anyone as long as you get what you want. In fact, the worse the better. An unsolved murder makes more headlines than a closed case."

"You'll never make those charges stick," Kelly said.

"Maybe not, but maybe Danny here will think twice about cooperating after he's spent a night in a cell with a bunch of crackheads and dope dealers."

Caldrovics sneered at him. "You can't do that—"

"I can and I will, you little weasel." Parker started pushing him toward the alley again.

Caldrovics looked at Kelly. "Jesus Christ, go call someone!"

Kelly's wide eyes darted back and forth from Caldrovics to Parker and back. "Wait. Wait. Wait," she said, holding up her hands to forestall them leaving.

"I don't have time for this, Kelly," Parker barked. "We're talking about a murderer who isn't finished killing people. He attacked the victim's daughter today, thanks to your asshole buddy here, who obligingly put her name in the newspaper this morning!"

Caldrovics started to defend himself again. "He could have known her any—"

Parker yanked on the handcuffs. "Shut up, Danny! I don't want to hear one more excuse come out of your mouth. You did what you did. Be a man and own it."

"What do you need to know from him, Parker?" Kelly asked.

"Where did he get his information? Who told him the daughter found the body?"

Kelly turned to Caldrovics. "You didn't get it from him? If he's the lead on the case, why didn't you get it from him?"

"I don't have to explain myself to you, Kelly."

Kelly stomped up to him and kicked him in the shin. "Are you stupid? I'm standing here trying to save your sorry, raggedy ass, and you're giving me lip?"

"He's a fucking moron," Parker declared.

"I guess." She shook her head and turned to walk away. "Do whatever you want with him, Parker. He's too stupid to live. And I was never here."

"Kelly! Jesus! For God's sake!" Caldrovics called after her.

She turned around and spread her hands. "You have information on a murder, Caldrovics. All he wants to know is who gave it to you. If you're so fucking stupid you didn't go through channels on a routine murder . . . You're going to last about three minutes working the crime beat. Why didn't you talk to Parker at the scene? He would have given you details. Why didn't you just ask him?"

Caldrovics didn't answer right away. Weighing his options, Parker thought. Searching for the lesser of evils.

Finally, he sighed heavily and said, "I didn't

go to the scene, all right? I caught it on the scanner. Fuck, it was raining, man. Why should I go out in the rain and stand around just to have somebody tell me the guy on the floor with his head smashed open is dead?"

"And how did you know his head was smashed open?" Parker asked. "That wasn't on the scanner. And why did you say the daughter found the body?"

Caldrovics looked away.

"Did you just make that up, Danny? Is that what you like to do? Write fiction? You're just pulling this newspaper gig until you can sell the big screenplay? It was a slow night, so you decided to embellish just for fun?"

"Why would I do that?"

"Because you can."

"You didn't go to the scene?" Kelly said, astounded. "What's that about? That's your job—you go to the scene, report on what happened. What's next? You wait to write a story until you see it on television?"

Caldrovics sulked. "I talked to a cop. What's the big deal?"

"It's a big deal," Parker said, "because you didn't talk to me. It's a big deal because, as far as I know, you didn't talk to anybody I know who was at the scene. It's a big deal because you put a piece of information in there that's news to me, and I want to know where it came from. What cop?"

Again with the big internal debate. Parker hadn't wanted to smack anybody in the head this badly in a long, long time. "He's with Robbery-Homicide. Why wouldn't I believe what he told me?"

Parker felt like he'd been struck hard over the top of his head. An enormous pressure ballooned behind his eyes and in his neck. "Kyle. That son of a bitch."

"Kyle who?" Caldrovics asked. "The guy I talked to is Davis."

"Who's Davis?" Parker asked. He turned to Kelly, who spent most of her time on high-profile cases, and probably knew the personnel at Parker Center much better than he did.

Kelly shrugged. "I don't know any Davis."

Parker looked at Caldrovics. "How do you know this guy?"

"From around. I met him at a bar down the street maybe a week ago. Can you take these cuffs off? I can't feel my hands."

"He showed you ID?" Parker asked, unlocking the cuffs.

"Yeah. I asked him what's it like on the big team. He told me about a couple of cases he'd worked in the past."

"You have a phone number for him?"

"Not on me."

Parker's cell phone rang. He checked the caller ID. Ruiz.

"Ruiz, I've told you a hundred times: No, I won't sleep with you."

She didn't laugh because she didn't have a sense of humor, he thought. But she didn't react at all, and instantly Parker felt a sense of dread prickle his skin.

"I just got called," she said. "I'm up, you know."

"I'll meet you at the scene. What's the address?"

"Speed Couriers."

26

Goddammit," Parker said on a long sigh. He felt the strength and energy drain from him with his breath. "Goddammit," he whispered.

A spotlight from Chewalski's radio car illuminated the scene in harsh white light, like the stage of some avant-garde performance artist.

Eta Fitzgerald lay in a heap on the wet, cracked pavement behind the Speed office. Or rather, her body lay there. There was no sense of the big personality Parker had met that morning. The force she had been was gone. What he was staring at now was just a shell, a carcass. Parker squatted down beside the body. Her throat had been slashed from ear to ear.

"That's a whole lotta woman," Jimmy Chew said.

"Don't," Parker said quietly. "Don't. Not this time."

"You know her, Kev?"

"Yeah, Jimmy, I knew her."

Which was a problem now. One of the first things he drilled into his trainees was not to attach emotionally to victims. Therein lay the road to madness. They couldn't make every case personal. It was too hard, too destructive. Easier said than done when you'd met the victim before the crime.

"Geez, I'm sorry," Chew said. "She a friend?"

"No," Parker said. "But she could have been, in another time, another place."

"She's got no ID on her. No pocketbook. I'm sure her cash is running all over town by now, buying rock cocaine and fifty-buck blowjobs. We found keys on the ground near the body. They fit the minivan. The van is registered to Evangeline Fitzgerald."

"Eta," Parker said. "She called herself Eta. She was the dispatcher here. Ruiz and I spoke with her this morning."

"That bike messenger, the one from last night, he worked here?"

"Yeah."

"Guess he's our guy, huh? The lawyer. The dispatcher. What they got in common is him."

Parker didn't say anything, but he didn't buy it. Why would Damon wait until the end of the day to kill her? He had to know the cops would have been on the messenger services first thing. The damage would have been done before the end of the workday—if Eta had chosen to give them any information. If Damon wanted to silence her, he would have killed her before she got to work, not as she was leaving.

Maybe he could have come back to rob her, but Parker doubted that too. Why would the kid risk coming back here at all? For all he knew, the place could have been under surveillance. And he supposedly had a large amount of cash from Lenny Lowell's safe. What would he want with the contents of the woman's wallet?

"She's got a family, kids," he said.

"The only people who deserve it are usually on the other end of the knife, I've found," Jimmy Chew said.

Parker stood and looked around. "Where's Ruiz? This is her call."

"She's not here yet. Probably taking extra time to sharpen her claws. You've got a real peach there, Kev."

"I don't have to like them, Jimmy," Parker said, walking away. "I just have to teach them something."

"Yeah, good luck with that."

"Anything for the press, Detective?" Kelly asked from behind the yellow tape.

Parker jammed his hands in his coat pockets and walked over. "It's not my case."

"And the detective in charge?"

"Isn't here yet." Parker glanced around to make sure Jimmy Chew wasn't in earshot. "Where's Caldrovics?"

Kelly shrugged. "Took a pass. Maybe he's busy reporting you to the authorities."

"He doesn't have a mark on him, except where you kicked him," Parker said. "And, by the way, thanks for the help."

"He deserved that, and you're welcome. Glad to do my civic duty by helping a policeman."

"I tried to impress that idea on Caldrovics, but he wasn't receptive."

Kelly made a face. "Kids these days. It's all me, me, me." She barely paused for a breath. "So what have you got for me, Parker? Big scoop?"

"The vic was a dispatcher for Speed Couriers. Apparent robbery. Her purse is gone."

Kelly scribbled in a notebook. "Does she have a name?"

"Pending notification of relatives." Parker took a breath of damp air that smelled of garbage, and let it out again, thinking of Eta's family, how they would take the news, how they would get along without her. He couldn't let Ruiz deliver the bad news. He could hear her now: "So, she's dead. Get over it."

"Kev?" Kelly was looking at him with concern.

"Lenny Lowell was waiting for a messenger last night. The messenger came from Speed Couriers. No one has seen him since."

That wasn't exactly true, but Kelly didn't need to hear every detail, and Parker still wasn't sure about Abby Lowell and her alleged encounter with Damon.

"Ruiz and I were here this morning trying to get information," he said. "None was forthcoming. His name is probably an alias. The address they had on file wasn't a residence."

"This messenger is your suspect? For both murders?"

"He's a person of interest."

A car roared down the alley, skidded to a halt behind Chewalski's radio car, stopping short of the rear bumper by three inches. The driver's door opened and Ruiz climbed out in head-to-toe skintight black leather.

"Where have you been?" Parker snapped. "Moonlighting as a dominatrix? You called me half an hour ago."

"Well, excuse me. I don't live in some trendy downtown loft. I live in the Valley."

"Why does that not surprise me?" Kelly muttered just loud enough for Parker to hear.

"Traffic on the 101 sucks," Ruiz went on. "Some moron dropped a dining room table off his truck. And then—"

Parker held up a hand. "Enough. You're here now. You don't need to torment us any more than that.

"Ruiz, this is Andi Kelly," he said, tipping his head toward the reporter. "She writes for the **Times.**"

Ruiz looked offended. "What's she doing here?"

Kelly pumped up the attitude and gave her the Valley Girl sneer. "Reporter, crime, story. Duh."

"Ladies, no catfights at the murder scene," Parker said. "It's your case, Ruiz. It's up to you to decide what you want the press to know. Try to remember they have their uses. In this case, I want you to run everything past me first. This murder could be related to my murder last night. We need to be on the same page. Do you know who the vic is?"

"The dispatcher."

The coroner's investigator had arrived and was walking slowly around Eta Fitzgerald's body, as if he couldn't decide where to start.

"It's your crime scene," Parker said. "Take it. Don't screw up, and try not to alienate more than three or four people. And remember, I'm watching you like a hawk. One wrong move and you're a meter maid."

Ruiz flipped him off and walked away.

"Yikes," Kelly said. "Someone at Parker Center **really** hates you."

"Honey, **everybody** at Parker Center really hates me." He flipped up the collar of his coat and resettled his hat. "I'll call you."

He started toward the scene.

"Hey, Parker," Kelly called before he'd gone ten feet. He looked at her over his shoulder. "Do you really live in a trendy downtown loft?"

"Good night, Andi," he said, and kept walking.

The coroner's investigator was going about his business of robbing the victim of the last of her dignity, cutting away her clothing to examine her body for wounds, marks, bruises, lividity.

"How long has she been dead, Stan?" Parker asked.

"Two or three hours."

The man groaned and strained to turn Eta Fitzgerald's body over. Two-hundred-plus pounds of literally dead weight. When she toppled, she knocked the investigator on his ass. Her throat had been severed nearly to her spine, and when she was rolled onto her back, her head almost didn't come with her.

Ruiz cringed and muttered, **"Madre de Dios."**

She turned milk white and came backward a step. Parker put a hand on her shoulder to steady her. "Your first cut throat?"

Ruiz nodded.

"You getting sick, doll?"

She nodded again, and Parker turned her and pointed her away from the immediate scene. "Don't puke on any evidence."

This was death at its most brutal. Parker knew plenty of seasoned veterans who tossed their dinner over a slit throat or a mutilation. There was nothing shameful in that. It was a horrific thing to see. That he had hardened himself to such sights sometimes made Parker wonder what it said about him. That he had learned to take his own advice and not make it personal, he supposed. That over time he'd developed the invaluable skill to disconnect the victim as a living person from the victim's corpse.

Even so, this one rocked him more than average. Hours ago he had heard one wisecrack after another come out of this big, vibrant woman. Now there was no voice, only an anatomy lesson on the inner workings of the human throat.

The edges of the gaping wound had peeled back like delicate layers of lace trim, revealing a lot of bright yellow adipose tissue, the connective tissue where fat is stored. It looked like fluorescent chicken fat under the harsh white light.

There wasn't much blood on or around the wound itself. A lot of it would have gone directly down the now partially exposed trachea into her lungs, drowning her. The carotid artery would have been spraying like a geyser. If it hadn't been washed away by the intermittent showers, the crime-scene people would find spatter maybe six to eight feet from the body. A lot of blood had pooled under her as she lay on the broken pavement exsanguinating. Her chest was stained with it where it had soaked through her clothes, partially obscuring the small tattoo of a flame-haloed red heart just above her left breast.

All that blood, and depending on where the killer had been standing, he might have walked away with not a drop on him.

Ruiz came back with an expression daring Parker to make a joke.

"Have you got uniforms checking these other buildings?" he asked. "Someone might have seen something."

She nodded.

"Who called it in?"

"I don't know."

Parker turned to Chewalski. "Jimmy?"

"One of our fine citizens," the officer said, nodding for them to follow him across the alley.

As they approached the loading area of a furniture store called Fiorenza, a dark, huddled figure emerged from inside a large discarded cardboard box. As the figure unfolded, he became a tall, thin black man with long, matted gray hair and layers of ragged clothes. His aroma preceded him. He smelled like he'd been in a sewer for a very long time.

"Detectives, this is Obidia Jones. Obi, Detectives Parker and Ruiz."

"I founded that poor woman!" Jones said, pointing across the alley. "I woulda tried to recirculate her, but I couldn't turn her over. As you can see, she's pacidermical in size. Poor creature, I axed her and axed her not to be dead, but she be dead anyway."

"And you called the police?" Ruiz said, dubious.

"It don't cost nothing to call 911. I do it every once in a while. There's a phone on the corner."

"Did you see what happened, Mr. Jones?" Ruiz asked, her face pinched against the smell of him.

"No, ma'am, I did not. I was indisposed of at the time of the hyenious act. I believe I'm consumptionating too much fiber in my diet."

"I didn't need to know that," Ruiz said.

The old man squinted at her, leaning down into her face. "I believe perhaps you might be lacking in fiber. This could account for your expression."

He looked at Parker for a second opinion.

"If it were only that simple," Parker said. "How did you come across the dead woman, Mr. Jones?"

"I came back to my habitat, and I seen her laying right there after that car pulled away."

"What car?"

"Big black car."

"And did you happen to see who was driving that car?" Parker asked.

"Not this time."

Ruiz rubbed her forehead. "What does that mean?"

"Oh, I seen him before," Jones said matter-of-factly. "He came by earlier."

"Would you know this guy if you saw him again?" Parker asked.

"He look like a pit bull dog," Jones said. "Square head, beady-eyed. Undoubtedly of white trash hermitage."

"We'll want you to take a look at some pictures," Parker said.

Jones arched a thick gray eyebrow. "At your station house?"

"Yeah."

"Tonight," he specified. "Whilst it's cold and wet out here?"

"If you don't mind."

"I don't mind much," he said. "Do you all get pizza in there?"

"Sure."

"Can I bring my bags along with me? All my accoutrementionables are in my bags."

"Absolutely," Parker said. "Detective Ruiz here will bring them for you in her car."

Jones looked at her. "There might be some fiberous foodstuffs in there for you. You're welcome to help yourself."

"Yeah, great," Ruiz said, glaring at Parker. "And Detective Parker can give you a ride."

"No," Parker said. "Mr. Jones would prefer to be chauffeured in the official police vehicle, I'm sure. Officer Chewalski might even run the lights for you," he said to Jones.

"That would be very classy," Jones said. "Indeed."

"Let's get your bags, Obi," Chewalski said. "We'll put them in the detective's trunk."

Ruiz looked up at Parker and mouthed, "I hate you."

Parker ignored her. "One last thing, Mr. Jones. Around the time of the murder, did you see anyone back here on a bicycle?"

"No, sir. All them bicycle boys was long gone before that."

"What about a small, boxy black car?"

"No, sir. Big car. Long and black as the grim reaper himself."

"Thank you."

"You are such an asshole," Ruiz said as they walked back toward the scene.

"Consider it your penance," Parker said.

"For being late?"

"For being you."

27

The apartment was quiet and dark, the only illumination a white glow that came and went like a searchlight as rain-swollen clouds scudded across the moon. Jace prowled the small space, a caged animal too aware that enemies might be moving ever closer.

Tyler had watched him closely after he'd come upstairs, his eyes somber, his mouth uncharacteristically silent. He had asked no questions about the new cuts and bruises. Jace thought maybe he should have told his brother something, but he hadn't volunteered the information, and Tyler hadn't asked, opting instead for accusatory stares. The tension in the apartment had felt like static electricity building and building until their hair should have been standing on end. At ten, Tyler had gone off to bed without a word.

Jace tried to shrug off the feelings of guilt. He would never do anything to put his brother in harm's way. That was the most important thing.

Tyler's fears and feelings had to come second to that. He practiced those lines in his head for when he would wake up his little brother to tell him he was leaving.

He packed quickly. A change of clothes and not much more stuffed into a backpack. He still didn't have a plan, but he knew what he knew: He couldn't stay here. Something would come to him, it always did. He'd been raised to think on the fly. He needed not to think of himself as prey being chased down by dogs. He needed to think from a position of strength.

He had what the killer wanted, and if it was worth killing for, then it had to be worth something to someone else too. Abby Lowell was the key to that answer. He didn't believe she didn't know what was going on; otherwise, why toss her apartment, why the warning on the mirror? **Next You Die.** It had to be meant to scare her into some action. What good would it be to threaten her if she didn't know what was going on?

He would have to lure her out somehow. Get her to meet him on neutral ground, somewhere with plenty of escape routes, somewhere he could see trouble coming. He would tell her he had the negatives, ask her what they meant to her. Ask her what they were worth to her.

Jace wondered what she'd told the police.

She'd mentioned a particular detective. What was his name? Parker. He wondered if that was the guy in the hat behind the Speed office. And he wondered what Parker knew, what he had put together, what Eta had told him.

He still didn't want to believe Eta had betrayed him. He wanted to contact her, talk to her. He wanted to be reassured.

"You're leaving."

Tyler stood in the doorway to the bedroom, wearing his Spider Man pajamas, his blond hair sticking up in all directions.

"You're leaving and you weren't even going to tell me."

"That's not true," Jace said. "I wouldn't leave without telling you."

"You told me you wouldn't leave at all."

"I said I would always come back," Jace corrected him. "I will."

Tyler was shaking his head, his eyes filling. "You're in trouble. You weren't gonna tell me that either, but I know."

"What do you know?"

"You treat me like a baby, like I'm stupid and can't figure anything out for myself. Like . . . like—"

"What do you know?" Jace said again.

"You're leaving. You could take me with you, but you're not going to, and I don't get to say anything about it because you don't think I should ever know what's going on!"

"You can't go with me, Tyler. I have to clear up some problems, and I have to be able to move fast."

"We could too go," Tyler argued. "We could go someplace nobody knows us, just like when Mom died."

"It's not that simple," Jace said.

"'Cause you're gonna go to jail?"

"What?" Jace dropped down on the futon. Tyler stood directly in front of him, his face tight with anger, a red flush mottling his pale skin.

"Don't lie," he said. "Don't pretend you didn't say it. I heard you say it."

Jace didn't bother to ask his brother if he'd been listening in on his conversation with Madame Chen. Obviously, he had, and Jace knew he shouldn't have been surprised. Tyler was notorious for turning up in places he shouldn't have been, and knowing things he shouldn't have known.

"I'm not going to jail," Jace said. "I said that to Madame Chen to scare her. She wants me to go to the cops or talk to a lawyer. I don't want to do that, and I have to make sure she doesn't do it for me."

"So CFS doesn't come and get me and put me in foster care."

"That's right, pal." Jace put his hands on his little brother's small shoulders. "I won't risk you. I would never risk you. Do you understand that?"

Tears glistened in Tyler's eyes as he nodded soberly.

"We look out for each other, right?"

"Then you should let me help you, but you won't."

Jace shook his head. "It's complicated. I need to figure out what's really going on."

"Then you should let me help you," Tyler insisted again. "I'm way smarter than you are."

Jace laughed wearily and mussed his brother's hair. "If this was about geometry or science, I'd come straight to you, Ty. But it's not. This is a whole lot more serious."

"Some man got killed," Tyler said quietly.

"Yes."

"What if you get killed too?"

"I won't let that happen," Jace said, knowing it was an empty promise. Tyler knew it too. Even so, Jace said, "I'll always come back."

One tear and then another skittered down his brother's face. The expression in his eyes was far older than he was. A deep, deep sadness, made all the more poignant by the weary resignation of past experience. In that moment Jace thought Tyler's soul must be a hundred years old or more, and that he had lived through one disappointment after the next.

"You can't come back if you're dead," Tyler whispered.

Jace pulled the boy close and held him tight, his own tears burning his eyes. "I love you, little guy. I'll come back. Just for you."

"You promise?" Tyler asked, his voice muffled against Jace's shoulder.

"I promise," Jace whispered, his throat aching, the promise he didn't know if he could keep like a jagged rock he couldn't swallow and wouldn't let go of.

They both cried for a while, then they sat there for a while longer, time stretching, meaningless, into the dark night. Then Jace sighed and stood his brother back from him.

"I have to go, pal."

"Wait," Tyler said. He turned and ran into his room before Jace could say anything, and came back seconds later with the pair of small two-way radios Jace had given him for Christmas.

"Take one," he said. "The batteries are new. Then you can call me and I can call you."

Jace took the radio. "I might be out of range. But I'll call you when I can."

He put his army fatigue jacket on and slipped the radio into a pocket. Tyler walked with him to the door.

"Don't get into any trouble," Jace said. "And mind Madame Chen. You got that?"

Tyler nodded.

Jace expected Tyler to tell him to be careful, but he didn't. He didn't say good-bye. He didn't say anything.

Jace touched his brother's hair one last time, turned, and went down the stairs.

Chinatown was silent now, the streets glistening like black ice under the streetlights. Jace climbed on The Beast and started slowly down the alley. One foot pressing down, and then the other, in a weary climb to nowhere. The Beast rocked from side to side with each step, until momentum became forward energy. He took a right at the end of the alley and headed toward downtown, where lights in the windows of tall buildings glowed like columns of stars.

And as Jace turned one corner, a five-year-old Chrysler Sebring turned another just a few blocks away. A big iron gate slid back on electronic command and the car slipped into its parking slot beside a former textile warehouse building that had been brought back from the edge of condemnation and converted into trendy lofts.

And on another block, a low-slung black sedan with a brand-new windshield turned a corner and prowled down a wet street, past a laundry and a greengrocer's and Chen's Fish Market.

Parker let himself into his loft, dropped his keys on the narrow black-walnut Chinese altar table that served as a console in the slate-floored entry hall. He didn't glance in the mirror above it. He didn't need to look to know that the day hung on him like a lead cloak. There was no energy left in him to feel anger or sadness or anything but numb.

The soft glow of the small halogen lights spotlighting the art on his walls led him down the hall to his dressing room and into the master bath. He turned on the steam shower, stripped out of his suit, and laid it across a chair.

He would send it to the cleaners tomorrow. The idea of wearing it again after having stood in that alley looking at Eta Fitzgerald's body wasn't acceptable to him. Even though the scene hadn't been something truly grotesque, like finding a dead body that had been left for days in a hot room, the scent of death was on it, the **idea** of Eta's death was on it.

The steam and pounding hot water melted some of it away—the smell of it, the weight of it—and soothed his muscles, warming away the chill both from without and from within.

The bedside lamps were turned on low—part of the elaborate electronic system a buddy had talked him into. Lights, music, room temperature—all were tied into a timed computer system so that he never came home to a cold, dark place.

The woman asleep in his bed was another matter. She had come of her own free will, let herself in, and made herself at home.

Parker sat down on the edge of the bed and looked at her, a little pleased, a little surprised, a little puzzled.

Diane blinked her eyes open and looked up at him.

"Surprise," she said softly.

"I am surprised," Parker said, touching her hair. "And to what do I owe the pleasure?"

She rubbed her hands over her face and scooted up against the pillows. "I needed to cleanse my palate of socialites. Decided I would find myself a hot metrosexual guy to hang out with."

Parker smiled. "Well, baby, I am the prince of
metrosexual chic. I have a closet full of Armani,
a medicine cabinet full of skin-care products. I
can whip up a dinner for four with no frozen in-
gredients, I can pick a good wine, and I'm not
gay—not that there's anything wrong with
that."

"I knew I'd come to the right place."

She sat up and stretched, not in the least
self-conscious about or self-promoting of her
naked state. That was part of Diane's appeal, there was no coy bullshit. She was a
strong, attractive woman, comfortable in her
own body.

"Did you get called to something?" she asked.

"Yeah. Ruiz's first homicide as lead."

"God help you," she said. "I don't like her."

"Nobody likes her."

"She's not a woman's woman."

"What does that mean?"

Diane rolled her eyes. "Men. You never get
this. It means don't turn your back on her.
Don't trust her, don't rely on her. It means she'll
be your best friend if she thinks she can get
something out of you, but if she can't, she'll
turn on you like a snake."

"I think we've already come to that point,"
Parker said.

"Good. Then you won't be surprised," she said. "Did she get an easy one?"

Parker shook his head. "Not really. It might be tied to the Lowell homicide last night."

"Really?" She frowned a little. "How so?"

"The vic is the dispatcher from the messenger service Lowell called at the end of the day. Somebody seems to be after something and is pretty damn pissed off not to be finding it."

"Did RHD show up again?"

"No. Too busy off hobnobbing on your side of town, I guess," Parker said. "How long did they stay at the party?"

"Just what I told you. They exchanged a few words with Giradello and left. What did that name mean to you?"

"Damon is the name of the bike messenger sent to Lowell's office last night."

"I thought Lowell was a robbery."

"I don't believe it," Parker said. "Maybe the perp stole the money out of Lowell's safe, but that wasn't what he went there for. Apparently he thinks the bike messenger has whatever that is."

"You don't think the bike messenger did it?"

"No. That doesn't track for me. I think the bike messenger is just the rabbit. I want the dog that's chasing him." His mood darkened again as he thought of Eta lying in that alley. "I **really** want him."

Neither of them spoke for a moment, as their respective wheels turned.

"Lowell called a messenger to pick something up," Diane murmured. "The messenger left with the package—"

"We assume."

"Someone killed Lowell, and now has killed someone connected to the bike messenger. The bike messenger still has the package. The killer is after the package."

"Smells like blackmail," Parker said.

"Hmmm" was all Diane said, lost in thoughts of her own.

Parker had always believed she would have made a hell of a detective. She was wasted poking at dead bodies for the coroner every day. But she liked the forensic side. She had been a criminalist with the Scientific Investigation Division for a long time before going to the coroner's office. She talked about going back to school to get a degree in medical pathology.

She sighed then and reached out and settled her hand on the curve between his neck and shoulder.

"Come to bed," she said quietly. "It's late. You can be the world's greatest detective again in the morning."

He nodded. "I'm not going to be good for anything," he said as he slipped beneath the covers.

"I'll settle for having you close," she said. "That's all I'm up for myself."

"I can manage that," Parker said, already falling asleep as he spooned her and kissed her hair.

28

Morning was a soft, sweet dream on the horizon to the east of Los Angeles. Narrow stripes of indigo, tangerine, and rose waiting to come into bloom. The offshore weather system that had brought the rain had cleared out, leaving the air washed fresh and the promise of Technicolor blue skies.

On the rooftop of the converted warehouse, a man moved slowly through the elegant, focused steps of tai chi. White Crane Spreads Its Wings, Snake Creeps Down, Needle at Sea Bottom. His concentration was on breathing, moving, inner stillness. His breath escaped as delicate clouds that dissipated into the atmosphere.

On another rooftop to the west, an old man and a child moved in unison, side by side, their individual energies touching, their minds completely separate. Meditation in motion. Slowly reach, slowly step, shift weight back. **Zuo xashi duli, shuangfeng guaner, duojuan gong.** One posture leading to another, to another. A slow-motion dance.

Under a freeway overpass at Fourth and Flower in downtown LA, Jace huddled inside a survival blanket, his army surplus coat arranged over the blanket to hide the silver stuff it was made of. The blanket looked like a big sheet of aluminum foil, but it held his body heat, and it folded down to the size of a sandwich.

He had dozed off and on for a couple of hours, but he couldn't say he'd slept. Crouched into a ball to stay warm and to draw as little attention to himself as possible, he felt as if his body had frozen into that position. Slowly he started to rise. His joints felt as if they were being wrenched apart.

A block down, at Fifth and Flower, messengers would be showing up for coffee and fuel at Carl's Jr. He would have sold his soul for a hot cup of coffee. The Midnight Mission at Fourth and Los Angeles served a full breakfast to anyone who wanted it.

Maybe he would go there later. He wanted to talk to Mojo, get the lowdown on what people were saying, what was going on at Speed, what Eta might have told the cops. Later the space under the bridge would fill with messengers hanging out, waiting for calls. They would park their motley assortment of bikes and perch themselves on the guardrail like a bunch of crows, and talk about everything from vegan diets to Arnold Schwarzenegger.

Of all the messengers, Mojo was the one Jace most respected and came closest to trusting. He came off like a crazy Rasta man with his voodoo and superstitions, but Jace knew him to be more crazy like a fox than crazy like Preacher John. Mojo had survived as a messenger for a lot of years. No one managed that by dumb luck. And every once in a while he would pull the mask back and give a glimpse of who he was behind it—an intelligent man with an enviable sense of calm at his core.

Mojo would give him the lowdown. If he could catch Mojo alone.

Jace folded his survival blanket and put it in his backpack. He went behind a concrete piling and took a whiz, then strapped on his pack, climbed on The Beast, and started down the street toward Carl's Jr. There was no traffic. The city was just waking up, stretching and yawning.

This was Jace's favorite time of day, now, when he could take a deep breath of clean air, when his head was still clear of noise and exhaust and the thousands of instant questions and answers that flash through the mind of a messenger as he dodged traffic, dodged pedestrians, made split-second decisions as to the shortest, fastest route to his delivery. At this early hour, the day still had a shot at being good. Usually.

He parked The Beast at the side of the restaurant, and ran the risk of leaving it unlocked, in favor of a quick getaway if he needed it. He couldn't go inside. Instead, he crossed Fifth and stood there on the corner with his collar up high around his face, his shoulders hunched, hands in pockets, stocking cap pulled down to his eyebrows, looking like a lot of guys on these downtown streets. No one would give him a thought at all, much less a second thought.

The first couple of messengers who showed rode for another agency—one that put its messengers in logo jerseys and windbreakers. Jace knew guys who had turned down the better pay simply because they didn't want to concede their individuality by dressing like drones. Jace would have worn a monkey suit for better pay, but agencies with uniforms didn't pay riders off the books.

He'd been standing maybe ten minutes when he saw Mojo coming down Fifth. Even though the sun wasn't really up yet, he wore his trademark Ray Charles shades. His ankles and shins were taped with bright green stretch tape over purple bike pants, and he wore several layers of ragged T-shirts and sweatshirts. He looked like a dancer who had hit hard times.

Jace started across the street as Mojo glided up onto the sidewalk at the alley entrance.

"Hey, buddy," he said. "Can you give me—"

"I got nothing for you, mon," Mojo said, braking. He swung his right leg over the back of the still-moving bike and dismounted gracefully. "I got nothing for you but good wishes."

Jace poked his head up out of his coat as he approached, hoping Mojo would recognize him. He glanced around to make sure there was no one else on the street. "Mojo, it's me. Jace."

Mojo stopped dead and stared at him. He pushed his shades up into his dreads and looked some more. He didn't smile.

"Lone Ranger," he said at last. "You look like the Devil been chasing your tail, and he caught you."

"Yeah. Something like that."

"Policemen came looking for you yesterday. Two different sets of them. First one asked me did I know you. I told him no one knows the Lone Ranger."

"What did Eta tell him?"

"She didn't know you neither," he said, his face gaunt and sad like the old paintings of Christ on the cross—if Christ had had a headful of dreadlocks. "For someone nobody knows, you are a very popular man, J.C."

"It's complicated."

"No, I don't think so. You killed a man or you didn't."

Jace looked him straight-on. "I didn't. Why would I do that?"

Mojo didn't blink. "Money is generally the great motivator."

"If I had money, I wouldn't be standing here. I'd be on a plane to South America."

He glanced nervously down the street, waiting for someone to come out of the restaurant and see him. "I need to talk to Eta, but I can't go back to Speed and I don't have her cell phone number."

"They got no telephones where Eta is, mon," Mojo said.

A strange tension crawled down Jace's back as he stared at Mojo's Jesus face. His eyes were puffy and rimmed in red, as if he had been crying. "What do you mean?"

"I came past Base on my way here. The alley is nothing but lines of yellow tape like a giant cat's cradle. A policeman was walking inside the lines."

Jace felt the kind of cold that had nothing to do with the weather. It was the kind of cold that came from deep within.

"No," he said, shaking his head. "No."

"I said to him, 'I work here, mon.' He said to me, 'Not today you don't, Rasta man.'" His eyes went glassy with tears. His voice thickened. "'A lady had her throat cut here last night.'"

Jace backed away a step, turned one way and then the other, looking for escape from this moment, escape from the horrible images spreading in his brain like bloodstains on cloth. "It wasn't her."

"Her van was sitting there. She didn't go home without it."

"Maybe it wouldn't start. Maybe she called a cab."

Mojo just watched him. Jace turned around in a circle. In his mind he was shouting for help, but like in a dream, no one could hear him. There was a huge pressure expanding inside his head, pressing against his eardrums, pressing against the backs of his eyes. He clamped his hands around his skull, as if to keep it from bursting open, to keep the images, the thoughts, from spilling out. He felt like he couldn't breathe.

Eta. She couldn't be dead. There was too much of her. Too much opinion, too much bluster, too much mouth, too much. Guilt rolled over him for thinking she might have betrayed him to the police. Jesus God, she was dead. Her throat had been cut.

He could see the black sedan sliding down the alley that morning. He could see Predator behind the wheel. The square head, the beady eyes, the mole on the back of his neck. He could feel the raw terror of being recognized. But the car had glided past him like the shadow of death; Predator hadn't spared him a glance.

"Bad neighborhood," Mojo said. "Bad things happen. Or maybe you know something we don't."

Jace barely heard him. Eta wasn't dead because they worked in a bad neighborhood. Eta was dead because of him. He didn't know why the weight of that didn't crush him where he stood.

He'd spent most of his life keeping people at a distance to protect himself, but those same people were now in danger—or dead—because of him. The irony tasted like bile in his mouth.

"Do you know something the rest of us don't, Lone Ranger?"

Jace shook his head. "No. I wish I did, but I don't."

"Then how come you running? You didn't kill a man. You didn't kill Eta—"

"Jesus Christ, no!"

"Then what are you running from?"

"Look, Mojo, I'm stuck in the middle of something I don't understand. The cops would be happy to throw my ass in jail and call it a day, but I'm not going there. I haven't done anything wrong."

"But you're looking for help?" Mojo raised his brows. "Is that why you're here talking to me? You wanted help from Eta, and now she's dead. That don't seem like a good deal."

"You don't know she's dead because of me," Jace said. **I know it, but you don't.** "She could have been mugged for her purse by some dope-head."

"Is that what you believe, J.C.?"

No, it wasn't. But he didn't say it. There was no point in saying it. Mojo had made up his mind already. Funny how he could still feel disappointed when he knew better than to expect anything from anybody.

"I don't want anything from you," Jace said. "And I sure as hell didn't want what's happened."

He started toward The Beast.

Mojo got in front of him. "Where you going?"

Jace didn't answer, but tried to step around him. Mojo blocked him, shoved him back a step with a hand to Jace's shoulder.

Jace pushed him back. "I wouldn't want to make you an accessory after the fact, Mojo. Don't worry about me. I can take care of myself."

"I'm not worried about you. I care about Eta. I care about what happened to Eta. Police come looking for you, now Eta's dead. I'm thinking you should talk with the police."

"I'll pass." Jace pulled his helmet on, put his left foot on the pedal, and pushed off, swinging his right leg over as the bike moved slowly forward.

"You don't care someone cut her throat?" Mojo said, his voice growing stronger, angrier. He mounted his own bike and came alongside Jace. They went over the curb and crossed Flower. "Someone has to pay for that."

"It's not going to be me," Jace said, picking up speed. "I don't know who killed her, and I can't go to the cops."

He kept his eyes on the road as he said it, not wanting Mojo to see the lie. He knew damn well who killed Eta. If he went to the cops, he could get with a composite artist and describe Predator down to the mole on the back of his neck. The guy probably had a record a mile long. His face was undoubtedly in the mug books. Jace could pick him out in a heartbeat. He could pick him out of a lineup.

The trouble was, if he went to the cops, he'd be tossed into a cell, and they wouldn't want to listen to anything he had to say about anything. They wanted him for Lenny, and he had no alibi for the time of the murder that could be corroborated by anyone other than the man who'd tried to kill him. They wanted him for Abby Lowell's break-in. She would happily identify him. Now Eta. He didn't know what time she'd been killed, didn't know whether he had an alibi or not. But he did know that the one thing all three people had in common— besides Predator—was him.

"You **won't** go," Mojo said angrily, keeping abreast of him. "Eta's dead. She has family, children—"

"And I don't, so what's the difference if I wind up in prison," Jace said, glancing over. He sat up straight, let go of the handlebars, and pulled his swim goggles up from around his neck and settled them in place.

"You don't care about no one but you."

"You don't know shit about me, Mojo. You don't know shit about what's going on. Stay out of it."

Jace raised up on his pedals and sprinted ahead, wanting to distance himself from Mojo, and from the guilt he was trying to impose. He wanted to outdistance the image in his head of

Eta Fitzgerald with her throat cut, her life running out on the oily, filthy ground behind Speed. He wanted not to think about what her last moments must have been like, what her last thoughts might have been.

The Beast swayed hard from side to side as he pumped. The new rear tire grabbed the road and propelled him forward. He took a right on Figueroa, where traffic was picking up. Produce delivery trucks, and Brinks trucks, and commuters coming into the city early to beat the worst of the crush on the freeways.

The smell of exhaust, the sounds of squeaking brakes and diesel engines were familiar, normal. As was the feel of speed beneath him. If nothing else in his life was normal, there was the smallest comfort of being in his element: feeling, seeing, hearing, smelling things he understood.

He glanced back to see if Mojo had taken the hint and backed off, but the other messenger was coming up on his left. Jace touched the brakes and dove around the corner, right onto Fourth, where his day had begun. Messengers had started to gather under the bridge. They registered as a blur of colors as he flew past.

Mojo was stuck at his left flank, his face grim. He motioned angrily for Jace to pull over. Jace gave him the finger and pumped harder. He was a decade younger than Mojo, but he was injured and exhausted. Mojo was sound and determined, and came up even with him, his U-lock in his right hand. He pointed with the lock for Jace to pull over, tried to crowd him over toward the curb, reached down and made to jam the lock into Jace's spokes.

Jace dipped right and jumped The Beast up onto the sidewalk as they crossed Olive, drawing a blast of horn from a car trying to make a right-hand turn onto Fourth. Pedestrians on the sidewalk jumped back, cursed him. He clipped the arm of a guy with a Starbucks cup in his hand, and coffee went into the air like a geyser.

Mojo was still in the street and pushing ahead of him, his eyes on the next intersection.

A million tiny, instant calculations went through Jace's brain like data in a computer—speed, velocity, trajectory, angles, obstacles.

A siren pierced his thought process. A black-and-white was coming up on Mojo, lights rolling. A voice cracked over a bullhorn: "LAPD! You on the bikes! Pull up!"

As they made the corner of Fourth and Hill, Mojo turned hard right, into Jace's path. Jace angled his front wheel to the left. The light on Fourth had turned yellow. The intersection was almost clear.

The Beast rocketed off the curb, just missing

Mojo's rear wheel. Airborne, Jace shifted his weight, turning the bike.

The cop car was at the corner, turning right from the outside lane, cutting off a truck. The Beast's rear tire landed just past the black-and-white's left front headlight. A loud crash sounded, and the cop car jumped forward as something hit it from behind.

Jace took the jolt from the landing, jumped on the pedals, and gunned the bike straight into the oncoming one-way traffic from Hill Street.

A chorus of horns. Tires screeching on pavement. He split the two lanes like a thread through the eye of a needle, just missing side mirrors and running boards. Drivers shouted obscenities at him. He prayed no one opened a door.

He kept going, turning, cutting through alleys, turning, moving. Not even a heat-seeking missile could have followed him. He was one of the fastest messengers in the city. This was his turf. He didn't even think. He just rode, burning off the adrenaline, sweating out the fear shaking down his arms and flailing in his chest.

Fucking Mojo, chasing him. Jesus H. One wrong move and they might both have ended up in a hospital, or in the morgue. Jace could have ended up in jail, hauled in for operating a bicycle in a dangerous manner, or something more serious, depending on how pissed off the cop had been. And it would have taken only a few minutes, maybe an hour, before they figured out they had the guy every cop in the city was looking for—if Mojo hadn't volunteered the information first.

That's what you get for trusting someone, J.C.

And what about what other people got for having him come to them? He thought again of Eta, and wanted to be sick.

Cruising through a green light, Jace checked the street sign, and might have laughed if he'd had it in him. Hope Street.

He pulled off at the Music Center Plaza, situated amid a trio of entertainment venues: the Mark Taper Forum, the Ahmanson Theater, and the Dorothy Chandler Pavilion, home of the Oscars until Hollywood had rejuvenated itself and reclaimed the awards.

The plaza was deserted. Nothing opened for another hour or so. Jace parked The Beast and sat down on a bench, trying to let go of all the tension in his body. He stared at the rise and fall of the many waterspouts around the **Peace on Earth** sculpture, and tried to clear his mind for just a moment.

The sculpture was allegedly famous. To Jace it looked like a monkey pile of people trying to hold up a giant artichoke that a dove had dive-bombed nose-first. All he could think looking at it was that the man who had created it had not lived in the same world he did, or the same world Eta Fitzgerald had lived in.

The sculpture was timeless. A thing without life that would live forever. A thing without emotion, meant to evoke emotion. It would sit on this spot forever, barring nuclear attack or the Big Quake.

Jace couldn't imagine that anyone would really care if it was there or not, but there it would remain. Instead, people would come and go, live and die, and years would pass, and some would be missed and some would never be thought of at all.

He tried to imagine what Eta would have had to say about **Peace on Earth,** but he couldn't hear her voice, and he would never hear her voice again. He could only put his head in his hands and cry for the loss of her.

29

Chen's Fish Market was five minutes from Parker's loft. According to the DMV, one of the Mini Coopers that may have fled the scene of Abby Lowell's break-in lived here. Parker pulled up in front and went to the public entrance first, finding the place hadn't yet opened for business. But in the loading bay two men were shoveling shaved ice for the coolers that would chill the day's deliveries.

Parker held up his badge. "Excuse me, gentlemen. I'm looking for a Lu Chen."

The men straightened immediately, one wide-eyed with fear, the other narrow-eyed with suspicion. The first had the round, doughy features of someone with Down syndrome. Parker addressed the other man. "I'm Detective Parker, LAPD. Is there a Lu Chen here?"

"Why?"

Parker smiled. "That was a yes or no question. Unless your name is Lu Chen."

"Lu Chen is my aunt."

"And you are?"

"Chi."

"Just Chi?" Parker asked. "Like Cher? Like Prince?"

The steel-eyed stare. No sense of humor.

"Is your aunt here?"

Chi stabbed his shovel into the pile of ice. Anger management issues. "I'll go see if she's in her office."

"I'll come with you," Parker said. The guy looked offended at the suggestion. Hell of a lot of attitude from someone who shoveled ice for a living.

Chi climbed up on the loading dock, then stood there with his hands on his hips, glaring at Parker. Not the day to have worn the Hugo Boss suit, Parker thought, but there it was. The gauntlet had been thrown down.

Parker boosted himself up onto the dock and dusted himself off, trying not to grimace as he looked at a streak of black dirt on the front of his jacket. His sour-faced tour guide turned and led him through part of the small warehouse space, down a narrow hall to a door marked OFFICE.

Chi knocked. "Aunt? A police detective is here to see you."

The door opened and a small, neat woman in a red wool blazer and black slacks stared out at them. Her expression was as fierce as her nephew's, but in a way that was strong rather than petulant.

"Detective Parker, ma'am." Parker offered his ID. "If I could have a moment of your time, please. I have a couple of questions for you."

"In regards to what, may I ask?"

"Your car, ma'am. You own a 2002 Mini Cooper?"

"Yes."

The nephew made a huff of disgust. Lu Chen looked at him. "Please leave us, Chi. I know you have work to do."

"More than usual," he said. "Being short-handed."

"Excuse us, then," she said pointedly, and the nephew turned and walked away. She turned to Parker. "Would you care for tea, Detective?"

"No, thank you. I just have a few questions. Is the car here?"

"Yes, of course. I park in back."

"Do you mind if I have a look?"

"Not at all. What is this all about?" she asked, leading him from the cramped office out the back to the alley.

Parker walked slowly around the car. "When was the last time you drove it?"

She thought for a moment. "Three days ago.

I had a charity luncheon at Barneys in Beverly Hills. Then, of course, it rained."

"You didn't take it out yesterday?"

"No."

"Did anyone else take it out? Your nephew, maybe?"

"Not that I know. I was here all day. Chi was here all day, as well, and he has his own car."

"Does anyone else have access to the keys?"

Now she began to look worried. "They hang in my office. What is this about, Detective? Have I violated some traffic law? I don't understand."

"A car matching the description of yours was reported leaving the scene of a crime yesterday. A break-in and assault."

"How dreadful. But I can assure you, it wasn't my car. My car was here."

Parker pursed his lips and raised his eyebrows. "A witness copied part of the license plate. It comes pretty close to matching yours."

"As do many, I'm sure."

She was a cool one, he had to give her that. He strolled along the driver's side to the rear of the car and tapped his notebook against the broken taillight. "As the car was leaving the scene, it was struck by a minivan. The taillight was broken."

"Such a coincidence. My car was struck while I was at my luncheon. I discovered the damage when I went to leave."

"What did the lot attendant have to say?"

"There was none."

"Did you report the incident to the police?"

"For what purpose?" she asked, arching a brow. "To garner their sympathy? In my experience, the police have no interest in such small matters."

"To your insurance company, then?"

"File a claim for so little damage? I would be a fool to give my insurance company such an invitation to raise my rates."

Parker smiled and shook his head. "You must be something on the tennis court, Ms. Chen."

"You may call me Madame Chen," she said, her back ramrod straight. Parker doubted she topped five feet, and still she somehow managed to look down her nose at him. "And I have no idea what you are talking about."

"My apologies," Parker said with a deferential tip of his head. "Madame Chen. You seem to have an answer for everything."

"Why would I not?"

He touched the scratch marks on the Mini Cooper's otherwise impeccable glossy black paint. "The minivan that struck the car leaving the crime scene was silver. The car that damaged your car was silver also."

"Silver is a popular color."

"Interesting thing about paint colors," Parker said. "They're particular to make. Ford's silver paint, for instance, is not Toyota's silver paint is not BMW's silver paint. They're chemically unique."

"How fascinating."

"Do you know a J. C. Damon?" Parker asked.

She didn't react to the sudden change of subject. Parker couldn't decide if that was genius or a miscalculation. An overreaction would have been more telling, he supposed.

"How would I know this person?" she asked.

"He's a bike messenger for Speed Couriers. Twentyish, blond, good-looking kid."

"I have no need of a bicycle messenger."

"That wasn't actually the question," Parker pointed out.

No response.

"J. C. Damon was the person driving the car that was leaving the scene of the crime."

"Do I seem like the sort of person to consort with criminals, Detective?"

"No, ma'am. But once again, you've managed not to answer my question."

Parker tried to imagine what possible connection this dignified steel lotus blossom might have to a kid like Damon, a ragtag loner, living on the fringes of society. There didn't seem to be any, and yet he would have bet money there was. This was the car. There were too many hits on crucial points for any of them to be coincidence, and what Madame Chen wasn't saying was a lot.

Parker leaned a hip against the car, making himself comfortable. "Between you and me, I'm not so sure this kid is a criminal," he confessed. "I think maybe he was in the wrong place at the wrong time, and now he's up to his neck in a serious mess and he doesn't know how to get out. Things like that happen."

"Now you speak like a social worker," Madame Chen said. "Is it not your job to make arrests?"

"I'm not interested in arresting innocent people. My job is to find the truth. I think he might be able to help me do that," Parker said. "And I might be able to help him."

She glanced away from him for the first time in their conversation, a pensive shading to her expression. "I'm sure a young man in such a situation may find it difficult to trust—particularly the police."

"Yes, I'm sure that's true," Parker said. "A young person with a happy background doesn't come to be in a situation like that. Life is tough for more people than not. But if a kid like that has someone in his life who can reach out to him . . . Well, that can make all the difference."

A small worry line creased between her brows. Parker figured she had to be pushing sixty, but her skin was as flawless as porcelain.

He reached into his coat pocket and pulled out a business card. "If for any reason you might need to reach me, ma'am, feel free to call me—anytime, day or night," he said, handing the card to her. "In the meantime, I'm afraid I'm going to have to impound your car."

Anger sparked her to attention again. "That is outrageous! I have told you my car has not left this spot in three days!"

"So you have," Parker conceded. "The thing is, I don't believe you. It matches the description, the plate number, the damage to the car I'm looking for. I'm afraid you've got the trifecta there, Madame Chen. A tow truck will come and take your car to be a guest of the LAPD until lab tests can be run."

"I'm calling my attorney," she declared.

"You have that right," Parker said. "I should also tell you that if the results of the tests come back the way I believe they will, there is a chance you could be charged as an accessory."

"That's ridiculous!"

"I'm just letting you know. It's not up to me. I wouldn't want to see that happen, Madame Chen. You strike me as a person who takes her responsibilities very seriously."

"I'm glad you think so highly of me that you would treat me like a common criminal," she snapped, turning on her heel and marching toward her office.

"I don't think you common in any way, Madame Chen," Parker said. "But for future reference, ma'am, Barneys' parking lot always has an attendant."

She gave him a look that might have melted lesser men.

Parker smiled. "I'm a regular."

Unimpressed, she stormed off and disappeared into the building.

Parker sighed and looked around. The Chen family had a nice little business going. Neat as a pin. Everything A-one. He had purchased prawns here once for a quiet dinner with Diane. Excellent quality.

Maybe he would do it again when this case was closed.

He had left Diane asleep in his bed, putting an orange on his vacated pillow and a note that read: **Breakfast in bed. I'll call you later. K**

It had been nice to fall asleep with her in his arms, and to wake up with her there. To do that more often seemed like a good idea. Not that he wanted something permanent, or legally binding. Neither of them wanted that. Rules and regulations altered expectations and issues of trust in a relationship, and not for the better, as far as he'd seen. But as he became more settled in his life outside the job, and more content with the reconstructed Kev Parker, stability and normalcy and connection were becoming more attractive to him.

He pulled his cell phone out and called Dispatch to have a black-and-white sent to sit on the Mini Cooper until he could get his warrant.

As he waited, he looked at the buildings across the alley. Plenty of windows overlooking the Chen lot. There were probably more than a few pairs of eyes glancing out even now. As soon as the black-and-white rolled in, the news would be all over Chinatown in a flash—among the Chinese, at least.

If he wanted to canvass the neighbors, he might find someone who had noticed the Mini Cooper missing, or perhaps had seen it leave or return. But Parker had no intention of doing that. He didn't want Madame Chen as an enemy, or perceiving him to be one. There was no need to air her business with the neighbors and fan the flames of gossip.

The sensation of being watched crept over Parker's skin. Not from above, but from straight on. His gaze swept the loading dock, the other side of the alley, and came to rest on a stack of wooden pallets sitting at the back of the next building.

Parker stuck his hands in his pockets and wandered—not toward the pallets, but across the alley, where tall bunches of purple irises and yellow sunflowers were being delivered in through the back door of a florist's shop.

He eased his way down the alley, the pallets in his peripheral vision. When he was just past them, he glanced back.

A small figure shifted position to keep him in sight, wedging between the pallets and the brick building.

Parker turned and looked straight at his little voyeur. A kid. Maybe eight or nine. Swallowed up in a faded black sweatshirt nine sizes too big for him, his face peering out from the depths of the hood, blue eyes that went wide as gaze met gaze.

"Hey, kid—"

The boy bolted before the words were even

out of Parker's mouth, and the chase was on. Quick as a rabbit, the kid zipped past Chen's lot, heading for the cover of a big blue Dumpster. Parker sprinted full-out after him, hit the brakes as the boy pulled a one-eighty, and skidded another ten feet before he could change directions.

"Kid! Stop! Police!" Parker shouted, sprinting back down the alley, his tie flipped over his shoulder, waving like a flag behind him.

The boy took a hard left into a parking lot wedged between a U of buildings. No way out Parker could see except to go in the back door of the center building. The door was closed.

The cars were parked nose-to-tail, two deep and four wide. Parker walked along behind the cars, his breath coming in hard, quick huffs. He set his hands at his waist and frowned at the fact that he was sweating. His shirt still had creases from the laundry. He hadn't worn it two hours and he would be sending it back.

A quick glimpse of blond hair and blue jeans caught his eye as the boy dashed between a green Mazda and a white Saturn, crouching down to half his already small size.

"Okay, junior," Parker said. "Come on out. I promise I won't arrest you. No handcuffs, no pistol-whipping . . ."

There was a rustling on the fine gravel beneath the cars. A glimpse of pant leg, a black sneaker disappearing under a Volvo.

Parker stayed along the back of the cars, pacing slowly back and forth.

"I just want to ask you a couple of questions," Parker said. "We could start with why you took off like that, but I'll give you that one. A freebie. For future reference: If you run, cops will chase. We're like dogs that way."

He followed the scuttling sound back to the other side of the lot. He bent over and looked beneath a white BMW X5 with vanity plates that read 2GD4U. Big blue eyes stared back at him over a button nose smudged with dirt.

"Kev Parker," he said, holding his badge down for the kid to see. "LAPD. And you are . . . ?"

"I have the right to remain silent."

"You do, but you're not under arrest. Is there some reason I should arrest you?"

"Anything I say can and will be used against me."

"How old are you?" Parker asked.

The kid thought about that for a moment, weighing the pros and cons of answering. "Ten," he said at last.

"You live around here?"

"You can't make me talk to you," the kid said.

"I know all about my rights against self-in-crim-i-nation as defined by the Fifth Amendment to the Constitution."

"A legal scholar. I'm impressed. What did you say your name was?"

"I didn't say. You really might as well not try to trick me," the boy said. "I watch cop shows all the time."

"Ah, you're wise to us."

"Plus, I'm probably a lot smarter than you are. I don't say that to make you feel bad or any-thing," he said earnestly. "It's just that I have an IQ of a hundred sixty-eight, and that's well above the average."

Parker chuckled. "Kid, you're a trip. Why don't you crawl out from under there? You can explain the Pythagorean Theorem to me."

"The square of the length of the hypotenuse of a right triangle equals the sum of the squares of the lengths of the other two sides. From the doctrines and theories of Pythagoras and the Py-thag-o-reans," he said, squeezing his eyes shut as he sounded out the clumsy word, "who developed some basic principles of math-ematics and astronomy, originated the doc-trine of the harmony of the spheres, and believed in me-tem-psy-cho-sis, the eternal re-currence of things, and the mystical significance of numbers."

Parker just stared at him.

"I read a lot," the boy said.

"I guess so. Come on, genius," Parker said, offering his hand. "All my blood is rushing to my head. Get out from under there before I have a stroke."

The boy scuttled out from under the car like a crab, stood up, and tried in vain to dust himself off. The sleeves of his sweatshirt had to be six inches longer than his arms. The hood had fallen back, revealing a shock of blond hair.

"I don't really consider myself to be a genius," he confessed modestly. "I just know a lot of stuff."

"Why aren't you in school?" Parker asked. "You already know everything, so they sprang you loose?"

The kid pushed back a sleeve and consulted a watch that was so big for him it looked like he had a dinner plate strapped to his arm.

"It's only seven thirty-four."

"Your school must be close by, huh?"

The boy frowned.

"And you live in the neighborhood, or you'd be more concerned about the time," Parker said. "You're observant. You're smart. I'll bet you know a lot about what goes on around here."

The one-shoulder shrug. The toe in the dirt. Eyes on the ground.

"You're below the radar," Parker said. "You can slip around, see things, hear things. Nobody even notices."

The other shoulder shrugged.

"So why were you watching me down there?"

"I dunno."

"Just because? You working your way up to becoming a Peeping Tom so you can spy on girls?"

The little face scrunched up in distaste. "Why would I want to do that? Girls are weird."

"Okay. So maybe you want to become a spy. Is that it?"

"Not really. I just have an in-sa-tia-ble curiosity."

"Nothing wrong with that," Parker said. "Do you know the Chens? From the fish market?"

Both shoulders.

"Do you know a guy around here by the name of J. C. Damon? He's a bike messenger."

The eyes went a little wider. "Is he in trouble?"

"Kind of. I need to speak with him. I think he might have some information that could help me with a big investigation."

"About what? A murder or something?"

"A case I'm working on," Parker said. "I think he might have seen something."

"Why won't he just come and tell you, if that's all?"

"Because he's scared. He's like you, running away from me because he thinks I'm the enemy. But I'm not."

Parker could see the wheels turning in the kid's head. He was curious now, and interested in the grudging way of someone pretending not to be.

"I'm not a bad guy," Parker said. "You know, some people blame first and ask questions later. There could be cops like that out there looking for this guy Damon. It'd be a whole lot better for him if he came to me before they get to him."

"What'll they do to him?"

Parker shrugged. "I don't know. I don't have any control over them. If they believe this guy's guilty, who knows what could happen?"

The kid swallowed hard, like he was swallowing a rock. Blond hair, blue eyes, good-looking kid. Just the way Parker had described Damon to Madame Chen. This one had been right there at the back of Chen's, watching, listening. His interest now went beyond the excuse of the kid's insatiable curiosity.

"Could they shoot him?" the boy asked.

Parker shrugged. "Bad things can happen. I'm not saying they will, but . . ."

He reached in a pocket, pulled out a business card, offered it to the kid. The boy snatched it as if he expected a manacle to snap around his wrist. One of those cop tricks he was wise to. He looked at the card, looked up at Parker from under his brows, then stuck the card in the pouch of the sweatshirt.

"If you see this guy Damon around . . ." Parker said.

The black-and-white radio car turned in at the end of the alley and stopped behind Chen's. The uniform got out and called to him.

"Detective Parker?"

Parker started to raise a hand. The kid was off like a shot.

"Shit!" Parker shouted, bolting after him.

The boy had run back into the U of buildings. No way out, Parker thought, closing in on him. There was only the narrowest of spaces between two of the buildings, a ray of sunlight as thin as a razor blade. The kid ran around the front row of cars. Parker tried to cut the angle, jumping up and skidding on his ass across the hood of a Ford Taurus. He reached out to grab the kid as he came off the car, but he landed badly, stumbled, and went down on one knee.

The kid didn't even slow down as he came to

the buildings. He ran into the crack of space, fitting exactly between the two walls.

Parker swore, turned sideways, sucked in his breath, and started in, cobwebs hitting his face, the brick snatching at his suit. The boy was out the other end and gone before Parker had made it a dozen feet.

"Hey, Detective?" the uniform called from the parking lot.

Parker emerged, scowling, picking spider-webs off the front of his jacket.

"Anything I can do for you?"

"Yeah," Parker said, disgusted. "Call Hugo Boss and send my apologies."

30

Ruiz sat at her desk with her head in her hand, her expression a mix of exhaustion, disgust, testiness, and fading hope. She had put her aromatic witness in Parker's chair, at Parker's desk, willing to suffer the stench in the name of revenge.

Obidia Jones appeared to have had a fine night's sleep in a holding cell. A late dinner from Domino's, coffee and pastry from Starbucks for breakfast. He paged through the mug books as if he were reading a magazine, occasionally remarking when he saw someone he knew.

"Personally, I prefer a heartier breakfast," he said, as he tore off a delicate piece of his danish. "Something substantiated to stick to a person's ribs. Something representing all your major food groups. A good big breakfast burrito."

Ruiz rolled her eyes.

Kray walked past with a sour look on his face. "Can't you take that somewhere else, Ruiz?

Why should the rest of us have to put up with that filthy stink?"

Ruiz looked at him. "As much time as you spend with your head up your ass, Kray, I'd think you'd be used to the smell by now."

Yamoto, standing by the coffeemaker, choked back a laugh and dodged the snake eyes his partner shot him.

"Bitch," Kray muttered under his breath.

"Say that a little louder," Ruiz taunted. "So I can file a harassment complaint against you. You can go through sensitivity training again. How many times would that be?"

Kray made a face and mimicked her like he was a five-year-old child.

Parker came into the squad, took three strides into the room, and was knocked back by the smell. When he saw Mr. Jones sitting in his chair, he turned a piercing look on Ruiz.

She smiled like a sly cat and said, "Touché."

"I think I've got the car," Parker said, ignoring her. "I've got to call an ADA for a warrant. If we're lucky, we'll have prints by noon."

"Where was it?" Ruiz asked.

"Chinatown. Doesn't make any sense now, but it's going to. I can feel it."

The anticipation was like a coffee buzz, like speed. He was moving faster, talking faster, thinking faster. The building high was almost better than sex.

"I love it when it all comes together," he said. He had run home from his encounter at Chen's Fish Market and changed suits. He wasn't about to put his ass in his own chair now. He went to Kray's desk and used the phone without asking, as if Kray weren't sitting right there.

"How's it going, Mr. Jones?" he asked as he waited for someone to pick up on the other end of his call.

"I'm very happy. You all are extremely magnimonious with your hospitality."

"Ms. Ruiz there treating you well?"

"She was kind enough to bring me coffee."

"We'll have to mark that on the calendar," Parker said. "She's never that nice to me."

"Must be your cologne," Kray grumbled.

"I don't need cologne," Parker said. "I smell like a fresh spring morning. But you could change that ugly shirt, cracker. How many days you been stewing in that thing? Yamoto, how many days has he been wearing that shirt?"

"Too many."

Scowling, Kray made a swipe at the telephone receiver. "Get off my goddam phone, Parker."

"Fuck you— No! Not you, sweetheart!" He

reached out and knocked one of Kray's messy piles of unfinished paperwork over the edge of the desk and mouthed the word "asshole" at Kray. "It's Kev Parker. Is this the astoundingly lovely Mavis Graves?"

Mavis Graves was sixty-three with upper arms the size of canned hams, but every lady loved a compliment.

"Mavis, doll, I need to speak to Langfield about a warrant. Is he in yet?"

Stevie Wonder came over the phone line. "My Cherie Amour."

Parker pointed a finger at Ruiz. "Did my court order for Lowell's safe-deposit box come through?"

"Not yet."

"Langfield. What do you need, Parker?"

"I need a warrant to search a car I believe may have been used to flee an assault."

"You believe?"

"A car matching the description was used for a getaway. I have a partial plate from a witness, and new damage to a taillight. The car leaving the scene got clipped by a van and broke a taillight."

"Where's the car? Did you find it abandoned?"

"No. The car's in Chinatown. It belongs to

one pissed-off lady who isn't being very forth-coming with me."

"What does she say about the car?"

"That the car was never used yesterday, and the taillight got broken in a parking lot in Beverly Hills."

"You have a suspect? Is she a suspect?"

"The woman isn't a suspect, but I think she knows more than she's saying. If I can get prints and put my suspect in the car . . ."

"So you're fishing?"

"It's the car."

"There aren't any other cars that match that description in LA?"

Parker heaved a sigh. "Whose side are you on, Langfield?"

"Mine. I'm not getting you a warrant you can only justify after you've done the search. The evidence will never make it past a judge. Can you connect your perp to this woman?"

"Not yet."

"So you're nowhere."

"I have the car, the damage to the car, the partial plate—"

"You've got nothing. You can't even sit and look at the car with what you've got."

"Well, thanks for pissing all over my parade," Parker said, rubbing at his temple. "You could

have come through on this, Langfield. Judge
Weitz would have signed off—"

"Judge Weitz is senile. I'm not bending rules
for you, Parker. You're the poster boy for what
happens when cops cut corners. I won't be a
party—"

Parker tossed the receiver down on Kray's
desk. Langfield was still preaching.

"Prick," Parker muttered, walking away,
working to gather himself. He had to keep his
eyes on the prize. He turned back, picked the
receiver back up. "There's paint marks on the
damage to this car. If I can match the paint to
the van that hit it—"

"You will have solved a traffic mishap. There's
still no reason to get inside the car."

"That's bullshit. It was leaving the scene of
the crime!"

"Do this ass-backward and anything you find
that could lead you to your perp is going to
get thrown out because the search was no
good. You want another one to take a walk because you—"

Parker threw the receiver down again. He
walked out of the squad, went into the men's
room, and washed his face in cold water, then
stood there holding his wrists under the faucet.

He stared at himself in the mirror, but he
didn't ask himself how long he was going to be

made to pay for the crime of arrogance. He didn't bother to go over the old ground that he'd been singled out as a scapegoat, and that it wasn't fair.

He never offered excuses. What had happened had happened. Even if other people wouldn't, he had to leave it in the past and own his present. He would find a way to get the car. He couldn't waste time and energy being angry that it wasn't a walk in the spring rain.

When he went back into the squad, Kray's phone was still off the hook, and playing "Isn't She Lovely."

Captain Fuentes came out of his office and crooked a finger. "Kev? Can I see you in here?"

Parker followed him and closed the door behind him. "I didn't do it. It's not mine. And I swear she was nineteen."

Fuentes, who was a good guy and had an easy sense of humor, didn't laugh. He had soulful black eyes that seemed to carry the sorrows of the world when he was serious like this.

"You look like you're about to tell me I have six weeks to live," Parker said.

"I got a call a little while ago. RHD is taking your homicide."

Parker shook his head. The rage seemed to start boiling in his feet and pushed its way upward. This was worse than being told he had six weeks to live. In six weeks' time he at least had the chance to try to save himself. He was losing his case, today, now, not six weeks from today. The first case he'd had in years that smelled big. The kind of case a detective made his chops on—or rode back out of purgatory.

"No," he said. "Not Lowell."

"There's nothing I can do, Kev."

"Did they give any explanation?" In his mind's eye he could picture the scene Diane had described to him over the phone. Bradley Kyle and his partner, Moose Roddick, and Tony Giradello with their heads together.

"Captain Florek told me they thought it might tie into something they already have."

I just overheard your name in a conversation. . . .

"That's all he said," Fuentes told him. "You know as well as I do, they don't need a reason. He could have said, 'Because the sky is blue,' and what could I do about it? I'm sorry, Kev."

No, not now, Parker thought. Not when it was all right there just beneath the surface. All he needed was to dig **just** a little harder, just a little longer.

"You can pretend we haven't had this conversation yet," he said.

"Kev—"

"I'm not here. You haven't seen me. I'm not on the radio. My cell phone isn't working."

"Kev, you're not going to close the case in the next three hours, are you?"

Parker said nothing.

"They want everything you've got," Fuentes said. "Pull it together and take it over to Parker Center."

"No."

"Kev—"

"I won't do it. I won't go over there. If Bradley Kyle wants this case, the little prick can come here and get it. I'm not going over there like some, some—"

Parker put a hand over his mouth and stopped himself before his control slipped any further. He took a deep breath and exhaled. He looked at Fuentes, willing him to say what he wanted to hear. Fuentes just looked at him with something much too close to pity in his eyes.

"You haven't seen me," Parker said quietly. "We haven't spoken."

"I can't put them off for long."

"I know." Parker nodded. "Whatever you can do. I appreciate it, Captain."

"Get out of here," Fuentes said, sitting down behind his desk. He settled a pair of reading glasses on the high bridge of his nose, and reached for some paperwork. "I haven't seen you. We haven't spoken."

Parker stepped out of Fuentes' office, closing the door behind him. Ruiz was watching him like a hawk. Good instincts, when she wanted to get out of her own way and use them, Parker thought.

She had Eta Fitzgerald's murder. Fitzgerald's murder was tied to Lowell's murder. He would stay in that way. Bradley Kyle wasn't going to be rid of him so easily.

Ruiz got out of her chair and came to him. "You've got your court order," she said quietly. "What's going on?"

"Robbery-Homicide is taking Lowell."

"Why?"

"Because they can."

Parker felt like he had bees in his head. He needed a strategy, had to move fast, had to make a break happen. He only had a few hours to live, in relation to this case.

"What are you going to do?" Ruiz asked.

Before Parker could formulate an answer, Obidia Jones let out a little yelp of excitement.

"That's him! That's your perpetuator, right there!" he said, poking a long, gnarled finger at a photograph in the book before him.

Parker and Ruiz both went to him, Ruiz

pinching her nose closed with thumb and fore-finger.

"Who've you got there, Mr. Jones?" Parker asked.

The old man slid his finger down from the face in the photograph, revealing exactly what Jones had told them: a head like a cinder block; small, mean eyes; five o'clock shadow. Eddie Boyd Davis.

"Only he had a piece of tape across his nose," Jones said. "Like someone maybe busted it for him."

"Mr. Jones, you are a fine citizen," Parker said. "I think Ms. Ruiz should kiss you full on the mouth."

Jones looked both scandalized and hopeful.

"But that would be against regulations," Ruiz said.

Parker looked again at the face of the man who had murdered Eta Fitzgerald in cold blood. He tapped his finger under the name, and spoke to Ruiz in a low voice.

"Dig up everything you can find on this mutt. I want to know if he has any connection to Lenny Lowell. And if Bradley Kyle comes in here, you don't know anything, and you haven't seen me."

"Wishful thinking," she muttered.

Parker's mind was already engaged elsewhere. "You're a doll," he said, patting her cheek.

He went through a couple of desk drawers, took out a file, pulled some papers from a wire tray on top of his desk. He grabbed the binder that was the murder book on the Lowell case, containing reports and official notes, sketches of the scene, Polaroids—everything to do with the homicide except for his personal notes. He put it all in a plastic mail carton he kept under his desk for just this purpose, then went around to Ruiz's desk to use her phone.

"You're not going to have seen me walk out of here with that container," he told Ruiz as he dialed Hollywood Division. "Right?"

"Right," she said, but there was a hesitation first.

"It's your case too," Parker said. "Lowell and Fitzgerald: If they take one, they take the other. Is that what you want?"

"It's Robbery-Homicide. They'll do whatever they want to do. We can't stop them."

Parker gave her the hard stare. "You sell me out to Bradley Kyle and you'll make an enemy you'll wish you didn't have."

"Jesus, I said all right," she said grudgingly. "Don't threaten me."

"What are you going to do?" he sneered. "Call Internal Affairs?"

"Fuck you, Parker. Just leave me out of it."

She would sell him out in a heartbeat, Parker thought, remembering what Diane had predicted. She would sell him out to Kyle because Kyle could get her noticed by the right people in RHD.

"LAPD, Hollywood Division. How may I direct your call?"

Parker said nothing and hung up the phone. He reached across the desktop, grabbed his dictionary, and dropped it on Ruiz's blotter.

"Your lesson for today," he said. "Look up the word **partner.** I'll call you later."

He grabbed the plastic box and left the room, then the building. He had only a few hours to live. He couldn't waste a minute.

31

Parker called Joel Coen from his car as he made his way to the City National Bank branch where Lenny Lowell's safe-deposit box lived.

Coen picked up on the second ring. Still young enough to be eager.

"Joel, Kev Parker. I've got something for you on the Lowell B&E, but you have to jump on it ASAP, got it?"

"What is it?"

"I've got your getaway car. It's sitting behind a fish market in Chinatown. Black Mini Cooper, damage to the left taillight, match on the partial plate."

"Geez, how'd you get that so fast?"

"I'm hyperactive. Do you know what color the minivan was?"

"Silver."

"That's it. I couldn't get a warrant—extenuating circumstances—but you won't have a problem. Call the DA's office and make sure you **do not** talk to Langfield. And when you get the car dusted for prints, make sure they go to Joanie at Latent. Tell her I sent you, and that she's looking for a match with my homicide."

"Got it."

"And move fast, Joel. There's a shitstorm coming. If Robbery-Homicide gets a sniff of this car, it's gone, and so's your case."

"RHD? Why would they—"

"Don't ask. The less you know, the better. Beat it over to Chinatown. I've got a unit sitting on the car."

He gave Coen the address, and ended the call as the bank came into sight. Half expecting to see Bradley Kyle and his partner waiting at the door, Parker parked his car and went inside, court order in hand.

The manager checked the document for crossed **t**'s and dotted **i**'s, and escorted him to the lower level, to the location of the boxes. Lowell's was the largest size available. They put the box on a long walnut table in a private room. Parker put on a pair of latex gloves, took a deep breath, and opened the lid.

Cool, green, cash money. Stacks of it. Stacks and stacks of hundred-dollar bills. Parker took them out and piled them on the table. Twenty-five thousand dollars. And under the money, at the bottom of the box, a small envelope containing a single photographic negative, and a bank deposit slip with numbers scribbled on the back.

"That slimy old son of a bitch," Parker murmured. He didn't have to know who was in the photograph to know what this was about. Blackmail.

Turning on one of his own clients. That had to be it. Lowell had put someone between a rock and a hard place and squeezed. That explained the pricey condo, the new Cadillac, the cash.

He held the negative up to the light. Two people, shot from a distance. They might have been shaking hands or exchanging something. It was impossible to tell.

The first line of numbers written on the deposit slip looked like an out-of-the-country phone number. The line of numbers below might be an account number, he guessed, and he thought back to finding the travel brochure on the floor of Lenny's office. The Cayman Islands. Lovely place to visit—or to hide money in a numbered account.

Parker put the negative and the slip back in the envelope. He asked the manager for a bank bag for the money, tagged it as evidence, and put everything in a brown paper Ralph's grocery sack he had brought in with him.

The elevator ride to the ground floor was silent. If the bank manager wondered what was going on, he didn't show it, and he didn't ask. He had probably seen cops take stranger things than money out of clients' boxes. Parker himself had once popped the lid of a suspected murderer's safe-deposit box and found a collection of mummified human fingers.

The elevator doors opened, framing a live portrait of Abby Lowell sitting on a marble bench, waiting. She had a hell of a wardrobe for a law student. Camel tweed wool suit with a slim skirt and a forties-inspired close-fitted jacket, belted at the waist with a thin band of brown crocodile. Matching shoes, matching bag. Maybe it paid to be the daughter of a blackmailer.

In one elegant move, she unfolded herself from the bench as Parker stepped out of the elevator. She looked directly at him, her expression calm but with an underlying quality of steel that had to scare the crap out of guys her own age.

"Did you find my father's papers?"

"And good morning to you, Ms. Lowell. I see you survived the night. Great suit. Prada?"

She didn't answer, but fell into step beside him as he started for the side door.

"Did you find my father's papers?" she asked again.

"In a manner of speaking."

"What does that mean?"

"Neither his will nor his life insurance policy was in the box," he said, sliding on his shades as they walked. The heels of her crocodile shoes clacked a staccato rhythm on the terrazzo floor.

"Then what do you have in that bag?"

"Evidence."

"Evidence of what? My father was the victim."

"Your father is dead," Parker said. "Anything I can find that will point to why he was killed or who killed him is evidence, as far as I'm concerned. Don't worry. You'll get it all back eventually—unless it turns out you killed him."

She snatched a breath to say something, thought better of it, tried again. Frustration knit her brow.

"What's the matter, Ms. Lowell? Can't figure out a way to ask the question without incriminating yourself?"

The doors whooshed open before them, and they stepped out into the shade of an overhang. The morning was already blindingly bright.

"I resent the implication," she said angrily. "I cared about Lenny."

"But you said yourself, he wasn't much of a father," Parker said. "When you were a kid, he dragged you along behind him like you were a piece of toilet paper stuck to the bottom of his shoe. That had to hurt. Little girls love their dads. They want to be loved back."

"I don't need to be psychoanalyzed by you," she snapped. "I pay someone quite handsomely to do that for me."

"You certainly have Beverly Hills taste, Ms. Lowell," Parker said. "Most students I know have beer budgets. Was Lenny footing the bill for your lifestyle? I wouldn't have guessed he made that kind of money defending the people he defended. Did he have some other source of income?"

"I have my own money," she said. "From my mother. Not that it's any of your business."

"Then maybe you were footing the bill for **his** lifestyle," Parker suggested. "Condo downtown, new Caddie . . ."

"And who pays for your lifestyle, Detective?" she asked pointedly. "Gucci loafers, Canali suit . . . I wouldn't have guessed you made that kind of money as a public servant."

Parker conceded the point with a tip of his head. "Touché, Ms. Lowell."

"Are you taking bribes?" she asked. "Fixing cases? Ripping off drug dealers?"

"No, but I believe your father was blackmailing someone," he said bluntly. "I just took twenty-five thousand dollars out of his safe-deposit box."

If she wasn't shocked, she was a fine actress, Parker thought. The brown eyes went wide, some of the color left her cheeks. She looked away, trying to collect herself. She covered by opening her handbag and fishing out a pair of Dior sunglasses.

"Where do you think all that money came from?" Parker asked.

He started across the parking lot, popping the trunk of his car with the remote. He didn't mention the negative, just to see if she would ask if he had found anything else in the box. But if she wondered, she was too smart to say anything.

Parker glanced at her as she followed him. "Any idea?"

"No."

"You're delusional if you think I'm a fool, Ms. Lowell." He put the paper sack in the trunk and shut the lid. "Your father is murdered and the killer calls you on your cell phone to tell you. He breaks into your apartment, tosses the place, threatens to kill you, but you claim you don't know what he's looking for. You're desperate to get into Lenny's safe-deposit box, then I find twenty-five K in the box and you claim to know nothing about it. Do you think I was dropped on my head as a child?"

She had no answer to that. She pressed an elegantly manicured hand to her lips, as she always seemed to do when a moment became too difficult for her. Her other arm banded across her stomach, holding herself.

Supporting, comforting herself, Parker thought. It was probably something she'd learned to do as a little girl while sitting as an afterthought beside her father at the racetrack. Whatever else he thought about her, he felt sorry for the lonely child she must have been.

She turned in a slow, small circle, not knowing where to go. Couldn't run, couldn't hide.

"Who was he blackmailing?" Parker asked.

"I don't believe that he was," she said, but she didn't look at him when she said it.

"Do you know a guy named Eddie Boyd Davis?"

She shook her head. She was fighting tears, fighting some internal battle Parker couldn't read.

"If you know something about this," he said, "now's the time, Abby. Bail now before it goes too far. Lenny's gone. His killer has you in his sights. A sack of money isn't worth dying for."

Her shoulders rose and fell as she let out a

slow, measured breath and composed herself again.

"Don't I pay taxes for you to serve and protect me?" she asked. "You're supposed to keep me from getting killed."

"I can't fight what I don't know, Abby."

"What don't you know?" she asked, impatient and frustrated. "Why can't you find that bike messenger?"

"I don't think the bike messenger had anything to do with it," Parker said.

"He attacked me!"

"It doesn't hold water."

"Are you calling me a liar?"

"If he killed your father for the money in the safe, why would he stick around to come and see you?" Parker asked.

"I don't know! Maybe he's just a psycho and he singled out Lenny and now me."

"That only happens in the movies, doll," Parker said. "The kid got sent to your father's office by chance. I think he was in the wrong place at the wrong time."

Even through the sunglasses he could see she was livid.

"Oh, I see," she said curtly. "He came into my home and attacked me, but he's just an innocent bystander? And I'm, what? The scheming femme fatale? Talk about fantasy. You have me cast in your own little film noir."

"It works that way," Parker said. "The way I see it is this: Lenny was blackmailing somebody and he got killed for it. And yes, I think you're in it up to your pretty little chin."

"I'd slap you if I didn't think you'd arrest me for it," she said.

"I wouldn't bother," Parker said. "If you don't come clean with this, I think I'm going to have plenty of better reasons to arrest you, Ms. Lowell."

She shook her head and looked away. "I can't believe this is happening."

"No? Well, you certainly seemed to take in stride the fact that someone beat your father's head in. I'd say you have a pretty skewed way of looking at things if you think I'm your worst problem."

She slapped him then, hard. The sting on his cheek and the ringing in his ear seemed to be one and the same.

Parker shook it off. "Well, I can't say I didn't give you permission to do that."

Her lips flattened in a line of disgust. "I am so through with you, Detective Parker."

She turned like a soldier and marched away, her crocodile bag clutched tightly under her

arm. She was parked five cars down. A blue
BMW 3 Series convertible. New. She turned
and faced him before she got in.

"Your captain will be hearing from me."

"I'm sure he'll look forward to that."

Parker watched her back out and drive away,
the first thing on her agenda to get him kicked
off the case.

"Sorry, doll," he muttered, climbing behind
the wheel of the Sebring. "Somebody already
beat you to it."

32

Parker turned in at the gates to the Paramount Studio lot and waved to the security guard.

"Good to see you, Mr. Parker."

"You too, Bill."

"You here to see Mr. Conners?"

"Not today. I need to see Chuck Ito. He's expecting me."

The guard made a note on his clipboard and waved Parker through.

Chuck Ito's office was a building toward the back of the lot. He worked as a film editor, but his hobby was still photography, and he had collected all the latest gizmos in his studio and had declared them as business expenses on his tax forms.

"Look what the cat dragged in." Ito's greeting. Parker had known him going on five years, and this was always his opening line.

"My suit takes offense at the implications of that remark," Parker said.

"So? It only speaks Italian," Ito said. "It doesn't know if I'm insulting it or not."

He checked his watch and grimaced. "We have to make this quick, Kev. I've got a meeting in ten with someone much more important than you."

Parker looked perturbed. "Who's more important than me?"

"Just about everyone."

"That's harsh."

Parker dropped into a chair and tossed the envelope from Lenny Lowell's safe-deposit box onto the desk.

Ito reached for it. "What have you got for me, Kev? Something I'll get arrested for?" He plucked the negative out and held it up to a light. "Who's in it?"

"I'd tell you, but then I'd have to kill you."

"So it's got something to do with your secret life as a woman?"

"I'm letting that slide in the interest of time," Parker said. "I'll knock you on your ass later. I need this developed ASAP."

Ito looked at him like he was stupid. "Go to the mall. They can do it in an hour."

"Or some kid making minimum wage will accidentally run it through a shredder. This is evidence in a homicide."

"Then why aren't you taking it to the LAPD lab if it's evidence?"

"You're kidding, right? I'd be lucky to get it back by Christmas, if ever. I think they have one person and he's only up to date on equipment through the tintype machine."

A mixture of truth and exaggeration. The general public has been led to believe that every crime lab in every city in the nation is just like the one on **CSI: Crime Scene Investigation,** when in truth none of them are. The great majority are understaffed, underfunded, and overloaded. In LA County, famous for making DNA evidence the talk of the world during the O. J. Simpson trial, there are three people who deal with DNA evidence. Most of the time their findings aren't even in until well after a trial is over.

Besides, Parker couldn't tell Ito he wasn't exactly supposed to have this piece of evidence. If he could get the thing developed, he could see who he was dealing with and have a bigger jump ahead of Robbery-Homicide. That was why he hadn't bagged and tagged the negative at the bank. He figured to get the thing developed, then seal it in the bag to be taken in as evidence, and no one would be the wiser.

"I need it ASAP."

"ASAP for me today is going to be more like late in the day. Dinnertime. I can have one of my assistants—"

"No. I can't have a lot of people handling this thing."

"I could go to prison for this, couldn't I?" Ito said.

Parker made a face. "Prison? Nah . . . the work farm, maybe. You don't have a record of prior convictions, do you?"

"Some friend you are," Ito said, pretending to be upset.

Parker got up and started toward the door. "It's fine," he said with a casual wave of the hand. "Just don't tell anyone you have it. If you get caught with it, I don't know you."

Blackmail. Parker stirred the word around in his mind as he drove back toward downtown. If Eddie Davis turned out to be one of the people in the photograph, then that gave Davis a strong motive to kill Lowell. If the two of them had been in on something together, one might have turned on the other out of greed. Another good motive.

Whichever way it went, Davis was after the negative. That was why he had ransacked Lenny's office, busted out the windows of his car. He would have done the same to Lowell's condo if not for the fact that it was in a secure building. It was probably Davis who had tossed Abby Lowell's place. The missing negative probably explained the implication in the note he had scrawled in lipstick on her bathroom mirror. **Next You Die** . . . If you don't give up the negative.

But there had to be more than one. Parker figured the one in the safe-deposit box would have been insurance, something Lenny could hold on to, just in case. And Parker had a hunch that the person holding them was J. C. Damon. He wondered if the kid had any idea what he had.

Parker's phone rang, breaking him out of his thoughts.

"Parker."

"Well, since you don't have any friends, I called one of mine." Andi Kelly. "There is no one named Davis in Robbery-Homicide."

"I know."

"How do you know?" She sounded offended not to have the scoop.

"Because I'm better than you are, doll."

Kelly laughed. "What bullshit."

"I know it because a witness identified Davis in a mug book this morning."

"He killed that woman last night?"

"Not my case," Parker said. "You'll have to talk to Ruiz."

"I don't like her."

"Nobody likes her," Parker said. "She's rude and abrasive and bratty. And she's not a woman's woman."

"How do you know about that? Men never get that."

"I'm in touch with my feminine side," Parker said.

"She'll sell you out for a dime and give back change," Kelly said.

"Well, there's definitely some truth in that," Parker muttered, wondering if Ruiz wasn't even at that very moment selling him out to Bradley Kyle, describing in detail every piece of paper Parker had taken with him when he'd gone.

"You're her training officer," Kelly said. "Usurp her power. Grab the case for yourself. What do you care if she hates you?"

"She already hates me."

"See?"

"Okay," Parker said with resignation. Kelly was like a Jack Russell terrier. If she wanted something, she was relentless in her pursuit. She would bite into a story and hang on, no matter what. "Yes, I like Davis for the murder last night."

"Why? What's his motive?"

"I'm still working on that," he hedged. "But it's a good bet that he went to Speed Couriers to get a line on the bike messenger."

"The bike messenger. Wasn't he a 'person of interest' last night?"

"He's still a person of interest. I just don't consider him to be a suspect. I need to get with him, talk to him, before RHD barges in and blows everything. They're taking the Lowell case."

"You're kidding. Why would they be interested?"

"That's what I'm trying to find out."

"And you'll let me know when you do?"

"You're the only pal I've got in this, Andi," Parker said seriously. "I've got bogies all around me. Don't make me think you're just using me like a cheap gigolo."

"I think you should know better, Kev," she said. "Nothing about you is cheap. I'd say I have your back, but I'd rather have your front. And I do like the idea of you playing the gigolo."

"You shameless tart."

"Yes. You know I'm pushing forty. I don't have time to mess around. Anyway, have I ever let you down?"

Parker ignored the opportunity to keep the innuendo going. "No. You haven't," he said on a sigh. "The head of Robbery-Homicide told my captain they feel the Lowell murder might relate to something they have ongoing."

Kelly was silent for long enough that Parker thought she might have lost the connection.

"And we're back to Bradley Kyle and Moose Roddick talking with Tony Giradello, your name coming up in the conversation," she said at last.

"That's right," Parker said. "I'm looking at a blackmail scheme here, Andi."

"Who versus who for what?"

"I don't know yet, but two people are already dead. And there's only one case Bradley Kyle has ongoing with stakes that high."

"Tricia Crowne-Cole."

33

Jace chained The Beast to a parking meter and went inside the bar. It was a small, dark, dank place with fishing nets and buoys and life preservers nailed to the walls. The place reeked of beer and cigarettes, blatantly defying the state's antismoking laws. A table of regulars felt free to stare with disapproval at any newcomer. They watched Jace all the way from the door to the bar.

Jace kept his head down and took a stool at the far end of the bar. He ordered a burger and a soda, ignoring his need for a good stiff belt of something to dull the physical and emotional pain.

The television that hung from the ceiling on the other end of the bar was tuned to Court TV. They were all over the Cole murder trial. Martin Gorman making a statement from a podium adorned with a bouquet of microphones. Then cut to ADA Giradello doing the very same thing in a different location.

A motion had been made by the defense to exclude any mention of Rob Cole's past—the drugs, the money, the women—on the grounds that evidence was only going to prejudice the jury. Giradello argued Cole's past should be admitted into evidence to establish a pattern of behavior. The judge ruled for the state. A serious blow to Gorman's case. He was complaining about Norman Crowne trying to buy justice, and complaining harder that it seemed to be working.

The burger arrived. Jace took a bite of it, still looking at the television. The ruling should have gone in favor of the defense, he thought. The probative value of the evidence didn't outweigh the prejudicial nature of the facts of Cole's past.

So Cole was a loser because of the drugs, the money, and the women, so what? None of that pointed to a violent offender. He had never tried to murder anyone before. There had never been any mention in the press of Cole physically abusing his wife. There was no pattern of escalating violent behavior. Jace figured if Cole had ever laid a finger on Tricia, Norman Crowne would have come down on him like a ton of bricks, and the gossip would have run like wildfire through LA.

But the ruling had gone for the prosecution,

and if that was an indicator of how the rest of the trial would go, Martin Gorman had his work cut out for him.

Gorman was probably right. Norman Crowne held tremendous sway over Los Angeles politics, and his pockets were virtually bottomless.

Jace thought back to the night he had picked up the package from Lenny. The television had been on with a report on the Cole case, and Lenny had said to him: **Martin's betting against the house in a rigged game. Money talks. Remember that.**

He wondered if Lenny knew those things because he had an inside track to information on the case, or because he was a blowhard who liked to talk himself into believing he had a more important role in the drama than he did or ever would. Maybe both.

Lenny for sure had the inside dirt on someone. The people in the negatives Jace wore taped to his belly. And what he had, what those negatives meant, was worth a lot to that person, or why bother to blackmail him or her.

Lawyers like Lenny didn't have big clients. There were no celebrities, no millionaires on his list. So if he wasn't defending the people in the negatives, then how would he know what to blackmail them for?

The only obvious choice was that someone, a

client, had let him in on something, and put him in the position to act on it.

The taped footage cut back to Giradello. He was a tough-looking son of a bitch. Not a man to cross. If Rob Cole had one brain cell in his head, he should be using it to figure out some way to avoid the ADA. Take a plea bargain. Hang himself in his jail cell. Anything.

Giradello pulled no punches in the courtroom. He went for the throat. He was going to make his chops on Rob Cole, maybe even launch his own political career from his vantage point on top of Rob Cole's bloody corpse. If he nailed Cole, he would have the undying gratitude of Norman Crowne.

Crowne and his son were asked to comment on the ruling. The old man was calm and dignified. The son, Phillip, was emotional. Ecstatic over the ruling, then melancholy about his sister, then angry with Cole, then back to melancholy. The display struck Jace as strange. He wondered if the lesser Crowne was on something.

"I think they should just leave Rob Cole alone," said one of the barflies, a peroxide blonde in a tube top, apparently so named for accentuating the tubular rolls of fat wrapped around her.

"You just want to fuck him, Adele." This

from a balding guy who had been wearing the same clothes so long, they were coming back in style.

"What's wrong with that? He's a whole lot cuter than you."

"He's a whole lot cuter than you too. I heard he's a fag. Anyway, I'm just saying, I'm sick of these celebrities thinking they can get away with murder. I hope the state fries his ass."

"They don't do that anymore, you moron. Now it's the spike. Lethal injection."

"That's too easy. When they used to strap a guy into ol' Sparky, he knew he was in for some serious pain."

"That's cruel and unusual."

"Who gives a shit? The creep is sitting in that chair because he killed somebody's kid, or wife, or whatever. Why should we make it easy on them?"

Jace tuned them out. He couldn't have cared less about Rob Cole. The guy was a loser. He couldn't act, and what was up with the lame bowling shirts?

He polished off the burger, then slid off the stool and went outside to a pay phone. He plugged in a quarter and punched in Abby Lowell's phone number. She answered on the third ring.

"Hello?"

"Ms. Lowell. You know me from yesterday in your apartment."

Silence. Then finally, "Yes?"

"I have something I think you might want. A package with some negatives in it."

"I don't know what you're talking about."

"Let's not play games," Jace said. "I've got the negatives your dad was using to blackmail someone."

She said nothing to that, but the silence seemed charged and heavy.

"I don't want them," Jace said. "They're nothing but trouble to me."

"What makes you think I want them?" she asked.

"Maybe you don't. Maybe I should give them to the cops."

Silence.

"They're worth money to somebody. I'm giving you first crack."

Another long silence passed. Finally, she said, "How much?"

"Ten thousand."

"That's a lot of money."

"No, it isn't. But I want out of this, and that's what I'll take for it."

Jace waited.

"Where and when?"

"Meet me at Pershing Square at five-fifteen. Come alone."

Jace hung up the phone and stood there, staring at nothing. The sun beat down on daily life in this nothing part of town. Cars drove past. People walked up and down. Signs in store windows advertised sales in two languages.

He had just set the stage for himself to commit extortion.

If Abby Lowell was in on the blackmail, she would pay to get the negatives and buy his silence. If he played it right, Jace could take her money—payback for Eta's family, and maybe a little insurance for himself and Tyler in case they had to get out of town. He could turn the cops on Abby; through her, the cops could get to Predator and that would be the end of it. He hoped.

All he needed was a little luck.

Lenny Lowell's voice echoed in the back of his mind: **It's better to be lucky than good, kid.**

34

Tyler ran straight to the fish market after his escape from Detective Parker. He found Madame Chen in her office, crying silently. When she saw his face peering into the room from behind the door, she swiped a tissue beneath her eyes and pulled herself together. Tyler had never seen her cry. It made him feel even more afraid than he already was.

"What's wrong?" he asked, creeping farther and farther into the room.

"I'm fine, little mouse. A moment of weakness only makes us see how strong we really are."

"Jace left," Tyler said.

"I know. We spoke for a long time last night."

Tyler didn't tell her that he'd heard most of it because he had been hiding in the broom closet. He knew Madame Chen would disapprove.

"I asked him not to go," Madame Chen said. "He thinks it is better his way. He wants to protect us, to solve his problem on his own."

"I don't like his way," Tyler said. He perched himself on the straight chair beside the desk, his knees tucked up against his chest. "What if he never comes back?"

"He will come back for you."

"Not if something bad happens and he gets killed or goes to jail or something."

"This is true," she said. "But bad things can happen anywhere, Tyler. We have no control of such things. We can only pray for good things."

"I don't believe in praying," Tyler said. "I've prayed lots of times, and nothing I ever asked for came true. I don't think God was listening."

"We must think positive thoughts, then," Madame Chen said. "We must center ourselves and think of gathering our chi into a ball and holding it tight in the center of us. Perhaps we can make a light so brilliant, it will guide JayCee back to us safely."

Tyler thought about that. He was more comfortable with the idea of the positive energy of chi. He had researched it in articles on the Internet, and had spoken about it at length with Grandfather Chen. It seemed a much more tangible, logical, scientific thing than believing in an invisible man who lived in the clouds and never answered any of Tyler's prayers. Chi was within him, he could control it. He found it ironic that Madame Chen's sour, angry nephew was called Chi. There was nothing positive about him.

It was the negative forces of energy in the world that frightened Tyler. No one could control anyone else's energy, particularly a little kid. Not even if he did have an IQ of 168.

"What are you thinking, little mouse?"

Tyler looked at her for a moment, trying to decide what he wanted to say. He had so many feelings swirling around inside of him, and he didn't know how to control all of them at once. If he tried to corral his fear for his brother, then his fear of Children and Family Services popped up. If he tried to conquer the anger he felt at Jace for leaving him, the fear of the uncertainty of his future popped up.

Finally, he simply said in a shaky voice, "I'm scared."

And then he was angry with himself for being such a baby.

"I know," Madame Chen said. "I am frightened too. We must all get through this together. Your brother is a good person. He has a good heart. True and brave. He will do the right thing, and he will come home to us. That is the only thing we should believe, Tyler. To worry about things that have not yet happened is to waste our energy for nothing."

"Yes, ma'am," Tyler said, wondering how he

was supposed to do that. There was a small garden on the roof of the building, tended to by Grandfather Chen. This was where he and Grandfather Chen went through the movements of tai chi every morning. Maybe, Tyler thought, he would go up there and Grandfather Chen would sit with him and they could meditate together.

A knock sounded at the office door, and Chi stuck his ugly head in without invitation. Tyler wondered if he had been listening in like he had the night before. Madame Chen gave him her sternest look.

"Chi, I know your mother taught you manners. What have you done with them? Thrown them out with the old fish heads? I should not have to scold you like a child when you are a grown man. Never open a door until you are asked in."

"I'm sorry, Aunt," he said without remorse. "There are more police detectives here to see you."

"Tell them I will be right out."

"Actually, they're right here behind me."

Madame Chen glared at her nephew, and said in Chinese, "Sometimes I think you are an apple full of worms, Chi."

The door swung fully open then, and Chi was herded into the room by the two men behind him. One was very large and frightening, with a flattop haircut and black-framed glasses. The other one looked like any businessman, except that his suit coat was a little too big in the shoulders. Like maybe he had borrowed it from a larger man.

Tyler didn't like the look in that one's eyes. He wanted to hop out of his chair and scurry out of the office to disappear into one of his hiding spaces. But when he slid out of the chair and started to inch his way to the door, the big man blocked his exit.

"Mrs. Chen—" the other one started.

"You may call me Madame Chen," she said in a frosty tone as she rose from her chair.

"**Madame** Chen," he tried again. "I'm Detective Kyle, and this is my partner, Detective Roddick. We're with the LAPD Robbery-Homicide Division. We'd like to ask you some questions about your car."

"Another one about the car," Chi commented.

Kyle turned to him. "Another?"

Madame Chen snapped a look at her nephew. "Chi, you may go now."

He tried to look smug, as if he was certain she wouldn't dress him down in front of these men. "I just thought I could—"

"Go. Now," she said firmly. Then in Chinese she said that he was a thorn in her side and if he didn't change his attitude she would pluck out the thorn and be rid of him.

Chi's face darkened, and he left the room looking humiliated and angry. Once again, Tyler tried to slip out, and once again the big guy blocked him.

Detective Kyle turned toward him. "And who are you?"

"I don't have to talk to you," Tyler said. "I'm just a kid."

"I only asked for your name. Is there some reason you think you might get in trouble for talking to me?"

"No, sir. I just don't like you, that's all."

"Tyler!" Madame Chen exclaimed. "Do not speak to anyone that way! How rude."

"I was only telling the truth."

"Telling the truth is a good thing, young man," Kyle said in a phony, patronizing tone. "So who are you?"

Tyler gave the man his most stubborn look.

"He is my son," Madame Chen announced.

The cops looked from Madame Chen to Tyler and back.

"Adopted," she amended.

The detectives looked at Tyler again. Eyes

wide and innocent, he started to rattle off his opinion of the two detectives in flawless Mandarin.

The detectives stared at him, then looked at each other. Madame Chen was trying not to laugh at what he was saying, the reprimand she delivered in Chinese losing all of its edge. Tyler started to giggle.

"Leave us now, Tyler," she said. "The gentlemen need to see me alone."

Dismissed, Tyler slipped out the office door and nearly ran into Chi, who had clearly been eavesdropping again.

Tyler looked up at his sour face. "Did you need something, Chi? I can go tell Madame Chen you're waiting for her."

"Why don't you mind your own business?" Chi said in a low voice. "I have more right to be here than you."

"Not today," Tyler said. "You are only a nephew. I am Madame Chen's adopted son. Didn't you hear that through the door?"

"Don't get comfortable with that idea," Chi warned. "Maybe it won't be long before you are gone from here. Your brother is a criminal. And when he goes to prison, people from Social Services will come and take you away. I'll make sure of that."

Tyler's worst nightmare. The fear and the

anger bubbled up inside his head, and into his throat. He wanted to cry. He wanted to scream. Instead, he hauled back and kicked Chi's shinbone as hard as he could.

Chi let out a yelp of pain, then a bunch of curse words, as he grabbed Tyler by the shoulders, his thick fingers digging in.

Tyler screamed as loudly as he could. "Don't hurt me! Don't beat me!"

The office door flew open and the two cops came out just as Chi started to shake him.

Madame Chen shouted, "Chi! What is the matter with you? Let him go!"

The cops didn't let him have any other option. The big one grabbed hold of Chi and yanked him backward as Kyle grabbed hold of Tyler and pulled him back.

Tyler crumpled into a little ball on the floor, sobbing.

The big cop slammed Chi up against the wall face-first, handcuffed him, and started to pat him down for weapons.

Madame Chen crouched down by Tyler and tried to comfort him in Chinese. Tyler sat up and let her put her arms around him. He pretended to be shaking with fear, hiccupping and trying to stop crying.

Madame Chen asked him if he was hurt. He shook his head no.

The big cop was reading Chi his rights. Madame Chen glared up at her nephew and told him in no uncertain terms he was a disgrace to the family. Tyler looked at Chi, made a face, and stuck out his tongue.

"I didn't do anything to him!" Chi exclaimed. "The little shit kicked me!"

Madame Chen marched over, reached up, grabbed her nephew's ear, and gave it a twist, all the while shouting at him in Chinese. Tyler had never seen her so angry.

"Ma'am," Detective Kyle said, trying to gently draw her away from Chi. "We'll take care of it. We'll take care of him."

"Good!" she said, still glaring at Chi. "Perhaps he will learn something in prison. A trade perhaps, which he can use when he gets out."

"You always favor them over me!" Chi shouted. "I am your family! I am your flesh and blood! I deserve—"

Furious, Madame Chen cut him off, going at him with more rapid-fire Chinese. The detectives looked at each other, frustrated by their inability to understand the words being exchanged. The one named Kyle looked down at Tyler.

"Can you tell us what they're saying? What did he mean when he said, 'You always favor them over me'?"

"Sometimes Chi is paranoid and de-lusion-al," Tyler said, rubbing at his sore shoulder. "You can look that up if you don't know what it is. I have a dictionary."

"I know what it is," Kyle said. "Why would you know about those things?"

"Because I'm smart, and I have an in-sa-tia-ble desire to learn new things."

Kyle didn't quite know what to say about that. Instead, he changed subjects. "Are you hurt? Do you need to go to the hospital?"

Tyler shook his head.

"Has this happened before? Has he hurt you before?"

"No. He didn't hurt me now either."

"Because you can tell me," Kyle said in that same condescending tone of voice he had used before. "You won't ever have to worry about him hurting you again."

"Are you going to put him in prison?" Tyler asked bluntly. "I don't think you should. He runs the fish market. He kind of needs to be here."

"We'll see," Kyle said. "He's going to jail right now."

"He's a liar and a troublemaker," Tyler said. "You should know that up front. You can't believe **anything** he says."

It was one thing to get Chi in trouble, sending him to jail was something else. Who knew what he might tell the police?

"He really didn't hurt me," Tyler said. "And I did kick him first."

"Why did you do that, son?" Kyle asked.

Tyler bristled a little at the word **son.** "Because he says mean things just to hurt people's feelings."

"He hurt your feelings? What did he say?"

"That he has more right to be here than I do because I'm adopted. But I don't think you should put him in jail for that."

"Child abuse is a crime," Kyle lectured, as if Tyler was slow-witted. "We have to take him in. And someone from Children and Family Services will probably come and talk to you."

Tyler looked up at Madame Chen, eyes wide.

"There is no need for any of this," she said to Kyle.

"Ma'am, if a child is in danger in his environment—"

"He is not in danger. Chi manages the fish market, he has little interaction with Tyler. There has been no incident such as this before, nor will it ever happen again. I have no interest in pressing charges."

"You don't have to, ma'am. The county and the state look out for the rights of children."

"I look out for my rights. And for the rights of my family," Madame Chen said firmly. "I neither need nor want help from you. What happened was an aberration. Familial rivalry, if you will. This is a family issue. There is no need to further burden the court system with a family squabble that was finished in five seconds.

"Is this the kind of case with which you fill your calendar, Detective Kyle?" she asked. "I was of the impression you are interested only in the big cases, the murders. Are there no murders for you to see to?"

"Uh, well, yes, ma'am," Kyle stammered.

"I assume you did not come here to arrest my nephew."

"No, ma'am."

"Then enough of this," Madame Chen declared. "You are costing me money and wasting all of our time. If you arrested every person who spoke harshly to a child, the prisons would be overflowing."

Kyle and Roddick looked at each other.

"Time is wasting," Madame Chen said impatiently.

Roddick watched Kyle for a signal. Kyle shrugged his shoulders and shook his head. "Fine, you're right, ma'am. We may have all overreacted."

Dealing with Chi was apparently more bother than it was worth. The big man undid

Chi's handcuffs. Chi rubbed at his wrists, sulking. Madame Chen told him to go back to work to earn his way back into her good graces.

"And for what reason did you come here in the first place, Detectives?" she asked.

"We have reason to believe your car might have been used in the commission of a crime. We'd like to take a look."

Madame Chen gave them a perturbed look. "Now I see how my tax dollars are wasted. The detective here before you already looked at the car. I told him it had been damaged in a parking lot. He insisted on taking it anyway. Then more police officers came, and they towed it away. And now I am an aging woman with no mode of transportation."

"What other detective came here first?" Kyle asked.

"Detective Parker," she said. "The car is gone. Perhaps you should talk to him as to its whereabouts."

Kyle went down the narrow hall and out the side door. There was no sign of a Mini Cooper.

"Detective Parker seems like a very nice man," Madame Chen commented. "Courteous, thorough, very well-dressed. I was angry with him for taking my car, but he was only doing his job. I have nothing to hide," she said, pulling

Tyler closer to her side, an arm around his shoulders.

Kyle ignored her. The muscles in his face flexed and tightened. He wasn't a happy man.

"Do you happen to know a young man named J. C. Damon?"

Madame Chen didn't blink. "Why would I know this person?"

"Maybe you've seen him in the vicinity. Early twenties, blond hair, blue eyes. He works as a bike messenger."

"I am a busy woman, in my office most of the time."

None of what she was saying was exactly a lie, nor was it exactly the truth. Tyler stood by her side looking as innocent as a lamb.

"How about you, son?" Kyle asked.

"You really shouldn't talk down to me, sir," Tyler said politely. "You might be embarrassed to find out I have an IQ of one sixty-eight."

The cops looked at each other again.

"Thank you for your time, ma'am," Kyle said. "We may call on you again once your car has been processed for evidence."

He took one long look at Tyler, at the blue eyes and the blond hair. Tyler held his breath. The detectives started toward the door.

Boo Zhu hurried from inside the warehouse

to the edge of the loading dock. He looked like Humpty Dumpty, Tyler had always thought. The bright sun made him squint like a mole. He turned one way and then the other.

"I know! I know!" he said excitedly, his thick tongue sticking out of his mouth. "I know JayCee!"

35

Parker left the Sebring in a red zone in front of the restaurant and went inside. The place was so dimly lit, for an instant he thought he'd gone blind. Then his eyes adjusted and he saw Diane, looking at her watch as she sat in a corner booth. The restaurant was at the front end of a nightclub that had been a swinging place in the days of the Rat Pack. It had never been redecorated. Most of the clientele in the main room had blue hair.

Once a month or so Diane met him there for lunch. The food was decent, it was quiet, and no one from either of their professions ever came there. They both preferred to keep their private lives private. Their monthly lunches were like little oases amid the chaos of their daily lives. Nice respites.

Parker kissed her cheek and apologized for keeping her waiting.

"I went ahead and ordered," she said, gesturing to the chopped salad on his side of the table. "Your usual."

"Perfect. Thanks." He slid into the booth, heaved a big sigh, and tried to idle the motor down. He was revving into high gear now. Things were happening. Time was short.

"It's been a hell of a day so far," he said, and proceeded to fill her in on the latest troop movements of the Evil Empire: Robbery-Homicide.

"They'll never give you a break, Kev," she said, picking at her salad.

"No, they never will. And you know what? Fuck 'em. I'll make my own breaks. If I can just stay ahead of them for a day or so . . ."

"You think you're that close to solving it?" she asked. Her elbows rested on the tabletop. She propped her head in one hand, looking drained.

Parker leaned across the table. "Are you all right?"

She rallied and brightened as if she'd just increased the volume on her energy level. Her mouth curved up at one corner. "I'm tired. All that social carousing and skulduggery I did for you last night. And I didn't even get a thank-you orgasm for my trouble."

"I'll make it up to you."

"Yeah, yeah, yeah . . . That's what you all say," she said with a wry smile.

"Yeah, but I've got the goods to back it up, baby," Parker said in his sexiest voice. One of the blue-haired ladies in the booth behind Diane leaned over to get a better angle for her eavesdropping. Parker caught her eye and winked at her.

Diane shook her head. "You're shameless."

Parker grinned. "Yes, I am. Aren't you glad?"

"I am." She poked the tines of her fork at a piece of shredded chicken. "So have you figured out who a guy like Lenny Lowell could possibly know who would be worth blackmailing?"

"Not yet, but I'm this close," he said, pinching a thumb and forefinger together. "And I ran off with the murder book, so it'll take Kyle and Roddick a while to catch up."

"This really must tie in to something big, for them to go to all this trouble with you."

"Their captain told my captain it relates to something they have ongoing. I can't connect the dots yet, but there's only one name that keeps coming to mind. Tricia Crowne-Cole."

Diane straightened in her seat. "What? Rob Cole killed his wife," she said firmly. "How could this possibly have anything to do with that? Are you delusional?"

"Somebody has been paying somebody else a lot of money to keep a secret."

"You don't even know that for certain."

"Actually, I do know that for certain."

"Rob Cole killed his wife," she said again. "You weren't there, Kevin. You didn't see what he did to her. It was personal, vicious—"

"She had other people in her life. The daughter, who might have been fucking her husband. The brother, who had to live in the shadow of perfect sister Tricia—"

Diane ticked her points off on her fingers. "Rob Cole is the one who's been indicted, the one going on trial, the one with no alibi and plenty of motive—"

"Tony Giradello could have a Pop-Tart indicted if he wanted—"

"Give me a break, Parker! There's no way Giradello goes forward with a trial this high-profile if he can't make it stick. He's still got egg on his face from the last time. The jury will be seated in a week. He's crossed every **t** and dotted every **i**, run every test, lined up every expert witness."

"Well, he's getting plenty of help with that, courtesy of Norman Crowne, isn't he?"

"And now you're a conspiracy nut! What have you been smoking?"

"Come on, Diane. You've said it yourself: It looks like Norman Crowne is buying justice. Who's to say he isn't buying silence too?"

"Tricia was the apple of his eye," she said.

"He couldn't have loved her more. There's no way he would pay to protect someone involved with her death."

"Even if that someone was his own grand-daughter?" Parker asked. "You know as well as I do, people will do incredible things in the name of love."

"I know that. I know that. But you are so off the mark here. You're seeing zebras. Rob Cole killed his wife."

"Well, we'll know for certain by tonight," Parker said. "I stole a negative out of Lowell's safe-deposit box, where he also had a whole lot of cash stashed. It's being developed as we speak. I don't think it's a baby picture of his daughter." He checked his watch and grimaced. He hadn't taken three bites of his salad, but hunger meant nothing to him now. Physical hunger had been swallowed up by the hunger to finish the hunt. The satisfaction would carry him for days.

"I've got to go," he said, digging bills out of his wallet. "As much as I love to see you get your back up, we'll have to finish this argument later."

Diane shoved her salad away and sat back, pouting.

"My God, you're gorgeous when you're pissed off," Parker said, sliding out of the booth. He bent and kissed her cheek. "Look, maybe I am way off the mark—"

"You are."

"I know Robbie is the guy you love to hate, doll, but you know what they say at the race-track: Only suckers bet the favorite."

She just stared at him, brows lowered.

"I'm not rooting against you," Parker said. "I'm rooting for me. If this plays out, I win. Do you hate Rob Cole more than you love me?"

Her face softened then, and she gave him a grudging smile. "I'll put a few bucks on you, long shot."

"You won't be sorry."

"We'll see."

"Are you scheduled to work later?" he asked. "Maybe you should call in. Take the day, get some rest."

"I'm off," she said. "Just doing some errands. The bank, the store . . ."

"I'll call you." Parker turned to go.

"Kev?"

Diane slid out of the booth as he turned toward her. She gave him a hug and whispered, "I'm sorry."

He stood back and smiled. "You're passionate. That's nothing to be sorry for."

The gorgeous winter-blue eyes glazed with a

very uncharacteristic sheen of tears. "I do love you, you know."

The old ladies in the next booth were staring openly, as enthralled as if they were at a dinner theater.

Parker couldn't have been more surprised if she'd hit him with a hammer. The **L** word. He grinned and made a joke because he was so stunned, he didn't know what else to do. "Why, Ms. Nicholson," he said, batting his eyelashes, "you've made me giddy."

She smiled and shook her head and waved him off. "Get out of here, you idiot."

Diane Nicholson loved him. He wasn't quite sure how he was supposed to take that. She loved him as a friend? He knew that. She loved him as in **loved** him? Hell of a time to have that sprung on him, Parker thought, though not with any rancor. Maybe his karma was turning around after all.

If he could close this case, make a big splash, he'd have the world by the tail.

He called Joanie at Latent and left a message asking her to look for Eddie Davis's name and address in the Rolodex that had been taken from Lowell's office and sent to Latent to be examined for fingerprints, to do it ASAP and then call him on his cell phone.

He had told Ruiz to check Davis out, but Parker didn't see himself calling her to ask if she had the info yet. Kyle and Roddick were sure to have been there by now. The hornet's nest had been well stirred, and he had no doubt she would be crawling all over Bradley Kyle.

Parker pulled the car over into the patch of dirt that served as a parking lot for a tiny Mexican joint in a weedy, dusty, semi-industrial part of town near the Los Angeles River. Dan Metheny had eaten lunch at this place every day Parker worked with him. Clearly Metheny had seen no reason to change that habit over the years.

He sat at one of the picnic tables beneath the corrugated tin overhang, a plate of fat and cholesterol in front of him. He watched Parker through silver-mirrored shades. In all the time Parker had known him, he had seen Metheny's eyes maybe twice.

"Hey, **GQ**," the old man said. "You here to show us common folk how to dress?"

Metheny had been on the job for about a hundred and twelve years, or so it seemed. A big, barrel-chested black (Metheny's own choice of words) man who ate too much red meat, drank too much bourbon, and smoked two packs a day. The stress of working South Central should have killed him, but he kept marching on. Too mean to die.

"I **am** the common folk," Parker said, taking the seat opposite.

"Kid, there's never been anything common about you. That's why everybody hates you."

"Well, that's good to know."

"Fuck 'em," Metheny growled. "It's lonely at the top."

"I wouldn't know. I've been spending all my time a few rungs down the ladder, getting shit on by the monkeys above me."

"Quit feeling sorry for yourself. Giradello would've had you working parking meters if he could have. But you're still a detective. You're still on the job. And you look like a goddam movie star. You've got nothing to whine about."

"Robbery-Homicide just yanked my murder away from me, and I have a trainee who would sooner stab me in the back with a stiletto heel than look at me."

"This chick Ruiz?" Metheny said around a mouthful of enchilada.

"Yeah."

"I asked a couple of guys I know working Latin gangs, and they never heard of her. I guess they could have forgot."

Parker shook his head. "Believe me, this one

doesn't go unnoticed. They would have remembered."

"Have you seen her personnel jacket?"

"It looks fine. I tried to call her last supervisor, but I was told the guy died. She probably cut out his heart and ate it as he bled to death at her feet."

Metheny was silent for a moment, thinking, all the lines of his bulldog face bending downward, accentuated by his thick salt-and-pepper Fu Manchu mustache.

"Dude, I don't like this," he said at last. "You know Alex Navarro? Alex knows every damn thing that goes on with the Latin gangs. If he doesn't know this chick, she wasn't there."

"So who the hell is she?" Parker asked. "And why is she riding around with me?"

Now he felt even more like he was being backed into a corner. Robbery-Homicide taking his case, Ruiz suddenly not who he thought she was.

"Could be she used a different name then," Metheny said. "You know how those undercover spooks are. They 'immerse' themselves in their roles," he said with a certain amount of disdain.

Metheny was an old-time cop from the kick-ass-and-take-names school. Everything was black or white for him. There were good guys and there were bad guys. He hit the streets armed with the law and about nine concealed weapons not approved of by the ACLU. A warrior for justice.

"Maybe," Parker conceded grudgingly, but he didn't believe it.

"Flush her out and call her bluff, man."

"Yeah."

There was nothing else to do. Parker knew he couldn't trust Ruiz. He might as well find out why. Find out how many enemies he really had.

He was already questioning the timing of it all. Ruiz had come on just days before the Lowell murder, and now she was selling him out to Robbery-Homicide, and Robbery-Homicide was taking the case for themselves. But how—even with the inside scoop on the blackmail—could anyone have known Lenny Lowell was going to be murdered?

He didn't like any of the possible explanations. He tried to tell himself he was being paranoid and building conspiracies where none existed. Only the killer could have predicted Lowell's death, and no one could have predicted who would be up on the board to take the case.

Metheny was watching him, watching the

thought process and the subtle changes in his face that went along with it.

"There's no such thing as coincidence, man," Metheny said. "Not with Robbery-Homicide. Those dudes don't saddle up for no reason."

"It doesn't make sense that Ruiz is connected to them," Parker said. "What would they need her for when they could take the case anytime they wanted?"

"Then what does make sense?" Metheny asked. "I once knew a guy who did giant chainsaw wood carvings from tree trunks. They were pretty damn good. He had this one of a moose. Looked just like a damn moose. You could practically smell it. I asked him how he did that, and he said to me, 'I start with a big hunk of tree trunk, and I carve away everything that doesn't look like a moose.'

"Chip away everything this mess couldn't be, and you're left with the truth. If Ruiz isn't who she says she is, then who is she? If she's not some kind of RHD spy, what's left?"

A sick, watery feeling trickled through Parker's body. He'd only ridden with Ruiz for a matter of days. She irritated him so badly, he hadn't paid much attention to what she was all about besides being a pain in the ass. But she'd known about his Jag, and she'd known about his loft, and she had commented more than once on the price of his wardrobe, and how easily he parted with money.

"What's left?" Metheny asked.

The words were sour in Parker's mouth. "Internal Affairs."

know JayCee!" Boo Zhu said, his tiny eyes bright with excitement. He laughed and snorted. His nose was running. Instead of wiping it, his abnormally long tongue swept across his upper lip.

"JayCee Ty! JayCee Ty!" Boo Zhu looked proudly at Chi, who was standing to one side on the dock trying to look as if he hadn't had a hand in Boo Zhu's announcement.

Detective Kyle turned to Madame Chen, standing just outside the doorway to the other part of the building. In the bright light she looked as pale as the white clapboard behind her.

"Who is this?" Kyle asked.

"The son of a cousin," Madame Chen said, crossing the small parking area. "He is challenged, as you can see."

Kyle looked up at him. "What's your name?"

"Boo Zhu! Boo Zhu know!"

"You know J. C. Damon?" Kyle asked.

Boo Zhu began to dance with all the grace of a bear, beside himself with pride that he had the answer to a question no one else seemed to have.

"Boo Zhu likes to please," said Madame Chen.

"Are you saying he doesn't know what he's talking about?"

"He knows that it will please you to say what he believes you want to hear." She flashed a glare at Chi. "He will tell you he knows the president if you ask him."

"JayCee Ty! JayCee Ty, ma'am!" Boo Zhu said, pointing a stubby finger toward the door to the office. "Yes, ma'am? Yes?"

Tyler darted back from the doorway. His heart was galloping so fast, he thought he might faint. Carefully, he dropped to the floor on his knees and crawled along the wall to the open window, then slowly raised his head until he could just see over the edge of the sill at the side of the window.

"Calm yourself, Boo Zhu," said Madame Chen.

"I good boy!"

"You're very good," Kyle said. "You know the answer, don't you?"

"Detective, please," said Madame Chen. "He is only a child in his mind. He doesn't understand."

"Who's Ty?" Kyle asked.

"Ty R! Ty R!" Boo Zhu exclaimed.

"Tyler?"

"Ty R, JayCee!"

"J. C. Damon?"

Boo Zhu had begun to sing a nonsense song to dance to, his euphoria blocking out all else.

Kyle turned to Chi. "What about you? Do you know J. C. Damon?"

Tyler's eyes filled with tears. He was so afraid, he thought he might wet his pants like a baby.

"If you don't already know this," Kyle said, "J. C. Damon is wanted for questioning in relation to a homicide, among other crimes. If you're protecting him, you're harboring a criminal. If he used your vehicle in the commission of a crime, you can be charged as an accessory."

Chi stared for a moment at his aunt. When he spoke, he spoke in Chinese. "You cannot risk yourself and the business, Aunt. Lying to the police is a serious offense."

"So is betrayal of family," Madame Chen returned.

"He is not family."

"You betray me, Chi. If you do this thing, I do not know you. I will not know you."

"We can go downtown," Kyle said. "I can get an interpreter. If I believe you're withholding information, you can be detained as material witnesses."

Madame Chen turned on him. "Do you think me a fool, Detective Kyle? I am an intelligent woman in two languages. You are a bully in only one. I am calling my attorney, who, as it happens, is the attorney for my business and for my family, including my nephew."

"You can't stop your nephew from talking to us," Kyle said. He turned again to Chi. "Do you know J. C. Damon?"

Chi looked at his aunt.

Tyler held his breath.

"I defer to my aunt's wisdom," Chi said humbly, bowing his head. "As matriarch of our family, she knows best. It is her wish we consult with our attorney."

Kyle turned once again to Boo Zhu, still locked in his own little world of bliss, singing to himself. "Boo Zhu? You know J. C. Damon?"

"This is outrageous!" Madame Chen said. "You will stop this immediately!"

"Yes," said Boo Zhu, but his smile of pride melted on his round face as he looked at Madame Chen. "Ty R bother? Yes, ma'am?"

Kyle ignored Madame Chen. "Tyler is J.C.'s brother?"

Boo Zhu looked at Madame Chen, his face mottling red as he began to worry he had done something wrong. "Yes, ma'am. Yes?"

Kyle turned to his partner. "Where's the kid?"

"He went inside."

"I want him out here. Now."

The big detective started toward the office.

Tyler bolted like a rabbit. On television the cops did all kinds of things they weren't supposed to do. Jace had always told him he couldn't trust them. He couldn't trust anyone but family. The life he knew depended on it.

Like a shot, he was down the hall and up the stairs. He ran like a whirlwind through the apartment, grabbed his backpack, grabbed the walkie-talkie Jace had given him.

He ran out of the apartment and up the last of the stairs, to the roof. The garden was empty. Grandfather Chen had gone to meet his cronies for their daily gossip.

Tyler crept on his belly to the edge of the roof, and looked down on the scene. The lot was empty. Only Boo Zhu remained, sitting on the edge of the loading dock, rocking himself and wailing.

Tyler felt bad for him. There was no doubt in his mind Chi had put Boo Zhu up to it, telling him everyone would be happy and proud of him if he told the policemen he knew Jace. Now Boo Zhu was upset and frightened. He wouldn't understand why everyone hadn't been delighted by his revelation. Or why Chi had abandoned him.

His heart pounding against his ribs like a hammer, Tyler strained to hear footsteps or voices below him, on the stairs or in the apartment. Maybe they were still looking for him downstairs. He would wait. Count to a hundred, maybe. When he could hear them getting close to the roof, he would go to the ground.

He swiped a hand across his face to brush away the tears that panic had brought to his eyes.

One hundred, ninety-nine, ninety-eight . . .

What if he didn't hear them coming? His pulse was pounding in his ears.

Ninety-seven, ninety-six, ninety-five . . .

Could they hold **him** as a material witness? In jail?

Ninety-four, ninety-three . . .

Would they call Children and Family Services right away?

Ninety-two . . .

If they took his walkie-talkie, he wouldn't be able to reach Jace.

Ninety-one.

If CFS took him, Jace would never be able to find him. Ever.

The tears beginning to come faster, Tyler scrambled back from the edge of the roof, ran to the other side of the building, and started down the fire escape. The iron was rusted. Some of the connections to the building were loose, the old bolts sheared off. It could hold Tyler's weight because he was small, but it rattled and shook, and he hoped no one could hear it.

His feet moved as fast as they could. He was quick, but he was scared, and fear caused mistakes. He stubbed the thick rubber toe of his sneaker and stumbled once, grabbing at the railing as he fell, scraping his knuckles, banging his elbow, then catching hold.

The last part of the escape was a ladder pulled up a dozen feet from the ground to stop people from climbing the stairs from below. Tyler grabbed hold with both hands and tried to force it down, but he wasn't strong enough, and it didn't move.

Without stopping to think about the danger, he climbed like a monkey to the other side of the ladder, the ground a long way below him. He would have been scared if he'd had time to look. Hanging on above his head with both hands, he jumped up and down on the rung below him. The ladder dropped a couple of inches, a couple of inches, then shot downward to its full length so fast, it took his breath away, then stopped so abruptly that Tyler kept falling, his momentum yanking his hands away from the ladder.

He fell the last five feet and hit the ground with a thud on his backside, his breath leaving him in one big huff.

Rolling over onto his hands and knees, Tyler pushed to his feet and braced himself against the brick wall until the earth stopped tilting beneath him.

The cops had gone inside. The alley was the only way to go. If he turned to the right, he would be on the street quickly, but he didn't trust that there wouldn't be a police car waiting. That was the direction the black-and-white cop car had come from earlier. If he turned left, he would have to dash past the lot. If Detective Kyle had come back outside . . . or Chi . . .

He turned left and crept along the back of the building, peering carefully around when he reached the corner. The lot and the loading dock were empty except for Boo Zhu, still lost in his misery. Tyler took three deep breaths and ran across the opening as fast as he could. He ducked behind the stack of wooden pallets where the other detective had found him. Detective Parker.

Tyler wondered why Kyle and Roddick had come and asked the same questions all over again. They hadn't even known the Mini Cooper had been taken away. Maybe they weren't real cops. Maybe they were bad guys. Maybe they had killed the guy Jace had been accused of killing.

Whoever they were, Tyler didn't like them. Parker had seemed like a nice guy, even if he was a cop. Kyle was just what Madame Chen had called him—a bully.

Sticking against the buildings like a tick, Tyler moved down the alley to the parking lot where Parker had caught him. He retraced his route down the narrow space between the two buildings, where Parker had lost him. His backpack scraped against the sides here and there.

At the opening to the sidewalk, Tyler crouched down and looked back toward the fish market. People were walking up and down the street. No one noticed him in the narrow opening, half hidden by a chalkboard sign advertising the specials of the day at the dim sum shop.

He saw Kyle and Roddick step out onto the sidewalk, making the people flow around them like a stream around boulders. They were dis-

cussing something, arms gesticulating. Kyle
pulled a cell phone out of his pocket and started
a conversation with someone on the other
end. Roddick planted his hands on his hips,
turned and looked down the street, directly—it
seemed—at Tyler.

Tyler held his breath. A thin woman with
long dark hair and movie-star sunglasses was
coming down the sidewalk walking a roly-poly
pug dog. The dog's bug eyes spotted Tyler and
bulged even larger. His nails scraped the sidewalk as he strained at the end of his leash, barking, trying to pull his owner closer to the dim
sum sign.

The woman frowned and tugged at the leash.
"Orson, no!"

Roddick was still staring down the street.

Orson the Pug kept barking. Tyler tried to
shush him. The thin woman spotted him then,
and hopped back, startled. Tyler stared up at
her with imploring eyes and a finger pressed to
his lips.

Roddick took a couple of steps, then Kyle
said something and stuck the phone back in the
pocket of his suit coat. They went to a car
parked in front of a fire hydrant and got in.

The woman with Orson the Pug dismissed
Tyler as unimportant, and kept walking. Orson
tried to linger, but had to give in to the leash

and move on. The detectives pulled into traffic and drove past without looking.

Tyler let his breath out in one big puff. His head swam and big spots swirled before his eyes. He leaned sideways against the building to his right and wondered how long it would take for his heart to stop going a hundred miles an hour.

He pulled his backpack off and dug around in the front pocket for the walkie-talkie.

"Scout to Ranger. Scout to Ranger. Do you read me?"

Nothing.

"Scout to Ranger. Are you out there, Ranger?"

Silence.

Tyler pressed the radio against his cheek and closed his eyes. The rush of urgency and excitement had bottomed out, and now a dark, oily kind of fear crept in to take its place. A kind of fear that made his stomach hurt and made him wish he weren't too big to crawl into a warm lap and feel strong, protecting arms around him.

The safety he had felt with the Chens was gone. Just like that, his home, his only family, had been found out and threatened. The only other safety he had ever known in his life was with his brother. Suddenly he had neither.

He had never felt so alone in his life.

He stared out at the street, where everyone

else was going on with their day, unaware that he was alone and afraid, and maybe nothing in his life would ever be the same.

Why am I me, instead of that guy delivering packages across the street? Why am I me, instead of that woman pushing the shopping cart? Why am I me, instead of that man getting out of his car?

He drove Jace crazy when he asked questions like that. **Why am I me, instead of someone else?** Why was this his life? No mother, no father. Why was the family he knew someone else's family? Jace told him there was no sense wondering things like that, but Tyler wondered anyway. Some questions didn't have answers, Jace said. Life was what it was, and all they could do was live it the best way they could.

Tyler wiped his nose on his sleeve and blinked back the threatening tears. He believed in his brother. He would try his best to do what Jace would do. No time for crying now. He had to clear his head to use his brain. There was no sense having an IQ of 168 if he wasn't going to use it when he needed it most.

So he closed his eyes and imagined locking all his fears in a box, and burying the box deep inside him. He needed to think like a hero now instead of waiting for one that might never come along.

37

I got the info on Davis," Ruiz said as Parker sat down at his desk. "Besides a few minor drug charges, he's got a history of assaults, with two convictions."

"Working off his drug debt by beating money out of the rest of the pipeheads who haven't paid," Parker speculated.

"He's been out of prison for about two years," Ruiz went on. "And his attorney of record for his last trial was Leonard Lowell."

Parker nodded. "Last known address?"

"He recently purchased a house in the Hollywood hills. He had to report the move to his parole officer."

"And if I go up there to check it out," Parker said, "will Bradley Kyle be there to greet me?"

He stared at his partner, waiting for an answer. Ruiz sighed and looked away.

"What do you want me to say, Parker? Robbery-Homicide can take anything they want—"

"Including my partner?"

"What's that supposed to mean?"

"It means I think your agenda and my agenda are not one and the same here."

Parker got out of his chair to pace, to try to burn off some of the anger.

"I'm not going to lie for you to Robbery-Homicide," Ruiz said. "What have you ever done for me? I've got to consider my own career."

"And which career is that?"

She stared at him, appearing confused and frustrated, with maybe a little bit of fear in her eyes.

"You want to work Homicide?" Parker asked, pacing back and forth, hands jammed at his waist, shoulders tense. "Or is this just a field trip for you?"

A couple of detectives on the other side of the room had turned to watch the escalating argument. Ruiz's eyes darted toward them.

"If you have something to say to me, Parker, I think we should take it into one of the interview rooms."

"Why the sudden modesty? You'll flash your cleavage in front of anyone, but you don't want them to know to whom they owe the pleasure?"

"You're fucking crazy!" she said, pushing to her feet. "Are you on crack?"

"Do you know Alex Navarro?"

Silence.

"I'll take that as a no," Parker said. "Alex Navarro is The Man working Latin gangs."

"Oh, yeah," she stammered. "I was too far down the food chain to have any contact with him."

"Alex Navarro can name every set of every gang in LA. If you asked him who got killed on June first five years ago, not only would he be able to answer that question, he would tell you every single detail of the case right down to what brand of underwear the vic had on when he went down. Navarro has absolutely no recollection of Officer Renee Ruiz working with the Gang Unit."

"So?" she challenged. He had to give her credit for cojones. "So I didn't work with him. What's the big deal?"

"You, Ms. Ravenous Ambition, who misses no opportunity to rub up against the nearest authority figure. You never made a move on the boss of bosses of your undercover task force?"

"Are you calling me a whore?" she said.

"That'd be a compliment," Parker snapped. "I'm calling you a liar."

"Fuck you, Parker!"

"I'm calling you a rat! Who put you here?" Parker shouted.

"What's the matter with you? Why are you doing this?"

"Because I'm pissed off," he said, getting in her face. To her credit, she didn't back down. "I don't like being played. What did you give Bradley Kyle when he came in here?"

"You fucking asshole. Why should I tell you anything?"

"What did you give him?"

"Everything you didn't take with you," she admitted.

"You told them about Davis, gave them his address?"

"I didn't have a choice."

"You **always** have a choice, Ruiz. You could have told them I had **everything** with me. You could have left out the information about Davis's house."

"They're taking the case!" she said, frustrated. "Don't you get that? It's not yours anymore, Parker. What's the difference if I gave them the information now instead of later? They still end up with the information."

Fuentes stuck his head out of his office. "What the hell is going on here?"

"He's crazy!" Ruiz said, then spouted off the

Spanish version in case Fuentes hadn't gotten it the first time.

"In my office," Fuentes said. "Both of you. Now."

"I've got to go," Parker said, starting to walk away. "I've got a job to do."

"In here, Kev. I mean it."

Parker stopped and weighed his pros and cons. Fuentes wouldn't do anything if he walked. But if he walked, Ruiz would have time to regroup. He wanted this over. Now.

They went into Fuentes' office, Ruiz going to one side of the room, Parker staying near the door. He didn't wait for Fuentes to set the tone. He faced the captain and said, "Where did she come from? Who assigned her here?"

"Don't be so paranoid," Fuentes said.

"He's out of his freaking mind," Ruiz said, crossing her arms tightly beneath her breasts.

Parker threw his hands up and turned around in a little circle. "Why will no one answer the damn question?"

"She came from the Gang—"

"Don't bullshit me!" Parker shouted. "I know she didn't come out of the Latin gangs task force."

"If you don't like the answers to your questions, stop asking them," Fuentes said, a little too calm. "It is what it is, Kev."

"Right. It is what it is," he said, nodding. "I know she's lying, therefore I can assume you're lying too."

Fuentes didn't bother to object. "She's your trainee. What difference does it make where she comes from? Your job is to train her."

"It matters if that's not the reason she's here," Parker said. "What are you, Ruiz? A Robbery-Homicide mole? An Internal Affairs rat? Take your pick of rodents."

Once again no one answered him. Ruiz and Fuentes exchanged looks that said they clearly knew something Parker didn't. He watched them, marveling at the fact that he could still expect something from someone, from Fuentes at least. He should have learned that lesson long ago. He thought he had. Maybe he had simply resigned himself, and now that he finally had a case where he could prove himself, the numbness was wearing off.

"Fuck this," he said, and turned to the door.

"Parker, where do you think you're going?"

"I've got a job to do."

"You're off Lowell," Fuentes said. "You have to hand everything over to Robbery-Homicide before they get really pissed off and decide to charge you with obstruction."

"They can do whatever they want," Parker said. "I don't know what their reasons are for

taking this, but I'm starting to put the pieces together and I don't like the picture I'm coming
up with. I'm not just going to hand them the
reins and walk off into the sunset."

"You could lose your career over this, Kev,"
Fuentes said. "Stay out of their way."

"I don't care," Parker said, resting his hand on
the doorknob. "Fire me if you want to, if you
don't want to take the heat. You can take my
job, but this case is mine, and I'm seeing it
through, even if I have to do it as a private
citizen."

"Kev—"

"You know, here's what you should do,"
Parker said. "Tell the brass I've finally flipped
my lid. I'll spend the next six months getting
my head examined by one of the department
shrinks. You can shrug it off. There's no impact
on you if I'm just bat-shit crazy."

Fuentes looked at him and sighed. "I'm not
your enemy, Kev," he said at last. "You have to
know when to walk away from something."

Parker turned to Ruiz. "Don't you have some
wiseass remark? Aren't you going to tell me this
will go on my permanent record? Whoever
you're working for is going to be grossly disappointed in you."

She had nothing to say to that, which was

easily the most telling moment he had ever spent with her.

"Good act, by the way," Parker said. "You turned me completely around. I never would have pegged you for a rat."

"You don't know what you're talking about," Ruiz said impatiently.

"On the contrary," Parker said. "I'm the authority on the subject of how to fuck over Kev Parker. I have years of experience.

"I'm leaving," he told them. "If there's no job for me when I come back, **c'est la vie.** God knows, I don't do this for the money."

"What **do** you do it for?" Ruiz asked pointedly.

"Is that what this is about?" Parker asked. He laughed, though it held no humor. "How does Parker afford a Jag? How does Parker buy a loft in Chinatown? How can Parker wear designer suits?"

"How do you?" she asked, blunt and unapologetic. "How do you afford your lifestyle on a detective's salary?"

"I don't," he said. "And the rest of that answer is no one's damn business."

"It is if you're getting that money—"

"You people are fucking amazing." He stared at her, incredulous, shaking his head. "I've never been anything less than a damn fine cop for more than half my life. I come here every day, work my cases a hundred and ten percent, train little pissant shits like you to work your way up to where I should have been for the last half a decade. And you have the gall to investigate me because I don't buy my suits at JC Penney?"

"I'm not apologizing to you for doing my job," Ruiz said, getting in his face. "In the last three years you've paid off two mortgages— yours and your parents'; you've purchased a loft in a luxury building in Chinatown; you've started wearing designer labels; you drive a Jaguar on your days off.

"You're not doing these things on what the LAPD pays you," she said. "How could you not think Internal Affairs would be interested in you?"

Parker felt his face getting hotter and hotter. "Do you have one complaint against me? Do you have anything on file against me?"

"As a matter of fact, yes," she said. "We have you screwing up a murder trial where a wealthy defendant walked away without so much as a slap on the wrist. Your income seems to have increased every year since. Do you need a pencil to connect those dots, Parker?"

"This is un-fucking-believable," Parker muttered. "IA has been watching me with their hairy eyeball all this time. Giradello couldn't get rid of me outright, couldn't make me quit, so you people are slithering in the back door for him?

"I'd ask you why you didn't just call me in and grill me," he said, "but I know how IA works. Persecute first, ask questions later."

"Would you have been any more cooperative than you're being now?" Fuentes asked.

"No. I haven't done anything wrong. I haven't done anything illegal. And what I do with my personal time is my personal business. I spent too many years with nothing but this job, and what did it get me? Ground down, and left flat."

"If you hated it so much, why didn't you just quit?" Ruiz asked.

Parker shook his head, then clutched it in his hands like a coconut, thinking it might just crack open from the sheer frustration of dealing with such narrow-minded stupidity.

"Did you even think about that before it came out of your mouth?" he asked, astonished that people could be so obtuse. "I don't hate the job. **I love the job!** Don't you get that? Why would I stay if I hated it and someone else was providing me with a six-figure income? Why wouldn't I tell you all to go fuck yourselves?"

Ruiz just stared at him, trying to look smug and superior, and pulling off neither.

"If you haven't figured out why I'm still with LAPD, knowing what you know about me, knowing what you were briefed on by whoever sent you here," Parker said, "you'll never get it."

In the old days he would have answered very differently. Back when it was all about him and his image and how many cases he could clear in a month. When all the flash had been stripped away from him, and he'd been forced to take a hard look at himself, it had gradually dawned on him that his career was really about something else, something deeper and more meaningful, more satisfying on a different level.

"What do you do it for, Ruiz?" he asked quietly. "The power? The control? The rush of climbing the ladder? I'll tell you right now, that's not enough. If the only goal is the big brass ring, what do you suppose happens to you after you catch it? What does it mean to you? What do you look back on? What do you have?"

"I have a career," she said.

"You have nothing," Parker said. "Look inside yourself. You have nothing. I know."

He looked at Fuentes, who couldn't quite meet his eyes. Just doing his job, Parker thought bitterly. The panacea for all people who couldn't otherwise justify their actions.

"I'm taking the rest of the day."

No one tried to stop him as he walked out the door.

38

The house where Eddie Davis lived in the Hollywood hills looked like something a pornographer might rent to shoot X-rated movies. Seventies hip, a little run-down, an angled flat roof, trapezoidal windows, and teal-green vertical blinds. There was a solid gate leading to the backyard, where Parker knew he would find a kidney-shaped pool, a big hot tub, and a tiki bar. The Eddie Davis Swinging Bachelor Pad.

It wasn't a high-end neighborhood. No mansions, no big celebs in the immediate area, but probably some mid-range screenwriters, an episodic television director or two. Still, it was probably by far the swankiest place Davis had ever lived in in his entire miserable life. All he needed was the porn actresses naked in his tacky hot tub, and Eddie would be in hog heaven. Good to see he was investing his blackmail money wisely.

Parker sat in his car, up the block. An elevated vantage point. He watched Davis's house for signs of life, as he waited on hold for his contact at the phone company. James Earl Jones tried to sell him on the idea of Verizon DSL.

"This is Patti. How can I help you?"

"Just the sound of your voice is a balm to my soul, doll."

He could hear the smile in her tone. "Kev Parker. If you could bottle that charm, you'd have something."

"Yeah, cheap cologne," Parker said. "I'm working on it in my free time. Listen, Patti, I need a favor. Can you fax me the local usage details for a possibly notorious criminal mastermind?"

He gave her Davis's name and address, along with his own home fax number.

"And you've got your warrant for this?"

"Not exactly."

"Kevin . . ."

"I do have courtside tickets to the Lakers–Spurs game next Friday."

"Courtside?"

"Primo. You'll be able to smell Jack Nicholson's breath."

"That's never really been a goal of mine."

"You'll be the envy of every Lakers fan in the city."

"I don't know," she said. "You know I shouldn't."

"No one will be the wiser, doll. None of this goes to court. I just need a break, is all," Parker said. "And doesn't your hubby deserve a little night on the town with his favorite girl?"

"He can have a million of them," Patti said. "I dumped the bastard. But my son would be delighted."

"They're yours for the taking. You know, they're yours either way," he said. Mr. Magnanimous. "Take your son and have a great time. I'm sorry things didn't work out for you."

"Oh, I think they probably did," she said, but her voice was no longer cheerful. "Everybody tells me I'm better off."

"Yeah, well, everybody can go through it for you too, then. Let them see what a good time you're having."

"Like you would know."

"I've learned from the experiences of my friends."

He let the silence hang, waiting for Patti to fill it.

"Tell me the warrant is on the way," she said with a sigh.

"The warrant is on the way. Call me if it gets lost en route," Parker said. "Pick the tickets up at Will Call. I'll leave your name."

There was no activity at Davis's place. No gardener in the yard. No cleaning woman parked in the driveway. Eddie could have been sleeping off his last murder, Parker supposed, his anger stirring again for Eta and for her family.

An absolutely senseless killing that would alter the lives of many people, and not for the better. And Eddie Davis was lying in bed scratching his balls, or down at Fat Burger, or doing whatever a mouth-breather like that did to pass the day. Sitting around picking his nose and trying to decide if he should go with a mutual fund or put his ill-gotten gains into a big crack-cocaine deal.

Parker eased his car down the hill, past Davis's driveway, parked, then walked back up to the house. Through the dirty glass panes in the garage door he could see an assortment of older motorcycles, most in various states of disrepair, and a brand-new red Kawasaki Ninja ZX12R sport bike. About twelve K worth of fuel-injected sexy beast. Another sign of Eddie's new prosperity. There was no big black sedan.

Parker boosted himself up on a big terra-cotta planter full of dead plants to look over the gate into the backyard.

Kidney-shaped pool. Tiki bar. Tacky hot tub. And an ugly orange chow chow that looked like it had mange. The dog got up and sauntered over, sat down and stared up at Parker, then turned to chew at one of the mangy bare spots on its coat.

Parker dropped back down and went to the front door of the house to peer in through the sidelights. The requisite porn-movie furniture—black leather, low-slung sectional sofa, cushions scattered on the living room floor around a Moroccan-looking coffee table made out of a giant hammered brass dish that was littered with beer cans and pizza boxes and open bags of Doritos. The only other piece of furniture in the room was a big, black, phallic, widescreen television flanked by enormous speakers.

Sliding doors to what was probably the master bedroom were located on the other side of the high wood-plank fence on the south end of the house. As Parker stood on another big pot of dead plants looking in, the chow chow came around from the other side of the house, sat down, and stared at him again. The dog's eyes were dark, emotionless dots in its big head. Eyes like a stone killer, Parker thought. The bastard would probably take his leg off if he swung it over the fence.

"Hey! Who the fuck are you?"

Parker hopped down from the planter. Eddie Davis stared at him from the driver's side of a black Lincoln Town Car pulled to the curb. He had the same eyes as the dog, and he looked like he'd been tossed into the middle of a hockey brawl—a piece of white tape across his nose, one eye swollen and red, scratches across one cheek.

"Steve," Parker called, grinning. "You Eddie? Rick sent me."

"Rick who?"

"You know. Rick from that thing at the beach. He told me you maybe got a bike for sale. A Kawasaki road bike, maybe ninety-eight, ninety-nine? If he's right, I've got money burning a hole in my pocket. I've got a hard-on for that bike, you wouldn't believe."

"Why were you looking over my fence?"

"I thought maybe you were back at the pool."

Davis seemed to contemplate whether his greed would outstrip his caution.

"Hey, if you want me to come back another time . . ." Parker offered, spreading his hands. "It'll have to wait until the end of next week, though. I'm on my way out of town on business. I just thought if I could drive by maybe I'd catch you. . . ."

Davis stared at him for a moment longer.

"It's your call," Parker said.

"Hold your coat open."

"Huh?"

"Hold your coat open."

To see if he was carrying. To see if he was a cop. Parker held his jacket open.

"Jesus, if you tell me you think I look like a cop, my tailor will kill himself!"

Davis didn't respond. Same sense of humor as the dog too. He put the Town Car in reverse, backed up, and pulled into the driveway.

Parker walked over, his senses sharpening with each stride, taking in the surroundings, the car, the license plate, a parking sticker on the lower right corner of the back window. He assessed Davis's body language as he got out of the car—tense, watchful. Parker had no doubt that Davis was carrying a weapon—a gun, a knife, the blade he'd used to cut Eta Fitzgerald's throat.

The homes in the neighborhood weren't densely packed together, but they were near enough that Parker thought Davis probably wouldn't risk killing him in his driveway in broad daylight.

"I don't know anybody named Rick," Davis said. His left eye was swollen nearly shut, and tearing. He pressed at it with a dingy handkerchief.

"Rick Dreyer," Parker said. "Venice Beach. The guy with the tats all up and down his arms and legs. You know. He does the great paint jobs. The guy's a genius with an airbrush."

The good eye narrowed. "I know of him."

Parker shrugged. "Maybe he's a friend of a friend or something."

Davis thought about that. The inner workings of his mind moved at the rate of grass growing. "Stench knows him."

Parker pushed his jacket open again and settled his hands at his waist. "Whatever," he said with a big I'm-your-pal grin. "Listen, Eddie, I've got a plane to catch, so . . ."

Davis pressed the button on the garage-door remote in his hand, and the door started up, grinding and groaning. He tipped his head by way of invitation for Parker to go in. Parker turned a bit sideways, wanting Davis in full view. The guy wasn't tall, but he was built like a refrigerator.

"So what do you want for this baby?" Parker asked.

"Eight thousand."

"Holy shit!"

Parker stopped abruptly. Davis went another two steps into the garage before he turned around. The sun hit him in the face and his eyes went shut.

Parker pulled his gun out of the belt holster

nestled at the small of his back, and, swinging with both arms, backhanded Davis as hard as he could across the face.

Davis's head snapped to his right, blood gushing from his already broken nose. He staggered backward, tripping over his own feet, falling. He hit the concrete ass-first, sprawling, arms flailing, the back of his head bouncing off the floor.

Anger and adrenaline pumping, Parker stepped over him, leaned down, stuck the SIG-Sauer in his face.

"Eddie Davis, you're under arrest for the murder of Eta Fitzgerald. One word out of your fucking mouth and I'll beat you to death. You would have the right to an attorney, but you killed him too, so you're shit out of luck. You got that?"

Davis groaned, turned onto his side, coughing, and spat out a mouthful of blood. "Jesus-fucking-Christ!"

Parker gave him a toe in the ribs, and Davis made a sound like a B-movie ninja warrior. "That's for cursing," Parker said. "Eta was an upright, churchgoing woman."

"Who the fuck is Eta?" He sounded like Marlon Brando in **The Godfather.**

"The mother of four and sole support of her family you cut and left in an alley last night like a sack of garbage, for no reason other than you are a miserable piece-of-shit excuse for a human being. Roll over. On your face."

Davis groaned, slowly turning onto his elbows and knees. Parker put a foot on his ass and shoved him down.

"What's going on in there?"

Parker glanced to the side. A shirtless older man who looked like an albino walrus sat at the curb in a golf cart and Bermuda shorts.

"Police busi—"

Parker's breath went out of him in a sudden whoosh as something hit him hard across the back and ribs. His body twisted away from the pain, and he tripped over Davis's legs and went down, cracking one kneecap hard on the concrete.

Davis rolled out from under him, struggled to his feet, and hit Parker twice as hard a second time across the back. Parker fell forward into a motorcycle. The bike fell over, hitting a second bike, then a third. They went down like dominoes.

Parker pushed off the bike and went sideways. The length of tailpipe Davis had gotten hold of just missed his head and clanged off a chrome fender.

Parker's gun was gone, lost in the mess of motorcycle parts on the floor. There was no time to look for it. Parker rolled and came up in a crouch on his feet.

Davis took another vicious swing at him with the pipe, but missed. He looked like a gargoyle now, face contorted, swollen, bleeding, foaming at the mouth. His eyes held the same dead-calm expression as before.

He rushed Parker, raising the pipe over his head. Parker ran backward into the nose of the Town Car, and rolled to the right as Davis brought the pipe crashing down, caving a dent in the hood of the car.

The old guy sat frozen in his cart, mouth agape.

Davis threw the pipe at Parker, got into the car, and gunned the engine. The tires spun and squealed, and the Town Car leapt backward, bashing into the front end of the golf cart, spinning it like a top.

Parker rushed into the garage, found the SIG, and ran back out and down the drive. The old guy had fallen out of his cart and was struggling to his feet. The cart was rolling down the hill on its own.

Limping, cursing, Parker gritted his teeth and ran for his car. With one hand, he caught hold of a roof-support post on a corner of the golf cart, and hopped onto the back end, where the clubs usually rode.

The cart raced downhill. Parker jumped off fifteen feet from his Sebring, and ran hard into the side of it.

"Fuck! Fuck! Fuck!" he shouted, tossing the SIG on the passenger's seat, turning the key in the ignition.

Davis's Town Car was nearly out of sight, skidding around a curve.

Parker peeled away from the curb and gunned the car down the hill. The golf cart swerved in front of him. He turned the wheel hard left, the back end of the Sebring fishtailing one way, then the other, taking out somebody's white mailbox and a planter of geraniums.

When he came around the curve, Davis was gone. The road branched off into canyon side streets like streams on a river. Parker spotted no black Town Car going down any of them.

He pulled to the side and called Hollywood Bureau, giving them a description of the car and of Eddie Davis, telling them that he was armed and extremely dangerous.

Eddie Davis. That close, and now he was gone, running. Parker couldn't know where he'd go. Vermin like Davis had holes everywhere. He would go to ground in one of them, and no telling when he'd come out.

Now he knew the cops were on to him. Maybe he would try to run. But he didn't have the negatives, and he was obviously willing to risk anything to get them.

The negatives were the key to luring him into a trap. Davis had no way of knowing Parker had the single negative Lenny had stashed.

Parker tried to call Ito to find out if he had developed the negative Lenny Lowell had hung on to for insurance, but he got Ito's voice mail instead. He left a message for Ito to call him ASAP, and hung up.

He needed to know what—or who—he was up against. Forewarned, forearmed. The clock was ticking for him to close the case on Lenny Lowell, and open a whole new can of worms. As comeback cases went, this one was shaping up to be a doozie. Ironic, Parker thought, that if he was right about the target of Lenny Lowell's blackmail scheme—and the reason for the blackmail itself—chances were good this case would be his last. In a city fueled by fame and power, this message would be something nobody wanted delivered: the truth.

39

The media encampment outside the court-house looked like some kind of techno-geek refugee camp. Lights on poles, generators, wire cable snakes running in all directions on the ground, guys in baggy shorts carrying video cameras with network logos, sound guys in headsets, on-air talent dressed to the nines from neck to waist. From the waist down: baggy shorts, sandals, sneakers.

News vans made their own parking lot. Satellite dishes raised up like strange, giant flowers turning their faces to the sun. Vendors sold cold drinks and cappuccinos, pita sand-wiches and burritos, ice cream and frozen fruit bars, vintage bowling shirts and "Free Rob Cole" T-shirts.

The print media were the coyotes of the bunch, roaming at large, not tethered to cables, no need for makeup or lights. Photographers with multiple cameras slung around their necks and ball caps on backward roamed the grounds, hunting for an angle that hadn't been used. Reporters perched here and there, smoking cigarettes, talking shop.

Parker punched Andi Kelly's number as he approached the scene.

"Andi Kelly."

"This is so 1994," Parker complained. "Hasn't anybody come up with anything new since O.J.? Isn't there something more exciting to report on?"

"Celeb criminals are hot again, Parker. It's retro reality TV. All the rage."

"What's next? The return of David Lee Roth and the hair bands?"

"The world's going to hell on a sled. Where are you?"

"Between the guy selling bootleg DVDs of Cole's television series and the Channel 4 news van. Where are you?"

"On the verge of a nervous breakdown."

"Meet me by the espresso guy."

"You're buying."

"Have you ever picked up a tab in your life?"

"Nope."

Parker paid for a double tall espresso for himself and a grande triple caramel macchiato with extra whipped cream for Kelly.

"You have the metabolism of a gnat," Parker observed.

"Yeah, it's great. What are you doing down here?"

"Talking to you," he said, but his gaze scanned the crowd, his radar up for any sign of Kyle or Roddick. He tipped his head away from the madness. "Take a walk with me. You won't miss anything, will you?"

She waved a hand at the courthouse and rolled her eyes. "Cole's inside, trying to look bereaved for the jury pool. Scintillating, I'm sure. He gets to show his full emotional range, from A to B."

They walked a short distance down the street, away from the carnival, turning to watch from a distance.

"You look a little rough around the edges, Kev," Kelly said.

"It's been a hell of a day so far."

"And the day ain't over yet," she said. "Have you had to face your friends from RHD?"

"I won't give them the satisfaction," Parker said, his gaze still scanning. He was in full-on hunting mode now, mind racing, pulse racing, blood pressure rising. He couldn't make himself stand still. Slowly shifting weight from one leg to the other was his pressure valve, spending a little steam to keep him from blowing up.

"I'm not a gracious loser," he said. "I took everything I had on the case and walked.

They've probably got an APB out on me even as we speak."

"So who knocked you around?" Kelly asked.

"Huh?"

"My keen investigative skills tell me someone wasn't playing nice on the playground." She leaned down and plucked at his pants leg where he'd landed on his knee in Davis's garage. A grease stain and a small three-corner tear marked the spot. Both legs were beige with dust over the expensive brown-with-blue-pinstripe fabric.

Parker's eyes widened as if he were seeing himself for the first time. "Aww, son of a . . . I'm suing this creep Davis when I catch him. This is Canali!"

"Well, how stupid are you? Why would you wear a designer suit to a dogfight?"

"I'm a detective. When am I ever in a fight?" Parker said, more bent out of shape than the piece of tailpipe Davis had used to beat on him.

"Well, today, apparently."

"Besides, my clothes are my disguise. No one thinks I'm a cop. I dress too well to be a cop."

"Can you write your suits off on your taxes, then?"

"My business manager says no."

"That sucks." Kelly shrugged. "Everything has a trade-off. So what happened?"

"Eddie Davis caught me poking around his place. I took the opportunity to arrest him. Then he took the opportunity to try to kill me. He's at large. Every cop in the city is looking for him now. Do you know anything interesting about him yet?"

"In the minute and a half since you asked me to vet the guy?"

"Here's what I know so far," Parker said. "He's a low-end petty criminal with delusions of grandeur. Until recently, he had a low-end defense attorney by the name of Lenny Lowell."

"Surprise, surprise."

Parker did another quick scan, only his eyes moving. A stocky guy in a wrinkled shirt and tie stood a little too near, lighting a cigarette. Parker went over to him and flashed his ID.

"Hey, pal, take a walk," he said.

The guy gave him attitude. "I'm having a cigarette here. Mind your own business."

Parker got in his face. "No. That's not how this works, ace. **You** mind **your** business over there," he said, jabbing a finger in the direction of the courthouse.

Kelly wedged herself in front of him and tried to move him back a step. "Kevin . . ." She glanced over her shoulder at the smoker. "Sorry. He started the patch last week."

Parker turned away from her and walked

down the block another fifteen yards. Kelly scurried to catch up.

"This is just a thought," she said, "but you could maybe take the testosterone down a notch."

Parker ignored her. "My friend who overheard my name in that conversation between Giradello and Kyle was at a fund-raiser for the DA. The prominent guest of the evening was Norman Crowne."

Kelly's brow furrowed as she tried to tie the pieces together. "A low-end lawyer like Lowell . . . a cheap thug like Davis . . . Those guys are less than ants in the world of someone like Norman Crowne."

"I think Lowell and Davis were blackmailing someone," Parker said. "I'm guessing Eddie got tired of sharing. So how does a goon like Eddie Davis, a known knee-buster, come up with someone to blackmail?"

"Sixty-two percent of relationships begin in the workplace," she quipped. Then realization dawned. "Oh, my God. You think someone hired Davis to kill Tricia Cole."

"And that someone couldn't be Rob Cole," Parker said. "Even he wouldn't be stupid enough to be in the house when the cops came. He would have been out establishing an alibi."

Kelly tried to digest the idea. Parker started to

pace, his own thought processes racing. Black cars were lined up at the curb with drivers at the wheel, and LAPD motorcycle cops were sitting on their bikes in front and behind, at regular intervals. Livery for the big heads that would be coming out of the courthouse soon. Three limos, a couple of Town Cars, a triple-black Cadillac Escalade with black-tinted windows.

Parker took in the details almost absently, just to keep his brain focused on something innocuous so he could breathe and rein in his energy for a moment. He paced back and forth past the same three cars a couple of times, then stopped abruptly. He wasn't even sure why, at first. Then slowly he turned back to walk past the last of the cars again.

"What is it?" Kelly asked, joining him.

On the lower right corner of the back window was a small purple circular sticker with a gold insignia and a row of black numerals. A parking sticker for a corporate lot. The scene came up in his memory: He was walking toward the black Lincoln Town Car, doing what he had been doing just now, taking in small details, filing them neatly away in his brain, but keeping his mind focused on the subject of most importance: Eddie Davis. He remembered the electric blue of the sky, the green of the grass, the black car, the license plate, the small parking sticker

on the lower corner of the back window. It was
no bigger than a quarter.

Parker's breathing was shallow and quick, and
he felt a strange light-headedness as he lowered
his gaze to the rear plate.

CROWNE 5.

40

Parker's first thought was a selfish one: **My career is over.**

"Eddie Davis is driving around in a black Lincoln Town Car," he said quietly.

"You're out of your mind, Kevin," Kelly said. "There's no way a hit man is riding around in a Crowne Enterprises vehicle."

Parker was already dialing his cell phone. As he spoke to the person on the other end of the line, he realized he was trembling. He had to press the phone against his ear to hold it steady. He imagined he heard a clock ticking as he waited for the information he'd requested.

Kelly was shaking her head, muttering to herself, "I can't get my brain wrapped around any of this. How does it work?"

"Crowne Enterprises has reported two black Lincoln Town Cars stolen in the past eighteen months," Parker said, sticking his phone back in his pocket.

"So Davis stole one."

Parker gave her a look. "Eddie Davis is walking along the street one night, decides he wants to steal a ride, and the car he rips off just happens to be a Town Car owned by Crowne Enterprises. What are the odds of that?"

Kelly frowned. "Well, if you put it that way . . ."

"You've been on this story since day one," Parker said. "If you had to pick a suspect other than Rob Cole, who would it be?"

She thought about it for a moment as she took her turn to glance around for spies. "Well, there's darling Caroline, who discovered her mother's body. Her relationship with Rob was certainly not father-daughter. They palled around like they were schoolmates. Of course, Robbie arrested development at about seventeen, so it probably seemed normal to him.

"And then there's Phillip, Tricia's brother. I suppose living in the shadow of St. Tricia had to get old. She was the apple of their father's eye, and Phillip . . . has always just sort of been there in the background.

"He had dinner with Tricia at Patina the night she was killed. A roomful of people saw them there, apparently having a serious discussion. He says she talked about divorcing Cole, that she was going to call a lawyer the following week. She hadn't spoken to anyone else about it, so we've only got Phillip's say-so."

She paused and looked away and made a face as if she was trying to decide whether or not to share something with him.

"You might as well tell me," Parker said. "I know there's something more in that brain of yours. I don't want to have to resort to torture."

"What kind of torture?" she asked, with a sultry look.

"The bad kind."

She sighed and said, "Okay. I heard a whisper once, back at the start of this mess, that Tricia had accused Phillip of skimming off one of the charities."

"Who told you?"

"It was a cousin of a woman whose husband's sister's uncle-in-law's housekeeper's daughter used to work at the Crowne Trust office. One of those deals. I dug on that story like a badger, but I never could substantiate it. Phillip has an alibi for the time of the murder, but if he hired it out . . ."

"He could have paid Davis with a Town Car," Parker speculated. "Then had to account for the missing fleet car and claimed it must have been stolen."

"But you're forgetting something here, Kev," Andi said.

"Which is what?"

"Rob Cole did it. He was there, in the house, passed-out drunk, when Tricia's body was discovered. He has no alibi. He's well-known for having an ugly temper. If Tricia wanted rid of him, then he would certainly have motive to want to be rid of her."

The first limo in line started its engine and rolled slowly forward, one of the motorcycle cops positioned in front of it, lights flashing.

"They must be coming out," Kelly said.

She started back toward the courthouse at a fast walk, which quickly broke into a trot. Parker went after her, his kneecap throbbing as he started to jog.

The media area was buzzing with a swarm of activity and excitement. Light stands moving, cables dragging, directions being shouted in English, Spanish, and Japanese.

Cole ironically had a big cult following in Japan, despite the fact that footage of a drunken Rob Cole cursing people of different ethnic persuasions—including the Japanese—while being escorted from a West Hollywood club aired regularly on news programs the world over.

Andi darted between and around people, her size an asset until she reached the last few impenetrable rows—the on-air talent for the networks and the local news stations. Parker followed her, holding up his ID and speaking in a serious, authoritative LAPD voice, telling people to step aside. He found Kelly because her head suddenly popped up between a pair of broad-shouldered men, then disappeared again. She was hopping up and down, trying to get a view of the courthouse main entrance.

She turned to Parker. "Bend over."

"What?"

"Bend over! I want to get up on your shoulders."

"What if I don't want you there?"

"Stop being such a baby, Parker. Hurry up."

He hoisted her up just before the doors opened and the first of the procession emerged: Norman Crowne and his entourage of attorneys and assistants and bodyguards.

Crowne had appeared regularly at the courthouse during the myriad pretrial hearings. Even while the voir dire was ongoing, and no one from his party was allowed into the courtroom, Norman Crowne had come to the courthouse as a show of support for his beloved daughter.

Parker had seen him in television interviews—a dignified, quiet man whose grief was almost palpable. It was a wrenching experience to watch him as he answered questions and spoke about Tricia. None of the emotion was forced or staged or disingenuous. It was raw, and he was clearly a very private man, uncomfortable trying to keep a too-small cloak of pride pulled over the worst of wounds.

It simply wasn't possible to imagine him having any connection to someone like Eddie Davis or needing to pay blackmail to a sleaze like Lenny Lowell.

On his arm: the granddaughter, Caroline, in a prim little suit with a jacket tailored to minimize the roundness of her figure. Parker knew enough about human psychology to know the idea of Caroline falling for her stepfather was not as far-fetched as it may have seemed on its face.

Caroline's biological father, by all accounts an abusive bastard, had bowed out of her life early on, leaving her with a void where a parent should have been, and a screwed-up idea of what made a good relationship. Then during Caroline's adolescence, when girls are struggling with hormones and budding ideas of their own sexuality, Rob Cole had come riding in to save poor Tricia from her loneliness.

He had looked past the mousiness, the awkwardly shy personality, straight to the billions of dollars behind her. But he had been a convincing Prince Charming, and everyone had loved him for it. Life was a fairy tale.

It wasn't hard to imagine that Caroline had bought into that fairy tale herself, or that she had developed a serious crush on her step-daddy. He had been, after all, a heartthrob at the time.

Psychologists claim girls are always in competition with their mothers for the attentions of dear old Dad. And when dear old dad turned out to be a weak, narcissistic, amoral, borderline personality, there was a recipe for trouble.

A couple of steps behind Caroline and her grandfather walked Norman Crowne's son, Phillip. The runt of the litter. Where the old man was considered slight of build, the son had more of a scrawny quality, thin and pale with thin, pale hair.

He was a VP of Crowne Enterprises, in charge of counting paper clips, or something to that effect. Norman was still the man in command, the man with his name in the papers. Perhaps that was why Phillip was so pale—he had spent his entire life standing in his father's shadow.

Tricia Crowne's brother had expressed more anger than pure grief at his sister's murder. He was the one who spoke of revenge more than justice. The idea that Tricia had been murdered morally offended him. The idea that Rob Cole had killed her offended him even more. Seeing Cole for what he was, Phillip Crowne had never warmed up to Cole as Tricia's husband. He loathed Cole the defendant.

It was difficult to imagine any of the Crownes even knowing of a person like Eddie Davis.

Parker watched the pack of them descend the steps. Two uniformed sheriff's deputies preceded them to the waiting car.

Mr. Crowne has no comment at this time.

My grandfather is very tired.

My father and the rest of us consider the judge's ruling this morning to be a triumph for justice.

They weren't all in the limo before the crowd's attention swung back to the courthouse. The Crownes and their opinions and emotions were instantly old news. Rob Cole and his cadre had emerged.

Cole's attorney: Martin Gorman, a big guy with red hair and a kind of Popeye-like expression. He towered over his client, keeping a hand on Cole's shoulder as if to guide or protect him.

Gorman's second chair, Janet Brown, was short, pudgy, with mouselike looks. A certain eerie resemblance to the victim. And, as such, a strategic member of Gorman's team. If a woman like Janet Brown could believe in Rob

Cole, defend him against charges that he had brutally murdered his wife, could he really be a bad man?

For the right price, Janet Brown would have posed as advocate to Caligula.

And then there was Rob Cole himself. A handsome grin with a whole lot of nothing behind it.

Cole was the kind of guy Parker took one look at and thought: **What an asshole.** Diane wasn't the only person who saw it. Parker recognized it instantly. He just didn't quite let on to Diane, because he found her animosity for the man both entertaining and intriguing. But Parker knew the animal. He had been Rob Cole once, only younger and much better-looking.

The difference was, a cute thirty-something jerk could still get a pass for arrogance. There was time for him to evolve into something better. A fifty-something jerk had passed the expiration date for change. Rob Cole would still be wearing fifties bowling shirts when he was seventy-five, and bragging to everyone at the rest home that that was his trademark and his public still loved it. The biggest recurring role of his career: starring as Rob Cole.

Cole played that part every day of his life. Every day was a three-act opera, and he was

Camille. He had put on his good-man-wrongly-accused persona for the media. Noble and stoic. The tight-lipped, serious expression, head held high. The salt-and-pepper hair cut military-short. The wraparound ultra-black shades, cool but understated.

Most people didn't want to search for a deeper level when they looked at the Rob Coles of the world. The facade was a showstopper, and that was as far as they went. The blessing and the curse of being a pretty face. The look was all people wanted to believe in, and because they didn't really care if there was anything behind it, the face began to believe there wasn't anything there to care about either. Good thing Rob had the face, or he wouldn't have anything.

Gorman had dressed him for the potential jury in an impeccably cut conservative charcoal suit, charcoal shirt, and striped tie. A strong but understated look, showing respect for the court and the gravity of the charges against him. No one would see the bowling shirts and the trim-fitting jeans until the verdict was old news. And hopefully not even then.

A lot of powerful people wanted Rob Cole's next look to be prison chambray. Only, Parker had a bad feeling that although Rob Cole might be an asshole, the one thing he wasn't—

no matter how many people wanted it—was guilty.

Parker's phone rang as Cole and his group passed him. Andi was up on his shoulders, twisting around, trying to turn him with her knees like he was an Indian elephant. He shifted positions and pulled his phone out of his pocket.

"Parker."

"Parker, it's me, Ruiz. Where are you? At a riot?"

"Something like that," Parker shouted, pressing his other ear closed with one finger. "What do you want? Besides my head on a platter."

"I was just doing my job."

"Yeah. I think Dr. Mengele said that too."

"Your bike messenger called."

"What?"

"I said, your bike—"

"No, I heard you. How do you know it was him?"

"He said his name was J. C. Damon."

"And?"

"He said to be at Pershing Square at five twenty-five."

"Hang on."

Parker reached up and swatted at Kelly. "Ride's over!"

She swung a leg around and slid down his back, patted his ass, and trotted over to her photographer. Parker walked away from the crowd.

"J. C. Damon called you and told you to tell me to be at Pershing Square at five twenty-five," he repeated. "You think I'm a fucking idiot, Ruiz? You think you pulled the big one on me and I fell for it, so I must be stupid?"

"It's not a setup."

"Right. And you're a virgin. Got anything else to sell me?"

"Look, fuck you, Parker," she said. "Maybe I felt guilty for two seconds and thought I'd do something decent. The guy called and asked for you, said he got your name from Abby Lowell. If you don't want it, go blow yourself. I'll call RHD."

"And you didn't tell any of this to Bradley Kyle already?"

"You know what? Fine," she said, disgusted. "You're not going to believe anything I tell you. Do what you want."

She hung up on him.

Parker slipped the phone back into his pocket and stood there, watching the last of the black cars drive away. The television news- people had already run back to their spots with the courthouse in the background to do their bits for the five o'clock news.

He would be a fool to trust Ruiz. Robbery-Homicide had taken the case. She had personally handed over whatever scraps he had left behind. She'd given them Davis's address. She was an IA rat. Nothing she said could be believed. Bradley Kyle had probably been standing right there when she'd called.

Andi broke away from the media pack and walked across the grass to him. "Well, that's all the fun I can have here," she said. "Let's go someplace romantic and you can tell me how one of the most beloved philanthropists in LA is hooked up with a homicidal maniac."

"I've got to take a rain check."

"Again with the rejection!" she said, rolling her eyes. "Where are you going? Are you seeing another reporter?"

"I'm going to Pershing Square."

"What's at Pershing Square besides dope dealers?"

"A circus," Parker said, starting toward his car. "You should bring a photographer. I think there might even be clowns."

41

Pershing Square is an oasis of green in the middle of downtown LA, a checkerboard area of the best and the baddest. Across Olive Street stood the grande dame of 1920s luxury: the Millennium Biltmore Hotel, where ladies in sweaters and pearls enjoyed high tea, and debutante balls were not a thing of the past. A block in the other direction, unemployed men with hungry eyes loitered outside of check-cashing places with heavy iron bars over the windows, and Hispanic women who only visited Beverly Hills through service entrances pushed baby carriages and shopped in cheap clothing stores where no one spoke English. Five blocks away, justice was doled out in federal and county courthouses, but here a crazy, homeless guy was taking a dump behind the statue of General Pershing.

The park was drawn out in rectangles of grass divided by strips of concrete and broad steps that transitioned one level to the next. Bright-

colored square concrete structures that had a
bunkerlike quality to them hid the escalators
down into the parking garage. A 120-foot purple concrete campanile jutted up in the middle
of it.

During the Christmas season an ice-skating
rink was featured at one end of the park. Only
in LA: people figure skating in seventy-degree
weather with a backdrop of palm trees. The rink
had been gone for a month.

Jace had always found the place too planned,
the lines too horizontal. There was too much
concrete in the middle of it. The sculptures
were cool—not so much the traditional statues,
but the huge rust-colored spheres that perched
here and there on concrete pedestals.

But the best thing about Pershing Square was
the openness of it. From his vantage point, Jace
could see most of the park. He could see people
coming, going, loitering. He could see the security guards who came up out of the underground garage periodically to look around, then
went back down to make sure no vagrants were
trying to get into the restrooms reserved for the
paying customers. Considering where the vagrants then relieved themselves, it seemed like a
policy worth reviewing.

The working day was over for the people in
suits who descended from the downtown tow-

ers to drive home to the Valley or the Westside, to Pasadena or Orange County. The word about downtown was that it was the hot new place to live, but Jace didn't see that many hipsters ready to rub shoulders with the indigenous homeless population, or that many yuppies ready to stroll their kids past the junkies hanging out in Pershing Square.

Fifteen feet away from him, two guys were making a deal on a little bag of something. A stoner with lime green hair was sitting on a park bench across the way. Over by the concrete fountain, a group of teenage boys were standing around playing Hacky Sack. A movie crew had been shooting in the area all day and were in the process of setting up lights in the square for a night shoot.

It was just past five. The sun had set behind the tall buildings. Only people on the Westside had daylight now. Pershing Square had been cast into the artificial dusk of the inner city— not day, not night. The lights had come on.

Jace had stashed The Beast between a couple of equipment trucks parked across the street from the square, on Fifth. He had been hanging around since about three o'clock, keeping his eyes open for anyone who looked like a cop coming into the park, watching for Predator to cruise past, waiting for Abby Lowell to show.

He had been all over the park, scouting vantage points, planning escape routes.

He figured she would show. If she was, as he believed, involved in the blackmail plot, she would come alone. She wouldn't want the cops looking at her, and Predator had threatened to kill her, so she couldn't be in on it with him. Whether or not she brought the money was something else.

The whole scheme was going to be all about timing. Timing, planning, thinking on his feet . . . and luck. He had taken triple care with the other factors, seeing as he hadn't had much of the last one.

Tyler would be worrying about him by now. Jace knew his brother had probably tried a hundred times to contact him on the walkie-talkie. Thinking about Tyler, he felt a terrible sadness. Even if this scheme worked, Jace didn't know that he would come out of it unscathed, that the cops wouldn't still have an interest in him, that they wouldn't then find out about Tyler. His instincts were telling him he and Tyler would have to run.

The idea of tearing his brother away from the Chens made him feel physically ill. Tyler was probably better off with them than he was with Jace, living like a hunted criminal, but Jace couldn't leave him. He had promised their mother he would look after his little brother, see that he was safe, see that he was never pulled into the cogs of the child welfare system. They were family. Jace was Tyler's only living family as far as Jace knew. He didn't count the bartender who had probably fathered the boy. Sperm Donor didn't qualify as family.

But Jace wondered if his reasons for sticking to his promise to Alicia weren't more self-serving than serving Tyler. His brother was all he had, his anchor, his only real escape from emotional isolation. Because of Tyler he had the Chens. Because of Tyler he had goals, and hope for a better future. Without Tyler he would be adrift, connected to no one.

Jace felt as if his heart were lying in his stomach, throbbing and soaking up acid like a sponge. He blocked all thoughts about the unfairness of their lives, and the fact that they had been through more than their share. There was no point in thinking about it, and no time. Abby Lowell had just emerged from the parking garage. . . .

She had changed out of the perfect Prada suit from the bank, opting for camel-tan slacks and boots, a black turtleneck sweater, and a pale aqua quilted vest. The girl had style.

Parker watched through high-powered field glasses as she walked toward the Fifth Street end of the park, where the kid with lime green hair sat on a bench. She was carrying a Louis Vuitton handbag, and a small nylon tote.

Parker stood in a beautifully appointed room on the fifth floor of the Biltmore, overlooking Olive Street. Pershing Square was stretched out before him. The field of play in a game he wasn't planning to join.

He didn't believe Ruiz with her cock-and-bull story of Damon calling in. And the fact that she and her RHD pals couldn't come up with a more viable setup than that was a sad commentary on the quality of that particular brain trust.

Parker's take was that Abby Lowell had gone to Robbery-Homicide, and RHD had set up this little tableau to seduce Parker, so they could throw a net over him and get him out of the way. If Damon really was going to show, if Bradley Kyle knew that somehow, there was no way they would have invited Kev Parker to the party.

As to what Ms. Lowell ultimately had up her sleeve, he wasn't exactly sure. She was in this thing up to her gorgeous big brown eyes, of that he had no doubt. But Eddie Davis was the muscle, and he had allegedly threatened to kill her.

Blackmailers were in it for two things: money

and power. It wasn't a group activity. The more
people involved, the more diluted the power became, and the more opportunity for mistakes of
some kind.

Across the street, Abby Lowell eyed the guy
with the green hair, went to the other end of the
bench, and sat down, putting the nylon tote on
her lap.

Payoff, Parker thought. That's how they were
setting it up: making it look like she was there
to pay off Damon in exchange for the negatives.

He scanned the perimeter of the park with
the field glasses, looking for Kyle or Roddick.
Then he tilted the glasses upward to check
rooflines. Habit. He wondered where Kelly had
taken herself off to. Probably downstairs in
Smeraldi's, eating a coconut-cream pie and
looking out the window to the square, waiting
for the action to start.

A movie crew was setting up equipment for a
night shoot, backlighting the sculptures to give
them a look that was mysterious or ominous,
depending on what the script called for. They
would be there half the night to get one scene.
It took for-bloody-ever to set up lighting and
get the cameras set to please the director of photography. Then, depending on director and
budget, it would take for-bloody-ever to shoot
the scene. They would rehearse it, talk about it,

rehearse it, talk some more. They would shoot it one way, then another, then do close-ups. The excitement of the movie business. Like watching people sleep.

Parker ran the glasses over the couple of equipment trucks he could see parked on Fifth. Nothing looked out of the ordinary.

Back in the park, Abby was waiting on the bench, tense. She gave the green-haired guy the skunk-eye, but the guy was stoned, and looked catatonic.

5:10.

On the low wall near the statues sat a guy in an army jacket, a black ball cap pulled low, his head down. For a moment he looked as out of it as the stoner on the bench. Then he turned his head a little to the side, toward Fifth Street. Toward Abby Lowell. Parker caught a brief glimpse of face in a wedge of light before it lowered again. Caucasian, young, beat-up.

Damon.

Parker had never seen the kid, and yet he knew in every fiber of his being it was J. C. Damon. There was a tension about the way the kid held himself as he sat there trying to look unconcerned. His gaze kept going back to the park bench, furtive, anxious, then moving to cover everything in his field of vision.

Parker drew a line with the glasses from

Damon back to Abby Lowell, then past Abby
Lowell to the area behind her, a wide half circle
with a radius of about twenty feet, looking for
cops. He widened the arc to include the area directly across from Damon. No sign of Kyle or
Roddick, or anyone Parker knew.

5:12.

Once again he swept the field glasses around
the area where Abby Lowell sat, where the kid
he believed to be Damon sat. From one to the
other, and back again.

Parker dropped the glasses around his neck,
turned, and hurried out of the room. He found
the stairs and raced down them, jogged into the
Olive Street lobby and out the door.

The street was backed up with traffic from
the Fifth Street light. Parker wove his way between the cars to get across, smacking a fist on
the hood of a Volvo when the driver honked
at him.

5:14.

As he came up from street level, he saw that
Damon had gotten down off the wall and was
moving toward Abby Lowell. The kid with the
green hair got up off the bench and turned
toward her as well.

Parker hurried his steps. Green Hair was not
part of the equation. The kid moved toward her,
one hand outstretched.

Damon kept coming.

Abby Lowell stood up.

In his peripheral vision, Parker caught someone else moving across the square, coming from the alcove hiding the escalators to the underground parking. Bulky trench coat, a little too long, collar up.

Bradley Kyle.

Parker hesitated.

A motorcycle engine revved nearby. Sound seemed magnified. The scene froze for an instant in Parker's head.

Then someone screamed, and all hell broke loose.

42

Jace didn't care about the kid with the green hair. The guy was just trying to panhandle. Besides, he created a little diversion. Abby was looking at him, worried, annoyed.

Jace's heart was thumping. Shove the envelope at her, grab the black bag, run like hell. He reached a hand inside his shirt and started to peel back the tape that held the envelope to his belly.

A sound like a chain saw starting registered in the back of his mind. Then a scream. Then everything seemed to happen at once.

"Freeze! Police!"

He didn't know where the shout had come from. His arms went out at his sides. Abby Lowell's eyes were ringed in white.

The kid with green hair had a gun.

"Down on the ground! Down on the ground!"

The motorcycle roared from the Olive Street side of the square, coming straight for them.

Jace didn't have time to even draw breath, or to think that the green-haired cop would shoot him. He lunged for Abby, knocking her to the park bench.

Jace fell into her sideways, just as the cycle hit the cop with the green hair, and blood exploded in every direction.

People were running now, shouting, screaming.

Guns were popping. He didn't know who was shooting, or who was being shot at.

Jace scrambled to get his feet under him. His eyes were on the cycle. Red bike, black mask, helmet. The driver had already swung it around, one-eighty, almost laying it down on the ground. It came back at Jace like a rocket. He went over the bench and ran for his life.

Parker started running the instant he saw the motorcycle. A red Kawasaki Ninja ZX12R. Eddie Davis. He had to have doubled back to his house before the Hollywood cops got there, ditched the Town Car, and grabbed the bike. The bike racing straight at Damon and Abby Lowell, and at the kid with the green hair, who had his back to the danger bearing down on him.

Parker sprinted, opened his mouth to shout.

He never heard the sound. The bike hit Green Hair. A nightmare scene of a body bending the wrong way, blood everywhere.

Davis hit the brakes and laid the cycle almost on its side. One-eighty. Up again and throttle wide open.

People were screaming. The movie crew scattered, some of them running toward the bike, some running toward the street, arms waving.

Parker pulled his gun.

To his right, Bradley Kyle had his weapon out, and was firing.

Damon went over the back of the park bench.

Abby Lowell tried to follow.

Davis roared past.

Parker fired. **BAM! BAM! BAM!**

The cycle swung hard right and went after Damon.

Jace heard him coming. He hit Fifth Street. It was empty. Traffic was detoured because of the movie people. The equipment trucks seemed a mile away. People were standing near them, staring at him. There was nothing they could do.

He veered right in a wide arc, so he could get

a look back without slowing down. The headlights blinded him. Way too close.

Four more strides to the trucks.

Three more strides.

He felt as if he wasn't moving, couldn't
breathe.

Two strides.

He cut between the trucks, took a hard left,
almost wiped out. Stumbling, stumbling, stumbling forward. Sheer will pulled him upright.

The cycle came up over the curb, onto the
sidewalk, and around the back side of the
trucks. Jace ducked between another pair of
trucks. He grabbed The Beast and mounted
from a run, fumbling to catch the pedals, to
start pumping.

If he could stay hidden by the trucks, if he
could get to the other side of Olive Street before
the motorcycle came around . . .

He stood on the pedals, ran on the pedals,
down Fifth to Olive, through the intersection,
horns blaring, lights coming at him, lucky he
didn't end up on a windshield. He jumped the
curb onto the sidewalk.

Glancing over his shoulder, Jace could see the
cycle racing up the opposite side of the street.
He would make it to the intersection before
Jace did.

The light at Olive and Fourth turned red. Nothing blocked the intersection. The motorcycle bounced off the curb, hit Fourth, screamed into a hard left turn.

Pumping, pumping, pumping, Jace's thighs felt as though they would burst. He willed more speed, but it didn't seem to come. The motorcycle ran the intersection and horns blasted as he split the oncoming cars on the one-way street.

Jace made the corner, went left, stuck close to the meters so he couldn't get pinned against the buildings if the cycle made it to the sidewalk. He could see his pursuer pushing between cars up ahead of him, trying to come across.

Turning left again, Jace cut through a small plaza with a fountain, and came to a halt. Before him was the precipitous drop of the Bunker Hill Steps, a stone double staircase with a waterfall running between the two sides. It dropped like a cliff down to Fifth Street, where traffic was now gridlocked. Sirens were screaming.

Jace looked down to the bottom. It would be his death or his salvation. He swallowed hard. Horns were still blasting behind him. He could hear the motorcycle getting closer.

Jace glanced back, saw the headlights coming, turned to the drop in front of him, took a deep breath, and went over the edge.

Several people rushed to the aid of the guy with green hair. Kyle ran past him, chasing the motorcycle, chasing Damon. Parker went to Abby Lowell. She lay over the back of the park bench, as if she had just turned to watch the action leave the park.

"Ms. Lowell? Are you all right?" he called above the noise. People were shouting, sirens were wailing.

Blood stained the back of her aqua vest. She'd caught a bullet. He rested a knee on the bench, bent over her, carefully swept her long hair back so he could see her face.

The brown eyes that rolled to look at him were wild with fear. Her breath was wheezing in the way of an asthmatic. "I can't move! I can't move! Oh, my God! Oh, my God!"

Parker didn't try to move her to see if the bullet had exited. She could bleed to death right in front of him, but if he turned her and a bone or bullet fragment shifted the wrong way, she would be a quadriplegic. Hell of a choice.

"We'll have an ambulance here in two minutes," Parker said, pressing two fingers to the side of her throat. Her pulse was galloping like a racehorse. "What did you feel? Did you feel something hit you from behind?"

"In my shoulder. Yes. In my back. Twice. Am I shot? Oh, my God. Am I shot?"

"Yes."

"Oh, my God!"

She was sobbing now, hysterical. No sign of the stoic, controlled woman trying to bravely deal with the fact that her murdered father lay on the floor at her feet.

"Why did you come here?" Parker asked. He pulled a clean handkerchief from his pocket, carefully reached under her, and felt for exit wounds. "Who set it up?"

She was crying so hard, she was gagging and choking herself.

"Who told you to be here?" Parker asked again. He pulled the handkerchief back, dyed red with blood.

"He did!" she said on a wail. "Oh, my God, I'm going to die!"

"You're not going to die," Parker said calmly. "The paramedics are here. They'll be with you in a minute."

The EMTs had run to the fallen Green Hair and were trying to revive him. He lay on the ground like a broken doll, staring at the afterlife.

"Hey!" Parker called. "I've got a GSW here! She's bleeding!"

One of the EMT crew looked up and acknowledged him. "Coming!"

Parker turned back to Abby. "Who called you? Who called Davis?"

She couldn't have cared less about what Parker wanted to know.

It didn't matter anyway. He had simply been shocked to see Damon show, and he wondered if the kid really had tried to reach out to him. And what it meant if he had.

He hoped he would get a chance to find out.

The Beast bounced and slipped on the stone steps. Going too fast. Jace touched the brakes, twisted a little sideways, angling the bike, trying to control his descent.

Déjà vu. He'd had this dream a hundred times. Out of control, hurtling down, his equilibrium rolling and tumbling in his head. He couldn't tell if he was right side up or ass over teakettle. Nausea rose in his throat.

The bike banged down the steps, back end threatening to overtake the front. Jace tried to make a correction, shifting his weight, and The Beast kicked out from under him and tumbled the last fifteen steps to the sidewalk. Jace rolled and bounced after it, trying to grab hold of something, anything to slow his fall.

He landed at the bottom, and immediately looked back up toward the fountain, toward Fourth Street. The motorcycle sat at the top. Even as he watched, the lunatic with the throttle in his hand made a decision, and the angle of the headlights tipped dramatically downward.

Crazy bastard.

Jace grabbed his bike up off the ground, climbed on, pointed it down Fifth. He raced around the corner at Figueroa, turning toward the Bonaventure Hotel. He checked back over his shoulder again and again. No motorcycle.

He lost himself then, in the same spot he had started his day, under the tangle of bridges that connected downtown to the Harbor Freeway. The place where, three days ago, he had hung out with the other messengers waiting for calls from their dispatchers, all of them complaining that it was going to rain.

His pursuer—if he survived his descent to Fifth Street—would assume Jace had turned down one street or another. He wouldn't think to look here. Jace hoped.

Jace hid the bike and himself behind a huge concrete footing, out of sight from the street. He stripped off his backpack and dropped it, stripped off his coat and threw it on the ground, so hot he thought he was going to vomit. His shirt was soaked with sweat, the kind that reeked of fear. He was shaking like a malaria victim. His legs gave way beneath him and he went down on his knees.

Shit like this only happens in the movies, he thought, bending forward, curling himself into a ball on the ground.

What the fuck? What the fuck? What the fuck **just happened?**

The images flashed through his head. He was going to have nightmares for the rest of his life. The panhandler with the green hair. The cops, the guns. The guy on the motorcycle.

Who the hell was he? Predator? He'd ditched the big gas hog for a rice burner? He had been scary enough in a car. With the motorcycle helmet, the extreme shape of the sport bike, he was a demon from hell for the **Matrix** age.

How had he known to be there? How had the cops known? It didn't make sense to Jace that Abby Lowell would have tipped off either of them. Why would she? She was in on it, whatever "it" was.

Jace had tried to call the detective she had told him was in charge of the case, Parker. But he hadn't gotten him, and even if the woman he'd spoken to had acted immediately, there'd been no time for them to get people set up in the park. The green-haired guy had been there an hour **before** Jace had made the call.

Abby Lowell had double-crossed him. She had thought she could get him arrested and walk away scot-free. So she had called Parker earlier in the day, probably right after Jace had spoken with her. But if she had set it up, she would have walked away without the negatives, and the negatives were what everybody wanted. The negatives were still in their envelope, still taped to Jace's belly.

And even if she had called in the cops, that still didn't explain Predator, if that was even who had been chasing him.

What the hell could he do now?

His pulse had slowed. His breathing had evened out. He was cold, the sweat dried on his skin by the chill of the night air. He wanted not to think, not to have to. He was alone. The light was weird under the bridge, dark, but dappled in spots with the diffused white glow from the streetlights above, like moonlight filtering down through a concrete forest. The hum of tires on the road above him was like white noise seeping into his exhausted brain.

He pushed himself up onto his knees, shrugged into his coat, reached for his back-pack, and dug out his space blanket. The walkie-talkie fell out of it as he unfolded the blanket.

Jace picked it up, turned it on, and held it next to his face, but he didn't press the call button.

His voice would telegraph his fear, his fear would leap across the airwaves, go into Tyler's ear, and frighten him to the core. Bad enough not to know what his big brother was up to, worse to know what he **was** up to, worse still to know that he was afraid.

What could he say to the kid anyway? He didn't know what to do. People were trying to kill him. Every way he turned, he only became more entangled in the mess, like he'd walked into a bramble bush.

I'm fresh out of plans, he thought. He felt hollow inside, like he was just a shell, and if someone was to give him a good kick, the shell would shatter into a million pieces and he would cease to exist.

"Scout to Ranger. Scout to Ranger. Come in, Ranger. Do you read me?"

The walkie-talkie crackled, speaking into the side of Jace's head. He didn't even jump. It was as if his mind had conjured his brother's voice.

"Ranger, do you copy? Come on, Jace. Be there."

He could hear the worry, the uncertainty in Tyler's voice. But he didn't answer. He couldn't. What could he say to Tyler after screwing up their lives this way?

He just squeezed his eyes shut tight, and whispered, "I'm sorry. I'm so, so sorry."

43

Tyler put the radio in his backpack and tried really hard not to start crying. He thought maybe he would pull out a granola bar and eat it to distract himself. It was suppertime anyway. But the idea of eating made him feel sick, so he didn't.

He went back inside the Central Library, his base of operations for most of the day. It somehow made him feel calmer to be in this big, solid, beautiful building full of things he loved, books. All that knowledge and wisdom and excitement and mystery around him, his for the small price of reading words.

But he was really tired now, and he still didn't have a plan that didn't involve superpowers, like Spider-Man had. And he doubted there was a single book in this building that could tell him what to do next. He kept thinking if only he could talk to Jace, but Jace hadn't answered a single radio call all day, and that made him worry.

Why would Jace have bothered to take the radio with him if he wasn't going to use it? Did the fact that he wasn't answering mean he was out of range, or that his batteries were dead? Or did the fact that he wasn't answering mean he **couldn't** answer? And if he couldn't answer, was it because he was in jail, or in a hospital because he'd been shot, or that he was dead?

Or maybe he was just plain gone—out of LA to Mexico or someplace—and Tyler would never see him again. Just like when their mother had died. She'd gone out the door with Jace to go to the hospital, and never came back. No good-bye, no I love you, no I'll miss you. Just gone.

That horrible empty feeling came over him from the inside out, like giant jaws opening to swallow him whole. Tyler pulled his feet up on the bench and hugged his arms around his knees, holding tight as his eyes welled up again.

Jace always told him he borrowed trouble. That wasn't true, Tyler thought, or else he would have for sure given it back to whoever he was supposed to have borrowed it from.

He had thought maybe if he went to the places he knew the bike messengers hung out, he would find Jace.

Jace never told him anything, but Tyler had long ago gotten on the Internet to find out everything he could about the bike messengers who worked downtown. He knew there were about a hundred messengers working for about fifteen different companies. He knew the "tag price" was the base price the client paid for the delivery. He knew the difference between being W-4 (having taxes withheld from salary) and 1099 (being an independent contractor).

Tyler knew that there were certain places that the messengers hung out together when they were between runs. So he had walked to the Spring Street station in Chinatown, taken the Gold Line train to Union Station, transferred to the Red Line, got off at the Pershing Square station, walked down Fifth to the corner at Fifth and Flower.

On one side of the street, messengers were hanging around in front of the library, but none of them was Jace. He went into the Carl's Jr. on the other side of the street and found plenty of weird-looking people—a bald guy with his head tattooed all over, Goth kids with piercings everywhere, green hair, pink hair, dreadlocks—but Jace was not among them.

At Fourth and Flower, Tyler walked up and down in front of the Westin Bonaventure Hotel, looking across the street at the messengers hanging out under the bridge, but he was afraid to go ask them if they'd seen his brother—afraid for himself, on account of they looked kinda scary, and afraid that if he said the wrong thing to the wrong person, he might get Jace in even bigger trouble. Maybe that person would rat him out to the cops or something.

But if Jace had been over there, looking back at the hotel, he for sure would have seen Tyler walking up and down. No one called to him, except a doorman from the hotel, who got suspicious. Tyler had beat it out of there in a hurry.

Over and over during the afternoon, he had gone back and forth between the hangout spots and the library, each time thinking this time he would see Jace, but he never did. He had tried and tried to get him on the radio, but he never had. Now it was dark, and he was afraid to go back down to Fourth Street.

Downtown was a busy place during the day, but once all the people in the office buildings went home, the only ones left on the streets were way scary—crazy, on drugs, looking for trouble. Not a place for a little kid to be walking around alone.

Madame Chen would be worried about him, he knew. Worried sick. The idea made him feel really guilty and bad. He had almost called her a couple of times during the day, but he didn't know what exactly he could tell her. He still didn't know. He didn't know what he was going to do.

He worried that maybe the detectives had bugged the Chens' phones, and if he called, the cops would be able to find him. He was already worried the Chens would be arrested for harboring a fugitive or something. And maybe the fish market was under surveillance, and the cops would see him if he tried to go back.

Tyler sat down on a bench near the restrooms. The library closed at eight. He supposed he could spend the night here if he could find a good hiding spot. But if he was stuck inside the building, he couldn't get radio reception, and what if Jace tried to reach him? Besides, Tyler could only imagine how creepy it was in here when the lights were out and everyone was (supposed to be) gone.

He was right back where he started: alone and scared.

Tyler stuck his hands inside the pockets of his sweatshirt and fingered the business card Detective Parker had given him. He didn't seem like a bad guy. He was kind of funny in a cool sort of way. And when he'd told Tyler he didn't want to see anything bad happen to Jace, Tyler had wanted to believe him. The other detective could have told him the sun comes up in the east, and Tyler would have been suspicious.

Always trust your instincts, Jace told him.

It was now 6:19. His instincts were telling him he wanted to go home. Maybe if he went up the fire escape onto the roof, he could sneak back into the building and let Madame Chen know he was okay. They would have to communicate with notes or sign language or something, in case the place was bugged, but then she would know he was okay, and he could sleep in his own bed, then sneak out really early and come back downtown to try again to find his brother. It wasn't a master plan, but it was a plan.

Tyler wiggled into the straps of his backpack and headed outside. There was some kind of commotion going on across Fifth Street, at the foot of the Bunker Hill Steps. People were standing around talking excitedly, gesturing wildly. Two police cars sat at angles to the curb, lights flashing. Traffic had come to a horn-honking standstill.

Whatever it was about, Tyler wanted no part of it. He hurried up the sidewalk toward Olive Street, his backpack bouncing against his butt as he went. The thing was heavy with his life essentials—granola bars, walkie-talkie, Game Boy, bottle of water, schoolbooks, comic books, and pocket dictionary.

Tyler imagined if he went up a really steep

hill, the thing would overpower him and flip him over backward, and he would have to lie there like a turtle until somebody turned him over. Tomorrow he would leave the schoolbooks at home.

He crossed Grand Avenue and kept going, but the traffic didn't get any better, and the closer he came to Olive Street and Pershing Square, the more people and cop cars and disorder there seemed to be.

The square was bright with floodlights and full of activity and yellow crime-scene tape and people shouting at one another. Tyler felt like he was walking onto a movie set, the scene seemed so unreal. He wound his way between people until he stood on the fringe of it all, eyes wide, ears open.

". . . and they were just standing there, and the next thing I knew . . ."

". . . **Freeze! Police!** And man, it was like . . ."

". . . insane! I thought it was part of the movie, even when . . ."

". . . the guy on the motorcycle. You mean that wasn't a stunt?"

". . . shooting . . ."

". . . screaming . . ."

". . . awesome cycle!"

Tyler had worked his way up to the yellow tape that was preserving the crime scene. He didn't see anyone in handcuffs. He didn't see anyone lying dead on the ground. But about twenty feet in front of him he saw two men having an argument, and he knew them both. Detective Parker and Detective Kyle. Good cop, bad cop.

Detective Kyle was so red in the face, he looked like his whole head was about to pop like a pimple. Detective Parker was so angry, a cop in a uniform got in front of him to hold him back from hitting Detective Kyle.

Pin prickles raced up Tyler's back and down his arms and inside his belly, and he felt weak in the knees. The two detectives had one case in common that Tyler knew about: Jace.

". . . shooting . . ."

". . . screaming . . ."

". . . **Bam!** And the guy is dead on the ground. . . ."

Tyler looked around to see if The Beast was propped up somewhere, or thrown on the ground.

"**. . . Bam! And the guy is dead. . . .**"

Tyler tried to back up a step, and banged into someone who had come up behind him. His head was swimming. He thought he was going to be sick.

Parker was still yelling at Kyle. Kyle was yelling back at him.

"I wasn't firing at her! How many times do I have to tell you that?" Kyle jabbed a finger at him. "None! That's how many times I have to tell you a goddam thing, Parker! You're not on this case, and if I have anything to do with it, you're not on the force."

"You don't have any power over me, Bradley," Parker barked back, leaning around the chubby cop who was still blocking him from getting to the other detective. "Nothing you could say or do could make any more impact on my life than a mouse dropping."

He stepped back, lifted his hands in front of him to show the guy in uniform he had no dangerous intent, then stepped around him. He leaned toward Detective Kyle and said something only the two of them could hear.

Then Parker turned, took three steps away, and looked right at Tyler.

44

Parker had stayed with Abby Lowell until the EMTs loaded her into the ambulance and drove away. She would go directly to surgery. It would be hours before anyone could talk with her, and by the time she was allowed visitors, Robbery-Homicide would have total control of who went in and out of her room.

A couple of motorcycle cops who had been dispatched to Pershing Square because of the movie shoot had taken off after Davis, who had taken off after Damon. LAPD choppers had been dispatched, and every news chopper in the city was swarming over the scene like vultures at the kill. The gridlocked traffic made it impossible for street units to join the pursuit, but that didn't stop them from running lights and sirens.

What a cluster fuck, Parker thought.

"What the hell are you doing here, Parker?" Bradley Kyle, red-faced, steam coming out of his ears, said.

"I know I declined your invitation to this

little soiree," Parker said, "but you can't seriously be all that surprised to see me, can you, Bradley?"

Kyle didn't bother to deny the accusation. Another black mark against Ruiz. He looked away and called out, "Did anyone get a plate number on the cycle?"

"It belongs to Eddie Davis," Parker said. "Did you invite him too? Were you setting up to reenact the shootout at the OK Corral?" he asked, the sarcasm like acid in his voice. "Congratulations, Wyatt Earp, you damn near managed to kill someone. Or did you mean to hit Damon? He's the perfect fall guy if he's dead."

"I didn't shoot anyone."

Parker looked around, feigning shock. "Did I miss the guy on the grassy knoll **again**? I didn't fire until Davis turned and was clear. You were shooting before I was."

Kyle wouldn't look at him.

"Are you going to try to tell me the dead guy did it?" Parker asked, incredulous. "His death grip pulled the trigger and shot Abby Lowell in the back—twice?"

Jimmy Chew stepped between them then, his back to Kyle. "Hey, fellas, let's cool it down. One dead cop at the scene is enough, right?"

"I wasn't firing at her!" Kyle shouted, like an

imbecile. Parker hoped the TV news crews had gotten that one on tape.

Kyle bobbed to one side of Chew just to jab a finger at Parker. "How many times do I have to tell you that? None! That's how many times I have to tell you a goddam thing, Parker! You're not on this case, and if I have anything to do with it, you're not on the force."

Parker laughed, the sound caustic with derision. "You don't have any power over me, Bradley. Nothing you could say or do could make any more impact on my life than a mouse dropping."

He held his hands up to Jimmy Chew to say he had no violent physical intent, and took a step back and then around the officer.

"Too bad Ruiz didn't come to the party," Parker said. "She could confiscate your weapon and start the IA investigation right now."

"Yeah?" Kyle sneered. "I hear she's got her hands full already."

"She's got nothing," Parker said. "She's wasting everybody's time, including mine. I haven't shot anybody. I'm not slinking around, Tony Giradello's lapdog, trying to keep this fucking shell game going."

"You don't know what you're talking about, Parker."

"Don't I? I know Eddie Davis is driving

around in a Lincoln Town Car just like the
Crowne Enterprises Town Cars. How do you
think that came to be, Bradley? I know Davis
and Lenny Lowell were blackmailing somebody,
and I've got a pretty damn good idea why. How
about you? What do you know about that?"

"I know you took all the paperwork on a
murder investigation and stole evidence out of
Lowell's safe-deposit box, including twenty-five-
thousand dollars cash," Kyle said. "That's a
felony."

"Bullshit," Parker said. "I had a court order.
The money is sealed, signed, and safe. It hasn't
made it to Property yet because I've been a little
busy getting stabbed in the back by my partner
and my captain, and trying to keep from letting
Robbery-Homicide screw me over again."

"You're interfering with an investigation,"
Kyle said. "I could have you arrested."

Parker stepped into Kyle's personal space, and
smiled like a snake.

"Go ahead, Bradley," he said softly. "You
cocksucking little weasel. Do it here, now. Every
media news source in LA is watching. Have
Jimmy here slap the cuffs on me, then you go
over there and explain to the reporters why you
had a conversation with Tony Giradello at the
DA's fund-raiser, using my name and Eddie
Davis's name in the same sentence."

Kyle didn't try to deny it, or to correct him. Diane hadn't been sure of the name, other than that it started with a **D.** Parker had made the jump to Damon, but that was before Eddie Davis had been identified by Obi Jones. "I don't have to explain myself. I'm doing my job."

"Yeah," Parker said. "There's a lot of that going around."

Disgusted, angry, he turned and started to walk away from Kyle, looking for Kelly in the crowd, and finding the kid from the alley staring at him with big eyes. Andi Kelly was standing right behind him.

Parker didn't want to react. He didn't want Bradley Kyle wondering what he was looking at.

His eyes went from the kid to Andi, back to the kid, back to Andi. Telepathy would have been a good thing, but he hadn't mastered it. Kelly probably thought he was having a seizure.

"Parker!" The voice came from behind him. Kyle. "You can't just go."

Parker glanced back at him. "Despite all the rumors I've heard about you, Bradley, you can't have it both ways. Not with me anyway. And as you pointed out: This isn't my case anymore."

"You're a police officer. You drew and fired your weapon."

"Un-fucking-believable," Parker muttered.

He looked at Jimmy Chew. "Hey, Jimmy, come here."

Chewalski came over and Parker unholstered and handed the officer his SIG. "You'll take that to Ballistics for the purpose of elimination in an officer-involved shooting. Let Internal Affairs know where it is."

"Will do, boss," Chew said, then gave Kyle a long you're-such-a-dick look and walked away.

Kyle looked like a spoiled kid who had thrown a fit and now all his friends were picking up their toys and going home.

"You're a witness," he said, pouting.

"Yeah," Parker said. "I'll be happy to come in tomorrow and give a long and detailed report on how you shot a woman in the back."

Turning away from Kyle, he tried to find his little friend again, but the kid had gone, and Kelly too. Parker ducked under the tape and walked away from the lights and the noise and the people. He was going back across the street to the Biltmore to sit in a civilized place and have a civilized drink.

He exited the square, stepped onto the sidewalk, and glanced left. The city was doing some kind of work to a retaining wall along that side of the park. As with most construction projects around town, someone had seen a need to throw up a lot of plywood and make a tunnel of sorts out of the sidewalk for twenty yards or so. A canvas for graffiti taggers, and a welcome haven at night for street people and rats. The kid was standing in the mouth of the tunnel.

Parker stopped and put his hands in his pockets and looked at the boy.

"Funny meeting you here," Parker said. "You get around for a kid. You don't work for Internal Affairs, do you?"

"No, sir."

"What brings you here?"

"The subway."

Parker gave a weary chuckle. "Everybody's a smart-ass." He sighed and took a couple of steps toward the tunnel. "Your mission, I meant. You're a ways from Chinatown, and, smart kid like you, you know this isn't a great place to be walking around after dark by yourself. Hell, **I** wouldn't walk around down here by myself. Where are your parents? They let you just run all over the city?"

"Not exactly." The boy nibbled on his bottom lip and looked everywhere but at Parker. "If I tell you something, will you promise not to arrest me?"

"That depends. Did you kill somebody?"

"No, sir."

"Are you a menace to society?"

"No, sir."

"Are you an enemy of the state?"

"I don't think so."

"Then, whatever you've done, I'll give you a pass," Parker said. "Looks like I'll be out of this job soon anyhow."

"I don't like that other guy," the boy confessed. "He's mean. I saw him at Chen's Fish Market this morning."

Parker arched a brow. "Really? And what was he doing there?"

"Well, he came to see Madame Chen's car, only some other cops had already taken it, which made him mad. And then he asked a bunch of questions, and was really rude."

"Mmm . . ." Parker leaned a little closer to confide, "I think he has self-esteem issues."

"He made Boo Zhu cry. Boo Zhu is de-vel-op-mentally challenged."

Parker loved the way the boy couldn't quite get his little mouth around big words. The words were all in his head, his tongue just hadn't matured as quickly as his intellect had.

"There you go," Parker said. "He's probably mean to small animals too. The kind of kid who went through a lot of hamsters, if you know what I mean."

The kid didn't, but he was too polite to say so. Odd little character.

"So what is it you want to tell me that I'm not going to arrest you for?"

The boy looked all around and up and down, looking for spies and eavesdroppers.

"I'll tell you what," Parker said. "I was just on my way across the street to grab some dinner. You hungry? You want to come? The cheeseburgers are on me."

"I'm an ovo-lac-to vegetarian," the kid said.

"Of course you are. All the tofu you can eat, then. Come on."

The boy fell into step beside him, but just out of reach. As they waited at the corner for the light to change, Parker said, "You know, I think we should be on a first-name basis by now. How about you?"

The sideways suspicious look.

"I can't figure out anything about you by just your first name," Parker said. "You can call me Kev."

The light changed. Parker waited.

The kid swallowed hard, took a big breath, let it out. "Tyler," he said. "Tyler Damon."

45

Tyler Damon gave Parker the saga of the Damon brothers, picking like a bird at a plate of pasta in Smeraldi's. The big blue eyes periodically made passes around the room and out to the Biltmore's Olive Street lobby, taking it all in like he'd fallen into an LA version of a Harry Potter book.

Parker's heart went out to him. The poor kid was terrified for his big brother, and terrified for himself. He had to feel like everything about his life was changing on a dime, and here he sat, telling it all to a cop.

"What's going to happen to us?" he asked miserably.

"You're going to be fine, Tyler," Parker said. "We need to find your brother so he'll be fine too. Can we make that happen?"

The skinny shoulders went up to his ears. He stared at his plate. "He hasn't answered any of my radio calls."

"He's been pretty busy today. I have a feeling we'll have better luck tonight."

"What if that guy with the motorcycle got him?"

"The guy with the motorcycle doesn't have the motorcycle anymore," Parker said. "According to what I was hearing across the street, your brother was hauling ass on that bike of his. The bad guy took a dive off the Bunker Hill Steps. He should have died."

"But he got away?"

"Your brother was long gone by then." Parker tossed some bills on the table and got up. "Come on, kiddo, let's blow this shack. You're riding shotgun."

Tyler Damon's eyes went huge. "Really?"

"You've got to be my partner. This isn't going to work without you."

"I have to call Madame Chen first."

"We'll call her from the car. She's not going to ground you or anything, is she?"

The boy shook his head. "I just don't want her to worry."

"We'll call her."

They went out through the main lobby, where Andi Kelly was loitering. Parker raised a hand and gave the universal sign for "I'll call you," but didn't pause. He needed Tyler

Damon's trust, and he wasn't going to get it by giving his attention to other people.

Parker's car sat in a red zone with an LAPD pass clipped to the sun visor. They got in, the boy trying not to make a big deal of being impressed with the convertible. Parker put the top up for privacy, and because, with the sun gone, it was damn cold. He made a mental note to take the kid out in the Jag after this mess was over.

"So," he said, "does Jace have a girlfriend?"

"No."

"A boyfriend?"

"No."

"Does he have any friends he might try to stay with?"

"I don't think so," Tyler said. "He's too busy to hang out."

The boy explained where he had been looking for his brother and why. Parker thought about it for a minute.

"Do you know if he was carrying much money with him?"

"We don't have very much money," the boy said.

"Credit cards?"

Tyler shook his head.

It wasn't likely Damon would have gone to a

hotel anyway, Parker thought. Too confined, too many people, too much potential for trouble.

He made a phone call to the Midnight Mission and asked a friend there if anyone matching Jace Damon's description had come in, and to call him back if a possibility did show up.

His next call was to Madame Chen to allay her fears that Tyler had been abducted, or worse. She asked to speak to the boy, and they conversed in Mandarin, Tyler glancing up at Parker every so often, Parker pretending not to listen. Then the boy handed the phone back to him.

"I need Tyler to help me tonight, Madame Chen. I have to find Jace before anyone else does, and I can't do that without Tyler."

Parker could tell by the quality of the silence that she didn't like the idea.

"I won't let anything happen to him," Parker promised.

"You will bring him back tonight?"

A question rather than an order. She was worried. Hell of a woman, Parker thought, taking these kids in literally off the street. He didn't know a single person who would have done the same, himself included.

"I'll bring him back as soon as I can."

Another silence. Her voice was strained when she spoke again. "He has school tomorrow."

Parker didn't point out the incongruity of what she'd just said. She only wanted for their lives to go back to normal.

"I'll bring him back as soon as I can," he said again. He wanted to tell her that he could script this and that everything would work out like a Hallmark movie, but he couldn't.

"Take care of him," she said. "Take care of them both."

"I will," Parker said, and ended the call.

Tyler was watching him, watching his face, trying to read him the way he would read about Pythagoras, or figure out a math problem. It had to be frustrating for him in a way, Parker thought: having that big 168 IQ, but still being a little kid with little kid fears, and no real power over his life.

"You got a nickname?" Parker asked.

The boy hesitated for a minute. Like maybe he had one he didn't want.

"On the radio, my name is Scout," he said, brightening. "Jace is Ranger."

Parker nodded. "Scout. I like that. Buckle up, Scout. Let's ride."

46

He needed to get rid of the negatives. Just get rid of them, get them to someone who didn't want to kill him. He'd been stupid to try to get something for them, but he had wanted someone to pay for Eta. To appease his own conscience, Jace supposed.

But no. This wasn't about him. He'd answered a call. He'd had no ulterior motive. It hadn't been his choice to be put in this position, just as it hadn't been Eta's choice. Other people had made choices with malice aforethought. He and Eta had just gotten in the way. Now he had to get out.

The evening chill had grown more damp. He could smell the ocean in it. When he wasn't sitting under a concrete bridge cocooned in a giant piece of Reynolds Wrap, Jace loved evenings like this. He liked to pull on a warm jacket and go up on the Chens' roof and look at the lights. He liked the soft, diffused quality of them when the ocean mist hung in the air. Standing on that roof was one of the few times he actually liked feeling alone.

He pushed to his feet, trying not to moan as stiff joints and tendons stretched reluctantly. He needed to keep moving or he wouldn't be able to move at all, and some junkie could stumble along and knock his head in for his space blanket.

Maybe if he could get the negatives to a reporter, to a TV station, he thought. Everyone in LA could find out about them together, decide together who was paying whom for what. Maybe this whole nightmare he was living could be made into a reality program. He should write the treatment himself, right now, get it off to an agent or a producer, or however that worked.

"Scout to Ranger, Scout to Ranger. Ranger, do you read me?"

The muffled voice came out of Jace's coat pocket. He steeled himself against the need to answer.

"Pick up, Ranger!" Tyler's voice pleaded. "Jace! Pick up! I'm in trouble!"

Parker grabbed the boy by the shoulders and pretended to jostle him. Tyler put his own hands around his throat and made a sound like he was being strangled.

"Tyler!"

"Ja—"

He clamped his hand over his mouth, cutting off the sound.

Parker snatched the walkie-talkie. "I want the negatives or the kid dies."

"Leave him alone, you motherfucker!"

"I want the negatives!" Parker shouted.

"You get the negatives when I get my brother."

Parker gave him instructions to meet them on the lowest level of the parking garage beneath the Bonaventure Hotel in half an hour.

"If you hurt him," Damon warned, "I'll kill you."

"If you fuck this up, like you fucked up Jace in the park," Parker said, "I'll kill you both."

He turned the radio off, and looked at his young cohort.

"That was mean," Tyler said.

Parker nodded. "Yeah, it was, but if you had just radioed him and told him to meet you because you had a cop sitting here telling you to, do you think he would have come?"

"No."

"You think he'll be mad?"

"Yes."

"Would you rather he was mad, or dead?"

The boy was silent for a moment as Parker

started the car and pulled away from the front entrance of the hotel.

"I wish this wasn't happening," Tyler said.

"I know."

They sat in silence for a moment, waiting for Jace to emerge from the gloom.

"Kev?" the boy asked in a small, shy voice.

"Yes, Scout?"

"When I asked you before what's going to happen to Jace and me . . . I meant, like, after it's over. Will Jace and I get to stay together?"

"What do you mean?"

"Jace always said that if anybody ever found out about us, Children and Family Services would come, and everything would change."

"You're my partner," Parker said. "I'd never rat you out."

"But that other detective knows I live with the Chens, and he knows Jace is my brother. And he's pretty pissed off at you."

"Don't worry about him, kid. Bradley Kyle is going to have a lot of other things to worry about. Trust me."

Tyler sat up, suddenly at attention. "There's Jace!"

"Okay. Down in your seat," Parker said, putting the car in gear. "He can't see you until we're down there."

They rolled into the garage, well behind Jace,

following from a distance, letting him move down from level to level to level.

"Does your brother own a gun?" Parker asked.

"No, sir."

"Chinese throwing stars?"

"No, sir."

"Is he schooled in the ways of killing men with his mind?"

"People can do that?" Tyler asked.

"I saw it in a ninja movie."

The boy chuckled a little. "That's not real."

"Perception is reality," Parker said.

Only a few cars occupied spaces on the lowest level. People who wanted to park nearest the elevators so they could become stuck in one during an earthquake while the building pancaked down on top of them.

Jace kept his bike in motion, like it was a shark that had to stay moving to live. Parker slowed his car to a stop and popped the automatic locks.

"Okay, Scout, you're on."

Jace sat on The Beast, barely moving, going just enough so that he wouldn't have to start from a dead standstill if he needed to move fast. Then suddenly Tyler was running to him.

"Tyler! Run!" Jace called. "Get in the elevator! Go to security!"

Tyler ran straight for him instead. Jace dumped the bike and grabbed his brother, shoving him toward the doors to the elevators. If Predator had them in his sights, he had no reason not to kill them both. The only good witness was a dead witness.

"Tyler! Go!"

Tyler spun around him in a circle. "Stop yelling! You have to listen to me for a change!"

What a fucking nightmare, Jace thought. He reached inside his coat, pulled out the envelope with the negatives in it, hurled it as hard as he could away from the two of them, and away from the guy getting out of the silver convertible Tyler had tumbled from.

Not Predator.

"You have to listen!" Tyler said again.

The guy at the car held his arms out to his sides. In one hand he held a badge.

Jace shoved Tyler behind him and moved a couple of steps backward. "What the fuck is this?"

"Jace, I'm Kev Parker. I'm here to help you out of this mess."

47

Eddie Davis had been told numerous times in his life that he would never amount to anything. The reasons varied. Some people blamed him, said he was stupid and lazy and didn't apply himself. Other people—his mother, specifically—had always blamed fate. Life just had it in for Eddie. Eddie chose to believe the second reason.

He had plenty of brains, lots of great ideas. Of course, none of them involved needing an education or doing any kind of hard work—that was what made them great ideas. Only an idiot would want to have to work. People were jealous of him because he had figured out that particular life mystery, and they turned on him every time. That was what happened again and again to screw up his life.

This fucking mess he was in now was a perfect example. He had masterminded a fucking brilliant plan. And the one person he should have been able to trust had turned on him. His own lawyer, for God's sake.

A person was supposed to be able to trust his lawyer. There was that confidential privilege thing, right? That had been the genius of the plan—he hooked his lawyer in when the game was already in motion. The murder had already happened. Whatever he told Lenny was confidential, so the lawyer couldn't rat him out. Eddie had needed someone to take the pictures of the client paying him off. He would split the money 70–30. Of course he deserved more since it was his idea and he had done the killing. The deal was too sweet for Lenny to resist.

They had milked the client a couple of times, then agreed to one final big payday in exchange for the negatives. It was then that Eddie had heard detectives were nosing around, asking questions about him. The detectives who had investigated the murder. That meant only one thing to Eddie: Lenny had dropped the dime on him and figured to end up with all the money and the one negative they had saved out in case they wanted to use it later on. Lenny would have cut him out of his own game, and run off to Tahiti or someplace no one would find him.

A man's lawyer was supposed to take his secrets to the grave, right?

Lenny Lowell had taken Eddie's there early. And it served him right.

Eddie had set up the final drop, told Lenny the client would be there, told the client nothing. His plan had been to intercept the negatives and kill the messenger as a warning to Lenny. Then he'd have the lawyer in his pocket to stand up for him, lie for him, give him alibis, do whatever Eddie needed him for in the future.

But everything had gone wrong because of the fucking bike messenger, and Eddie had been so damned mad. And it was all Lenny's fault anyway, so if he couldn't kill the messenger, he might as well kill Lenny. Get the lawyer to give up the last negative, then beat his head to a pulp. There was just something so satisfying in beating a head in.

"Ouch!" Eddie howled, twisting around to give the bitch stitching him an ugly look. "Fucking cunt! That hurts!"

The woman averted her eyes and apologized in Mexican. At least, it sounded like an apology.

He turned back around, and took a pull on the tequila bottle and a drag on his cigarette. One of the cops had nicked him good. The bullet had torn a gash in his side about three inches long, and it felt like it had maybe chipped a rib. If the bullet had hit a couple of inches to the left, it would have taken out a kidney, and he'd be dead. He should figure he was lucky, but he didn't.

If he was lucky, his fucking twelve-K Jap Ninja wouldn't be scrap metal at the bottom of the fucking Bunker Hill Steps. The only lucky thing about it was that he hadn't broken his neck, and he'd been able to jack a car and get the hell out of there.

Now he sat in this shithole, backdoor, spic "clinic" in East LA, getting stitched up by some bitch who probably spent her days cleaning toilets for white people.

Hector Munoz, the guy who ran the place, sure as hell wasn't a doctor, but he would keep his mouth shut for a couple hundred bucks, and he always had a good supply of Oxycodone—Eddie's drug of choice.

The cell phone Eddie had left lying on the metal table beside him—the table with all the needles and scissors and the bedpan he was using for an ashtray—went off. He knew who it was. He'd been waiting for the call. He'd been working on his lie for two hours. His client was expecting the negatives. Now Eddie had to break the news that that wasn't going to happen.

He grabbed the phone. "Yeah?"

"You can have the negatives." He'd never

heard the voice before, young, male. The bike messenger. "I just don't want to die, that's all. It's not worth it. I thought Abby Lowell would pay for them. I never figured she'd call the cops. She told me she was in it with you—"

"How the fuck did you get this phone number?"

"From her."

He sounded scared. He should be. This kid had caused Eddie nothing but grief. He'd wrecked a windshield, wrecked the Ninja, cost Eddie time and money. Shit, he'd had to kill two extra people because of this little fuck. And now the kid thought he could shake him down.

"What do you want?" Eddie snapped.

Nurse Ratched jabbed him with the needle again. He swung around and backhanded her, knocking her into the metal table, making a lot of noise. The woman put her hands over her face and started to cry.

"Tie the fucking knot and get the fuck away from me!"

She started blabbering and jabbering. Hector Munoz cracked the door open from the other side of his business—a strip club featuring a naked all-girl Mariachi band. He smiled nervously, his thin mustache rippling over his upper lip like a worm.

"Eddie? **Muchacho?**"

"Shut the fucking door!"

Eddie put his phone against his head again. "What do you want?"

"I want out," the kid said. "I just want out. I don't even know who's in the fucking pictures. I just knew if the negatives were worth killing for, they had to be worth money. Throw me a couple grand. Enough for me to get out of town—"

"Shut the fuck up," Eddie snapped. "Be at Elysian Park in twenty minutes."

"Go out there so you can kill me? Fuck that. I've got what you want. You can come to me."

"Where are you?"

"Under the bridge at Fourth and Flower."

"How do I know you won't set me up?"

"With the cops? They think I killed the lawyer, why would I call them? If I wanted cops, I would have stayed in Pershing Square."

"I still don't like it," Eddie said.

"Then don't come. You know what? Forget it. Maybe I can sell them to a tabloid or something."

"All right. Don't get your balls in a twist. There's gotta be cops all over down there still. It's too risky. I'm driving a stolen car, for Christ's sake."

"That's your problem."

Eddie wanted to reach through the phone and choke the little shit. "Look, I can get you five grand, but you have to give me a couple hours to get the money, and the meet has to be somewhere cops aren't driving by every three minutes."

Eddie thought about it for a minute. He wanted a place where there wouldn't be a lot of people around at this time of night. Had to have escape routes and good access to a freeway. "Olvera Street Plaza. Two hours. And, kid? Double-cross me, and I'll skin your dick and feed it to you while you bleed to death. You got that?"

"Yeah. Whatever. Just bring the money."

Eddie ended the call and got off the exam table. The door cracked open again, and Hector slithered in. He was skinny and oily, and shook all over like a shit-ass Chihuahua dog. The little Mexican chick hurried up to him and rattled off a lot of gibberish, gesturing at Eddie. Eddie took a last drag on his cigarette, and shrugged into his shirt.

"Hector, I need to borrow your car."

Hector smiled that nervous smile again. "Sure, man, whatever." He pulled a set of keys out of his pants pocket and tossed them to Eddie. "It's the blue Toyota with the flames all down the sides."

"Great."

"What you gonna do, man?"

Eddie looked at him with his dead eyes and said, "I'm gonna go kill somebody. I'll see you later."

48

On weekends the plaza on Olvera Street is ringed with tourists and Mexican families watching Aztec dancers or listening to Mariachi bands. On a weeknight in the dead of winter, there are no tourists, only transients looking for a park bench to sleep on.

Jace paced a slow half circle at the edge of the plaza, feeling like a goat that had been staked out as lion bait, waiting for the guy who had tried repeatedly to kill him. Waiting for the guy who had twisted his life into a nightmare, who had murdered an innocent woman. Jace let his outrage singe the edges of his fear. He would be a part of taking down Eta's killer. He had argued with Parker to be in on it. It was his duty to Eta.

The wind was rustling the leaves of the big fig trees, putting him on edge as he tried to sharpen his ear for the sound of a shoe scraping on pavement, the hammer of a gun being cocked.

Jace had brought Tyler here a million times.

It was an easy walk from Chinatown, and an in-expensive day out for people with limited re-sources. Free shows, an outdoor market of stalls with cheap trinkets and T-shirts.

The park was supposedly the heart of LA's original 1781 settlement. In a city where change and all things cutting-edge rule, the adobe structures and old tile walkways gave the im-pression of being in another world. And Tyler, who absorbed detail and history like a sponge, loved it.

If anything happened to that kid, Jace was going to dismember Kev Parker with his bare hands. There had been no time to take Tyler home. They had to set up, get into their posi-tions, and do it before Davis could arrive. He had asked for a couple of hours. There was no way of knowing what he meant to do with that time. His intentions could have been the same as theirs, to get here early with a plan.

Parker had given Tyler the job of lookout, and left him in the car with his walkie-talkie.

A big black guy was lying on his side on a bench Jace had walked past twice, sleeping, snoring, reeking of bourbon. He looked like a sea lion flopped on the beach, the moonlight washing over him and the rags he had covered himself with. Another innocent bystander unwittingly waiting to die, Jace thought. He knocked the guy on his shoes.

"Hey, buddy, wake up. Get up."

The man didn't move. Jace grabbed hold of an ankle and gave a yank. "Hey, mister, you need to get out of here."

The old drunk just went on snoring. Jace moved away from him. If he was that dead to the world, he was probably as safe as he could be here. Jace walked away.

A dot of light flashed at him from across the plaza. Parker. Davis was coming.

The excitement building in Eddie's gut was a lot like the anticipation of sex. A fist of tension, all his nerve endings starting to buzz. He loved his work.

He loved that he was so fucking smart. He'd come up with the perfect plan to cut away all the loose ends of this deal and ride off into the sunset. He could already see himself stretched out on the beach in Baja with a cigar, a bottle of tequila, and some topless Mexican babe ready to do whatever freaky, kinky thing he wanted her to do.

He could see the kid pacing around the plaza, probably ready to shit his pants. Stupid kid.

Except that he probably wasn't so stupid that he hadn't brought a gun or something this time to protect himself.

What he hadn't brought with him was cops. Eddie had done his recon. No plainclothes cop–looking cars in the area. You could always tell cops by the shit rides the city gave them. The place was deserted except for a few homeless losers with their shopping carts parked next to benches.

Eddie himself was traveling light. The only thing he carried with him was his knife.

Parker had given Jace a gun, a .22 caliber handgun he had taken out of a case in the trunk of his car. It seemed a pretty wild thing for a cop to do, but Jace had figured out quickly that Kev Parker was not a mainstream kind of guy. He was riding around in a convertible with no police radio, only a scanner. He didn't have a partner—not with him anyway. They had stopped en route and picked up a crazy woman who was a newspaper reporter.

If Jace hadn't looked at Parker's ID, he wouldn't have believed the guy was a cop at all. First of all, he dressed too well to be a cop. Even his shoes looked expensive, and that was one thing you could always count on with cops—the bad shoes.

Still, Jace didn't like the idea of trusting him. This was all happening too fast. But he didn't see that he had any choice. The only way he was getting out of this mess alive was for someone to take Eddie Davis out.

He could see Davis coming, the shape of a small vending machine in a long dark coat. His palms started to sweat and acid rose in his throat like the red stuff in a thermometer.

It would be over in the next few minutes. Jace's only hope was that he would live to tell the tale.

Parker watched Eddie Davis through night-vision binoculars as he crossed the plaza. LAPD may not have been able to afford pens that didn't leak, but Parker had no such budget limitations. He kept a small treasure trove of gadgets in the trunk of his car.

Clipped to the bridge of the binoculars was a small, wireless parabolic microphone that fed him sound through a discreet earphone. In his other ear was an earbud for the walkie-talkie that connected him to Tyler, in the car.

He had left the boy with Andi Kelly, and didn't know which one was more liable to keep the other out of trouble. They had picked Kelly up on their way. If Parker's hunch paid off, she was going to get one hell of a story.

"Where's the money?" Jace asked. Davis was still ten feet away.

"It's on the way."

"What? You never said anything about anybody else," Jace said. He was trembling. The guy standing in front of him was a murderer.

"You never asked," Davis said. "I don't carry that kind of cash around. What did you think? That I'd rob an ATM?"

He looked like something from **Dawn of the Dead** as he stood there with the streetlight washing over him. He had a strip of white tape across his nose. One eye was almost swollen shut, and he looked like someone had hit him across the left side of his face with a brick.

He stood with his arms crossed, casual, like they were a couple of strangers chatting while they waited for a bus.

"So where are the negatives?"

"They're safe," Jace said. He rubbed his hand over the gun in his pocket. He didn't know anything about using a gun. Parker had said, **What's to know? Point and shoot.**

"There must be someone big in those pictures to be worth all this, for people to be killed over them," Jace said now.

Davis smiled like a crocodile. "The killing's the fun part."

He started to take a step closer.

Jace pulled the .22 out of his pocket. "You're fine right there. I don't want you coming any closer."

Davis gave a little huff. "You're some pain in the ass, kid. How do I know you've even got the negatives? Maybe you came here to rob me."

"Maybe I came here to kill you," Jace said. "That woman you murdered at Speed Couriers? She was a good person."

"So?" Davis shrugged. "I just do my job. It's nothing personal."

Jace wanted to shoot him then, just **Bam!** point-blank in the face. That was what he deserved. No need for the taxpayers to waste a nickel on him.

This is for Eta. . . .

"I hope my brother doesn't get killed." Tyler tried to sound matter-of-fact about it. The truth was, he was so scared, he thought he might throw up.

"Kev won't let that happen."

They sat hunched down in the front seat of Parker's car. Well, Andi was hunched more than he was. It didn't take that much hunching for Tyler to be pretty much out of sight.

"Are you his girlfriend?" he asked.

"Naw . . . Kev's a loner. Until this week, I hadn't seen him in a long time," she said. "He's a good guy. He didn't used to be, but he is now. He used to be a jerk."

"And then what?"

"And then he took a long look at himself and he didn't like what he saw. I'm pretty sure he's the first man in recorded history to make the decision to grow and change, and actually pull it off."

"He seems pretty cool—for a cop."

"You don't like cops?"

Tyler shook his head.

"Why is that?"

He shrugged with one shoulder. "'Cause that's how it is."

He turned away to avoid her trying to figure him out. Headlights flashed as a car turned toward them.

Tyler jumped in his seat, fumbled for the walkie-talkie, pressed the call button.

"Scout to Leader, Scout to Leader! Bogie! Bogie!"

If there was one thing Parker hated, it was a wild card, unless the wild card was himself. Davis had called in a ringer, and what the hell was that about? He didn't need help getting a pack of negatives from one kid, and there was no way he was actually going to pay for them.

He touched the button on his mike. "Roger that. We've got a bogie coming in."

Countdown to showtime.

"You're a real piece of shit," Jace said.

Davis didn't react. "Yeah, people tell me that all the time." He went to reach inside his coat. "I want a smoke."

"Keep your hands where I can see them," Jace ordered.

Davis gave a big sigh. "Amateurs."

"Yeah," Jace said. "Amateurs make mistakes. Get jumpy. Pull the trigger when they don't mean to."

That smile crawled across Davis's wide face again. "You want to kill me so bad, you can taste it. Maybe you've got a future in my business."

Jace said nothing. The creep was trying to yank his chain, distract him. His arms were getting tired holding the gun out in front of him. Where the hell was the guy with the money?

Headlights bobbed nearby. He almost made the mistake of turning to look.

The air around them seemed as thick as the ocean. Hard to breathe. The only sound he could hear was the black guy snoring on the park bench.

"Here comes the money, honey," Davis said.

Parker waited for the new member of the troupe to appear. At Tyler's alert, his sensitivity to every stimulus heightened to an almost unbearable level. Every sound seemed louder. The touch of the night air on his skin was too much. He was more aware of his breathing, of his heart tripping faster.

His money was on Phillip Crowne.

The daughter, Caroline, may have had motive, but he couldn't see a girl that age being able to pull it off—having her mother killed, setting up her lover to take the fall, and keeping it all quiet. No. Young women in love were all about passion and drama and over-the-top demonstrations of both.

Nor would Rob Cole have taken the fall for

her. Guys like Cole didn't take responsibility for
their own actions, let alone someone else's. If
Rob Cole had thought that Caroline had murdered Tricia, he would have been singing that
song at the top of his lungs.

Parker liked the brother for it. Andi Kelly had
told him Phillip Crowne had been seen having
dinner with his sister the night she was killed.
The dinner conversation had been serious.
Phillip claimed Tricia had talked about divorcing Cole, but the discussion could just as easily
have been about Tricia wanting to blow the
whistle on her brother's siphoning of funds
from the charitable trust.

No one had ever been able to prove Phillip
had been helping himself—but then, everyone
had been focused on stringing up Rob Cole.
A celebrity scandal was so much more interesting than plain old vanilla embezzling. There was
nothing sexy or exciting about Phillip Crowne,
while going after Rob Cole had all the ingredi-
ents of America's favorite pastime: tearing down
the idol.

Besides, Rob Cole had motive, means, and
opportunity. He'd been right there at the scene
of the crime when it had happened. He had no
viable alibi for the time of the murder. Parker
was willing to bet Phillip Crowne hadn't gotten
more than a perfunctory look from RHD, if

that. And it hadn't hurt him to be the son of one of the most influential men in the city either. Norman Crowne backed the DA. Phillip Crowne and Tony Giradello had known each other since law school.

If Eddie Davis and Lenny Lowell had been blackmailing Phillip, was it such a stretch to imagine Phillip Crowne going to his old buddy Giradello for a favor? It wasn't that difficult for Parker to imagine Giradello selling justice to Crowne. There wasn't a man on the planet hungrier or more ambitious than Anthony Giradello.

All of it fell into place like the heavy, glossy pieces of an expensive puzzle. Giradello couldn't let a couple of mutts like Davis and Lowell bring down his well-heeled pal, or ruin the trial that would make his own name a household word. If he sent in Bradley Kyle and Moose Roddick, who also stood to benefit from convicting Rob Cole, he could manipulate the situation, make it go away.

Parker's blood went cold at the idea that maybe Kyle hadn't meant to miss anybody he'd been shooting at in Pershing Square. Davis was a big loose end. Jace Damon had the negatives. Abby Lowell was a wild card.

He had wished for a case to make a comeback. This one was an embarrassment of scandalous riches and human tragedy. He thought of Eta Fitzgerald and her four motherless children, and wished he could trade the case to give her back her life. But the best he could do was nail her killer and the people whose actions had ultimately been the catalyst for her murder.

A figure was walking toward the plaza, toward Davis and Damon. The moment of truth was at hand.

Parker raised his glasses and focused in . . . and the world dropped from under him.

49

Jace didn't recognize the person coming toward them, coming from behind Eddie. From a distance, the light was too poor. And as the person drew nearer, Jace caught only an on-again, off-again glimpse over Davis's shoulder.

"This guy had better have the money," he said.

Davis glanced over his shoulder. Jace kept the .22 trained on him, but pulled it back and held it in front of himself at waist height.

Davis opened his stance, turning a half step so he could see his benefactor and still see Jace from the corner of his eye.

The other person spoke. "Where are the negatives?"

"Where's the money?" Jace asked, allowing himself only a second to register the fact that the third person in their group turned out to be a woman.

She looked at Davis. "Who's he?"

"Middleman," Davis said.

"Can't you do anything right?"

"I did okay killing Tricia Cole for you."

"And I paid you for that. And that's all I've done since," she said. Her voice was tense and trembling and angry. "Pay and pay and pay."

"Hey," Davis said. "You want to run with the dogs, that's how it goes, honey. It's not like calling a flunky to kill a snake in your yard. You had someone whacked. There's consequences."

"I can't do this anymore," she said, choking back tears. "It has to stop. I want it to stop. I never meant for all this to happen. I just wanted him to pay. But when do **I** stop paying?"

"Now," Davis said. "This is it. Jesus Christ, knock off the waterworks. The kid has the negatives. You pay him his five grand, you pay me my finder's fee, and that's the end of it. Cole goes to trial next week. You did your part making sure he doesn't have an alibi. Giradello can't wait to hang him."

"Where's the money?" Jace asked again, impatient and jittery.

The woman held a black nylon gym bag in her left hand. She swung it out to the side and let go of the handle. The bag hit the ground maybe four feet away.

Jace looked over at it. He nodded to Davis and motioned with the gun. "See what's in it."

Davis went to the bag, squatted, and unzipped it. "Here it is, kid. See for yourself."

Jace took a step to the side and tried to see inside the bag without bending over.

It happened so fast, he barely had time to register the flash of light on the blade as Davis came at him and rammed the knife into his belly.

Parker screamed into the mike, "Go, go, go!" Throwing the binoculars aside, he bolted out of cover and ran.

Even as he shouted, "Police!" Diane Nicholson pulled a gun and shot Eddie Davis in the head.

Dan Metheny rolled off the park bench, weapon in hand, shouting, "Freeze, motherfucker!"

But Diane was already running, and kept running as Metheny fired off five quick shots.

Parker screamed at him, "Don't shoot! Don't shoot!"

He pointed at the ground as he ran past and shouted at Metheny, "Keep him alive!"

He sprinted after Diane as hard as his legs would pump, shouting her name over and over.

She had twenty yards on him, and was athletic and fast. She was going to make it to her car.

She skidded around her Lexus, yanked open the door, and got in.

The engine fired as Parker drew close, then the car was coming at him.

Parker went up on the hood, losing his gun, grabbing on with both hands as Diane spun the wheel. The turn was lurching and awkward, and threw Parker off the side like a bull in a rodeo.

He hit the ground and skidded and rolled, coming up on his feet.

But the Lexus didn't make it a hundred yards. Jimmy Chewalski's black-and-white came screaming from the other direction and skidded to a stop, blocking her escape.

Parker reached the back of the car, panting, as Diane flung herself out of it. She stumbled, went down on her knees, scrambled back up, and turned to face him. A gun was in her hand.

"Diane," Parker said. "Jesus Christ, drop the gun."

Chewalski and his partner both had their weapons out, and were yelling.

Standoff.

Diane looked at them, looked at Parker. Her

expression was one of anguish, and a kind of pain Parker had never imagined until now. He thought that her face was mirroring the emotions tearing through him.

"God, Diane, please," he begged. "Drop the gun."

Diane felt as if she were standing outside of her body, watching this happen to someone else.

She was holding a gun. Cops were pointing their guns at her.

She had shot a man in the head.

She had paid a man to kill her former lover's wife.

She had no idea who this person was, this person inside of her who could do those things.

Her need for his love had turned her into something she hated. She had told him more than once she would do anything for him—lie for him, die for him, subjugate her pride, give up all she had. The idea made her sick.

"Diane, please," Parker said, holding out a hand to her. The emotions on his face broke her heart. "Put the gun down."

How could I have done this? she asked herself. **How could I have come to this?**

It was too late for answers. It was too late to change any of it. It was too late. . . .

50

Tyler felt all his blood drain to his feet when the shooting started.

"Jace!" he shouted. He grabbed the radio and pressed the button. "Scout to Leader! Scout to Leader!"

He turned to Andi Kelly. Her eyes looked as wide as his felt.

The person from the Lexus ran out of the park, running for the car that was left way down the street from them. Someone came chasing after, closing ground. He sprinted through a cone of light from a street lamp. Parker.

"Jace! Jace!" Tyler screamed his brother's name over and over. He shoved open the car door and started running for the plaza as fast as his legs could carry him.

"Tyler!" Andi Kelly called.

She caught him from behind, grabbing him by the arm. Tyler struggled and kicked and yanked, shouting, "Let me go! Let me go!"

But the woman didn't let go. Instead, she

pulled him against her and held tight. His screams became sobs, and he went limp in her arms.

They call it "suicide by cop." Someone wants to die but doesn't have the guts to stick the gun in their own mouth and pull the trigger, so they get the cops to do it for them. If the person wants it badly enough, there isn't any way to stop them. All that person has to do is turn the gun on the cops and start shooting.

Parker's heart was in his throat as he held his hand out to Diane. "Diane. Honey. Please put the gun down."

The despair in her face was a terrible thing to see. She was giving up right before his eyes. He took a step closer.

Behind him, Jimmy Chew said, "Kev, don't get close." Chew was worried Diane would turn the gun on Parker.

Parker took another step.

The streetlight shone silver over the tears on her cheeks. She looked at him and said, "I'm so sorry. I'm so, so sorry. . . ."

He took another step.

Shaking and weak, she tried to lift the gun out to the side. It wobbled in her hand like a dying bird.

"It's okay," Parker whispered. Stupid thing to say. What was okay about any of this? What would be okay after this moment had passed? Nothing. But he said it again anyway. "It's okay, honey. It's okay."

The gun dropped from her limp hand, and she melted into his arms, sobbing.

Parker held her as tightly as he could. He was shaking. Tears burned his eyes. He held her and rocked her.

Behind them, he could hear the radio chatter coming from the black-and-white. Chew's partner was calling for backup, asking to have a supervisor and detectives sent.

Parker hoped to God they didn't send Ruiz, or Kray.

An ambulance siren was already wailing, coming from the other side of the plaza. Metheny also would have called them in, and requested backup, and asked for detectives and a supervisor. In a very short time the plaza would be ablaze with lights, alive with people. He wished he could make it all recede and go away. He didn't want people seeing this. Diane was a proud and private person. She wouldn't want anyone seeing her like this.

It was a strange thought, he supposed. She had shot a man in the head. She had as much as confessed to having paid Eddie Davis to murder

Tricia Crowne-Cole. But he didn't know the person who had done those things. He knew the woman he held. He wished he had known her better.

Jimmy Chew put a hand on his shoulder. "Kev," he said quietly. "They're coming."

Parker nodded. He led Diane to the black-and-white and put her in the backseat. Chew handed him a blanket from the trunk of the car, and Parker wrapped it around her and kissed her cheek, and whispered something to her that even he didn't understand.

As he straightened away from the interior of the car, he turned to Chewalski and said, "Jimmy—uh—can you just see that no one bothers her? I—uh—have to go over there. . . ."

"Sure, Kev."

Parker nodded and tried to say thank you, but his voice didn't work. He walked a few steps away, rubbed his hands over his face, took a deep breath, and let it out. He had a job to do. That was the only thing that was going to keep him from falling apart.

He walked away from the black-and-white without looking back, and returned to the plaza, where Metheny knelt on the ground, with Eddie Davis's head in his big hands.

"Is he alive?" Parker asked.

"So far."

Metheny pressed a thumb against bullet holes on either side of Davis's forehead. Diane's shot had gone in one side and out the other, straight through the frontal lobes. Davis appeared to be surprised, but Parker couldn't tell if he was actually conscious or not. Still, he was breathing.

Metheny looked up at him. "I feel like the damn little Dutch boy plugging the dike. If I take my thumbs away, this guy's brains are gonna run out."

"Eddie. Can you hear me?" Parker asked, leaning down to him. Davis didn't respond. "Shit."

"That chick was a wild card, man," Metheny said. "Did you see that coming?"

"No," Parker said. "I didn't."

"I didn't get a good look at her. Do you know who she is?"

Parker didn't answer. He didn't know what to say.

He stepped over Davis and went to Jace Damon. The kid was lying on his back, staring up.

"Knocked the wind out of you?" Parker asked.

The kid nodded.

Parker kneeled down and helped him onto his hands and knees. Jace sat back on his heels and wheezed.

"You shouldn't have stepped that close to him," Parker said. "I told you not to get close. I gave you the gun so you'd stay back from him. Of course, it wasn't loaded. . . ."

Damon turned his head and glared at him, mouthing the word "What?"

"Jesus, I'd never give a loaded gun to a civilian. Get my ass fired," Parker muttered. "Not that that won't happen anyway. Metheny had your back."

The kid finally got his breath. "Who the hell is Metheny?"

Parker nodded in his former partner's direction. "I didn't want you to know he was there. I didn't want you glancing over at him, tipping Davis."

"Well, thanks for thinking about me," Jace said. He struggled to get a deep breath. "I think I broke a rib."

He sat up a little more on his heels and opened his coat, revealing the light-colored Kevlar vest Parker had strapped him into. **And thank God,** was all Parker could think. The kid had taken the force of Davis's blow with the knife, and could well have broken a rib, but the blade hadn't penetrated the material of the vest, which was five times stronger than steel.

"Just sit still and try to relax," Parker told him as the ambulance came into sight. "We'll get an

EMT to check you out after they take care of your friend here."

He put a hand on Jace's shoulder. "That was a really brave thing you did, Jace."

"For Eta," Jace said. "Partly anyway."

Parker nodded. "I know. But it's not your fault she died. That's on Davis. His choice."

"But if I'd turned myself in—"

"How about if Davis and Lowell hadn't cooked up the blackmail scheme? How about if none of this had happened? How about if we could all fly to Mars and start over? There are a lot of what-ifs on that list before it gets to you."

The kid nodded, but with his eyes pointed at the ground, the guilt still weighing on him.

"Jace," Parker said. "You don't know me. You don't know I'm not just full of shit. But I'm telling you, you did what you believed you had to do through all of this. Not what was easiest or best for you. You did what you did, and you're owning it. And I don't know ten men who would be brave enough to do that."

"Jace!"

The excited shriek arrived about a nanosecond before Tyler hurled himself at his brother.

Parker leaned over and ruffled the boy's hair. "Good work, Scout."

Tyler beamed up at him. "Me and Andi let the air out of the tires on that Lexus!"

Parker turned to Andi, who shrugged and made a face, waiting for him to yell at her. Instead, he took a few steps away from the boys, and rested his hands on his hips.

"Well, this is a hell of a mess," he said.

Kelly studied his face, sober as a judge. "Who's down there, Kev? Phillip?"

"Diane Nicholson."

"What? I don't understand."

"Yeah, well, that makes two of us," Parker said. He looked across the plaza as an ambulance arrived and EMTs piled out of it. "It looks like she hired Davis to kill Tricia, and she set up Rob Cole to take the fall."

"Oh, my God. Diane Nicholson? From the coroner's office?"

"Yes."

"Why?"

He shook his head. He watched the paramedics swarm around Eddie Davis.

"What the hell happened?" one of them asked. "Ice pick? Twin ice picks?"

"Shot," Metheny said. "Through-and-through."

The paramedic turned Davis's head one way, then the other. "The poor man's lobotomy."

"He won't miss it," Metheny said. "He wasn't using that part anyway."

It was something Parker would have said himself, but the black humor every cop he knew used to diffuse the stress wasn't there for him. Numbness had begun to set in. Thank God.

Kelly touched his hand. "Kev? Are you all right?"

"No," he whispered. "I'm not."

And he turned and walked away.

51

Ruiz caught the call to the shooting. She showed up in a white suit and strappy sandals. Parker, sitting back against the hood of a black-and-white, didn't have the energy to comment.

She walked up to him, shaking her head in frustration. "What the fuck were you thinking?"

"Shut up."

"Excuse me?"

"I said, shut up," Parker said calmly. "I don't need a bunch of crap from you, Ruiz."

The no-bullshit sharpness of his tone set her back a step.

"You put a civilian in harm's way," she said.

"He's not going to sue the city, if that's what you're worried about," Parker said. "The kid had a stake in this. He wanted to do it for Eta. Despite all recent evidence to the contrary, there are a few people left in the world who know the meaning of honor and duty."

"Don't bag on me, Parker," she bitched. "You

could be blackmailing the preppie killer. You could be up to your ass in drug money, for all we know."

"'All you know' doesn't amount to much, does it?" he said. "Tell me, was Kyle standing right there when you called and tipped me on Pershing Square? Nice and close, so you could hang up the phone, turn your head, and give him a blowjob?"

She didn't answer, and that spoke volumes.

"Who tipped Kyle?"

Ruiz opened her handbag, took out a cigarette, and lit it. "I did," she said on a stream of blue smoke. "Damon really did call for you."

"And you called Davis, so RHD could set up the whole thing," Parker said. "In a public park at rush hour. An uncontrollable situation in an uncontrolled environment. I would say that trumps what I did."

He reached out and yanked the cigarette from her lips. "Don't smoke at a crime scene, Ruiz. Haven't I taught you anything?"

He crushed the cigarette beneath the toe of his shoe, took it to a trash can, and threw it away.

"Parker! I'm not done talking to you!" she said, doing the high-heel jog to catch up with him. "I need to get your statement. I have to file the preliminary report."

Parker looked at her like she smelled. "They couldn't send a real detective?"

"I'm on the rotation until my paperwork from IA comes through."

"Well, that's your problem. I've said everything I have to say to you."

He started to walk away again, then. hesitated. "That's not exactly true."

Ruiz waited, stiffening for a tirade.

"I doctor scripts for Matt Connors."

He might have told her he was a hermaphrodite. Her expression would have been the same. "What?"

"My big secret," Parker said. "I doctor scripts and serve as a technical consultant to Matt Connors."

"The movie guy?"

"Yeah. The movie guy."

"Jesus!" she breathed. "Why didn't you just tell us?"

Parker smiled a bitter, crooked smile and walked away, shaking his head. In this town, he probably would have gotten a promotion if he'd let on he was connected in the industry. He hadn't wanted the attention. All he had wanted from LAPD was a chance to make it back from purgatory, and to do it through his own sweat and brainpower.

He could have held Renee Ruiz down and

explained that to her nine thousand times, and she would never have understood.

The bitter irony was, in fighting for his own resurrection, he had ultimately revealed the fall of a woman he cared about. Yin and yang. Everything in life came with a price.

"I want my money back," he mumbled as he approached Bradley Kyle.

Kyle stood amid a tiny forest of evidence markers, trying to boss one of the SID people around. He turned and smirked at Parker. "You really screwed the pooch this time, Parker. Or is that a poor choice of words? I hear you and Nicholson—"

Parker hit him so hard with a right cross, Kyle spun halfway around before he hit the dirt. Everyone stopped what they were doing, but no one made a move toward him.

Parker turned to Moose Roddick and said, "All the paperwork on the Lowell homicide is in my trunk. Come and get it."

The news vans had rolled in. The choppers were swarming. They were just in time for breaking in live on the eleven o'clock news. But they wouldn't have the story behind what had happened here. That shit would hit the fan tomorrow, and the feeding frenzy would begin.

Rob Cole was about to get another fifteen minutes of fame. The Good Man Wrongly

Accused would be set free. Or, from a more cynical standpoint, an idiot too stupid to escape being framed for murder was about to be let back into the gene pool.

Parker didn't know the whole story himself, but he was willing to bet Rob Cole was not the hero, and he knew there wouldn't be a happy ending.

He turned his cell phone on as he walked toward his car, and hit the button for voice mail. He had one message. Ito saying he had the photograph ready.

52

Diane sat on a chair in a front corner of the interview room, her feet tucked up, her arms around her legs, her cheek pressed to her knees. No makeup, no veneer of control. Parker had never seen anyone look more vulnerable. Not in the vulnerable way of a child who trusts, but in the way of a grown woman who knows better but has no defenses left.

Parker closed the door behind him and sat on the edge of the table.

"Hi."

"Hi," she said in a voice so small and thin, it seemed to have come from another room.

She had stretched the sleeves of her black sweater to the point that only the tips of her fingers showed. She used the sweater to dab at the tears that fell at random. Her gaze moved from point to point around the small white room, not lighting on anything for more than a few seconds. Not touching his face at all.

"Are you cold?" he asked, already slipping off his jacket.

It wouldn't have mattered if she had said no. He wanted the excuse to touch her. He wrapped the jacket around her shoulders and touched her cheek with his fingertips.

"Who's watching?" she asked, looking across the room at the two-way mirror set into the wall.

"No one. It's just us. Do you have an attorney?"

She shook her head.

"I'll take care of it."

"Kev, you don't have to—"

"It's done."

She sighed and looked away. "Thank you."

"So . . . you hired Eddie Davis to kill Tricia Crowne-Cole, and set up Rob Cole to take the fall," Parker said. Drained of energy himself, he didn't think he could project his voice any farther than the next chair. "That's a pretty harsh sentence for having a married guy hit on you."

She looked away and closed her eyes. The only sound in the room was the annoying buzz of the fluorescent lighting. It was late. Parker had gotten her shipped to Central Division before RHD could make a move. The territorial dispute was being left until morning. Spending the night in one holding cell was pretty much the same as spending the night in another. And no one was going to question her without an attorney present.

"It's just us, Diane," he said. "I'm not here as a cop. Hell, I probably won't even be a cop by this time tomorrow. I'm just here as me. Your friend."

"I play it through in my head," she murmured. "It's not me. I can't believe it's me in those memories. I'm too smart, too cynical. I'm too sharp a judge of character. I've listened to women friends cry about this guy or that guy, and the promises they made, and the excuses the women made to cover when none of it happened. And I would think, **What's wrong with her? How stupid is she? What kind of self-respecting woman would stand for that? How pathetic can she be?**

"And then I found out. It's some kind of insanity. The intensity, the passion, the unbridled joy. It's like a drug."

"What's **it?**" Parker asked.

"Love. The kind people write about, but no one really believes in. I always wanted to know what it was like to feel that, to have someone feel it for me."

"Cole told you he did."

"No one has ever made me feel the way you

make me feel. No one has ever understood me the way you understand me. I've never loved anyone the way I love you." Her mouth twisted in a bitter smile. "I know. I know. **What's wrong with her? How stupid is she?** I look back now, and I say the same thing. **How pathetic am I?** But I believed everything he told me because I felt the same way. I said the same things, and I meant them. I wanted to believe he meant them too. I should have seen him coming a mile away."

She rested her head on her knees again, her eyes staring at nothing.

"He's an actor," Parker said. "He's been playing that role for a long time."

"The poor, misunderstood bad boy from the wrong side of the tracks," she said. "Victim of his own popularity. Trapped in a loveless marriage. He's finally found the love of his life. If only we could be together. But I was married . . . and he was married . . . and Tricia was 'fragile.' And then suddenly I wasn't married . . . and things became difficult . . . and Tricia was practically suicidal, he said . . . and he had an obligation . . . and he had to sacrifice himself . . . and do what was right. . . ."

She closed her eyes and the fluorescent lights hummed. Parker thought she might have fallen asleep, and he didn't even care. It wouldn't be

long before everything changed, and she would
be surrounded by people, and there would be
no late-night chats, just the two of them in a
room alone.

Very softly, she sang a few bars of a song she'd
once heard on the radio. **"I never believed it
could happen to me. Something like this
only happens to dumb girls."**

"Why kill Tricia?" Parker asked. "Why not
Cole? He deserved it."

"You can't know the rage I felt," she whispered. "My marriage was already falling apart
when I met Rob. I was vulnerable, lonely. He
knew just how to prey on those feelings. And
then, when Joseph died . . . The guilt was terrible. Not that I'd caused his death, but that I
hadn't been a very good partner, that I'd cheated
him, and cheated on him. And Rob knew just
what to do with those feelings too.

"I trusted him. I gave him everything I was.
How dare he take that gift and break it?"

She was trembling. She squeezed her eyes
shut, straining against an inner pain Parker
knew he couldn't imagine. He waited for the
moment to pass with the sad patience of someone knowing nothing good was coming and
there wasn't anything he could do about it.

"And then one day, I got in an elevator at the
Crowne building. I was there . . . something to

do with Joseph's pension. And there was Tricia," she said. "Just the two of us riding up to the highest floors in the building. And she stood there looking at me with this smug, evil, superior look on her face."

"She knew?"

"Oh, yes," she said, laughing without humor. "She knew. She knew everything. She knew things she couldn't possibly have known without having witnessed them happening."

Parker's blood went cold as the implication of what she was telling him sank in.

Diane's mouth twisted in a bitter smile. "You see, I wasn't a game just to Rob Cole. I was a game to them both."

"Oh, Jesus," Parker breathed. Nausea washed over him.

Fat tears rolled like pearls down Diane's cheeks. "And she said, in this voice I'd never heard before: **'He always comes back to me.'** And there was nothing fragile about her."

Parker could picture the scene in his mind. Diane would have pretended not to react, because she was proud and controlled. While inside she would have shattered like glass.

"A couple of days later I got a package in the mail. A videotape of me and Rob in bed together, him telling me all those things I wanted to hear, wanted to believe. Then there they were, the two of them—Tricia and Rob—reenacting that very same scene, line for line, and laughing about it afterward."

Parker's stomach turned at the cruelty.

Diane unfolded herself from the chair and began to move around, her arms banded around her as if she were in a strait jacket.

"Something inside me just broke. It was as if some hidden, festering wound had opened and poisoned me," she said. "I started drinking. A lot. I was in a bar one night crying to the bartender. There was a man two stools down, listening. He told me he could help me, for a price."

"Eddie Davis," Parker said.

"I think about it now, and I can't believe any of that happened. I can't believe I hired a killer, and I came up with a plan, and I went through with that plan. It was all like a weird nightmare.

"I asked Rob to come to my house for dinner the night Tricia was killed. To talk about things, I told him, smooth everything over between us. No hard feelings. He actually thought we could still be friends. He said it the day he told me he couldn't leave poor pathetic Tricia, that his feelings for me had changed, that the sex had been really great but that everything else was over. But couldn't we still be friends?"

She laughed at that. "Why do men think that can happen? That they can lead a woman on, and lie to her, and treat her like shit, but she should be a sport about it in the end. That's delusional. Sociopathic. Cruel."

Parker said nothing. There was no excuse to make for what Rob Cole had done.

"It was so easy," she said, her eyes blank as she looked back into her mind and watched the memory unfold. "He drank too much, because he always drinks too much. It's part of Rob's drama, that the pressure of being him is such that he has to self-medicate in order to tough it out. I slipped some GHB into his last drink. Not a lot. Just enough to know that by the time he got home, he would be ready to pass out. Driving drunk was nothing new to him. I'm sure he wasn't even aware of the drug taking hold. He would have thought he'd just had one too many.

"Later that night I got called to go to a murder scene."

"Tricia," Parker said.

"Davis had killed her with Rob right there in the house. He staged it to look like Rob did it."

"And Cole didn't have an alibi because he was there, and he couldn't very well tell anyone he'd been with a lover scorned just prior to the murder. Even he wouldn't be so stupid. He had to know you'd be called as a corroborating witness, and you'd crucify him."

Methodical, cool, smart. Those were words he would have applied to Diane, but never in this context.

"Why kill Tricia, though?" Parker asked. "Why not Rob? He was the more immediate evil, the one who had carried out the abuse."

"Because to die quickly wasn't punishment enough. But to send him to prison . . . where he would have to wake up every morning and face a life in hell, where being Rob Cole would never, ever be an advantage, or a ticket to do whatever he wanted with no threat of conse-quences . . ."

She was right. Rob Cole's minor celebrity, his too-good looks and cocky attitude, would not have served him in a place like San Quentin. He would have been a target, and he wouldn't have had any power to do anything about it.

"And the blackmail?"

"Started shortly after. I had money. Joseph left me very well taken care of. Davis thought he deserved a bonus because he'd done such a fine job. I paid him. But then he wanted more. He sent me a photograph of me paying him off. The trial was coming up. Everyone said

Giradello had a slam dunk. Davis said he could ruin it."

"By incriminating himself?" Parker said.

"He didn't care. He said he'd disappear, go underground. But that wouldn't stop him from putting the photographs and the story out there. He actually liked the idea of having people know he had killed Tricia and gotten away with it. He thought he could sell his story to the movies while living a dashing life of international intrigue.

"I gave him Joseph's Lincoln. That wasn't enough."

She went to the darkened glass and stared at her reflection.

And then there was her lover, Parker thought, investigating the crime, piecing the story together, working to tie two seemingly disparate crimes together. His big comeback case. He wanted to throw up.

"I offered them two hundred and fifty thousand dollars to sell me the negatives outright, but then everything went wrong, and it just got worse and worse. . . ."

She continued to stare at her reflection, as if she was trying to recognize someone she couldn't quite remember.

"I just wanted him to pay," she said softly, her

voice strained. "I wanted them both to pay for what they'd done to me. I wanted Rob to be punished. I wanted him to hurt the way I hurt."

The last threads of her control shredded, and tears came in a torrent. Sobs tore loose from the depths of her soul. The sounds were of something dying inside her.

Parker turned her to him then, and held her as gently as he would a child. He couldn't connect the woman he knew to the things she'd done. As she had said, the person who had committed those acts couldn't have been her. And yet the woman he knew would pay, and there was nothing he could do about it . . . except hold her, and be there for her as her demons raked her with their claws.

53

Parker left the building and just stood for a while in the night air. It was closer to morning than to midnight. The empty streets were shiny black, wet with sea mist. No one was around. He wondered what would happen if he just walked away and never came back.

The thought was fleeting. He wasn't the type to walk away from anything, God help him. He could only be thankful that for now all he could feel was numbness.

Andi Kelly was curled in the passenger seat of his car, huddled in a microfleece jacket he kept in the backseat. She jumped awake like a jack-in-the-box as Parker unlocked the doors and let himself in.

"As a car thief," he said, "you're a very good writer."

"I stole your little plastic emergency key earlier. It let me in the door, but it wouldn't start the engine."

She turned sideways on the seat and just

stared at him for a moment. Parker started the engine and turned on the heater. The dash lights glowed green.

"How are you doing, Kev?"

"No comment."

"Off the record."

"No comment. I can't talk about this, Andi. Not now. It's too raw."

"You don't have to," she said. "I just wanted to offer. I'm a good listener."

"How can that be?" he teased gently. "You never shut up."

"I'm multitalented. I can juggle a little bit too."

"Well, you'll always have something to fall back on."

"Diane Nicholson is a friend?" she asked carefully.

Parker nodded. He focused his stare on the odometer—something mundane, unimportant—in the hopes that the tide of emotion rising inside him would recede a bit. He hurt. For Diane, and because of her.

"I'm really sorry, Kev."

He nodded again, a pressure building in his head, behind his eyes.

Andi picked up her bag from the floor of the car, rummaged through it, pulled out a flask, and offered it to him. "Have a wee nip, as my grandfather used to say to us as children. Hell of a baby-sitter, Granddad. He taught us how to play poker so he could cheat us out of our allowance money."

Parker managed a chuckle, took the flask, and poured a shot of very good scotch down his throat.

"Eddie Davis is conscious and talking," Andi said. "Your pal Metheny was right—he really wasn't using that frontal lobe after all. Brains are miraculous little globs of gross, disgusting goo. Unnamed hospital sources say he'll be released in a matter of days."

"That sucks," Parker said. "He's not worth the powder to blow him up, and he walks away from getting shot in the head. Rob Cole fucks up people's lives right and left, and he'll walk out of jail tomorrow, a free man."

"Well, it turns out he didn't kill anybody," Andi said.

That wasn't exactly true, Parker thought, but he didn't say it.

"You know he'll sell his story for a movie of the week and insist on playing himself."

"Stop. You're making me wish **I'd** gotten shot in the head," Parker said. "Any word on Abby Lowell?"

"She's stable. They won't know until the swelling goes down around the spinal cord whether she has any permanent damage. A day or two."

They were quiet for a moment. Diana Krall's smoky voice drifted from the stereo speakers, reflective and sad. The perfect sound track for the night.

"I feel like the whole damn world has blown apart, and we'll each drift on our own little rock and scatter like dust in the wind," Parker said.

"That's not true. You're not alone, Kev," Andi said. "None of us is."

"I'm not convinced that's a good thing."

"You're done in. Go home. Sleep for a couple of days. Call if you decide you want company," she said, and waggled her eyebrows.

Parker smiled reluctantly. "I'm glad we found each other again, Andi."

"Me too."

"I'll walk you to your car."

"I'm right here," she said, gesturing to a silver Miata, the next car down.

She leaned over and kissed his cheek, and gave him a hug around the shoulders. "Take care of yourself, Kevin."

He nodded. But as he drove the deserted streets home to Chinatown, he found himself thinking that he wished he didn't have to take care of himself. He had won the battle and lost the war. This was a night for a soft place to fall, but the person he most wanted to share his victory with was gone. Lost to him. Lost to herself. Forever. And there was nothing to do but mourn.

54

Another gorgeous Southern California morning. Sunshine, traffic jams, and sensationalism.

Every early news show of every television station in the city was running footage of "Peril in Pershing Square," followed by "Shootout on Olvera Street." Much of the Pershing Square fiasco had been caught on videotape by a USC film student, who had been in the park to make a documentary about the movie crew that had been setting up for a shoot on the site.

Every station had reporters live at the scenes, where absolutely nothing was happening at six in the morning, and no one had anything of any real value to say.

"Regurgitating and rehashing sketchy facts and supposition—live at [crime scene of choice] this is [reporter's name here] for channel whatever news."

Television journalism in the new millennium.

Parker watched TV with the sound muted, reading the closed- captioning for Diane's name, which appeared again and again. Every cop and SID tech and paramedic at the scene knew her. There had been no shortage of people willing to step into the glare of the lights and make some comment, or express their shock. The upper-right-hand corner of the screen on every channel had her booking photo already.

It hurt to see it, to see the emptiness in her eyes, the pallor of her skin. The vibrant, strong woman he knew was not there. This was some other Diane. This was the Diane she had spoken of, a stranger even to herself. In this Diane lived fear and fury, and the kind of raw pain that drove otherwise good people to cross lines they otherwise would not. This Diane had committed murder by proxy. This Diane had shot a man in the head. This Diane had planned and executed the plan to frame a man for a capital crime punishable by death.

In this Diane lived the need for love, the hunger for connection, the vulnerability of a child. This Diane had been used and abused by a sexual sociopath in a cruel and heartless game.

Parker walked away from the plasma-screen TV and went up onto the roof to stretch, to close everything out of his mind and walk through the movements that had helped to calm and center him every day for the past few years. Today the dance was tense with anger, the energy—the chi—blocked by the strength of his emotions.

When the frustration had tried his patience long enough, he gave up and just stood there for a long time, looking out over Chinatown, listening to the sounds of the city awakening and beginning the day.

One of the things he loved most about LA was the overriding sense that every day was new, brimming with the possibility of dreams coming true. Today, all he could feel was the opposite of hope. Today, he would in all likelihood lose the career he had fought so hard to resurrect. Today, a woman he loved would be charged with murder, and a morally bankrupt, emotional rapist would be set free with an unspoken endorsement to go on with his life as if nothing had ever happened.

Parker released a heavy sigh and went back inside to prepare to face it all. The best thing to do with a bad day: get through it and end it, and hope the next day would somehow be better.

Parker made his first stop of the day the hospital. One, because it was early, and he had a better chance of avoiding anyone from Robbery-Homicide. They would certainly interview Abby Lowell that day, but there was no urgent need to do it right away. Eddie Davis wasn't going anywhere. And two, because he still had a badge, and the badge would get him in to see her with no questions asked.

She was a ghostly figure under the white sheet, the machines monitoring her vital signs the only things that indicated life. Staring up at the television growing out of the ceiling, her face was blank, her eyes expressionless. She was watching the **Today** show. An NBC news reporter was standing in Pershing Square talking about the incident, the film student's footage was rolling, and Katie Couric looked concerned as she asked the reporter if there had been any bystander casualties.

"Your fifteen minutes is starting," Parker said, tapping the face of his watch.

Abby's eyes darted toward him. She didn't say anything. Parker pulled a stool over to the side of the bed and perched on it.

"I'm told your prognosis is good," he said. "You have feeling in all extremities."

"I can't move my legs," she said.

"But you know they're there. That's a good sign."

She just looked at him for a moment, trying

to decide what to say. Her gaze flicked to the television and back. "Thank you for staying with me in the park last night. That was a very kind thing for you to do."

"You're welcome." He gave her a crooked smile. "See? I'm not all bad."

"You're pretty bad," she said. "You treated me like a criminal."

"I can apologize now," Parker said. "But it's my job to be suspicious of people. Nine times out of ten I'm proven right."

"And the tenth time?"

"I'll send flowers."

"Did you get the bike messenger?"

He nodded. "He didn't have anything to do with your father's death."

"He tried to sell me the negatives. I thought he was in on it with Davis."

"Why would you have wanted them?"

"Should I have an attorney present?" she asked.

Parker shook his head. "It's not against the law to purchase negatives. Are you in them?"

"No."

"Did you have any part in the blackmail scheme?" He wasn't sure she didn't. Her behavior through it all had been less than innocent.

"I found out what Lenny was up to," she

said. "I wouldn't have thought he could surprise or disappoint me anymore. I was wrong."

"It's hard to learn that lesson with someone you care about."

"I didn't want it to be true. I confronted him, begged him to put a stop to it, like that would have changed the fact that he was guilty of blackmail. He told me he would. He told me he had gotten caught up in it, that he was afraid of Eddie."

"How did he get involved in the first place?"

"Davis was already a client. He came to Lenny and confessed to the murder, bragged about it. He didn't think Lenny could do anything because of privilege. Then he asked Lenny to help him with the blackmail. He needed someone who wouldn't rat him out to take the photographs."

"And Lenny said yes," Parker said. The lure of money had been too much for him, and/or having had a confessed perpetrator of a brutal murder make the offer made it too scary to refuse.

A nurse came into the room and gave Parker the eye as she looked at the machines and checked on Abby, trying to move him along. He could see by the strain on Abby's face that she was running out of gas.

"Did Lenny give up Davis to the DA's office? He wanted the last big payoff to himself?"

Tears brimmed over her lashes. The machine monitoring her heart rate began to beep a little faster. "I did," she confessed in a small, hoarse whisper. "I thought if Giradello could go after Davis . . ."

Then Davis would have been arrested for Tricia Crowne-Cole's murder. The negatives showed only Davis and Diane. Maybe they wouldn't find anything against Lenny, except the word of a hit man. But Davis had had other plans.

"Did you speak to Giradello himself?"

"No. To his assistant."

"Did you give your name?"

"I couldn't."

And how seriously would Anthony Giradello take an anonymous tip on a case that was a lock to convict, and a lock to launch his own political career? Not very. He had a vested interest in sending Rob Cole away. It was a wonder he'd even bothered to put Kyle and Roddick into the field to nose around.

Parker looked at Abby Lowell lying there looking young and frightened and crushed at the losses she had suffered. And he could see her at five or six in his mind's eye, with that same expression as she sat in the corner of some bookie joint, left there by her father like she was a piece of luggage he would pick up on his way out.

Her eyes closed. The nurse scowled at Parker. He murmured a good-bye and walked out the door.

55

I think the unemployment office is in a different building," Andi Kelly said, as Parker walked toward her through the waiting mob outside the Criminal Courts Building, where Rob Cole and his dream team would be emerging shortly to tell the world he was a free man.

Parker had taken off his tie and opened the collar of his shirt. His suit was rumpled from sitting in a Parker Center conference room for two hours. "Suspended," he said. "Thirty days without pay."

"Never mind that you cleared about three cases for them in one fell swoop."

"I didn't ask pretty please if I could."

Actually, the words that had been tossed around the conference room by the chief of detectives, the head of Robbery-Homicide, and Bradley Kyle (who had a raccoon's mask of bruising from Parker breaking his nose at the Olvera Street Plaza), among others, had been words like **insubordinate, dangerous, rogue.**

Parker had brought up the subject of Robbery-Homicide's shadowy involvement in the Lowell homicide investigation, and had been brushed off. He had pointed out that a lot of people could have been killed at Pershing Square. No one wanted to hear it. He mentioned that Kyle had shot a woman in the back. Internal Affairs would investigate the shooting. Kyle would be on desk duty pending the outcome and would likely be suspended afterward.

At least Parker had the satisfaction of knowing Bradley Kyle would not be advancing his career. He would probably be sent down from Robbery-Homicide, or fired if the brass could get around the union. And then the lawsuits would come rolling in from Abby Lowell, from any civilian standing in Pershing Square when the shooting had started.

When Parker's sentence had been pronounced, the chief of detectives had asked him if he had anything he wanted to say. Parker stood up and asked Bradley Kyle directly, why, if Giradello had been given a reason to suspect Eddie Davis for the Crowne homicide, had he not had them pull Davis in for questioning before he killed someone else.

They had all looked at one another like they were trying to pass a hot potato with telekinesis.

They hadn't taken the threat of Eddie

Davis seriously enough on the weight of an anonymous tip. And certainly, Tony Giradello wouldn't have wanted it to get out that another suspect was being questioned practically on the eve of his making his opening statement to the jury, telling them Rob Cole was, without a doubt, a brutal murderer.

So Kyle and Roddick had dragged their feet, and a lot of people had paid a terrible price for it.

"I quit," he told Andi. "I took off my service weapon, took out my ID, left it all on the table, and walked."

Kelly was wide-eyed. "Whoa. Intense."

"Yeah."

"But you worked so hard to make it back, Kev. And after they get done being pissed off, they're going to see—"

"I don't need them to see anything, Andi," he said, shaking his head. "They don't matter. I thought I had to prove something, and I did, to myself. There's nothing left for me to prove. I can move on with my life."

"Wow," she said. "That's one of the most mentally healthy things I've ever heard any-one say."

The commotion began at the courthouse doors and rolled through the crowd on a wave. The doors swung open and Good Man Wrongly

Accused emerged with his entourage. Parker wanted to slap the smirk off his face.

Rob Cole was as deserving of punishment as any felon in the system, but the press, who had vilified him from his arrest to this day, would now hail him as some kind of accidental hero. Cole was no more a hero than any idiot who fell down a well and had to be rescued by a huge team of county workers, at taxpayers' expense. In both cases, the fool would be the one to do all the morning news and late-night talk shows. He'd be a guest on **Larry King,** and be asked to judge the Miss America Pageant.

What a country.

The press conference was brief and nauseating. Parker stood behind Andi, in a prime spot just behind a knot of television news talent. Then Cole moved to one side of the podium to greet his adoring public and sign autographs.

Parker stood at the edge of the madness, watching women hurl themselves at Cole, screaming his name. It turned his stomach.

He glanced to his right. There was a tall, striking woman with short sandy hair standing just a few feet away, waiting her turn, but not screaming. Not screaming, not smiling, just staring at Rob Cole with pale gray eyes as cold as ice. A sense of unease scratched at the back of Parker's neck.

To his left, Andi made a comment, and he had to lean over and have her repeat it.

In that split second, the woman with the gray eyes pulled a gun from her handbag, pointed it at Rob Cole's chest, and started shooting.

The surprise on Cole's face was the thing that would stick with Parker most. Robbie's shining moment of victory, snatched away from him, just like that.

The scene was chaos. People screaming, people running. From the corner of his eye Parker could see a couple of sheriff's deputies coming, weapons drawn. Everyone immediately surrounding the shooter had dropped to the ground.

The woman just stood there, gun in hand.

Parker launched himself at her a split second before one of the deputies discharged his weapon. He knocked her flat to the ground. The gun flew out of her hand. She was sobbing now, saying over and over, "Look what he did to me!"

A subsequent search of the home of Rob Cole and Tricia Crowne-Cole yielded a treasure trove of X-rated videotapes. Most of Cole with other women—Diane and the brunette among them—having sex with them, having dinner with them, telling each of them she was his soul mate, that no one had ever made him feel the way she made him feel. Making promises he never intended to keep to vulnerable, needy women.

And there were the tapes of Cole and Tricia, shot in their bedroom. Cole naked, Tricia looking grotesque in lingerie intended for a younger, trimmer woman. Tricia mocking the current other woman, begging him to love her, begging him to stay. The two of them laughing like a pair of jackals.

And a fresh scandal was born.

The press demanded to know why the tapes hadn't turned up during the initial investigation of Tricia's murder, but there had been no reason to look for them. Contrary to what television dramas teach the American public, search warrants are specific as to what is being looked for. In the investigation of Tricia Crowne-Cole's death, there had been no reason to search for anything. They had the victim, the prime suspect in the house with the victim. Rob Cole had motive, means, and opportunity. And the murder weapon had been left on the remains of the victim's face. What more could Robbery-Homicide have asked for?

Parker watched the news reports and thought maybe there was a God after all, though nothing could ever mend the damage that had been done, the lives that had been ruined. He hired Harlan Braun, attorney to the stars, to represent Diane. One of the other women who had been victimized was filing a class-action civil suit on behalf of all the victims, suing the estate of Tricia Crowne-Cole for suffering and extreme emotional distress.

She was doing all the talk shows too.

On Sundays, Parker would go visit Diane in jail.

Andi Kelly was writing a book.

The laws of nature dictate nothing go to waste when an animal is killed. Rob Cole was feeding the scavengers, all eager to pick their teeth with his bones.

In the end, there would be nothing left of Cole but his infamy. He deserved nothing better.

56

Jace sat in a chair on the roof of the Chens' building, watching Tyler and Grandfather Chen play with a pair of remote-control cars. Both the old man and the boy were laughing and grinning and chattering at each other in Mandarin as they worked the controls, and the cars careened around in a mad race. For the first time in what seemed like forever, an easy smile spread across Jace's face.

It was a perfect Saturday morning. The sun was already warm and felt good on his body. After several days of rest, the aches had begun to subside, and some of the tension had left him. It was difficult to justify sweating over life's details when he was so very aware he was lucky to have a life.

Parker had taken him to the Robbery-Homicide offices in Parker Center the day before so Jace could give his statement of everything that transpired in those few very long days. Jace hadn't wanted to go, the old suspicions and fears hanging on with talons. He'd held his breath practically the whole time, waiting for someone to ask him about Tyler and the Chens, but it hadn't happened.

Parker had told him the cops wouldn't be interested in his private life. LAPD had enough on its agenda without dabbling in social services. And Social Services was too entangled in its own tentacles to go sniffing around LAPD. The system at work. Besides, Parker had said, if Jace really was nineteen or twenty-one, or any of the ages he chose to tell people, he was legally an adult, and entitled to custody of his brother.

The focus of the interview had been narrow and on point. What had happened and when it had happened. Just the facts.

Parker had stayed right there with him the whole time, asking some questions himself, but also interjecting bits of humor here and there, helping Jace stay calm and focused. Parker was a good man, maybe even someone Jace thought he could want to know and trust.

Afterward, Parker had taken him out to lunch, and filled him in on where the case was. Eddie Davis was being charged with four counts of murder, beginning with the murder-for-hire of Tricia Crowne-Cole. A one-man crime spree, fueled by greed and the sheer joy of taking lives.

The fact was, three of those lives, including Eta's, could have been spared if Assistant District Attorney Anthony Giradello had pushed to have Eddie Davis picked up immediately after Abby Lowell had called and tipped him off regarding Davis's involvement in the Crowne murder.

An investigation was under way.

The most important thing to Jace was that he was out of it, and his odd little patchwork family was safe. Family—he liked the sound of that. He thought he might actually try to open up to the idea.

Where he would go from here, he wasn't sure. The broken rib and his other injuries would keep him quiet for another few days. He wouldn't go back to being a messenger. The stress would be too much for Tyler, wondering every five seconds if his brother was being run down in the street, or chased by someone like Eddie Davis.

Jace probably should have been anxious about what the future would hold, but for the time being, he was content to watch his little brother being a kid. He was content to think that they had a home, and a family, and to know that family didn't have much to do with blood, but had everything to do with heart.

Parker turned the green vintage racing Jag down the alley and parked behind the Chens', in the slot where Madame Chen's Mini Cooper had sat the first time he had come here. Madame Chen emerged from her office in pristine white cotton slacks and a black silk twin set, her hair perfectly coiffed.

"You are replacing my car, Detective Parker," she said with a sly smile. "How kind of you."

"I **will** replace your car, Madame Chen," he said.

"And when will this miraculous thing happen? Before I am as old as my father-in-law and too blind to drive on the streets?"

"Today," he promised. "The Hollywood police are finished with your car. I called them personally to have them bring it back to you today."

She pretended to pout. "But now I like this car better. You will trade perhaps?"

Parker laughed. "You have an appreciation for fine things, Madame Chen."

"Of course," she said, her dark eyes twinkling. "My tastes are very simple, Detective. I like only the best."

"Then you'll say yes if I ask you to be my girl-friend?"

A blush tinted the apples of her cheeks. "I will say no such thing . . . until you take me for a ride in that car."

Parker put his arms around her and gave her a hug. She protested and chattered at him in Chinese, but when he stood back, she was blushing and trying not to giggle like a schoolgirl.

"I'll take you for a drive up the coast one day," he promised. "We'll have lunch and I'll try to ply you with wine and charm. I'm full of charm, you know."

She gave him a look. "You are certainly full of something, Detective Parker."

"Kev!"

Tyler's shout came over the side of the roof. Half a second later, the boy came bursting out the door.

"Wow! Cool car!"

"You think?" Parker said. "I came to take you and your brother for a ride."

"Excellent!"

Ten minutes later they were on the road, the Jag growling beneath them, the wind in their hair, Tyler and Jace squished together in the passenger's seat, sharing one seat belt.

"Isn't this illegal?" Tyler yelled.

Parker cut him a quick glance. "What are you? A cop?"

"Uh-huh. I have a badge now."

Parker had given the boy an honorary junior detective's badge in appreciation for his exemplary service the night they had nailed Eddie Davis.

He found he liked playing uncle very much. Tyler Damon was a terrific little person. And Jace was something too. Brave and good. Both of them were damned amazing, considering the tough lives they'd had.

Parker suspected Jace had been born an adult. At nineteen he had a larger sense of duty and responsibility than ninety percent of the people Parker knew. Jace had geared his life to raising and protecting his little brother, doing what he had to do for Tyler to have a better life. Working two jobs and taking the train to Pasadena City College a couple of times a week to work toward getting a degree.

It seemed to Parker that no one deserved a break more than Jace Damon did. And he was about to give him one.

He turned the Jag in at the entrance to the Paramount lot and pulled up at the guard shack.

"Hey, Mr. Parker. Good to see you."

"You too, Bill. My young friends and I are here to see Mr. Connors."

"Who's Mr. Connors?" Tyler asked.

"A buddy of mine," Parker said. "Matt Connors. I do a little work for him on the side."

Jace looked over at him, suspicious. "Matt Connors the movie director?"

"Writer, director, producer. Matt wears a lot of hats."

"What kind of work do you do for him?"

"I . . . consult," Parker hedged. "I was talking with him last night. He's anxious to meet you."

"Why?"

"Because you've got a hell of a story to tell, kid," Parker said. "And you might as well tell it to Matt Connors."

He parked the Jag and they all piled out. Having been alerted by Bill at the gate, Connors met them at the car.

Matt Connors was good-looking in a younger Paul Newman kind of way—forty-five, handsome enough to work in front of the camera, but smart enough not to. On the list of successful people in Hollywood, Connors's name was not far down the list from people like Spielberg.

"Kev Parker, my long-lost friend and script savior!" Connors rejoiced, throwing his arms around Parker. Then he stepped back and said, "Where the hell are your notes on **Prior Bad Acts**?"

"I've been a little busy saving the city from violence and corruption," Parker said.

Connors rolled his eyes. "Oh, **that.** Are these your deputies?" he asked, looking at Jace and Tyler.

"More like secret undercover agents," Parker said. "This is Jace Damon and his brother, Tyler. I was telling you about them."

"Right," Connors said, sizing them up as if he was already casting their roles in his head.

The three of them shook hands. Jace looked suspicious of the whole setup. Tyler was wide-eyed.

"Can we see somebody doing special effects on a computer?" Tyler asked. "I've been reading all about the latest technology in computer animation, and . . ."

The boy rattled on like an audio encyclopedia.

"Tyler has an IQ of one sixty-eight," Parker remarked.

Connors's brows went up. "Wow. That's more than you and me put together."

"So we get to look around?" Jace asked. He was already looking, Parker noticed, and trying very hard not to appear excited about it. .

Connors spread his arms wide. "Matt Connors, personal tour guide, at your service, gentlemen. Let's take a walk. I'll show you where all the magic happens."

They started down the lot, Parker and Connors flanked by the two boys, the California sun spilling over them like molten gold, the world of dreams spread out before them.

"So, Kev," Connors said. "What have you got to say for yourself?"

Parker put a hand on Connors's shoulder and said, "My friend, have we got a story for you. And for a generous price that would put him through college and graduate school, I'm guessing Jace here would be happy to tell it to you."

Connors nodded, turned to Jace, and said, "How about it, kid? You want to be in the movie business?"

Jace stared at him, his brain stalling out. "A movie? About me? About what just happened?"

"Right," Connors said. "I already have the perfect title. We'll call it **Kill the Messenger**. . . ."

LIKE WHAT YOU'VE SEEN?

If you enjoyed this large print edition of
Kill the Messenger, look for other Random House
Large Print books available from Tami Hoag.

Dark Horse (hardcover)
0-375-43182-9 ($28.95/$43.95C)

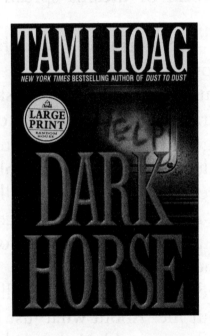

Large print books are available wherever
books are sold and at many local libraries.

All prices are subject to change, check with your
local retailer for current pricing and availability.
For more information on these and other large print titles
visit www.randomhouse.com/large print.